DEXTER BY DESIGN

DEXTER BY DESIGN

JEFF LINDSAY

THORNDIKE
WINDSOR
PARAGON

This Large Print edition is published by Thorndike Press, Waterville, Maine, USA and by BBC Audiobooks Ltd, Bath, England.
Thorndike Press, a part of Gale, Cengage Learning.
Copyright © 2009 by Jeff Lindsay.
The moral right of the author has been asserted.

The text of this Large Print edition is unabridged.
Other aspects of the book may vary from the original edition.
Set in 16 pt. Plantin.
Printed on permanent paper.

LIBRARY OF CONGRESS CATALOGING-IN-PUBLICATION DATA

Lindsay, Jeffry P.
    Dexter by design / by Jeff Lindsay.
      p. cm. — (Thorndike Press large print core)
    ISBN-13: 978-1-4104-2083-1 (alk. paper)
    ISBN-10: 1-4104-2083-3 (alk. paper)
    1. Forensic scientists—Fiction. 2. Vigilantes—Fiction. 3. Serial murderers—Fiction. 4. Miami (Fla.)—Fiction. 5. Psychological fiction. 6. Large type books. I. Title.
PS3562.I51175D46 2009b
813'.54—dc22   2009034256

BRITISH LIBRARY CATALOGUING-IN-PUBLICATION DATA AVAILABLE

Published in 2009 in the U.S. by arrangement with Doubleday, an imprint of Knopf Doubleday Publishing Group.
Published in 2010 in the U.K. by arrangement with The Orion Publishing Group Ltd.

U.K. Hardcover: 978 1 408 46060 3 (Windsor Large Print)
U.K. Softcover: 978 1 408 46061 0 (Paragon Large Print)

Printed in the United States of America
1 2 3 4 5 6 7 13 12 11 10 09

For LTF
with all my love

ONE

Pardonnez-moi, monsieur. Où est la lune? Alors, mon ancien, la lune est ici, ouvre la Seine, énorme, rouge, et humide. Merci, mon ami, I see it now. *Et actualment,* name of a dog, it is a night for the moon, a night made just for the sharp pleasures of the moonlight, the dance macabre between Dexter of the Dark and some special friend.

But *merde alors!* The moon is over la Seine? Dexter is in Paris! *Quelle tragédie!* The Dance is not possible, not in Paris! Here there is no way to find the special friend, no sheltering Miami night, no gentle welcoming ocean waters for the leftovers. Here there is only the taxis, the tourists, and that huge and lonely moon.

And Rita, of course. Rita everywhere, fumbling with her phrase book and folding and unfolding dozens of maps and guidebooks and pamphlets, all promising perfect happiness and, miraculously, delivering it

7

— to her. Only to her. Because her newly wedded Parisian bliss is strictly a solo act, and her newly acquired husband, former high priest of lunar levity, Dexter the Drastically Deferred, can only marvel at the moon and hold tightly to the impatiently twitching Dark Passenger and hope that all this happy insanity will end soon and send us back to the well-ordered normal life of catching and carving the other monsters.

For Dexter is used to carving freely, with a neat and happy hand that now must merely clutch at Rita's while he marvels at the moon, savoring the irony of being on a Honeymoon, wherein all that is sweet and lunar is forbidden.

And so, Paris. Dexter trudges meekly along in the wake of the Good Ship Rita, staring and nodding where these things are required and occasionally offering a sharp and witty comment, like, "Wow," and "Uh-huh," as Rita trammels through the pent-up lust for Paris that has surged in her all these many years and now, at last, has found consummation.

But surely even Dexter is not immune to the legendary charms of the City of Light? Surely even he must behold the glory and feel some small synthetic twitch stirring in response, somewhere in the dark and empty pit where a soul should go? Can Dexter truly come to Paris and feel absolutely nothing?

Of course not. Dexter feels plenty; Dexter feels tired, and bored. And Dexter feels slightly anxious to find someone to play with sometime soon. The sooner the better, to be perfectly honest, since for some reason Being Married seems to sharpen the appetites somewhat.

But this is all part of the bargain, all part of what Dexter must do in order to do what Dexter does. In Paris, just like at home, Dexter must *maintenez le disguisement.* Even the worldly-wise French might pause and frown at the thought of a monster in their midst, an inhuman fiend who lives only to tumble the other monsters off the edge and into well-earned death. And Rita, in her new incarnation as blushing bride, is the perfect *disguisement* for all I truly am. No one could possibly imagine that a cold and empty killer would stumble meekly along behind such a perfect avatar of American tourism. Surely, not, *mon frère. C'est impossible.*

For the moment, alas, *très impossible.* There is no hope of slipping quietly away for a few hours of much-deserved recreation. Not here, where Dexter is not known and does not know the ways of the police. Never in a strange and foreign place, where the strict rules of the Harry Code do not apply. Harry was a Miami cop, and in Miami all that he spake was just as he ordained it to be. But Harry spake no French, and so the risk is far too high here, no matter how strongly the pulse of darkness may throb in the shadowy backseat.

A shame, really, because the streets of Paris are made for lurking with sinister intent. They are narrow, dark, and possess no logical order that a reasonable person can detect. It's far too easy to imagine Dexter, wrapped in a cape and clutching a gleaming blade, sliding through these shadowed alleys with an urgent appointment somewhere nearby in one of these same old buildings that seem to lean down at you and demand that you misbehave.

And the streets themselves are so perfect for mayhem, made as they are out of large blocks of stone that, in Miami, would long ago have been pried out and flung through the windshield of passing cars, or sold to a building contractor to make new roads.

But this is not Miami, alas. This is Paris. And so I bide my time, solidifying this vital new phase of Dexter's disguise, hoping to live through only one week more of Rita's dream honeymoon. I drink the French coffee — weak by Miami standards — and the *vin de table* — disturbingly, reminiscently, red as blood — and marvel at my new wife's capacity for soaking up all that is French. She has learned to blush very nicely as she says *table pour deux, s'il vous plaît,* and the French waiters instantly understand that this is a brand-new two and, almost as if they all got together ahead of time and agreed to feed Rita's romantic fantasies, they smile fondly, bow us to a table, and all but break into a chorus of "La Vie en rose."

Ah, Paris. *Ah, l'amour.*

We spend the days trudging through the streets and stopping at terribly important map references. We spend the nights in small and quaint eating spots, many of them with the added bonus of some form of French music playing. We even attend a performance of *The Imaginary Invalid* at the Comédie Française. It is performed entirely in French for some reason, but Rita seems to enjoy it.

Two nights later she seems to enjoy the show at the Moulin Rouge just as much. She seems, in fact, to enjoy nearly everything about Paris, even riding a boat up and down the river. I do not point out to her that much nicer boat rides are available at home in Miami, boat rides that she has never shown any interest in, but I do begin to wonder what, if anything, she might be thinking.

She assaults every landmark in the city, with Dexter as her unwilling shock troop, and nothing can stand before her. The Eiffel Tower, the Arc de Triomphe, Sacré-Coeur, the cathedral of Notre-Dame; they all fall to her fierce blond focus and savage guidebook.

It begins to seem like a somewhat high price to pay for *disguisement,* but Dexter is the perfect soldier. He plods on under his heavy burden of duty and water bottles. He does not complain about the heat, his sore feet, the large and unlovely crowds in their too-tight shorts, souvenir T-shirts, and flip-flops.

He does, however, make one small attempt to stay interested. During the Hop-on-Hop-off Bus Tour of Paris, as the taped program drones out the names of the different fascinating locations with massive historical significance in eight languages, a thought comes unasked for into Dexter's slowly suffocating brain. It seems only fair that here in the City of Eternal Accordion Music there is some small cultural pilgrimage available to a long-suffering monster, and I know now what it is. At the next stop, I pause at the door of the bus and ask the driver a simple and innocent question.

"Excuse me," I say. "Do we go anywhere near the Rue Morgue?"

The driver is listening to an iPod. He pulls one earbud out with an annoyed flourish, looks me over from head to toe, and raises an eyebrow.

"The Rue Morgue," I say again. "Do we go by the Rue Morgue?"

I find myself speaking in the too-loud tones of the American nonlinguist, and I stumble to a stop. The driver stares at me. I can hear tinny hip-hop music coming from the dangling earbud. Then he shrugs. He launches into a brief and passionate explanation of my complete ignorance in very rapid French, pops the earbud back in, and opens the door to the bus.

I follow Rita off the bus, meek, humble, and mildly disappointed. It had seemed like such a simple thing to make a solemn stop at the Rue Morgue, to pay my respects to an important cultural landmark in the world of Monsters, but it is not to be. I repeat the question later, to a taxi driver, and receive the same answer, and Rita interprets with a somewhat embarrassed smile.

"Dexter," she says. "Your pronunciation is

terrible."

"I might do better in Spanish," I say.

"It wouldn't matter," she says. "There is no Rue Morgue."

"What?"

"It's imaginary," she says. "Edgar Allan Poe made it up. There is no *real* Rue Morgue."

I feel like she has just said there is no Santa Claus. No Rue Morgue? No happy historical pile of Parisian corpses? How can this be? But it is certain to be true. There is no questioning Rita's knowledge of Paris. She has spent too many years with too many guidebooks for any possibility of a mistake.

And so I slide back into my shell of dumb compliance, the tiny flicker of interest killed as dead as Dexter's conscience.

With only three days left before we fly back home to the blessed malice and mayhem of Miami, we come to our Full Day at the Louvre. This is something that has raised mild interest even in me; after all, merely because I have no soul does not mean I don't appreciate art. Quite the opposite, in fact. Art is, after all, all about making patterns in order to create a meaningful impact on the senses. And isn't this just exactly what Dexter does? Of course, in my case "impact" is a little more literal, but still

— I can appreciate other media.

So it was with at least a mild interest that I followed Rita across the huge courtyard of the Louvre and down the stairs into the glass pyramid. She had chosen to go this alone and forsake the tour groups — not out of any distaste for the grungy mobs of gaping, drooling, woefully ignorant sheep who seemed to coalesce around each tour guide, but because Rita was determined to prove that she was a match for any museum, even a French one.

She marched us right up to the ticket line, where we waited for several minutes before she finally bought our tickets, and then we were off into the wonders of the Louvre.

The first wonder was immediately obvious as we climbed out of the admissions area and into the actual museum. In one of the first galleries we came to, a huge crowd of perhaps five large tour groups was clustered around a perimeter marked by a red velvet rope. Rita made a noise that sounded something like "mrmph" and reached for my hand to drag me past. As we walked rapidly past the crowd I turned for a look; it was the *Mona Lisa.* "It's so tiny," I blurted out.

"And very overrated," Rita said primly.

I know that a honeymoon is meant to be a

time for getting to know your new life partner, but this was a Rita I had never encountered before. The one I thought I knew did not, as far as I could tell, ever have strong opinions, especially opinions that were contrary to conventional wisdom. And yet, here she was calling the most famous painting in the world overrated. The mind boggled; at least, mine did.

"It's the *Mona Lisa*," I said. "How can it be overrated?"

She made another noise that was all consonants and pulled on my hand a little harder. "Come look at the Titians," she said. "They're much nicer."

The Titians were very nice. So were the Rubenses, although I did not see anything in them to explain why they should have a sandwich named for them. But that thought did make me realize I was hungry, and I managed to steer Rita through three more long rooms filled with very nice paintings and into a café on one of the upper levels.

After a snack that was more expensive than airport food and only a little tastier, we spent the rest of the day wandering through the museum looking at room after room of paintings and sculptures. There really were an awful lot of them, and by the time we finally stepped out into the twilit courtyard again my formerly magnificent brain had been pounded into submission.

"Well," I said as we sauntered across the flagstones, "that was certainly a full day."

"Oohhh," she said, and her eyes were still large and bright, as they had been for most of the day. "That was absolutely incredible!" And she put an arm around me and nestled close, as if I had been personally responsible for creating the entire museum. It made walking a bit more difficult, but it was, after all, the sort of thing one did on a honeymoon in Paris, so I let her cling and we staggered across the courtyard and through the gate into the street.

As we turned the corner a young woman with more facial piercings than I would have thought possible stepped in front of us and thrust a piece of paper into Rita's hands. "Now to see the real art," she said. "Tomorrow night, eh?"

"Merci," Rita said blankly, and the woman moved past, thrusting her papers at the rest of the evening crowd.

"I think she probably could have gotten a few more earrings on the left side," I said as Rita frowned at the paper. "And she missed a spot on her forehead."

"Oh," said Rita. "It's a performance piece."

Now it was my turn to stare blankly, and I did. "What is?"

"Oh, that's so exciting," she said. "And we don't have anything to do tomorrow night. We're going!"

"Going where?"

"This is just perfect," she said.

And maybe Paris really is a magical place after all. Because Rita was right.

Two

Perfection was in a small and shadowed street not too far from the Seine, in what Rita breathlessly informed me was the Rive Gauche, and it took the form of a storefront performance space called Réalité. We had hurried through dinner — even skipping dessert! — in order to get there at seven-thirty, as the flyer had urged. There were about two dozen people inside when we got there, clustered together in small groups in front of a series of flat-screen TV monitors mounted on the walls. It all seemed very gallery-like, until I picked up one of the brochures. It was printed in French, English, and German. I skipped ahead to the English and began to read.

After only a few sentences I felt my eyebrows climbing up my forehead. It was a manifesto of sorts, written with a clunky passion that did not translate well, except possibly into German. It spoke of expanding the frontiers of art into new areas of perception, and destroying the arbitrary line between art and life drawn by the archaic and emasculated Academy. And even though some pioneering work had been done by Chris Burden, Rudolf Schwarzkogler, David Nebreda, and others, it was time to smash the wall and move forward into the twenty-first century. And tonight, with a new piece called *Jennifer's Leg,* we were going to do just that.

It was all extremely passionate and idealistic, which I have always found to be a very dangerous combination, and I would have found it a little funny — except that Someone Else was finding it so, more than a little; somewhere deep in the dungeons of Castle Dexter I heard a soft and sibilant chuckle from the Dark Passenger, and that amusement, as always, heightened my senses and brought me up on point. I mean, really; the Passenger was enjoying an *art* exhibit?

I looked around the gallery with a different sort of awareness. The muted whispering of the people clustered by the monitors no longer seemed to be the hush of respect toward art. Now I could see an edge of disbelief and even shock in their near silence.

I looked at Rita. She was frowning as she

read, and shaking her head. "I've heard of Chris Burden, he was American," she said. "But this other one, Schwarzkogler?" She stumbled over the name — after all, she had been studying French all this time, not German. "Oh," she said, and she began to blush. "It says he . . . he cut off his own —" She looked up at the people around the room, staring silently at something or other on the screens. "Oh my God," she said.

"Maybe we should go," I suggested, as my inner friend's amusement climbed steadily up the scale.

But Rita had already moved to stand in front of the first screen, and as she saw what it showed her mouth dropped open and began to twitch slightly, as if she was trying and failing to pronounce a very long and difficult word. "That's . . . that's . . . that's —" she said.

And a quick look at the screen showed that Rita was right again: it really was.

On the monitor a video clip showed a young woman dressed in an archaic stripper's costume of bangles and feathers. But instead of the kind of sexually provocative pose the outfit might have called for, she stood with one leg up on the table and, in a short and soundless loop of about fifteen seconds, she brought a whirring table saw down on her leg and threw her head back, mouth wide open in anguish. Then the clip jumped back to the start and she did the whole thing again.

"Dear God," Rita said. Then she shook her head. "That's . . . that's some kind of trick photography. It HAS to be."

I was not so sure. In the first place, I had already been tipped off by the Passenger that something very interesting was going on here. And in the second place, the expression on the woman's face was quite familiar to me from my own artistic endeavors. It was genuine pain, I was quite sure, real and extreme agony — and yet, in all my extensive research I had never before encountered someone willing to inflict this much of it on themselves. No wonder the Passenger was having a fit of the giggles. Not that I found it funny: if this sort of thing took hold, I would have to find a new hobby.

Still, it was an interesting twist, and I might have been more than willing to look at the other video clips under ordinary circumstances. But it did seem to me that I had some kind of responsibility toward Rita, and this was clearly not the sort of thing she could see and still maintain a sunny outlook. "Come on," I said. "Let's go get some dessert."

But she just shook her head and repeated, "It HAS to be a trick," and she moved on to the next screen.

I moved with her and was rewarded with another fifteen-second loop of the young woman in the same costume. In this one she actually appeared to be removing a chunk of flesh from her leg. Her expression here moved into dumb and endless agony, as if the pain had gone on long enough that she was used to it, but it still hurt. And strangely enough, this expression reminded me of the face of the woman at the end of a movie Vince Masuoka had shown at my bachelor party — I believe it was called *Frat House Gang Bang.* There was a gleam of I-Showed-You satisfaction visible through the fatigue and the pain as she looked down at the six-inch patch between her knee and her shin where all the flesh was peeled off to reveal the bone.

"Oh my God," Rita murmured. And for some reason she moved on to the next monitor.

I do not pretend to understand human beings. For the most part I try to maintain a logical outlook on life, and this is usually a real disadvantage in trying to figure out what people really think they're doing. I mean, as far as I could tell, Rita truly was as sweet and pleasant and optimistic as Rebecca of Sunnybrook Farm. The sight of a dead cat beside the road could move her to tears. And yet here she was, methodically moving through an exhibit that was clearly far worse than anything she had ever imagined. She knew that the next clip would be more of the same, graphic and appalling beyond belief. And yet, instead of sprinting for the exit, she was calmly moving on to the next screen.

More people drifted in, and I watched them go through the same process of recognition and shock. The Passenger was clearly enjoying things, but to be perfectly truthful, I was beginning to think that the whole affair was wearing a little thin. I could not really get into the spirit of the event and feel any sense of fun from the audience's suffering. After all, where was the point? Okay, Jennifer cut off pieces of her leg. So what? Why bother inflicting enormous pain on yourself when sooner or later Life would certainly get around to doing it for you? What did it prove? What happened next?

Still, Rita seemed determined to make herself as uncomfortable as possible, moving relentlessly from one video loop to the next. And I could think of nothing else to do but follow along in her wake, nobly enduring as she repeated "Oh God. Oh my God" at each new horror.

At the far end of the room, the largest clump of people stood looking at something on the wall that was angled away so we could only see the metal edge of the frame. It was clear from their faces that this was a real doozy, the climax of the show, and I was a little impatient to get to it and get things over with, but Rita insisted on seeing every clip along the way first. Each one showed the woman doing more dreadful things to her leg, until finally, in the last one, a slightly longer clip that showed her sitting still and staring down at her leg, there was nothing left but smooth white bone between her knee and her ankle. The flesh on the foot was left intact, and looked very odd at the end of the pale length of bone.

Even odder was the expression on Jennifer's face, a look of exhausted and triumphant pain that said she had clearly proved something. I glanced again at the program, but I found nothing to say what that something was.

Rita had no apparent insight, either. She had fallen into a numb silence, and simply stared at the final clip, watching it three times before shaking her head a last time and moving on as if hypnotized to where the larger group of people stood clustered around the Something in the metal frame at the far end of the room.

It proved to be by far the most interesting piece in the exhibit, the real clincher as far as I was concerned, and I could hear the Passenger chuckling agreement. Rita, for the first time, was unable even to muster another repeat of "Oh my God."

Mounted on a square of raw plywood and set in a steel frame was Jennifer's leg bone. The whole thing this time, including everything from the knee down.

"Well," I said. "At least we know for sure it isn't trick photography."

"It's a fake," Rita said, but I don't think she believed it.

Somewhere outside in the bright lights of the world's most glamorous city, the church bells were striking the hour. But inside the little gallery there was very little glamour, and the bells sounded unusually loud — almost loud enough to cover another sound, the sibilance of a small familiar voice letting me know that things were about to get even more interesting, and because I have learned that this voice is almost always right, I turned around to look.

Sure enough, the plot was thickening even as I glanced at the front of the room. Because as I watched, the door swung open, and with a rustle of spangles, Jennifer herself came in.

I had thought the room was quiet before, but it had been Mardi Gras compared to the silence that followed her as she clumped down the length of the room on crutches. She was pale and gaunt. Her stripper's costume hung loosely from her body, and she walked slowly and carefully, as if she was not yet used to the crutches. A clean white bandage covered the stump of her newly missing leg.

As Jennifer approached us where we stood in front of the mounted leg bone, I could feel Rita shrink back, away from any possible contact with the one-legged woman. I glanced at her; she was nearly as pale as Jennifer, and she had apparently given up breathing.

I looked back up. Just like Rita had done, the rest of the crowd, with their unblinking eyes fixed on Jennifer, edged away from her path, and she finally came to a halt only a foot in front of her leg. She stared at it for a long moment, apparently unaware that she was depriving an entire roomful of people of oxygen. Then she raised one hand off the crutches, leaned forward, and touched the leg bone.

"Sexy," she said.

I turned to Rita, thinking I might whisper *"ars longa,"* or words to that effect. But it was no use.

Rita had fainted.

THREE

We arrived home in Miami on a Friday evening, two days later, and the mean-spirited surge of the crowd in the airport as they cursed and shoved one another around the baggage carousel nearly brought a tear to my eye. Someone tried to walk off with Rita's suitcase, and then snarled at me when I took it away, and this was all the welcome I needed. It was good to be home.

And if any further sentimental greeting was necessary, I got it bright and early on Monday morning, my first day back at work. I stepped off the elevator and bumped into Vince Masuoka. "Dexter," he said, in what I am sure was a very emotional tone of voice, "did you bring doughnuts?" It was truly heartwarming to realize that I had been missed, and if only I had a heart, I am sure it would have been warmed.

"I no longer eat doughnuts," I told him. "I only eat *croissants.*"

Vince blinked. "How come?" he said.

"Je suis Parisien," I said.

He shook his head. "Well, you should have brought doughnuts," he said. "We got a really weird one out on South Beach this morning, and there's no place out there to get doughnuts."

"Quel tragique," I said.

"Are you gonna stay like this all day?" he said. " 'Cause this could be a really long one."

It was, in fact, a long one, made longer by the mad crush of reporters and other gawkers who already stood three deep at the yellow crime-scene tape strung up around a chunk of beach not too far from the southernmost tip of South Beach. I was already sweating when I worked my way through the crowd and onto the sand, over to where I saw Angel Batista-No-Relation already down on his hands and knees about twenty feet from the bodies, examining something that no one else could see.

"What's weird?" I asked him.

He didn't even look up. "Tits on a frog," he said.

"I'm sure you're right. But Vince said there's something weird about these bodies."

He frowned at something and bent closer

30

to the sand.

"Don't you worry about sand mites?" I asked him.

Angel just nodded. "They were killed somewhere else," he said. "But one of them dripped a little." He frowned. "But it's not blood."

"How lucky for me."

"Also," he said, using tweezers to put something invisible into a plastic bag, "they got . . ." And he paused here, not for any reason connected with unseen objects, but as if to find a word that wouldn't frighten me, and in the silence I heard a rising whir of stretching wings from the dark backseat of the Dexter-mobile.

"What?" I said, when I could stand it no longer.

Angel shook his head slightly. "They got — arranged," he said, and as if a spell had broken, he jerked into motion, sealing his plastic bag, placing it carefully to one side, and then going back down on one knee.

If that was all he had to say on the subject, I would clearly have to go see for myself what all the sibilant silence was about. So I walked another twenty feet to the bodies.

Two of them, one male and one female, apparently in their thirties, and they had not been chosen for their beauty. Both were

31

pale, overweight, and hairy. They had been carefully arranged on gaudy beach towels, the kind so popular with tourists from the Midwest. Casually spread open on the woman's lap was a bright pink paperback novel with the kind of gaudy cover that people from Michigan love to carry around on vacation: *Tourist Season.* A perfectly ordinary married couple enjoying a day at the beach.

To underline the happiness they were supposed to be experiencing, each of them had a semitransparent plastic mask stuck onto their face and apparently held in place with glue, the kind of mask that gave the wearer's face a large and artificial smile while still allowing the actual face to show through. Miami, the home of permanent smiles.

Except that these two had somewhat unusual reasons to smile, reasons that had my Dark Passenger burbling with what very nearly sounded like a case of the giggles. These two bodies had been split open from the bottom of the rib cage down to the waistline, and then the flesh had been peeled back to show what was inside. And I did not need the surge of sibilant hilarity that rose up from my shadowy friend to appreciate that what was inside was just a little bit out of the ordinary.

All of the standard-issue messiness had been removed, which I thought was a very nice start. There was no awful gooey heap of intestines or other glistening horrible guts. Instead, all the dreadful bloody gunk had been scooped out. The woman's body cavity had then been neatly and tastefully converted into a tropical fruit basket, the kind that might welcome special guests to a good hotel. I could see a couple of mangoes, papayas, oranges and grapefruits, a pineapple, and of course some bananas. There was even a bright red ribbon attached to the rib cage, and poking up out of the middle of the fruit was a bottle of cheap champagne.

The man had been arranged with a somewhat more casual diversity. Instead of the bright and attractive fruit medley, his emptied gut had been filled with a huge and gaudy pair of sunglasses, a dive mask and snorkel, a squeeze bottle of sunscreen, a can of insect repellent, and a small plate of *pasteles,* Cuban pastries. It seemed like a terrible waste in this sandy wilderness without doughnuts. Propped up on one side of the cavity was some kind of large pamphlet or brochure. I could not see the cover, so I bent over and looked closer; it was *The South Beach Swimsuit Calendar.* A grouper's head peeked out from behind the calendar, its gaping fishy face frozen into a smile that was eerily similar to the one on the plastic mask glued to the man's face.

I heard the hiss of feet through the sand behind me and turned around.

"Friend of yours?" my sister, Deborah, said as she walked over and nodded at the bodies. Perhaps I should say Sergeant Deborah, since my job requires me to be polite to someone who has reached her exalted rank in the police force. And polite I generally am, even to the point of ignoring her snarky remark. But the sight of what she held in her hand wiped away all my political obligations. Somehow, she had managed to come up with a doughnut — a Bavarian cream, my favorite — and she took a large bite. It seemed horribly unfair. "What do you think, bro?" she said through a mouthful.

"I think you should have brought me a doughnut," I said.

She bared her teeth in a large smile, which did not help anything, since her gums were lined with chocolate frosting from the doughnut in question. "I did," she said. "But I got hungry and ate it."

It was nice to see my sister smile, since it was not something she had been doing much of for the last few years; it just didn't seem to fit in with her cop self-image. But I was not filled with the warm glow of brotherly affection at seeing her — mostly because I was not filled with doughnut, either, and I wanted to be. Still, I knew from my research that the happiness of one's family was the next-best thing, so I put the best possible face on it.

"I'm very happy for you," I said.

"No you're not, you're pouting," she said. "What do you think?" And she crammed the last chunk of Bavarian cream into her mouth and nodded down at the bodies again.

Of course, Deborah, of all people in the world, had the right to ask for the benefit of my special insight into the sick and twisted animals who killed like this, since she was my only relative and I was sick and twisted myself. But aside from the slowly fading amusement of the Dark Passenger, I had no particular insight into why these two bodies had been arranged like a welcome message from a very troubled civic booster. I listened intently for a long moment, pretending to study the bodies, but I neither heard nor saw anything, except a faint and impatient clearing of the throat from the shadows inside Chateau Dexter. But Deborah was expecting some sort of pronouncement.

"It seems awfully contrived," I managed to say.

"Nice word," she said. "What the fuck does that mean?"

I hesitated. Usually my special insight into unusual homicides makes it easy for me to develop an idea of what kind of psychological chaos produced the heap of human leftovers in question. But in this case, I was drawing a blank. Even a true expert like myself has limits, and whatever trauma created the need to turn a pudgy woman into a fruit basket was beyond me and my interior helper.

Deborah looked at me expectantly. I didn't want to give her any casual chatter that she might take for genuine insight and charge off in the wrong direction. On the other hand, my reputation required that I offer some kind of learned opinion.

"It's nothing definite," I said. "It's just that —" And I paused for a moment, because I realized that what I had been about to say actually was a genuine insight, and the small encouraging chuckle from the Passenger confirmed it.

"What, goddamn it?" Deborah said, and it was something of a relief to see her return to her own cranky normality.

"This was done with a kind of cold control you don't see normally," I said.

Debs snorted. "Normally," she said. "Like, what — normal like you?"

I was surprised at the personal turn her remarks were taking, but I let it go. "Normal for somebody who could do this," I said. "There needs to be some passion, some sign that whoever did this was really, uh — *feeling* the need to do it. Not this. Not just like, what can I do after that's fun."

"This is fun for you?" she said.

I shook my head, irritated that she was deliberately missing the point. "No, it's not, that's what I'm trying to say. The *killing* part is supposed to be fun, and the bodies should reveal that. Instead, the killing wasn't the point at all, it was just a means to an end. Instead of the end itself . . . Why are you looking at me like that?"

"Is that what it's like for you?" she said.

I found myself somewhat taken aback, an unusual situation for Dashing Dexter, always ready with a quip. Deborah was still coming to terms with what I was, and what her father had done with me, and I could appreciate that it was difficult for her to deal with on a daily basis, especially at work — which for her, after all, involved finding people like me and sending them to Old Sparky.

On the other hand, it was truly not something I could talk about with anything approaching comfort. Even with Deborah, it felt like discussing oral sex with your mother. So I decided to sidestep ever so slightly. "My point," I said, "is that this doesn't seem to be about the killing. It's about what to do with the bodies afterward."

She stared at me for a moment, and then shook her head. "I would love to know what the fuck you think that means," she said. "But even more, I think I would love to know what the fuck goes on in your head."

I took a deep breath and let it out slowly. It sounded soothingly like a sound the Passenger might make. "Look, Debs," I said. "What I'm saying is, we're not dealing with a killer — we're dealing with somebody who likes to play with *dead* bodies, not live ones."

"And that makes a difference?"

"Yes."

"Does he still kill people?" she asked.

"It sure looks like it."

"And he'll probably do it again?"

"Probably," I said over a cold chuckle of interior certainty that only I could hear.

"So what's the difference?" she said.

"The difference is that there won't be the

38

same kind of pattern. You can't know when he'll do it again, or who he'll do it to, or any of the things you can usually count on to help you catch him. All you can do is wait and hope you get lucky."

"Shit," she said. "I never was good at waiting."

There was a little bit of a commotion over where the cars were parked, and an overweight detective named Coulter came scuffling rapidly over the sand to us.

"Morgan," he said, and we both said, "Yeah?"

"Not you," he told me. "You. Debbie."

Deborah made a face — she hated being called Debbie. "What?" she said.

"We're supposed to partner on this," he said. "Captain said."

"I'm already here," she said. "I don't need a partner."

"Now you do," Coulter said. He took a swig from a large soda bottle. "There's another one of these," he said, gasping for breath. "Over at Fairchild Gardens."

"Lucky you," I said to Deborah. She glared at me and I shrugged. "Now you don't have to wait," I said.

FOUR

One of the great things about Miami has always been the total willingness of its residents to pave everything. Our Fair City began as a subtropical garden spot teeming with wildlife, both animal and vegetable, and after only a very few years of hard work all the plants were gone and the animals were dead. Of course their memory lingers on in the condo clusters that replaced them. It is an unwritten law that each new development be named after whatever was killed to build it. Destroy eagles? Eagle's Nest Gated Community. Kill off the panthers? Panther Run Planned Living. Simple and elegant and generally very lucrative.

I don't mean to suggest by this that Fairchild Gardens was a parking lot where all the Fairchilds and their tulips had been killed. Far from it. If anything, it represented the revenge of the plants. Of course you had to drive past a certain number of Orchid

Bays and Cypress Hollows to get there, but when you arrived, you were greeted by a vast natural-looking wilderness of trees and orchids nearly devoid of hedge-clipping humanity. Except for the busloads of tourists, of course. Still, there were actually one or two places where you could look at a genuine palm tree without seeing neon lights in the background, and on the whole I usually found it a relief to walk among the trees and vegetate far from the hurly-burly.

But this morning the parking area was overflowing when we arrived, since the Gardens had been closed with the discovery of Something Awful, and the crowds of people who had scheduled a visit had backed up at the entrance, hoping to get inside so they could mark it off on their itinerary, and maybe even see something horrible so they could pretend to be shocked. A perfect vacation visit to Miami: orchids and corpses.

There were even two elfin young men with video cameras circulating through the crowd and filming, of all things, the people standing around and waiting. And as they moved they called out, "Murder in the Gardens!" and other encouraging remarks. Perhaps they had a good parking spot and didn't want to leave it, since there was absolutely no place left to park anything larger than a unicycle.

Deborah, of course, was a Miami native, and a Miami cop; she pushed her motor-pool Ford through the crowd and parked it right in front of the main entrance to the park, where several other official cars were already parked, and jumped right out. By the time I got out of the car, she was already talking to the uniformed officer standing there, a short and beefy guy named Meltzer, who I knew slightly. He was pointing down one of the paths on the far side of the entrance, and Deborah was already headed past him along the trail to which he had pointed.

I followed as quickly as I could. I was used to tagging along behind Deborah and playing catch-up, since she always rushed onto a crime scene. It never seemed quite politic to point out to her that there was really no need to hurry. After all, the victim wasn't going anywhere. Still, Deborah hurried, and she expected me to be there to tell her what she thought of it. And so, before she could get lost in the carefully tended jungle, I hurried after her.

I finally caught up to her just as she skidded to a halt in a small clearing off the main trail, in an area called Rain Forest. There was a bench where the weary nature lover could pause and recuperate amid the blooms. Alas for poor panting Dexter, breathing hard now as a result of racing pell-mell after Debs, the bench was already occupied by someone who clearly needed to sit down far more than I did.

He sat beside running water in the shade of a palm tree, dressed in baggy cotton shorts, the flimsy kind that have somehow become okay to wear in public recently, and he wore the rubber flip-flops that invariably go with the shorts. He also had on a T-shirt that said I'M WITH BUTTHEAD, and he was draped with a camera and pensively clutching a bouquet. And although I say pensively, it was a very different kind of pens-ing, because his head had been neatly removed and replaced with a gaudy spray of tropical flowers. And in the bouquet, instead of flowers, was a bright and festive heap of intestines, topped by what was almost certainly a heart and surrounded by an appreciative cloud of flies.

"Son of a bitch," Deborah said, and it was hard to argue with her logic. "Son of a goddamn bitch. Three of 'em in one day."

"We don't know for sure that they're connected," I said carefully, and she glared at me.

"You want to tell me we got TWO of these assholes running around at the same time?" she demanded.

"It doesn't seem very likely," I admitted.

"You're goddamned right it doesn't. And I'm about to have Captain Matthews and every reporter on the Eastern Seaboard on my ass."

"Sounds like quite a party," I said.

"So what am I supposed to tell them?"

"We are pursuing a number of leads and hope to have something more definite to tell you shortly," I said.

Deborah stared at me with the look of a large and very angry fish, all teeth and wide eyes. "I can remember that shit without your help," she said. "Even the reporters can remember that shit. And Captain Matthews *invented* that shit."

"What kind of shit would you prefer?" I asked.

"The kind of shit that tells me what this is about, asshole."

I ignored my sister's name-calling and looked again at our nature-loving new friend. There was an air of studied ease to the position of the body that created a very large contrast to the fact that it was actually a very dead and headless former human being. It had apparently been posed with extreme care, and once again I got the distinct impression that this final die-orama was more important than the actual killing had been. It was a little bit disturbing, in spite of the mocking chuckle from the Dark Passenger. It was as if someone admitted they went through all the bother and mess of sex only in order to smoke a cigarette.

Equally disturbing was the fact that, as at the scene where the first two bodies were displayed, I was getting no hints at all from the Passenger, beyond a kind of disconnected and appreciative amusement.

"What this seems to be about," I said hesitatingly, "is making some kind of statement."

"Statement," Deborah said. "What kind of statement?"

"I don't know."

Deborah stared at me for a moment longer, then shook her head. "Thank God you're here to help," she said, and before I could think of some suitable remark that would defend me and sting her a little at the same time, the forensic team bustled into our peaceful little glen and began to photograph, measure, dust, and peer into all the tiny places that might hold answers. Deborah immediately turned away to talk to Camilla Figg, one of the lab geeks, and I was left alone to suffer in the knowledge that I had failed my sister.

I am sure the suffering would have been terrible if I was capable of feeling remorse, or any other crippling human emotion, but I am not built for it, and so I didn't feel it — or anything else except hunger. I went back out to the parking area and talked to Officer Meltzer until someone came along who could give me a ride back to the South Beach site. I had left my kit there, and had not even made a start on looking for any blood evidence.

I spent the rest of the morning shuttling back and forth between the two crime scenes. There was very little actual spatter work for me to do, no more than a few small, nearly dry spots in the sand that suggested the couple on the beach had been killed elsewhere and brought out onto the beach later. I was pretty sure we had all assumed this already, since it was very unlikely that somebody would do all that chopping and rearranging quite so publicly, so I didn't bother to mention this to Deborah, who was already in a pointless frenzy, and I didn't want any more of it aimed at me.

The only real break I got all day was at almost one o'clock, when Angel-No-Relation offered to drive me back to my cubicle, and stop along the way at Calle Ocho for lunch at his favorite Cuban restaurant, Habanita. I had a very nice Cuban steak with all the trimmings, and two *cafecitas* with my flan dessert, and I felt a whole lot better about myself as I headed into the building, flashed my credentials, and stepped into the elevator.

As the elevator doors slid shut I felt a small flutter of uncertainty from the Passenger, and I listened hard, wondering if this was a reaction to the morning's carnival of carnage, or perhaps the result of too many onions on my steak. But I could get nothing more from it beyond a certain tensing of black invisible wings, very often a sign that things were not what they should be. How this could happen in an elevator I did not know, and I considered the idea that the Passenger's recent sabbatical in the face of Moloch might have left it in a mildly dithering and unsettled state. It would not do, of course, to have a less than effective Passenger, and I was pondering what to do about that when the elevator doors opened and all questions were answered.

As if he had known we would be aboard, Sergeant Doakes stood glaring and unblinking at the exact spot where we stood, and the shock was considerable. He had never

47

liked me; had always had the unreasonable suspicion that I was some kind of monster, which of course I was, and he had been determined to prove it somehow. But an amateur surgeon had captured Doakes and removed his hands, feet, and tongue, and although I had endured considerable inconvenience in trying to save him — and really, I did help save most of him — he had decided his new, trimmed-down form was my fault, and he liked me even less.

Even the fact that without his tongue he was now incapable of saying anything that was minimally coherent was no help; he said it anyway, and the rest of us were forced to endure what sounded like a strange new language made up of all *G* and *N* sounds, and spoken with an urgent and threatening delivery that made you look for an emergency exit even while you strained to understand.

And so I braced myself for some angry gibberish and he stood there looking at me with an expression that is usually reserved for grandmother-rapers, and I began to wonder if I could possibly just push past him, and nothing else happened until the elevator doors began to close automatically. But before I could escape back downstairs, Doakes shot out his right hand — actually a gleaming steel claw — and stopped the doors from closing.

"Thank you," I said, and took a tentative step forward. But he did not budge and he did not blink, and without knocking him down, I did not see how I could get by.

Doakes kept his unblinking, loathing stare on me and brought up a small silver thing about the size of a hardcover book. He flipped it open to reveal that it was a small handheld computer or PDA and, still without looking away from me, he jabbed at it with his claw.

"Put it on my desk," said a disjointed male voice from the PDA, and Doakes snarled a little more and jabbed again. "Black with two sugars," the voice said, and he poked again. "Have a nice day," it said, really a very pleasant baritone that should have come from a happy and pudgy white American man instead of this glowering dark cyborg so bent on revenge.

But at least he finally had to look away, down to the keyboard of the thing he held in his claw, and after staring for a moment at what was clearly a cluster of prerecorded sentences, he found the right button.

"I am still watching you," said the happy baritone voice, and the cheerful and positive tone should have made me feel very good about myself, but the fact that it was Doakes saying it by proxy somehow spoiled the effect.

"That's very reassuring," I said. "Would you mind watching me get off the elevator?"

For a moment he thought he did mind, and he moved his claw to the keyboard again. But then he remembered that it hadn't worked out too well before to poke it without looking, so he glanced down, punched a button, and looked up at me as the cheerful voice said, "Motherfucker," in a tone that made it sound like "Jelly doughnut." But at least he moved aside slightly so I could get by.

"Thank you," I said, and because I am sometimes not a very kind person, I added, "And I will put it on your desk. Black with two sugars. Have a nice day." I stepped past him and headed down the hall, but I could feel his eyes on me all the way to my cubicle.

FIVE

The ordeal of the working day had been nightmarish enough, from being stranded without doughnuts in the morning all the way through the terrifying encounter with what was left of Sergeant Doakes, vocally enhanced version. Even so, none of this prepared me for the shock of arriving home.

I'd been hoping for the warm and fuzzy glow of a good meal and some downtime with Cody and Astor — perhaps a game of Kick the Can out in the yard before dinner. But as I pulled up and parked at Rita's house — now My House, too, which took some getting used to — I was surprised to see the two small and tousled heads sitting in the front yard and apparently waiting for me. Since I knew full well that *SpongeBob* was on TV right now, I could not imagine what would make them sit out here, instead of in front of the TV. So it was with a growing sense of alarm that I climbed out of my car and approached them.

"Greetings, citizens," I said. They stared at me with a matched set of mournful looks, but said nothing. That was to be expected from Cody, who never spoke more than four words at a time. But for Astor, it was alarming, since she had inherited her mother's talent for circular breathing, which allowed them both to talk without pausing for air, and to see her sit there without speaking was almost unprecedented. So I switched languages and tried again. "What up, yo?" I asked them.

"Poop van," said Cody. Or at any rate, that's what I thought I heard. But since none of my training had prepared me to respond to anything remotely like that, I looked over at Astor, hoping for some hint about how I should react.

"Mom said we get to have pizza, but it's the poop van for you, and we didn't want you to go away, so we came out here to warn you. You're not going away, are you, Dexter?"

It was a small relief to know that I had heard Cody right, even though that now meant that I really was dealing with trying to make sense of "poop van." Had Rita really said that? Did it mean that I had done something very bad that I didn't know about? That didn't seem fair — I liked to remember and enjoy it when I do something bad. And one day after the honeymoon — wasn't that just a little abrupt?

"As far as I know, I'm not going anywhere," I said. "Are you sure that's what your mom said?"

They nodded in unison and Astor said, "Uh-huh. She said you'd be surprised."

"She was right," I said, and it really didn't seem fair. I was totally at a loss. "Come on," I said. "We'll go tell her I'm not going." They each took one of my hands and we went inside.

The air inside the house was filled with a tantalizing aroma, strangely familiar and yet exotic, as if you sniffed a rose and instead smelled pumpkin pie. It was coming from the kitchen, so I led my small troop in that direction.

"Rita?" I called out, and the clatter of a pan answered me.

"It's not ready," she said. "It's a surprise."

As we all know, surprise is usually ominous, unless it is your birthday — and even then, there are no guarantees. But I pushed bravely into the kitchen anyway, and found Rita wearing an apron and fussing over the stove, a lock of blond hair falling unnoticed down across her forehead.

"Am I in trouble?" I asked.

"What? No, of course not. Why would —
damn it!" she said, sticking a singed finger
into her mouth, and then stirring the con-
tents of the pan furiously.

"Cody and Astor say you're sending me
away," I said.

Rita dropped her stirring spoon and
looked at me with an expression of alarm.
"Away? That's silly, I — why would I . . ."
She bent to pick up the spoon and jumped
to the skillet to stir again.

"So you didn't call the poop van?" I said.

"Dexter," she said, with a certain amount
of stress in her voice, "I am trying to make
you a special meal, and I'm working very
hard not to ruin it. Can this please wait until
later?" And she jumped to the counter and
grabbed a measuring cup, and then rushed
back to the skillet.

"What are you making?" I said.

"You liked the food so much in Paris,"
she said, frowning and slowly stirring in
whatever was in the measuring cup.

"I almost always like the food," I said.

"So I wanted to make you a nice French
meal," she said. "Coq au vin." She said it
with her best Bad French accent, *caca van,*
and a very small lightbulb came on in my
head.

54

"Caca van?" I said, and I looked at Astor. She nodded. "Poop van," she said.

"Damn it!" said Rita again, this time trying vainly to stick a burned elbow into her mouth.

"Come along, children," I said in a Mary Poppins voice. "I'll explain it outside." And I led them through the house, down the hall, and out into the backyard. We sat together on the step and they both looked at me expectantly.

"All right," I said. "Caca van is just a misunderstanding."

Astor shook her head. Since she knew absolutely everything, a misunderstanding was not possible. "Anthony said that *caca* means 'poop' in Spanish," she said with certainty. "And everybody knows what a van is."

"But coq au vin is French," I said. "It's something your mother and I learned about in France."

Astor shook her head, a little doubt showing on her face. "Nobody speaks French," she said.

"Several people speak it in France," I said. "And even over here, some people like your mother think they speak it."

"So what is it?" she asked.

"It's chicken," I said.

They looked at each other, then back at me. Oddly enough, it was Cody who broke the silence. "Do we still get pizza?" he asked.

"I'm pretty sure you do," I said. "So how about rounding up a team for Kick the Can?"

Cody whispered something to Astor, and she nodded. "Can you teach us stuff? You know, the other stuff?" she said.

The "other stuff" she referred to was, of course, the Dark Lore that went with training to be Dexter's Disciples. I had discovered recently that the two of them, because of the repeated trauma of life with their biological father, who regularly beat them with furniture and small appliances, had both turned into what can only be described as My Children. Dexter's Descendants. They were as permanently scarred as I was, forever twisted away from fuzzy puppy reality and into the sunless land of wicked pleasure. And they were far too eager to begin playing wicked games, and the only safe way out for them was through me and onto the Harry Path.

And truthfully, it would be a very real delight to conduct a small lesson tonight, as a baby step back in the direction of resuming my normal life, if I can use those two words together when talking about me. The

56

honeymoon had strained my imitations of polite behavior beyond all their previous limits, and I was ready to slither back into the shadows and polish my fangs. Why not bring the children along?

"All right," I said. "Go get some kids for Kick the Can, and I'll show you something you can use."

"By playing Kick the Can?" Astor said with a pout. "We don't want to know that."

"Why do I always win when we play Kick the Can?" I asked them.

"You don't," Cody said.

"Sometimes I LET one of you win," I said loftily.

"Ha," Cody said.

"The point is," I said, "I know how to move quietly. Why could that be important?"

"Sneak up on people," Cody said, a lot of words in a row for him. It was wonderful to see him coming out of his shell with this new hobby.

"Yes," I said. "And Kick the Can is a good game to practice that."

They looked at each other, and then Astor said, "Show us first, and then we'll go get everybody."

"All right," I said, and I stood up and led them to the hedge between their yard and the neighbors'.

It was not dark yet, but the shadows were getting longer as we stood there in the shaded grass beside the hedge. I closed my eyes for just a moment; something stirred in the dark backseat and I let the rustling of black wings rattle softly through me, feeling myself blend in with the shadows and become a part of the darkness —

"What are you doing?" Astor said.

I opened my eyes and looked at her. She and her brother were staring at me as if I had suddenly started to eat dirt, and it occurred to me that trying to explain an idea like becoming one with the darkness might be a tough sell. But it had been my idea to do this, so there was really no way around it.

"First," I said, trying to sound casually logical, "you have to make yourself relax, and feel like you're a part of the night around you."

"It's not night," Astor said.

"Then just be a part of the late afternoon, okay?" I said. She looked dubious, but she didn't say anything else, so I went on. "Now," I said. "There's something inside you that you need to wake up, and you need to listen to it. Does that make sense to you?"

58

"Shadow Guy," said Cody, and Astor nodded.

I looked at the two of them and felt something close to religious wonder. They knew about the Shadow Guy — their name for the Dark Passenger. They had it inside them as certainly as I did, and were familiar enough with its existence to have named it. There could be no doubt about it — they were already in the same dark world I lived in. It was a profound moment of connection, and I knew now that I was doing the right thing — these were my children and the Passenger's and the thought that we were together in this stronger-than-blood bond was almost overwhelming.

I was not alone. And I had a large and wonderful responsibility in taking charge of these two and keeping them safely on the Harry Path to becoming what they already were, but with safety and order. It was a lovely moment, and I am quite sure that somewhere music was playing.

And that really should have been how this day of turmoil and hardship ended. Really and truly, if there were any justice at all in this wide wicked world, we would have frolicked happily in the evening's heat, bonding and learning wonderful secrets, and then ambling in to a delicious meal of

French food and American pizza.

But of course, there is no such thing as justice, and most of the time I find myself pausing to reflect that it must be true that life does not really like us very much, after all. And I should not have been surprised when, just as I reached out a hand to each of them, my cell phone began to warble.

"Get your ass down here," Deborah said, without even a hello.

"Of course," I said. "As long as the rest of me can stay here for dinner."

"That's funny," she said, although she didn't sound very amused. "But I don't need another laugh right now, because I am looking at another one of those hilarious dead bodies."

I felt a small inquisitive purr from the Passenger, and several hairs on the back of my neck stood up for a closer look. "Another?" I said. "You mean like the three posed bodies this morning?"

"That's exactly what I mean," she said, and hung up.

"Har-de-har-har," I said, and put my phone away.

Cody and Astor were looking at me with an identical expression of disappointment. "That was Sergeant Debbie, wasn't it?" Astor said. "She wants you to go to work."

"That's right," I admitted.

"Mom is going to be really mad," she said, and it hit me that she was probably right — I could still hear Rita making furious cooking noises in the kitchen, punctuated with the occasional "damn it." I was hardly an expert on the subject of human expectations, but I was pretty sure she would be upset that I was going to leave without tasting this special and painfully prepared meal.

"Now I really am on the poop van," I said, and I went inside, wondering what I could possibly say and hoping some inspiration might hit me before Rita did.

Six

I was not at all certain I was going to the right place until I got there and pulled up in front — it had seemed like such an unlikely destination before I got to where I could see the yellow crime-scene tape, the lights of the patrol cars flashing in the dusk, and the growing crowd of gawkers hoping to see something unforgettable. It was almost always crowded at Joe's Stone Crab, but not in July. The restaurant would not open again until October, which seemed like a long wait even for Joe's.

But this was a different crowd tonight, and they weren't here for stone crabs. They were hungry for something else tonight, something Joe would most likely prefer to take off his menu.

I parked and followed the trail of uniformed officers around to the back, where tonight's entrée sat, leaning back against the wall beside the service door. I heard the sibilant interior chuckling before I actually saw any details, but as I got close enough, the lights strung up by the forensic team showed me plenty worth an appreciative smile.

His feet were crammed into a pair of those black glove-leather shoes that are usually Italian, and most often worn for the sole purpose of dancing. He also wore a pair of very nice resort-style shorts in a tasteful cranberry color, and a blue silk shirt with a silver embossed palm-tree pattern on it. But the shirt was unbuttoned and pulled back to reveal that the man's chest had been removed and the cavity emptied out of all the natural and awful stuff that should go in there. It was now filled instead with ice, bottles of beer, and what appeared to be a shrimp-cocktail ring from the grocery store. His right hand was clutching a fistful of Monopoly money, and his face was covered with another of those glued-on plastic masks.

Vince Masuoka crouched on the far side of the doorway spreading dust in slow even strokes across the wall, and I stepped over beside him.

"Are we going to get lucky tonight?" I asked him.

He snorted. "If they let us take a couple

of those free beers," he said. "They're really cold."

"How can you tell?" I asked.

He jerked his head toward the body. "It's that new kind, the label turns blue when it's cold," he said. He wiped his arm across his forehead. "It's gotta be over ninety out here, and that beer would taste great right now."

"Sure," I said, looking at the improbable shoes on the body. "And then we could go dancing."

"Hey," he said. "You want to? When we're done?"

"No," I said. "Where's Deborah?"

He nodded to his left. "Over there," he said. "Talking to the woman who found it."

I walked over to where Debs was interviewing a hysterical Hispanic woman who was crying into her hands and shaking her head at the same time, which struck me as a very difficult thing to do, like rubbing your belly and patting your head. But she was doing it quite well, and for some reason Deborah was not impressed with the woman's wonderful coordination.

"Arabelle," Debs was saying. "Arabelle, please listen to me." Arabelle was not listening, and I didn't think my sister's vocal tone of combined anger and authority was well calculated to win over anyone — especially not someone who looked like she had been sent over from a casting office to play the part of a cleaning woman with no green card. Deborah glared at me as I approached, as if it was my fault that she was intimidating Arabelle, so I decided to help.

It is not that I think Debs is incompetent — she is very good at her job; it's in her blood, after all. And the idea that to know me is to love me is one that has never crossed the shadowed threshold of my mind. Just the opposite, in fact. But Arabelle was so upset, it was clear that she was not filled with the thrill of discovery. She was instead several steps over the edge into hysteria, and talking to hysterical people, like so much of ordinary human interaction, takes no particular empathy or liking for people, happily for Dark and Dismal Dexter. It was all technique, a craft and not an art, and that put it squarely inside the expertise of anyone who has studied and copied human behavior. Smile in the right places, nod your head, pretend to listen — I had mastered it ages ago.

"Arabelle," I said in a soothing voice and with the proper Central American accent, and she stopped shaking her head for a moment. *"Arabelle, necitamos descubrir este monstre."* I looked over at Debs, and said,

"It is a monster that did this, right?" and she snapped her chin up and down in a nod of agreement.

"Digame, por favor," I said soothingly, and Arabelle very gratifyingly lowered one hand from her face.

"Sí?" she said shyly, and I marveled once again at the power of my totally smarmy synthetic charm. And in two languages, too.

"En inglés?" I said with a really good fake smile. *"Por qué mi hermana no habla español,"* I said, nodding at Deborah. I was sure that referring to Debs as "my sister," rather than "the authority figure with a gun who wants to send you back to El Salvador after she has seen you beaten and raped," would help to open her up a little bit. "Do you speak English?"

"Lee-tell beet," she said.

"Good," I said. "Tell my sister what you saw." And I took a step back, only to find that Arabelle had shot out a hand and clamped it onto my arm.

"You no go?" she said shyly.

"I stay here," I said. She looked at me searchingly for a moment. I don't have any idea what she was looking for, but she apparently thought she saw it. She let go of my arm, dropped both hands to clasp them in front of her, and faced Deborah, standing almost at attention.

I looked at Deborah, too, and found her staring at me with a look of disbelief on her face. "Jesus," she said. "She trusts you and not me?"

"She can tell that my heart is pure," I said.

"Pure what?" Debs said, and she shook her head. "Jesus. If she only knew."

I had to admit there was some truth in my sister's ironic observation. She had only recently discovered what I am, and to say that she was not quite comfortable with it was a bit of an understatement. Still, it had all been sanctioned and set up by her father, Saint Harry, and even in death his was not an authority that Debs would question — nor would I, for that matter. But her tone of voice was a little sharp for someone who was counting on me for help, and it stung just a little. "If you like," I said, "I can leave and let you do this alone."

"No!" said Arabelle, and once again her hand flew over and attached itself to my arm. "You say that you stay," she said, accusation and near panic in her voice.

I raised an eyebrow at Deborah.

She shrugged. "Yeah," she said. "You stay."

I patted Arabelle's hand and pried it off me. "I'll be right here," I said, adding, *"Yo espero aquí,"* with another completely artificial smile that for some reason seemed to reassure her. She looked into my eyes, smiled back, took a deep breath, and faced Debs.

"Tell me," Debs said to Arabelle.

"I get here same hour, like every time," she said.

"What hour is that?" Deborah asked.

Arabelle shrugged. "Five o'clock," she said. "Threes time a week now, because is close *en julio,* but they wan keep it clean. No coke-roachess." She looked at me and I nodded; coke-roachess bad.

"And you went to the back door?" Deborah asked.

"Esway, es—" She looked at me and made an awkward face. *"Siempre?"*

"Always," I translated.

Arabelle nodded. "Always back door," she said. "Frawnt ees close *hasta octobre.*"

Deborah cocked her head for a moment, but then got it: front closed until October. "Okay," she said. "So you get here, you go around to the back door, and you see the body?"

Arabelle covered her face again, just for a moment. She looked at me and I nodded, so she dropped her hands. "Yes."

"Did you notice anything else, anything unusual?" Debs asked, and Arabelle looked

68

at her blankly. "Did you see something that shouldn't be there?"

"*El cuerpo,*" Arabelle said indignantly, pointing at the corpse. "He no shood be there."

"And did you see anybody else at all?"

Arabelle shook her head. "Nobody. Me only."

"How about nearby?" Arabelle looked blank, and Deborah pointed. "Over there? On the sidewalk? Anybody at all over there?"

Arabelle shrugged. "*Turistas.* Weeth cameras." She frowned and lowered her voice, speaking confidentially to me. "*Creado que es posible que estan maricones,*" she said, shrugging.

I nodded. "Gay tourists," I said to Deborah.

Deborah glared at her, then turned it on me, as if she could scare one of us into thinking up another really good question. But even my legendary wit had run dry, and I shrugged. "I don't know," I said. "She probably can't tell you any more than that."

"Ask her where she lives," Deborah said, and an expression of alarm flitted across Arabelle's face.

"I don't think she'll tell you," I said.

"Why the fuck not?" Deborah demanded.

"She's afraid you'll tell *la migra,*" I said,

and Arabelle visibly jumped when I said it. "Immigration."

"I know what the fuck *la migra* means," Deborah snapped. "I live here, too, remember?"

"Yes," I said. "But you refused to learn Spanish."

"Then ask her to tell *you*," Deborah said.

I shrugged and turned to Arabelle. *"Necesito su dirección,"* I said.

"Por qué?" she said rather shyly.

"Vamos a bailando," I said. We'll go dancing.

She giggled. *"Estoy casada,"* she said. I'm married.

"Por favor?" I said, with my very best hundred-watt totally fake smile, and I added, *"Nunca por la migra, verdadamente."* Arabelle smiled, leaned forward, and whispered an address in my ear. I nodded; it was in an area flooded with Central American immigrants, several of them here legally. It made perfect sense for her to live there, and I was certain she was telling me the truth. *"Gracias,"* I said, and as I started to pull away, she grabbed my arm again.

"Nunca por la migra?" she said.

"Nunca," I said. Never. *"Solamente para hallar este matador."* Only to find this killer.

She nodded as if that made sense, that I

needed her address to find the killer, and gave me her shy smile again. *"Gracias,"* she said. *"Te creo."* I believe you. Her faith in me was really quite touching, especially considering that there was no reason for it at all, beyond the fact that I had given her a completely phony smile. It made me wonder if a career change was in order — perhaps I should sell cars, or even run for president.

"All right," Deborah said. "She can go home."

I nodded at Arabelle. *"Va a su casa,"* I said.

"Gracias," she said again. And she smiled hugely and then turned and almost ran for the street.

"Shit," Deborah said. "Shit shit SHIT."

I looked at her with raised eyebrows, and she shook her head. She seemed deflated, the anger and tension drained out of her. "I know it's stupid," she said. "I just hoped she might have seen something. I mean —" She shrugged and turned away, looking in the direction of the body in the doorway. "We'll never find the gay tourists, either. Not in South Beach."

"They can't have seen anything anyway," I said.

"In broad daylight. And nobody saw any-thing?"

"People see what they expect to see," I

71

said. "He probably used a delivery van, and that would make him invisible."

"Well, shit," she said again, and this didn't seem like a good time to criticize her for such a limited vocabulary. She faced me again. "I don't suppose you got anything helpful from looking at this one."

"Let me take some pictures and think about it," I said.

"That's a no, right?"

"It's not a stated no," I said. "It's an implied no."

Deborah held up a middle finger. "Imply this," she said, and she turned away and trudged back to look at the body.

SEVEN

It is surprising, but true: cold coq au vin really doesn't taste as good as it should. Somehow the wine gives off an odor of stale beer, and the chicken feels slightly slimy, and the whole experience becomes an ordeal of grim perseverance in the face of bitterly disappointed expectations. Still, Dexter is nothing if not persistent, and when I got home around midnight, I worked through a large portion of the stuff with truly stoic fortitude.

Rita did not wake up when I slipped into bed, and I did not dawdle overlong on the shores of sleep. I closed my eyes, and it seemed like almost immediately the clock radio beside the bed began to scream at me about the rising tide of dreadful violence threatening to overwhelm our poor battered city.

I pried open an eye and saw that it really was six o'clock and time to get up. It didn't seem fair, but I dragged myself out of bed and into the shower, and by the time I reached the kitchen, Rita had breakfast on the table. "I see you had some of the chicken," she said, a little grimly, I thought, and I realized a little blarney was called for.

"It was wonderful," I said. "Better than what we had in Paris."

She brightened a little, but shook her head. "Liar," she said. "It never tastes right when it's cold."

"You have the magic touch," I said. "It tasted warm."

She frowned and brushed a lock of hair off her face. "I know you have to, you know," she said. "I mean, your job is . . . But I wish you could have tasted it when — I mean, I really do understand," she said, and I was not sure I could say the same thing. Rita put a plate of fried eggs and sausage in front of me and nodded at the small TV set over by the coffeemaker. "It was all over the news this morning, about . . . that's what it was, wasn't it? And they had your sister on, saying that, you know. She didn't look very happy."

"She's not happy at all," I said. "Which doesn't seem right, since she has a really challenging job, and her picture is on TV. Who could ask for more?"

Rita did not smile at my lighthearted jest. Instead, she pulled a chair over next to mine and, sitting down and clasping her hands in her lap, she frowned even deeper. "Dexter," she said, "we really need to talk."

I know from my research into human life that these are the words that strike terror into men's souls. Conveniently enough, I have no soul, but I still felt a surge of discomfort at what those ominous syllables might mean. "So soon after the honeymoon?" I said, hoping to deflect at least some small bit of seriousness.

Rita shook her head. "It's not — I mean . . ." She fluttered one hand, and then let it drop back into her lap. She sighed deeply. "It's Cody," she said at last.

"Oh," I said, without even a clue of what sort of "it" Cody might be. He seemed perfectly all right to me — but then, I knew better than Rita that Cody was not at all the small and quiet human child he seemed to be, but instead a Dexter-in-training.

"He still seems, so . . ." She shook her head again and looked down, her voice dropping. "I know his . . . father . . . did some things that . . . *hurt* him. Probably changed him forever. But . . ." She looked up at me, her eyes bright with tears. "It isn't right that . . . he should still be like this.

Should he? So quiet all the time, and . . ." She looked down again. "I'm just afraid for what . . . you know." A tear fell onto her lap and she sniffled. "He might be . . . you know . . . permanently . . ."

Several more tears joined the first one, and even though I am generally helpless in the face of emotion, I knew that some kind of reassuring gesture was called for here.

"Cody will be fine," I said, blessing my ability to lie convincingly. "He just needs to come out of his shell a little bit."

Rita sniffled again. "Do you really think so?"

"Absolutely," I said, putting a hand over hers, as I had seen in a movie not too long ago. "Cody is a great kid. He's just maturing a little slower than others. Because of what happened to him."

She shook her head and a tear hit me on the face. "You can't know that," she said.

"I can," I told her, and oddly enough, now I was actually telling the truth. "I know perfectly well what he's going through, because I went through it myself."

She looked at me with very bright, wet eyes. "You — you never talked about what happened to you," she said.

"No," I said. "And I never will. But it was close enough to what happened to Cody, so

I do know. Trust me on this, Rita." And I patted her hand again, thinking, *Yes, trust me. Trust me to turn Cody into a well-adjusted, smoothly functioning monster, just like me.*

"Oh, Dexter," she said. "I do trust you. But he's so . . ." She shook her head again, sending a spray of tears around the room.

"He'll be fine," I said. "Really. He just needs to come out of his shell a little bit. Learn to be with other kids his own age." *And learn to pretend to be like them,* I thought, but it didn't seem terribly comforting to say aloud, so I didn't.

"If you're sure," Rita said with a truly enormous snuffle.

"I'm sure," I said.

"All right," she said, reaching for a napkin off the table and blotting at her nose and eyes. "Then let's just . . ." *Sniffle. Honk.* "I guess we'll just think of ways to get him to mix with other kids."

"That's the ticket," I said. "We'll have him cheating at cards in no time."

Rita blew her nose a last, long time.

"Sometimes I couldn't tell that you're being funny," she said. She stood up and kissed me on the top of the head. "If I didn't know you so well."

Of course, if she really knew me as well as she thought, she would stab me with a fork and run for her life, but maintaining our illusions is an important part of life's work, so I said nothing, and breakfast went on in its wonderfully soothing monotony. There is a real pleasure in being waited upon, especially by someone who really knows what she's doing in the kitchen, and it was worth listening to all the chatter that went with it.

Cody and Astor joined us as I started my second cup of coffee, and the two of them sat side by side with identical expressions of heavily sedated incomprehension on their faces. They didn't have the benefit of coffee, and it took them several minutes to realize that they were, in fact, awake. It was Astor, naturally enough, who broke the silence.

"Sergeant Debbie was on TV," she said. Astor had developed a strange case of hero worship for Deborah, ever since she found out that Debs carried a gun and got to boss around big beefy uniformed cops.

"That's part of her job," I said, even though I realized it would probably feed the hero worship.

"How come you're never on TV, Dexter?" she said accusingly.

"I don't want to be on TV," I said, and she looked at me like I had suggested outlawing ice cream. "It's true," I said. "Imagine if everybody knew what I look like. I couldn't walk down the street without people pointing at me and talking behind my back."

"Nobody points at Sergeant Debbie," she said.

I nodded. "Of course not," I said. "Who would dare?" Astor looked like she was ready to argue, so I put my coffee cup down with a bang and stood up. "I'm off to another day of mighty work defending the good people of our city."

"You can't defend people with a micro-scope," Astor said.

"That's enough, Astor," Rita said, and she hustled over to plant another kiss on me, on the face this time. "I hope you catch this one, Dexter," she said. "It sounds awful."

I rather hoped we would catch this one, too. Four victims in one day seemed a little bit overzealous, even to me, and it would certainly create a citywide atmosphere of paranoid watchfulness that would make it almost impossible for me to have any quiet fun of my own.

So it was with a real determination to see justice done that I went in to work. Of course, any real attempt at justice would have to start with the traffic, since Miami drivers have long ago taken the simple chore of going from one place to another and turned it into a kind of high-speed, heavily armed game of high-stakes bumper cars. It's even more interesting because the rules change from one driver to the next. For example, as I drove along in the tight bundle of cars on the expressway, a man in the next lane suddenly started honking his horn. When I turned to look, he flipped me off, yelled, *"Maricón!"* and forced his way in front of me, and then over on to the shoulder, where he accelerated away.

I had no idea what had caused the display, so I simply waved at his car as it vanished in a distant concerto of honking and shouting. The Miami Rush-Hour Symphony.

I arrived at work a little bit early, but the building was already buzzing with frantic activity. The press room was overflowing with more people than I had ever seen before — at least, I assumed they were people, although with reporters you can never be sure. And the true seriousness of the situation hit me when I realized that there were dozens of cameras and microphones and no sign of Captain Matthews.

More unprecedented shocks awaited: a uniformed cop stood at the elevator and demanded to see my credentials before he let me past, even though he was a guy I knew slightly. And even more — when I finally got to the lab area, I found that Vince had actually brought in a bag of croissants.

"Good lord," I said, gazing at the flakes of crust that covered Vince's shirtfront. "I was just kidding, Vince."

"I know," he said. "But it sounded kind of classy, so . . ." He shrugged, which caused a trickle of croissant flakes to fall off him and onto the floor. "They make 'em with chocolate filling," he said. "And ham and cheese, too."

"I don't think they'll approve of that in Paris," I said.

"Where the fuck have you been?" Deborah snarled from behind me, and she snatched up a ham-and-cheese croissant.

"Some of us like to sleep from time to time," I said.

"Some of us don't *get* to sleep," she said. "Because some of us have been trying to work, surrounded by camera crews from fucking Brazil and who knows where." She took a savage bite of croissant and, with a full mouth, looked at the rest of it in her hand and said, "Jesus Christ, what is this thing?"

"It's a French doughnut," I said.

Debs threw the rest of it at a nearby trash can and missed by about four feet. "Tastes like shit," she said.

"Would you rather try some of my jelly roll?" Vince asked her.

Debs didn't even blink. "Sorry, I'd need at least a mouthful, which you ain't got," she said, and she grabbed my arm. "Come on."

My sister led me down the hall to her cubicle and flung herself into the chair at her desk. I sat in the folding chair and waited for whatever onslaught of emotion she might have prepared for me.

It came in the form of a stack of newspapers and magazines that she started to throw at me, saying, "*L.A. Times. Chicago Sun-Times. New York* Fucking *Times. Der Spiegel. Toronto Star.*"

Just before I vanished completely under a pile of papers, battered insensible, I reached across and grabbed her arm, stopping her from flinging the *Karachi Observer* at me. "Debs," I said. "I can see them better if they're not wedged into my eye sockets."

"This is a shit-storm," she said, "like no shit-storm you have ever seen before."

Truthfully I had not seen many actual shit-storms, although one time in middle school Randy Schwartz flushed a cherry bomb down a full toilet in the boys' restroom, forcing Mr. O'Brien to go home early to change clothes. But clearly Debs was in no mood for fond reminiscence, even though neither of us had liked Mr. O'Brien. "I gathered that," I said, "from the fact that Matthews is suddenly invisible."

She snorted. "Like he never existed."

"I never thought we'd see a case so hot the captain didn't want to be on TV," I said.

"Four fucking bodies in one fucking day," she spat out. "Like nothing anybody has ever seen, and it lands in my lap."

"Rita says you looked very nice on television," I said encouragingly, but for some reason that caused her to slap at the pile of newspapers and knock several more onto the floor.

"I don't wanna BE on fucking television," she said. "Fucking Matthews has thrown me to the lions, because this is absolutely the biggest, most badass god-awful goddamn story in the whole fucking world right now, and we haven't even released any pictures of the bodies but somehow everybody knows there's something weird going on, and the mayor is having a shit fit, and the fucking GOVERNOR is having a shit fit, and if I personally do not solve this thing by lunchtime the whole fucking state of Florida is going to fall into the ocean and I am going to be underneath it when it happens." She slapped at the pile of newspapers and this time at least half of them fell to the floor. That seemed to take all the fury out of her, because she slumped over and suddenly looked drained and exhausted. "I really need some help here, bro. I hate it like hell that I have to ask you, but . . . if you could ever really figure one of these out, this is the time."

I wasn't really sure what to make of the fact that suddenly she hated like hell to ask me — after all, she had asked before, several times, apparently without hate. She seemed to be getting a little odd and even snarky lately on the subject of my special talents. But what the hell. While it is true that I am without emotion, I am not immune to being manipulated by it, and the sight of my sister so obviously at the end of her rope was more than I could comfortably sidestep. "Of course I'll help, Debs," I said. "I just don't know how much I can really do."

"Well, fuck, you have to do something," she said. "We're going under here."

It was nice that she said "we" and included me, although I had not been aware until right now that I, too, was going under. But the added sense of belonging did very little to jar my giant brain into action. In fact, the huge cranial complex that is Dexter's Cerebral Faculty was being abnormally quiet, just as it had been at the crime scenes. Nevertheless, it was clear that a display of good old team spirit was called for, so I closed my eyes and tried to look like I was thinking very hard.

All right then: if there were any real, physical clues, the tireless and dogged heroes of forensics would find them. So what I needed was some kind of hint from a source that my coworkers could not tap — the Dark Passenger. The Passenger, however, was being uncharacteristically silent, except for its mildly savage chuckling and I wasn't sure what that meant. Normally, any display of predatory skill would evoke some kind of appreciation that quite often provided a small stab of insight into the killing. But this time, any such comment was absent. Why?

Perhaps the Passenger was not yet settled back in comfortably after its recent flight. Or perhaps it was still recovering from the trauma — although this didn't seem likely, judging by the growing power of my Need.

So why the sudden shyness? If something wicked transpired under our nose, I had come to expect a response beyond amusement. It had not come. Therefore . . . nothing wicked had happened? That made even less sense, since we quite clearly had four very dead bodies.

It also meant that I was, apparently, on my own — and there was Deborah staring at me with a very hard and expectant glare. So back up a step, Oh great and grim genius. Something was different about these killings, beyond the rather gaudy presentation of the bodies. And *presentation* was exactly the right word — they were displayed in a way calculated to make a maximum impact.

But on whom? Conventional wisdom in the psychopathic killer community would say that the more trouble you go to show off, the more you want an adoring audience. But it is also common knowledge that the police keep such sights under tight wraps — and even if they didn't, none of the news media would run pictures of such terrible things; believe me, I have looked.

So who could the presentations be aimed at? The police? The forensics wonks? Me? None of these were likely, and beyond them and the three or four people who had discovered the bodies, nobody had seen anything, and there had been only the tremendous outcry from the entire state of Florida, desperate to save the tourist industry.

A thought snapped my eyes open, and

there was Deborah staring at me like an Irish setter on point.

"What, goddamn it?" she said.

"What if this is what they want?" I said.

She stared at me for a moment, looking quite a bit like Cody and Astor when they've just woken up. "What's that mean?" she finally said.

"The first thing I thought about the bodies was that it wasn't about *killing* them. It was about playing with them afterward. Displaying them."

Debs snorted. "I remember. It STILL doesn't make any sense."

"But it does," I said. "If somebody is trying to create an *effect*. To have an *impact* in some way. So look at it backward — what impact has this already had?"

"Aside from getting media attention all over the world —"

"No, NOT aside from that. That is exactly what I mean."

She shook her head. "What?"

"What's wrong with media attention, sis? The whole world is looking at the Sunshine State — at Miami, tourist beacon to the world —"

"They're looking, and they're saying no fucking way am I going anywhere near that slaughterhouse," Debs said. "Come on,

Dex, what's the fucking point? I told you . . . Oh." She frowned. "You're saying somebody did this to attack the tourist industry? The whole fucking *state?* That's fucking nuts."

"You think somebody did this who isn't nuts, sis?"

"But who the hell would do that?"

"I don't know," I said. "California?"

"Come on, Dexter," she snarled. "It has to make sense. If somebody does this, they have to have SOME kind of motive."

"Somebody with a grudge," I said, sounding a lot more certain than I felt.

"A grudge against the whole fucking state?" she said. "Is *that* supposed to make sense?"

"Well, not really," I said.

"Then how about if you come up with something that does make sense? And like, right now? Because I don't see how this could get much worse."

If life teaches us anything, it is to flinch away and roll under the furniture whenever anyone is foolish enough to utter those fell words. And sure enough, the dreadful syllables were barely out of Deborah's mouth when the phone on her desk buzzed for her attention, and some small and rather nasty voice whispered in my ear that this would be a great time to wedge myself under the desk in the fetal position.

Deborah snatched up the phone, still glaring at me, and then suddenly turned away and hunched over. She muttered a few shocked syllables that sounded like, "When? Jesus. Right," and then she hung up and turned a look on me that made her previous glare seem like the first kiss of springtime. "You motherfucker," she said.

"What did I do?" I said, rather surprised by the cold fury in her voice.

"That's what I want to know," she said.

Even a monster reaches a point at which irritation begins to trickle in, and I believe I was very close to that point. "Deborah, either you start speaking complete sentences that actually make sense, or I'm going back to the lab to polish the spectrometer."

"There's a break in the case," she said.

"Then why aren't we happy?"

"It's at the Tourist Board," she said.

I opened my mouth to say something witty and cutting, and then I closed it again.

"Yeah," Deborah said. "Almost like somebody had a grudge against the whole state."

"And you think it's me?" I said, beyond irritation now and all the way to open-mouthed astonishment. She just stared at me. "Debs, I think somebody put lead in your coffee. Florida is my home — you want me to sing 'Swanee River'?"

It might not have been the offer to sing that animated her, but whatever it was, she looked at me for another long moment and then jumped up. "Come on, let's get over there," she said.

"Me? What about Coulter, your partner?"

"He's getting coffee, fuck him," she said. "Besides, I'd rather partner with a warthog. Come on," she said. For some reason, I did not actually swell with pride at being slightly better than a warthog, but when duty calls, Dexter answers, and I followed her out the door.

EIGHT

The Greater Miami Convention and Visitors' Bureau was in a high-rise building on Brickell Avenue, as befitted its status as a Very Important Organization. The full majesty of its purpose was reflected in the view from its windows, which showed a lovely slice of downtown and Government Cut, a swath of Biscayne Bay, and even the nearby arena where the basketball team shows up from time to time for some really dramatic losses. It was a wonderful view, almost a postcard, as if to say, *Look — this is Miami: we weren't kidding.*

Very few of the bureau's employees seemed to be enjoying the view today, however. The office resembled a giant oak-lined bees' nest that somebody had poked with a stick. There could not have been more than a handful of employees, but they were flitting in and out of doors and up and down the hallway so rapidly it looked like there were hundreds of them in constant motion, like crazed particles in a whirring jar of oil. Deborah stood at the receptionist's desk for two full minutes — a lifetime, as far as her sense of patience was concerned — before a large woman paused and stared at her.

"What do you want?" the woman demanded.

Debs immediately flashed her badge. "I'm Sergeant Morgan. From the police?"

"Oh my God," the woman said, "I'll get Jo Anne," and disappeared through a door on the right.

Deborah looked at me as if it was my fault and said, "Jesus," and then the door slammed open again and a small woman with a long nose and a short haircut came barreling out.

"Police?" she said with real outrage in her voice. She looked beyond us and then back to Deborah, looking her up and down. "YOU'RE the police? What, the pinup police?"

Of course Deborah was used to having people challenge her, but usually not quite so brutally. She actually blushed a little before she held up her badge again and said, "Sergeant Morgan. Do you have some information for us?"

"This is no time for politically correct," the woman said. "I need Dirty Harry, and they send Legally Blonde."

Deborah's eyes narrowed and the pretty red flush left her cheeks. "If you'd like, I can charge you with obstructing an investigation."

The woman just stared. Then there was a yell from the back room and something large fell over and broke. She jumped a little, then said, "My God. All right, come on," and she vanished through the door again. Deborah breathed out hard, showing a few teeth, and then we followed.

The small woman was already disappearing through a door at the end of the hall, and by the time we caught up with her she was settling into a swivel chair at a conference table. "Sit down," she said, waving at the other chairs with a large black remote control. Without waiting to see if we sat, she pointed the remote at a big flat-screen TV, and said, "This came yesterday, but we didn't get around to looking at it until this morning." She glanced up at us. "We called right away," she said, perhaps still trembling with fear from Deborah's threat. If so, she was controlling her trembles remarkably well.

"What is it?" Deborah said, sliding into a chair.

I sat in one next to her and the woman said, "The TV. Lookit."

The TV blinked into life, went through a few wonderfully informative screens asking us to wait or select, and then blurted into life with a high-pitched scream. Beside me, Deborah jumped involuntarily.

The screen lit up and an image leaped into focus: from an unmoving position above, we saw a body lying against a white porcelain background. The eyes were wide and staring and, to someone of my modest experience, obviously dead. Then a figure moved into view and partially blocked the body. We saw only the back, and then the upraised arm holding a power saw. The arm went down and we heard the whine of the blade biting into flesh.

"Jesus Christ," Deborah said.

"It gets worse," said the short woman.

The blade whirred and growled, and we could see the figure in the foreground working hard. Then the saw stopped, the figure dropped it onto the porcelain, reached forward, pulled a huge heap of terrible gleaming guts out, and dropped them where the camera could see them best. And then large white letters appeared on the screen, superimposed on the heap of intestines:

THE NEW MIAMI: IT WILL RIP YOUR GUTS OUT.

The picture held for a moment, and then the screen went blank.

"Wait," the woman said, and the screen blinked again, and then new letters glowed to life.

THE NEW MIAMI — SPOT #2

Then we were looking at sunrise on a beach. Mellow Latin music played. A wave rolled in on the sand. An early-morning jogger trotted into the frame, stumbled, and then came to a shocked halt. The camera moved in on the jogger's face as it went from shock to terror. Then the jogger lurched into a sprint, up away from the water and across the sand toward the street in the distance. The camera moved back to show my old friends, the happy couple we had found disemboweled on the sand at South Beach.

Then a jump cut took us to the first officer on the scene as his face crumpled and he turned away to vomit. Another jump to faces in the crowd of onlookers craning their necks and freezing, and several more faces, coming faster and faster, each expression different, each showing horror in its own way.

Then the screen whirled, and began to show a frozen shot of each face we had seen, lined up in little boxes until the screen was filled with them and looked like a page from a high school yearbook, with a dozen shocked mug shots in three neat rows.

Again the letters glowed into life:

THE NEW MIAMI: IT WILL GET
TO YOU.

And then the screen went dark.

I could think of almost nothing to say, and a glance at my companions showed that I was not the only one. I thought of criticizing the camera technique just to break the awkward silence — after all, today's audience likes a little more movement in the shot. But the mood in the room didn't really seem conducive to a discussion of film technique, so I stayed quiet. Deborah sat clenching her teeth. The short woman said nothing, just looked out the window at the beautiful view. Then, finally, she said, "We're assuming there's more. I mean, the news said there were four bodies, so . . ." She shrugged. I tried to see around her and out the window at whatever was so interesting to her, but saw nothing more than a speedboat coming up Government Cut.

"This got here yesterday?" Deborah said. "In the regular mail?"

"It came in a plain envelope with a Miami postmark," the woman said. "It's on a plain disc, just like the ones we have here in the office. You can get them anywhere — Office Depot, Wal-Mart, whatever."

She said it with such disdain, and with such a lovely expression of true humanity on her face — something between contempt and indifference — that I had to wonder how she could make anyone like *anything*, let alone make millions of people want to come to a city partially inhabited by someone like her.

And as that thought clattered onto the floor of my brain and echoed across the marble, a small train chugged out of the Dexter Station and onto the tracks. For a moment I just watched the exhaust billow up out of the smokestack, and then I closed my eyes and climbed on board.

"What," Deborah demanded. "What have you got?"

I shook my head and thought it through one more time. I could hear Deborah's fingers tapping on the table, and then the clatter of the remote as the short woman put it down, and the train finally came up to cruising speed and I opened my eyes. "What if," I said, "somebody wants negative publicity for Miami?"

"You said that already," Deborah snarled, "and it's still stupid. Who could have a grudge against the whole fucking state?"

"But if it's not against the state?" I said. "What if it's only against the people who *promote* the state?" I looked pointedly at the short woman.

"Me?" the short woman said. "Somebody did this to get to *me?*"

I was touched by her modesty and gave her one of my warmest fake smiles. "You, or your agency," I said.

She frowned, as if the idea of someone attacking her agency instead of herself was ridiculous. "Well . . ." she said dubiously.

But Deborah slapped the table and nodded. "That's it," she said. "NOW it makes sense. If you fired somebody, and they're pissed off."

"Especially if they were a little bit off to begin with," I said.

"Which most of these artsy types are anyway," Deborah said. "So somebody loses their job, stews about it for a while, and hits back like this." She turned to the short woman. "I'll need to see your personnel files."

The woman opened and closed her mouth a few times and then started shaking her head. "I can't let you see our files," she said.

Deborah glared at her for a moment and then, just when I was expecting her to argue, she stood up. "I understand," she said. "Come on, Dex." She headed for the door and I stood to follow.

"What — where are you going?" the woman called out.

"To get a court order. And a warrant," she said, and turned away without waiting for a reply.

I watched as the woman thought she might bluff it out, for a good two and a half seconds, and then she jumped up and ran after Debs, calling, "Wait a sec!"

And that is how, only a few minutes later, I happened to be sitting in the back room in front of a computer terminal. Beside me at the keyboard was Noel, a preposterously skinny Haitian American man with thick glasses and severe facial scars.

For some reason, whenever there is computer work to do Deborah calls on her brother, Digitally Dominant Dexter. And it is true that I am quite accomplished in certain areas of the arcane lore of finding things with a computer, since it has proved very necessary for my small and harmless hobby of tracking down the bad guys who slip through the cracks in the justice system and turning them into a few nice and tidy garbage bags full of spare parts.

But it is also true that our mighty police department has several computer experts who could have done the work just as easily without raising the question in the department of why a blood spatter expert was such a good hacker. These questions can eventually turn awkward and make suspicious people ponder, which I do like to avoid at work, since cops are notoriously suspicious people.

Still, complaining is no good. It draws just as much attention, and in any case the entire police force was used to seeing the two of us together and, after all, how could I say no to my poor little sister without receiving a few of her famous powerful arm punches? Besides, she had been somewhat cranky and distant lately, and beefing up my HLQ, or Helpful-Loyal Quotient, could not possibly hurt.

So I played Dutiful Dexter and sat with Noel, who was wearing far too much cologne, and we talked about what to look for.

"Look," Noel said with a thick Creole accent, "I give you a list of all who are fired for what, two years?"

"Two years is good," I said. "If there aren't too many."

He shrugged, a task that somehow looked painful with his bony shoulders. "Less than a dozen," he said. He smiled and added, "With Jo Anne, many more just quit."

"Print the list," I said. "Then we check their files for any unusual complaints or threats."

"But also," he said, "we have a number of independent contractors to design projects, no? And sometimes they do not get the bid, and who can say how unhappy they are?"

"But a contractor could always try again on the next project, right?"

Noel shrugged again, and the motion looked like he was endangering his ears with his too-sharp shoulders. "Per'aps," he said.

"So unless it was some sort of final blowup, where the bureau said we would never ever use you under any circumstances, it's not as likely."

"Then we stick to the fired ones," he said, and in just a few moments he had printed out a list with, as he said, less than a dozen names and Last Known Addresses on it — nine, to be exact.

Deborah had been staring out the window,

but when she heard the printer whirring into action, she stalked over and leaned on the back of my chair. "What've you got?" she demanded.

I took the sheet of paper from the printer and held it up. "Maybe nothing," I said. "Nine people who were fired." She snatched the list from my hand and glared at it as if it was withholding evidence. "We're going to cross-check it against their files," I said. "To see if they made any threats."

Deborah gritted her teeth, and I could tell she wanted to run out the door and down the avenue to the first address, but after all, it would certainly save time to prioritize them and put any real zingers at the head of the list. "Fine," she said at last. "But hurry it up, huh?"

We did hurry it up; I was able to eliminate two workers who had been "fired" when Immigration had forced them out of the country. But only one name moved right to the top of the list: Hernando Meza, who had become obstreperous — that's the word the file used — and had to be removed from the premises forcibly.

And the beauty part? Hernando had designed displays at airports and cruise terminals.

Displays, like what we had seen at South

Beach and Fairchild Gardens.

"Goddamn," Deborah said when I told her. "We got a hot one, right off the bat."

I agreed that it looked worthwhile to stop and have a chat with Meza, but a small and nagging voice was telling me that things are never this easy, that when you get a hot one right off the bat, you usually end up right back on the bat again — or dodging as the bat comes straight at your face.

And as we should all know by now, anytime you predict failure you have an excellent chance of being right.

NINE

Hernando Meza lived in a section of Coral Gables that was nice, but not too nice, and so, protected by its own mediocrity, it hadn't changed much over the last twenty years, unlike most of the rest of Miami. In fact, his house was only a little more than a mile from where Deborah lived, which practically made them neighbors. Unfortunately, that didn't seem to influence either one of them into acting in a neighborly way.

It started right after Debs knocked on his door. I could tell by the way she was jiggling one foot that she was excited and really thought she might be onto something. And then when the door made a kind of mechanical whirring sound and opened inward to reveal Meza, Deborah's foot stopped jiggling and she said, "Shit." Under her breath, of course, but hardly inaudible.

Meza heard her and responded with, "Well, fuck YOU," and just stared at her with a really impressive amount of hostility, considering he was in a motorized wheel-chair and without the apparent use of any of his limbs, except possibly for a few fingers on each hand.

He used one of the fingers to twitch at a joystick on the bright metal tray attached to the front of his chair, and it lurched a few inches forward. "The fuck you want?" he said. "You don't look smart enough to be Witnesses, so you selling something? Hey, I could use some new skis."

Deborah glanced at me, but I had no actual advice or insight for her, so I simply smiled. For some reason, that made her angry; her eyebrows crashed together and her lips got very thin. She turned to Meza and, in a perfect Cold Cop tone of voice, she said, "Are you Hernando Meza?"

"What's left of him," Meza said. "Hey, you sound like a cop. Is this about me running laps naked at the Marlins game?"

"We'd like to ask you a couple of questions," Debs said. "May we come in?"

"No," he said.

Deborah already had one foot lifted, her weight leaning forward, anticipating that Meza, like everyone else in the world, would automatically let her come in. Now she lurched to a pause and then stepped back half a step. "Excuse me?" she said.

"Noooooo," Meza said, drawing out the word as if he was talking to an idiot who didn't understand the concept. "Noooo, you may not come in." And he twitched a finger on the chair's controls and the chair jerked toward us very aggressively.

Deborah jumped wildly to one side, then recovered her professional dignity and stepped back in front of Meza, although at a safe distance. "All right," she said. "We'll do it here."

"Oh, yeah," Meza said, "let's *do it* here." And flipping his finger on the joystick, he made the chair pump a few inches forward and backward several times. "Yeah baby, yeah baby, yeah baby," he said.

Deborah had clearly lost control of the interview with her suspect, which the cop handbook frowns upon. She jumped off to the side again, completely flustered by Meza's fake chair sex, and he followed her around in his chair. "Come on, Mama, give it up!" he called in a voice somewhere between a chortle and a wheeze.

I'm sorry if it sounds like I am feeling something, but I sometimes get just a little twinge of sympathy for Deborah, who really does try very hard. And so, as Meza whirled his chair in a stuttering arc of minilurches at Debs, I stepped behind him, leaned down to the back of his chair, and pulled the power cable off the batteries. The whine of the engine stopped, the chair thumped to a halt, and the only remaining sounds were a siren in the distance and the small clatter of Meza's finger rattling against the joystick.

At its best, Miami is a city of two cultures and two languages, and those of us who immerse ourselves in both have learned that a different culture can teach us many new and wonderful things. I have always embraced this concept, and it paid off now, as Meza proved to be wonderfully creative in both Spanish and English. He ran through an impressive list of standards, and then his artistic side took full flower and he called me things that had never before existed, except possibly in a parallel universe designed by Hieronymus Bosch. The performance took on an added air of supernatural improbability because Meza's voice was so weak and husky, but he never allowed that to slow him. I was frankly awed, and Deborah seemed to be, too, because we both simply stood and listened until Meza finally wore down and tapered off with, "Cocksucker."

I stepped around in front and stood beside Debs. "Don't say that," I said, and he just glared at me. "It's so pedestrian, and you're much better than that. What was that part, 'turd-sucking bag of possum vomit'? Wonderful." And I gave him his due with some light applause.

"Plug me in, *pedo de puta*," he said. "We see how funny you are then."

"And have you run us over with that sporty SUV of yours?" I said. "No thanks."

Deborah lurched up out of her stunned appreciation of the performance and back into her alpha role. She pushed me to one side and resumed her stone-faced staring at Meza. "Mr. Meza, we need you to answer a couple of questions, and if you refuse to cooperate, I will take you down to the station and ask them there."

"Do it, cunt," he said. "My lawyer would love that."

"We could just leave him like this," I suggested. "Until someone comes along and steals him to sell for scrap metal."

"Plug me in, you sack of lizard pus."

"He's repeating himself," I said to Deborah. "I think we're wearing him down."

"Did you threaten to kill the director of the Tourist Board?" Deborah asked.

Meza started to cry. It was not a pretty sight; his head flopped nervelessly to one side and mucus drooled from his mouth and nose, joined the tears, and began to march across his face. "Bastards," he said. "They shoulda killed ME." He snuffled so weakly that it had no effect at all except for the thin wet noise it made. "Looka me, looka what they done," he said in his hoarse, husky voice, a croak with no edge to it.

"What did they do to you, Mr. Meza?" Debs said.

"Looka me," he snuffled. "They did this. Looka me. I live in this *chingado* chair, can't even pee without some *maricón* nurse to hold my dick." He looked up, a little defiance once again showing through the mucus. "Woun't you wanna kill those *puercos,* too?" he said.

"You say they did this to you?" Debs said.

He sniffled again. "Happened on the job," he said a little defensively. "I was on the clock, but they said no, car accident, they don't pay for it. And then they fire me."

Deborah opened her mouth, and then closed it again with an audible click. I think she had been about to say something like, "Where were you last night between the hours of three-thirty and five," and it occurred to her that he had most likely been right here in his powered chair. But Meza was sharp if nothing else, and he had noticed, too.

109

"What," he said, snuffling mightily and actually moving a small stream of mucus, ever so slightly. "Somebody finally killed one of those *chingado maricones?* And you don't think it could be me 'cause I'm in this chair? Bitch, you plug me in, I show you how easy I kill somebody piss me off."

"Which *maricón* did you kill?" I asked him, and Deborah elbowed me, even though she still had nothing to say.

"Whichever one is dead, motherfucker," he wheezed at me. "I hope it's that cocksucker Jo Anne, but fuck, I kill them all before I finish."

"Mr. Meza," Deborah said, and there was a slight hesitation in her voice that might have been sympathy in somebody else; in Debs, it was disappointment at realizing that this poor blob of stuff was not her suspect. And once again, Meza picked up on it and went on the attack.

"Yeah, I did it," he said. "Cuff me, cunt. Chain me to the floor in the backseat with the dogs. Whatsa matter, you afraid I'll die on you? Do it, bitch. Or I kill you like I kilt those asshole suckers at the board."

"Nobody killed the board," I said.

He glared at me. "No?" he said. His head swiveled back to Deborah, mucus flashing in the sunlight. "Then what the fuck you

110

harassing me for, shit pig?"

Deborah hesitated, then tried one last time. "Mr. Meza," she said.

"Fuck you, get the fuck off my porch," Meza said.

"It seems like a good idea, Debs," I said.

Deborah shook her head with frustration, then blew out a short, explosive breath. "Fuck," she said. "Let's go. Plug him in." And she turned and walked off the porch, leaving me the dangerous and thankless job of plugging Meza's power cord back in to the battery. It just goes to show what selfish and thoughtless creatures humans are, even when they're family. After all, she was the one with the gun — shouldn't she be the one to plug him in?

Meza seemed to agree. He began running though a new list of graphically vulgar surrealism, all directed at Deborah's back. All I rated was a quick, muttered, "Hurry up, faggot," as he paused to catch his breath.

I hurried. Not out of any desire to please Meza, but because I did not want to be standing around when he got power back to his chair. It was far too dangerous — and in any case, I felt that I had spent enough of my precious and irreplaceable daylight listening to him complain. It was time to get back out into the world, where there were monsters to catch, even a monster to be, and with luck, there was also at some point a lunch to eat. None of this could happen if I remained trapped on this porch dodging a motorized chair with mouth to match.

So I pushed the power connection back on the battery and vaulted off the porch before Meza realized he was plugged in again. I hurried to the car and climbed in. Deborah slammed the car into gear and accelerated away even before I got the door closed, apparently worried that Meza might disable the car by ramming it with his chair, and we were very quickly back in the warm and fuzzy cocoon of Miami's homicidal traffic.

"Fuck," she said at last, and the word seemed like a soft summer breeze after listening to Meza, "I was sure he was going to be it."

"Look at the bright side," I said. "At least you learned some wonderful new words."

"Go shit up a rope," Debs said. After all, she wasn't exactly new to this herself.

TEN

There was time to check two more names on the list before we broke for lunch. The address for the first one was over in Coconut Grove, and it took us only about ten minutes to get there from Meza's house. Deborah drove just slightly faster than she should have, which in Miami is slow, and therefore a lot like wearing a "Kick Me" sign on your back. And so even though the traffic was light, we had our own sound track along the way, of horns and hollering and gracefully extended middle fingers, as the other drivers swooped past us like a school of ravenous piranha darting around a rock in the river.

Debs didn't seem to notice. She was thinking hard, which meant that her brow was furrowed into such a deep frown that I felt like warning her that the lines would become permanent if she didn't unclench. But past experience had taught me that interrupting her thought process with that kind of caring remark would invariably result in one of her blistering arm punches, so I sat silently. I did not really see what there was to think about so thoroughly: we had four very decorative bodies and no clue who had arranged them. But of course, Debs was the trained investigator, not me. Perhaps there was something from one of her courses at the academy that applied here and called for massive forehead wrinkling.

In any case, we were soon at the address on our list. It was a modest old cottage off Tigertail Avenue, with a small and over-grown yard and a FOR SALE sign stuck in front of a large mango tree. There were a half-dozen old newspapers scattered across the yard, still in their wrappers, and only half visible through the tall and untended grass of the lawn.

"Shit," said Deborah as she parked in front of the place. It seemed like a very sharp and succinct summary. The house looked like it had not been lived in for months.

"What did this guy do?" I asked her, watching a brightly colored sheet of newsprint blow across the yard.

Debs glanced at the list. "Alice Bronson," she said. "She was stealing money from an office account. When they called her on it, she threatened them with battery and murder."

"One at a time, or together?" I asked, but Debs just glared at me and shook her head.

"This won't be anything," she said, and I tended to agree. But of course, police work is composed mostly of doing the obvious and hoping you get lucky, so we unbuckled our seat belts and kicked through the leaves and other lawn trash to the front door. Debs pounded on the door mechanically and we could hear it echo through the house. It was clearly as empty as my conscience.

Deborah looked down at the list in her hand and found the name of the suspect who was supposed to live here. "Ms. Bronson!" she called out, but there was even less response, since her voice did not boom through the house like her knocking did.

"Shit," Debs said again. She pounded one more time with the same result — nothing.

Just to be absolutely sure, we walked around the house one time and peered in the windows, but there was nothing to see except some very ugly green-and-maroon curtains left hanging in the otherwise bare living room. When we circled back around to the front again, there was a boy beside our car, sitting on a bicycle and staring at us. He was about eleven or twelve years old and had long hair plaited into dreadlocks and then pulled back into a ponytail.

"They been gone since April," he said. "Did they owe you guys money, too?"

"Did you know the Bronsons?" Deborah asked the boy.

He cocked his head to one side and stared at us, looking a lot like a parrot trying to decide whether to take the cracker or bite your finger. "You guys cops?" he said.

Deborah held up her badge and the boy rolled forward on his bike to take a closer look. "Did you know these people?" Debs said again.

The boy nodded. "I just wanted to be sure," he said. "Lots of people have fake badges."

"We really are cops," I said. "Do you know where the Bronsons went?"

"Naw," he said. "My dad says they owed everybody money and they prolly changed their name or went to South America or something."

"And when was that?" Deborah asked him.

"Back in April," he said. "I already said."

Deborah looked at him with restrained irritation and then glanced at me. "He did," I told her. "He said April."

116

"What did they do?" the boy asked — a little too eagerly, I thought.

"Probably nothing," I told him. "We just wanted to ask them a few questions."

"Wow," the kid said. "Murder? Really?"

Deborah made a strange little shake of her head, as if she was clearing away a cloud of small flies. "Why do you think it was murder?" she asked him.

The boy shrugged. "On TV," he said simply. "If it's murder, they always say it's nothing. If it's nothing, they say it's a serious violation of the penal code or something like that." He snickered. "PEEnal code," he said, grabbing at his crotch.

Deborah looked at the kid and just shook her head. "He's right again," I said to her. "I saw it on *CSI*."

"Jesus," said Debs, still shaking her head.

"Give him your card," I said. "He'll like that."

"Yeah," the boy said, smirking happily, "and tell me to call if I think of anything."

Deborah stopped shaking her head and snorted. "Okay, kid, you win," she said. She flipped him her business card, and he caught it neatly. "Call me if you think of anything," she said.

"Thanks," he said, and he was still smiling as we climbed into the car and drove away, although whether because he really did like the card, or because he was just pleased to have gotten the best of Deborah, I couldn't say.

I glanced at the list beside her on the seat. "Brandon Weiss is next," I said. "Um, a writer. He wrote some ads they didn't like, and he was fired."

Deborah rolled her eyes. "A writer," she said. "What did he do, threaten them with a comma?"

"Well, they had to call in security and have him removed."

Deborah turned and looked at me. "A writer," she said. "Come on, Dex."

"Some of them can be quite fierce," I said, although it seemed like a bit of a stretch to me, too.

Deborah looked back at the traffic, nodded, and chewed on her lip. "Address?" she said.

I looked down at the paper again. "This sounds more like it," I said, reading off an address just off North Miami Avenue. "It's right in the Miami Design District. Where else would a homicidal designer go?"

"I guess you would know," she said, rather churlishly I thought, but not much more than normal, so I let it go.

"It can't possibly be worse than the first

two," I said.

"Yeah, sure, third time's a charm," Deborah said sourly.

"Come on, Debs," I said. "You need to show a little enthusiasm."

Deborah pulled the car off the highway and into the parking lot of a fast-food spot, which surprised me a great deal because, in the first place, it wasn't quite lunchtime and, in the second place, the things this place served were not quite food, no matter how fast.

But she made no move to go into the restaurant. Instead, she slammed the gear lever into park and turned to face me. "FUCK it," she said, and I could tell that something was bothering her.

"Is it that kid?" I asked. "Or are you still pissed off about Meza?"

"Neither," she said. "It's you."

If I had been surprised by her choice of restaurants, I was absolutely astonished at her subject matter. Me? I replayed the morning in my head and found nothing objectionable. I had been the good soldier to her crabby general; I had even made fewer than normal insightful and clever remarks, for which she should really be grateful, since she was usually the target for them.

"I'm sorry," I said. "I don't know what you mean."

"I mean *YOU*," she said, very unhelpfully. "All of you."

"I still don't know what you mean," I said. "There isn't that much of me."

Deborah slammed the palm of her hand on the steering wheel. "Goddamn it, Dexter, the clever-ass shit doesn't work for me anymore."

Have you ever noticed that every now and then you'll overhear an amazingly clear declarative sentence when you're out in public, spoken with such force and purpose that you absolutely yearn to know what it means, because it is just so forceful and crystalline? And you want to follow along behind whoever just spoke, even though you don't know them, just to find out what that sentence means and how it would affect the lives of the people involved?

I felt like that now: I had no idea at all what she was talking about, but I really wanted to know.

Happily for me, she didn't keep me waiting.

"I don't know if I can do this anymore," she said.

"Do what?"

"I am riding around in a car with a guy

who has killed what, ten, fifteen people?"

It's never pleasant to be so grossly under-estimated, but it didn't seem like the politic thing to correct her. "All right," I said.

"And I am supposed to CATCH people like you, and put them away for good, except you're my BROTHER!" she said, slamming her hand on the wheel to empha-size each syllable — which she didn't really need to do, since I heard her very clearly. And I finally understood what all her recent churlishness had been about, although I still had no idea why it had taken until now for her to blow up on the subject.

My sister had only recently found out about my little hobby, and upon reflection, I realized that there were many sound reasons for her to disapprove. Of course there was the act itself, which I freely admit is not for everyone. Add to that the fact that all I was had been sanctioned, even con-structed, by her father, Saint Harry of the Blue Suit; Harry, whose clean and shiny path she thought she had been following. And now she had discovered that there was an alternative path, stamped out by those same hallowed feet, and this path went into the dark places in the forest and reveled in them. All she was stood firmly against everything that made up wonderful me, and both of us designed by the same blessed hand. It was rather biblical when you thought about it.

And there was a great deal to what she said, of course, and if I had really been as smart as I think I am, I would have known that at some point we were going to have this conversation, and I would have been ready for it. But I had foolishly assumed that there is nothing in the world as powerful as the status quo, and Deborah had caught me by surprise. Besides, as far as I could see, there had been nothing in the recent past that would trigger this kind of confrontation; where do these things come from?

"I'm sorry, Debs," I said. "But, uh, what do you want me to do?"

"I want you to *stop* it," she said. "I want you to be somebody else." She looked at me, and her lips twitched, and then she looked away again, out the side window and away beyond U.S. 1 and over the elevated People Mover rails. "I want you . . . to be the guy I always thought you were."

I like to think I am more resourceful than most. But at the moment, I might as well have been bound and gagged and tied to the railroad tracks. "Debs," I said. Not much, but apparently the only shot I had in the chamber.

"God*DAMN* it, Dex," she said, slapping the steering wheel so hard the whole car trembled. "I can't even talk about it, not even to Kyle. And you —" She slapped the steering wheel again. "How do I even know you're telling the truth, that Daddy set you up like this?"

It's probably not accurate to say my feelings were hurt, since I'm pretty sure I don't have any. But the injustice of the remark really did seem painful. "I wouldn't lie to you," I said.

"You lied to me every day of your life that you didn't tell me what you really are," she said.

I am as familiar with New Age philosophy and Dr. Phil as the next guy, but there comes a point where reality absolutely has to intrude, and it seemed to me that we had reached it. "All right, Debs," I said. "And what would you have done if you knew who I really was?"

"I don't know," she said. "I still don't know."

"Well then," I said.

"But I ought to do *something*."

"Why?"

"Because you *killed* people, goddamn it!" she said.

I shrugged. "I can't help it," I said. "And they all really deserved it."

"It isn't right!"

"It's what Dad wanted," I said.

A group of college-age kids walked past the car and stared at us. One of them said something and they all laughed. Ha ha. See the funny couple fighting. He will sleep on the couch tonight, ha ha.

Except that if I couldn't persuade Deborah that all was exactly as it should be, world without end, I might very well sleep in a cell tonight.

"Debs," I said. "Dad set it up this way. He knew what he was doing."

"Did he?" she said. "Or are you making that up? And even if he *did* set it up, was he right to do it that way? Or was he just another bitter, burned-out cop?"

"He was Harry," I said. "He was your father. Of course he was right."

"I need more than that," she said.

"What if there isn't any more?"

She turned away at last, and didn't beat on the steering wheel, which was a relief. But she was silent for long enough that I began to wish she would. "I don't know," she said at last. "I just don't know."

And there it was. I mean, I could see that it was a problem for her — what to do with the homicidal adopted brother? After all, he was pleasant, remembered birthdays, and gave really good presents; a productive member of society, a hardworking and sober guy — if he slipped away and killed bad people now and then, was it really such a big deal?

On the other hand, she was in a profession that generally frowned on that kind of thing. And technically, it was supposed to be her job to find people like me and escort them to a reserved seat in Old Sparky. I could see that it might pose something of a professional dilemma, especially when it was her brother who was forcing the issue.

Or was it?

"Debs," I said. "I know this is a problem for you."

"Problem," she said. A tear rolled down one cheek, although she did not sob or otherwise seem to be crying.

"I don't think he ever wanted you to know," I said. "I was never supposed to tell you. But . . ." I thought about finding her taped to the table with my real genetic brother standing over her, holding one knife for him and one for me, and realizing I could not kill her no matter how much I needed to, no matter how close it would have brought me to him, my brother, the

only person in the world who really understood me and accepted me for what I am.
And somehow, I couldn't do it. Somehow,
the voice of Harry had come back to me
and kept me on the Path.

"Fuck," Deborah said. "What the fuck was
Daddy thinking?"

I wondered that sometimes, too. But I also
wondered how people could possibly believe
any of the things they said they did, and
why I couldn't fly, and this seemed to be in
the same category. "We can't know what he
was thinking," I said. "Just what he did."

"Fuck," she said again.

"Maybe so," I said. "What are you going
to do about it?"

She still didn't look at me. "I don't know,"
she said. "But I think I have to do something."

We both sat there for a very long moment
with nothing left to say. Then she put the
car in gear and we rolled back out onto the
highway.

ELEVEN

There are really very few better conversation stoppers than telling your brother you're considering arresting him for murder, and even my legendary wit was not equal to the task of thinking of something to say that was worth the breath spent on it. So we rode in silence, down U.S. 1 to 95 North and then off the freeway and into the Design District, just past the turnoff for the Julia Tuttle Causeway.

The silence made the trip seem a lot longer than it really was. I glanced once or twice at Deborah, but she was apparently absorbed in thought — perhaps considering whether to use her good cuffs on me or just the cheap extra pair in the glove compartment. Whatever the case, she stared straight ahead, turning the wheel mechanically and moving in and out of traffic without any real thought, and without any attention wasted on me.

We found the address quickly enough, which was a relief, since the strain of not looking at each other and not talking was getting to be a bit much. Deborah pulled up in front of it, a sort of warehouse-looking thing on Northeast Fortieth Street, and pushed the gear lever into park. She turned off the engine and still did not look at me, but paused for a moment. Then she shook her head and climbed out of the car.

I guess I was supposed to just follow along like always, Little Deb's hulking shadow. But I do have some small smidgen of pride, and really: If she was going to turn on me for a paltry few recreational killings, should I be expected to help her solve these? I mean, I don't need to think that things are fair — they never are — but this seemed to be straining at the bounds of decency.

So I sat in the car and didn't really watch as Debs stalked up to the door of the place and rang the buzzer. It was only out of the uninterested corner of my eye that I saw the door open, and I barely noticed the boring detail of Deborah showing her badge. And from where I sat unwatching in the car, I couldn't really tell if the man hit her and she fell over, or whether he simply pushed her to the ground and then disappeared inside.

But I was mildly interested again when she struggled to one knee, then fell over and did not get up again.

I heard a distinct buzzing in Alarm Central: something was very wrong and all my huffishness with Deborah evaporated like gasoline on hot pavement. I was out of the car and running up the sidewalk as fast as I could manage it.

From ten feet away I could see the handle of a knife sticking out of her side and I slowed for a moment as a shock wave rolled through me. A pool of awful wet blood was already spreading across the sidewalk and I was back in the cold box with Biney, my brother, and seeing the terrible sticky red lying thick and nasty on the floor and I could not move or even breathe. But the door fluttered open and the man who had knifed Deborah stepped out, saw me, and went to his knees reaching for the knife handle, and the rising sound of wind that fluttered in my ears turned into the roar of the Dark Passenger spreading its wings and I stepped forward quickly and kicked him hard in the side of the head. He sprawled beside her, face in the blood, and he did not move.

I knelt beside Deborah and took her hand. Her pulse was strong, and her eyes fluttered open. "Dex," she whispered.

"Hang on, sis," I said, and she closed her eyes again. I pulled her radio from its holster on her belt and called for help.

A small crowd had gathered in the few minutes it took for the ambulance to get there, but they parted willingly as the emergency medical techs jumped out and hurried to Deborah.

"Whoof," the first one said. "Let's stop the bleeding fast." He was a stocky young guy with a Marine Corps haircut, and he knelt beside Debs and went to work. His partner, an even stockier woman of about forty, quickly got an IV bag into Deborah's arm, sliding the needle in just as I felt a hand pulling my arm from behind.

I turned. A uniformed cop was there, a middle-aged black guy with a shaved head, and he nodded at me. "You her partner?" he asked.

I pulled out my ID. "Her brother," I said. "Forensics."

"Huh," he said, taking my credentials and looking them over. "You guys don't usually get to the scene this fast." He handed back my ID. "What can you tell me about that guy?" He nodded to the man who had stabbed Deborah, who was sitting up now and holding his head as another cop squatted beside him.

"He opened the door and saw her," I said. "And then he stuck a knife in her."

"Uh-huh," the cop said. He turned away to his partner and said, "Cuff him, Frankie."

I did not watch and gloat as the two cops pulled the knife wielder's arms behind him and slapped on cuffs, because they were loading Deborah into the ambulance. I stepped over to speak to the EMS guy with the short hair. "Will she be all right?" I asked.

He gave me a mechanical and unconvincing smile. "We'll see what the doctors say, okay?" he said, which did not sound as encouraging as he might have intended.

"Are you taking her to Jackson?" I asked.

He nodded. "She'll be in the ICU trauma when you get there," he said.

"Can I ride with you?" I asked.

"No," he said. He slammed the door shut, ran to the front seat of the ambulance, and got in. I watched as they nosed out into traffic, turned on the siren, and drove away.

I suddenly felt very lonely. It seemed far too melodramatic to bear. The last words we had spoken were not pleasant, and now they might very well prove to be our Last Words. It was a sequence of events that belonged on television, preferably on an

131

afternoon soap opera. It did not belong in the prime-time drama of Dexter's Dim Days. But there it was. Deborah was on her way to intensive care and I did not know if she would come out of it. I did not even know if she would get there alive.

I looked back at the sidewalk. It seemed like an awful lot of blood. Deborah's blood.

Happily for me, I did not have to brood too long. Detective Coulter had arrived, and he looked unhappy even for him. I watched him stand on the sidewalk for a minute and look around, before he trudged over to where I stood. He seemed even more unhappy as he looked me over from head to toe with the same expression he had used on the crime scene.

"Dexter," he said. He shook his head. "The fuck you do?"

For a very brief moment I actually started to deny that I'd stabbed my sister. Then I realized he couldn't possibly be accusing me, and indeed, he was merely breaking the ice before taking my statement.

"She shoulda waited for me," he said. "I'm her partner."

"You were getting coffee," I said. "She thought it shouldn't wait."

Coulter looked down at the blood on the pavement and shook his head. "Coulda waited twenty minutes," he said. "For her partner." He looked up at me. "It's a sacred bond."

I have no experience with the sacred, since I spend most of my time playing for the other team, so I simply said, "I guess you're right," and that seemed to satisfy him enough that he settled down and just took my statement with no more than a few sour glances at the bloodstain left by his sacred partner. It took a very long ten minutes before I could finally excuse myself to drive to the hospital.

Jackson Memorial Hospital is well known to every cop, felon, and victim in the greater Miami area, because they have all been there, either as a patient or to pick up a coworker who was one. It is one of the busiest trauma centers in the country, and if practice truly makes perfect, the ICU at Jackson must be the very best at gunshot wounds, stab wounds, blunt-object wounds, beating injuries, and other maliciously inflicted medical conditions. The U.S. Army comes to Jackson to learn field surgery, because over five thousand times every year someone comes to the trauma center with the closest thing you can find to front-line combat wounds outside of Baghdad.

So I knew Debs would be in good hands

if she got there alive. And I found it very hard to imagine that she could possibly die. I mean, I was very well aware that she *could* die; it does happen to most of us, sooner or later. But I could not picture a world without a Deborah Morgan walking around and breathing in it. It would be like one of those thousand-piece jigsaw puzzles with a large center piece missing. It would just seem wrong.

It was unsettling to realize just how used to her I was. We certainly never exchanged tender feelings or gazed dewy-eyed at each other, but she had always been there, my whole life, and as I drove to Jackson it occurred to me that things would be very different if she died, and not quite as comfortable.

I didn't like thinking about it. It was a very strange sensation. I could not recall ever getting this maudlin before. It was not just realizing that she might die, since this was something that I did have some small experience with. And it was not merely the fact that she was more or less family, since I had been through that before, too. But when my foster parents died, I'd had a long illness and the certain knowledge that they were dying to prepare me. This was so sudden. Perhaps it was just the unexpected nature of the shock that made me feel so very nearly emotional.

Luckily for me, it was not a very long drive — the hospital was only a couple of miles away — and I pulled into the parking lot after only a few minutes of racing through traffic with one hand on the horn — which most Miami drivers usually ignore anyway.

All hospitals are the same on the inside, even down to the color the walls are painted, and on the whole they are not truly happy places. Of course, I was quite pleased to have one here at the moment, but I was not filled with a sense of pleasant expectation when I walked into the trauma unit. There was an air of animal resignation to the people waiting, and a sense of perpetual, bone-numbing crisis on the faces of all the doctors and nurses as they bustled back and forth, and this was only countered by the un-hurried, bureaucratic, clipboard-wielding officiality of the woman who stopped me when I tried to push through and find Deborah.

"Sergeant Morgan, knife wound," I said. "They just brought her in."

"Who are you?" she said.

Stupidly thinking it might get me past her quickly, I said, "Next of kin," and the woman actually smiled. "Good," she said.

"Just the man I need to talk to."

"Can I see her?" I said.

"No," she said. She grabbed me by the elbow and began to steer me firmly toward an office cubicle.

"Can you tell me how she's doing?" I asked.

"Have a seat right here, please," she said, propelling me toward a molded plastic chair that faced a small desk.

"But how is she?" I said, refusing to be bullied.

"We'll find out in just a minute," she said. "Just as soon as we get some of this paper-work done. Sit down, please, Mr. — is it Mr. Morton?"

"Morgan," I said.

She frowned. "I have Morton here."

"It's Morgan," I said. *"M-O-R-G-A-N."*

"Are you sure?" she asked me, and the surreal nature of the whole hospital experience swept over me and shoved me down into the chair, as if I had been smacked by a huge wet pillow.

"Quite sure," I said faintly, slumping back as much as the wobbly little chair allowed.

"Now I'll have to change it in the computer," she said, frowning. "Doggone it."

I opened and closed my mouth a few times, like a stranded fish, as the woman pecked at her keyboard. It was just too much; even her laconic "doggone it" was an offense to reason. It was Deborah's life on the line — shouldn't there be great fiery gouts of urgent profanity spewing from every single person physically able to stand and speak? Perhaps I could arrange for Hernando Meza to come in and teach a workshop on the correct linguistic approach to impending doom.

It took far longer than seemed either possible or human, but eventually I did manage to get all the proper forms filled out and persuade the woman that, as next of kin AND a police employee, I had every right in the world to see my sister. But of course, things being what they are in this vale of tears, I did not really get to see her. I simply stood in a hallway and peeked through a porthole-shaped window and watched as what seemed like a very large crowd of people in lime-green scrubs gathered around the table and did terrible, unimaginable things to Deborah.

For several centuries I simply stood and stared and occasionally flinched as a bloody hand or instrument appeared in the air above my sister. The smell of chemicals, blood, sweat, and fear was almost overwhelming. But finally, when I could feel the earth turning dead and airless and the sun growing old and cold, they all stepped back from the table and several of them began to push her toward the door. I stepped back and watched them roll her through the doors and down the hall, and then I grabbed at the arm of one of the senior-looking men who filed out after. It might have been a mistake: my hand touched something cold, wet, and sticky, and I pulled it away to see it splotched with blood. For a moment I felt light-headed and unclean and even a little panicky, but as the surgeon turned to look at me I recovered just enough.

"How is she?" I asked him.

He looked down the hall toward where they were taking my sister, then back at me. "Who are you?" he asked.

"Her brother," I said. "Is she going to be all right?"

He gave me half a not-funny smile. "It's much too soon to tell," he said. "She lost an awful lot of blood. She could be fine, or there could be complications. We just don't know yet."

"What kind of complications?" I asked. It seemed like a very reasonable question to me, but he blew out an irritated breath and shook his head.

"Everything from infection to brain damage," he said. "We're not going to know anything for a day or two, so you're just going to have to wait until we do know something, okay?" He gave me the other half of the smile and walked away, in the opposite direction from where they had taken Deborah.

I watched him go, thinking about brain damage. Then I turned and followed the gurney that had carried Deborah down the hall.

TWELVE

There were so many pieces of machinery around Deborah that it took me a moment before I saw her in the middle of the whirring, chirping clutter. She lay there in the bed without moving, tubes going in and out of her, her face half covered by a respirator mask and nearly as pale as the sheets. I stood and looked for a minute, not sure what I was supposed to do. I had bent all my concentration on getting in to see her, and now here I was, and I could not remember ever reading anywhere what the proper procedure was for visiting nearest and dearest in the ICU. Was I supposed to hold her hand? It seemed likely, but I wasn't sure, and there was an IV attached to the hand nearest me; it didn't seem like a good idea to risk dislodging it.

So instead I found a chair, tucked away under one of the life-support machines. I moved it as close to the bed as seemed proper, and I settled down to wait.

After only a couple of minutes there was a sound at the door and I looked up to see a thin black cop I knew slightly. Wilkins. He stuck his head in the door and said, "Hey. Dexter, right?" I nodded and held up my credentials.

Wilkins nodded his head at Deborah. "How is she?"

"Too soon to tell," I said.

"Sorry, man," he said, and shrugged. "Captain wants somebody watching, so I'll be out here."

"Thank you," I said, and he turned away to take up his post at the door.

I tried to imagine what life would be like without Deborah. The very idea was disturbing, although I could not say why. I could not think of any huge and obvious differences, and that made me feel slightly embarrassed, so I worked at it a little harder. I would probably get to eat the coq au vin warm next time. I would not have as many bruises on my arms without her world-famous vicious arm punches. And I would not have to worry about her arresting me, either. It was all good. Why was I worried?

Still, the logic was not terribly convincing. And what if she lived but suffered brain damage? That could very well affect her career in law enforcement. She might need full-time care, spoon-feeding, adult diapers — none of these things would go over well on the job. And who would do all the endless tedious drudgery of looking after her? I didn't know a great deal about medical insurance, but I knew enough to know that full-time care was not something they offered cheerfully. What if I had to take care of her? It would certainly put a large dent in my free time. But who else was there? In all the world, she had no other family. There was only Dear Dutiful Dexter; no one else to push her wheelchair and cook her pablum and tenderly wipe the corners of her mouth as she drooled. I would have to tend to her for the rest of her life, far into the sunset years, the two of us sitting and watching game shows while the rest of the world went on its merry way, killing and brutalizing one another without me.

Just before I sank under a huge wave of wet self-pity I remembered Kyle Chutsky. To call him Deborah's boyfriend was not quite accurate, since they had been living together for over a year, and that made it seem like a bit more. Besides, he was hardly a boy. He was at least ten years older than Debs, very large and beat-up, and missing his left hand and foot as the result of an encounter with the same amateur surgeon who had modified Sergeant Doakes.

To be perfectly fair to me, which I think is very important, I did not think of him merely because I wanted someone else to take care of a hypothetically brain-damaged Deborah. Rather, it occurred to me that the fact that she was in the ICU was something he might want to know.

So I took my cell phone from its holster and called him. He answered almost immediately.

"Hello?"

"Kyle, this is Dexter," I said.

"Hey, buddy," he said in his artificially cheerful voice. "What's up?"

"I'm with Deborah," I said. "In the ICU at Jackson."

"What happened?" he said after a slight pause.

"She's been stabbed," I said. "She lost a lot of blood."

"I'm on my way," he said, and hung up.

It was nice that Chutsky cared enough to come right away. Maybe he would help me with Deborah's pablum, take turns pushing the wheelchair. It's good to have someone.

That reminded me that I had someone — or perhaps I was had. In any case, Rita would want to know I would be late, before she cooked a pheasant soufflé for me. I called her at work, told her quickly what was up, and hung up again as she was just getting started on a chorus of oh-my-Gods.

Chutsky came into the room about fifteen minutes later, trailed by a nurse who was apparently trying to make sure he was perfectly happy with everything from the location of the room to the arrangement of IVs. "This is her," the nurse said.

"Thanks, Gloria," Chutsky said without looking at anything but Deborah. The nurse hovered anxiously for a few more moments, and then vanished uncertainly.

Meanwhile, Chutsky moved over to the bed and took Deborah's hand — good to know I had been right about that; holding her hand was, indeed, the correct thing to do.

"What happened, buddy?" he said, staring down at Deborah.

I gave him a quick rundown, and he listened without looking at me, pausing briefly in his hand-holding to wipe a lock of hair away from Deborah's forehead. When I had finished talking, he nodded absently and said, "What did the doctors say?"

"It's too soon to tell," I said.

He waved that away impatiently, using the gleaming silver hook that had replaced his left hand. "They always say that," he said. "What else?"

"There's a chance of permanent damage," I said. "Even brain damage."

He nodded. "She lost a lot of blood," he said, not a question, but I answered anyway.

"That's right," I said.

"I have a guy coming down from Bethesda," Chutsky said. "He'll be here in a couple of hours."

I couldn't think of very much to say to that. A guy? From Bethesda? Was this good news of some kind, and if so, why? I could not come up with a single thing to distinguish Bethesda from Cleveland, except that it was in Maryland instead of Ohio. What kind of guy would come down from there? And to what end? But I also couldn't think of any way to frame a question on the subject. For some reason, my brain was not running with its usual icy efficiency.

So I just watched as Chutsky pulled another chair around to the far side of the bed, where he could sit and hold Deborah's hand. And after he got settled, he finally looked directly at me. "Dexter," he said.

"Yes," I said.

"Think you could scare up some coffee? And maybe a doughnut or something?"

The question took me completely by

145

surprise — not because it was such a bizarre notion, but because it *seemed* like one to me, and it really should have been as natural as breathing. It was well past my lunchtime, and I had not eaten, and I had not thought of eating. But now, when Chutsky suggested it, the idea seemed wrong, like singing the real words to "Barnacle Bill" in church.

Still, to object would seem even stranger. So I stood up and said, "I'll see what I can do," and headed out and down the hall.

When I came back a few minutes later, I had two cups of coffee and four doughnuts. I paused in the hallway, I don't know why, and looked in. Chutsky was leaning forward, eyes closed, with Deborah's hand pressed to his forehead. His lips were moving, although I could hear no sound over the clatter of the life-support machinery. Was he praying? It seemed like the oddest thing yet. I suppose I really didn't know him very well, but what I did know about him did not fit with the image of a man who prayed. And in any case, it was embarrassing, something you didn't really want to see, like watching somebody clean their nostrils with a fingertip. I cleared my throat as I came in to my chair, but he didn't look up.

Aside from saying something loud and cheerful, and possibly interrupting his fit of religious fervor, there was nothing really constructive for me to do. So I sat down and started on the doughnuts. I had almost finished the first one when Chutsky finally looked up.

"Hey," he said. "What'd you get?"

I passed him a coffee and two of the doughnuts. He grabbed the coffee with his right hand and passed his hook through the holes in the doughnuts. "Thanks," he said. He held the coffee between his knees and flipped the lid off with a finger, dangling the doughnuts from his hook and taking a bite out of one of them. "Mmp," he said. "Didn't get any lunch. I was waiting to hear from Deborah, and I was going to maybe come eat with you guys. But . . ." he said, and trailed off, taking another bite of the doughnut.

He ate his doughnuts in silence, except for the occasional slurp of coffee, and I took advantage of the time to finish mine. When we were both done we simply sat and stared at Deborah as if she was our favorite TV show. Now and again one of the machines would make some sort of odd noise and we would both glance up at it. But nothing actually changed. Deborah continued to lie with her eyes closed, breathing slowly and raggedly and with the Darth Vader sound of the respirator as an accompaniment.

I sat for at least an hour, and my thoughts didn't suddenly turn bright and sunny. As far as I could tell, neither did Chutsky's. He did not burst into tears, but he looked tired and a little gray, worse than I had ever seen him except for when I rescued him from the man who cut off his hand and foot. And I suppose I did not look a great deal better, although it was not the thing I worried about the most, now or at any other time. In truth, I did not spend a great deal of my time worrying about anything — planning, yes, making sure that things went just right on my Special Nights Out. But worrying truly seemed to be an emotional activity rather than a rational one, and until now it had never furrowed my forehead.

But now? Dexter worried. It was a surprisingly easy pastime to pick up. I got the hang of it right away, and it was all I could do to keep from chewing my fingernails.

Of course she would be all right. Wouldn't she? "Too soon to tell" began to seem more ominous. Could I even trust that statement? Wasn't there a protocol, a standard medical procedure for informing next of kin that their loved ones were either dying or about to become vegetables? Start out by warning them that all may not be right — "too soon to tell" — and then gradually break it to them that all is forever unwell?

But wasn't there some law somewhere that required doctors to tell the truth about these things? Or was that just auto mechanics? Was there such a thing as truth, medically speaking? I had no idea — this was a new world for me, and I didn't like it, but whatever else might be true, it really was too soon to tell, and I would just have to wait, and shockingly, I was not nearly as good at that as I would have thought I'd be.

When my stomach began to growl again, I decided it must be evening, but a glance at my watch told me that it was still only a few minutes short of four o'clock.

Twenty minutes later Chutsky's Guy from Bethesda arrived. I hadn't really known what to expect, but it was nothing like what I got. The Guy was about five-six, bald and potbellied, with thick gold-framed glasses, and he came in with two of the doctors who had worked on Deborah. They followed him like high school freshmen trailing the prom queen, eager to point out things that would make him happy. Chutsky leaped to his feet when the Guy came in.

"Dr. Teidel!" he said.

Teidel nodded at Chutsky and said, "Out," with a head motion that included me.

Chustky nodded and grabbed my arm, and as he pulled me out of the room Teidel and his two satellites were already pulling back the sheet to examine Deborah.

"The guy is the best," Chutsky said, and although he still didn't say the best what, I was now assuming it was something medical.

"What is he going to do?" I asked, and Chutsky shrugged.

"Whatever it takes," he said. "Come on, let's get something to eat. We don't want to see this."

That did not sound terribly reassuring, but Chutsky obviously felt better about things with Teidel in charge, so I followed along to a small and crowded café on the ground floor of the parking garage. We wedged ourselves in at a small table in the corner and ate indifferent sandwiches and, although I didn't think to ask him, Chutsky told me a little about the doctor from Bethesda.

"Guy's amazing," he said. "Ten years ago? He put me back together. I was in a lot worse shape than Deborah, believe me, and he got all the pieces back in the right place and in working order."

"Which is almost as important," I said,

and Chutsky nodded as if he was listening to me.

"Honest to God," he said, "Teidel is the best there is. You saw how those other doctors were treating him?"

"Like they wanted to wash his feet and peel him grapes," I said.

Chutsky gave one syllable of polite laugh, "Huh," and an equally brief smile. "She's gonna be okay now," he said. "Just fine."

But whether he was trying to convince me or himself, I couldn't say.

THIRTEEN

Dr. Teidel was in the staff break room when we got back from eating. He sat at a table sipping a cup of coffee, which somehow seemed strange and improper, like a dog sitting at a table and holding a pawful of playing cards. If Teidel was going to be a miraculous savior, how could he do ordinary human things, too? And when he looked up as we came in, his eyes were human, tired, not at all brimming with the spark of divine inspiration, and his first words did not fill me with awe, either.

"It's too soon to be certain," he said to Chutsky, and I was grateful for the slight variation in the standard medical mantra. "We're not at the real crisis point yet, and that could change everything." He slurped from his coffee cup. "She's young, strong. The doctors here are very good. You're in good hands. But a lot can still go wrong."

"Is there anything you can do?" Chutsky

asked, sounding very uncertain and humble, like he was asking God for a new bicycle.

"You mean a magic operation or a fantastic new procedure?" Teidel said. He sipped coffee. "No. Not a thing. You just have to wait." He glanced at his watch and stood up. "I have a plane to catch."

Chutsky lurched forward and shook Teidel's hand. "Thank you, Doctor. I really appreciate this. Thanks."

Teidel pried his hand away from Chutsky's. "You're welcome," he said, and headed for the door.

Chutsky and I watched him go. "I feel a lot better," Chutsky said. "Just having him here was major." He glanced at me as if I had said something scornful, and said, "Seriously. She's going to be okay."

I wished that I felt as confident as Chutsky. I did not know that Deborah was going to be okay. I really wanted to believe it, but I am not as good at kidding myself as most humans are, and I have always found that if things have a choice of directions, they are most likely to go downhill.

Still, it was not the sort of thing I could say in the ICU without causing a certain amount of negative feeling to be directed toward me, so I mumbled something appropriate and we went back to sit at Deborah's bedside. Wilkins was still at the door, and there had been no change in Deborah that I could see, and no matter how long we sat or how hard we looked at her, nothing happened, except for the *hum, click, ping* of the machinery.

Chutsky stared at her, as if he could make her sit up and speak by the power of his gaze. It didn't work. After a time he switched his stare to me. "The guy who did this," he said. "They got him, right?"

"He's locked up," I said. "At the detention center."

Chutsky nodded and looked like he was going to say something else. He looked toward the window, sighed, and then went back to staring at Deborah.

Dexter is known far and wide for the depth and sharpness of his intellect, but it was nearly midnight before it occurred to me that there was no point in sitting and staring at Deborah's unmoving form. She had not leaped to her feet from the Uri Geller intensity of Chutsky's gaze, and if the doctors were to be believed, she was not going to do anything at all for some time: in which case, instead of sitting here and slowly sagging into the floor and morphing into a hunched, red-eyed lump, it made more sense for Dexter to totter off to bed for a few squalid hours of slumber.

Chutsky offered no objection; he just waved his hand and muttered something about holding down the fort, and I staggered out of the ICU and into the warm and wet Miami night. It was a pleasant change after the mechanical chill of the hospital, and I paused to breathe in the flavor of vegetation and exhaust fumes. There was a large chunk of evil yellow moon floating in the sky and chuckling to itself, but I did not really feel its pull. I could not concentrate at all on the joyous matching gleam a knife blade would give off or the wild nighttime dance of shadowy delight I should be longing for. Not with Deborah lying unmoving inside. Not that it would be wrong — I just didn't feel it. I didn't feel anything at all except tired, dull, and empty.

Well, I couldn't cure the dull and empty, and I couldn't cure Deborah, but at least I could do something about the tired part.

I went home.

I woke up early, with a bad taste in my mouth. Rita was already in the kitchen and she had a cup of coffee in front of me before I could even settle into a chair. "How is she?" she said.

"It's too soon to tell," I said, and she nodded.

"They always say that," she said.

I took a large slug of the coffee and stood back up. "I'd better check and see how she is this morning," I said. I grabbed my cell phone from the table by the front door and called Chutsky.

"No change," he said, in a voice that was rough with fatigue. "I'll call you if anything happens."

I went back to the kitchen table and sat, feeling like I might fall into a coma myself at any minute. "What did they say?" Rita asked.

"No change," I told her, and I slouched forward into the coffee cup.

Several cups of coffee and six blueberry pancakes later I was somewhat restored and ready to go to work. So I pushed back from the table, said good-bye to Rita and the kids, and headed out the door. I would go through the motions like always, and let the ordinary rhythm of my artificial life lull me into synthetic serenity.

But work was not the sanctuary I had expected. I was greeted everywhere with sympathetic frowns and hushed voices asking, "How is she?" The entire building seemed to be throbbing with concern and echoing with the battle cry of "It's too soon to tell." Even Vince Masuoka had gotten into the spirit. He had brought in doughnuts — the second time this week! — and in a spirit of pure sympathetic kindness he had saved me the Bavarian cream.

"How is she?" he asked, handing me the doughnut.

"She lost a lot of blood," I told him, mostly for the sake of some variety before I wore out my tongue from saying the same thing so many times. "She's still in ICU."

"They're pretty good at this stuff at Jackson," he said. "Lots of practice."

"I'd rather have them practice on someone else," I said, and ate the doughnut.

I had been in my chair for less than ten minutes when I got a call from Captain Matthews's executive assistant, Gwen. "The captain wants to see you right away," she said.

"Such a beautiful voice . . . It can only be that radiant angel Gwen," I said.

"He means right now," she said, and hung up. And so did I.

I was in the captain's outer office in just under four minutes, looking at Gwen in person. She had been Matthews's assistant forever, all the way back to when she was called a secretary, and for two reasons. The first was that she was incredibly efficient. The second was that she was incredibly plain, and none of the captain's three wives had ever been able to find the slightest objection to her.

The combination of these two things made her irresistible to me, as well, and I was unable to see her without letting some lighthearted jest fly out from my frothy wit. "Ah, Gwendolyn," I said. "Sweet siren of South Miami."

"He's waiting for you," she said.

"Never mind him," I said. "Fly away with me to a life of beautiful debauchery."

"Go on in," she said, nodding at the door. "In the conference room."

I had assumed that the captain would want to express official sympathy, and the conference room seemed like a strange place to do that. But he was the captain and Dexter is a mere underling, so I went on in.

Captain Matthews was, indeed, waiting for me. He stood just inside the door to the conference room, and as I stepped inside he pounced on me. "Morgan," he said. "Just, um — this is entirely unofficial, so . . ." He waved a hand, then placed it on my shoulder. "Help us out here, son," he said. "Just — you know," and with no further surreal stage direction he led me to a seat at the table.

There were several people already seated,

most of whom I recognized, and none of whom was particularly good news. There was Israel Salguero, who was head of Internal Affairs; he was bad news all by himself. But he was also joined by Irene Cappuccio, who I knew only by sight and reputation. She was the senior lawyer for the department, and rarely called in unless somebody had filed a credible and substantial lawsuit against us. Sitting beside her was another department lawyer, Ed Beasley.

Across the table was Lieutenant Stein, information officer, who specialized in spinning things to keep the whole force from looking like a rampaging gang of Visigoths. Altogether, this was not a group calculated to make Dexter sink into a chair wrapped in a soft cloud of tranquillity.

There was a stranger sitting in one of the chairs by Matthews, and it was clear from the cut of his apparently expensive suit that he was not a cop. He was black, with a look of important condescension on his face and a shaved head that gleamed so brightly I was sure he used furniture polish, and as I watched he twitched his arm so that the sleeve rolled up to reveal a large diamond cuff link and a beautiful Rolex watch.

"So," Matthews said as I hovered above a

chair fighting down a sense of panic. "How is she?"

"Too soon to tell," I said.

He nodded. "Well, I'm sure we all, ah, hope for the best here," he said. "She's a fine officer, and her dad was, uh — your dad, too, of course." He cleared his throat and went on. "The, uh, doctors at Jackson are the best, and I want you to know that if there's anything the department can do, um . . ." The man beside him glanced up at Matthews, and then at me, and Matthews nodded. "Sit down," he said.

I hooked a chair back away from the table and sat, with no idea what was going on, but an absolute certainty that I wouldn't like it.

Captain Matthews confirmed my opinion right away. "This is an informal conversation," he said. "Just to, ah, ahem . . ."

The stranger turned his large and brittle eyes on the captain with a somewhat withering expression, and then looked back at me. "I represent Alex Doncevic," he said.

The name meant absolutely nothing to me, but he said it with such smooth conviction I was sure it ought to, so I just nodded and said, "Oh, all right."

"In the first place," he said, "I am demanding his immediate release. And in the

160

second . . ." He paused here, apparently for dramatic effect and to let his righteous anger build up and spill out into the room. "In the second place," he said, as if he was addressing a crowd in a large hall, "we are considering a lawsuit for punitive damages."

I blinked. They were all looking at me, and I was clearly an important part of something a little bit dire, but I really had no idea what it might be. "I'm sorry to hear that," I said.

"Look," Matthews said. "We're just having an informal, preliminary conversation here. Because Mr. Simeon here, ah — has a very respectable position in the community. Our community," he said.

"And because his client is under arrest for several major felonies," Irene Cappuccio said.

"*Illegally* under arrest," Simeon said.

"That remains to be seen," Cappuccio told him. She nodded at me. "Mr. Morgan can possibly shed some light on that."

"All right," said Matthews. "Let's not, uh." He put both hands on the conference table, facedown. "The important thing is, just — uh, Irene?"

Cappuccio nodded and looked at me. "Can you tell us *exactly* what happened yesterday, leading up to the assault on

Detective Morgan?"

"You know you would never get away with that in court, Irene," Simeon said. "Assault? Come on."

Cappuccio looked at him with a cold, unblinking stare for what seemed like a very long time, but was probably only about ten seconds. "All right," she said, turning back to me. "Leading up to the time his client stuck a knife in Deborah Morgan? You're not denying he stabbed her, are you?" she said to Simeon.

"Let's hear what happened," Simeon said with a tight smile.

Cappuccio nodded to me. "Go on," she said. "Start at the beginning."

"Well," I said, and that was all I could really say for the moment. I could feel the eyes on me and the clock ticking, but I couldn't think of anything more cogent to say. It was nice finally to know who Alex Doncevic was; it's always good to know the names of people who stab your family members.

But whoever else he might be, Alex Doncevic was not the name on the list Deborah and I had been investigating. She had knocked on that door to find someone named Brandon Weiss —

— and been stabbed by someone else altogether, who had panicked into attempted murder and flight at the mere sight of her badge?

Dexter does not demand that life must always unfold in a reasonable manner. After all, I live here, and I know that logic does not. But this made no sense at all, unless I accepted the idea that if you knock on doors at random in Miami, one out of three people who answer is prepared to kill you. While this idea had its own very great charm, it did not really seem terribly likely.

And on top of that, at the moment *why* he did it was not as important as the fact that Doncevic had stabbed Deborah. But why that should cause a gathering of this magnitude, I had no idea. Matthews, Cappuccio, Salguero — these people did not get together for coffee every day.

So I knew that something unpleasant was happening, and that whatever I said was going to affect it, but since I didn't know what "it" was, I didn't know what to say to make things better. There was just too much information that did not add up to anything, and even my giant brain could not quite cope. I cleared my throat, hoping it would give me a little time, but it was over in just a few seconds and they were all still looking at me.

"Well," I said again. "Um, the beginning? You mean, um . . ."

"You went to interview Mr. Doncevic," Cappuccio said.

"No, um — not really."

"Not really," said Simeon, as if one of us must not know what the words meant. "What does that mean, 'not really'?"

"We went to interview someone named Brandon Weiss," I said. "Doncevic answered the door."

Cappuccio nodded. "What did he say when Sergeant Morgan identified herself?"

"I don't know," I said.

Simeon glanced at Cappuccio and said, "Stonewalling," in a very loud whisper. She waved it off.

"Mr. Morgan," she said, and glanced down at the file in front of her. "Dexter." She gave me a very small facial twitch that she probably thought was a warm smile. "You're not under oath here, and you're not in any kind of trouble. We just need to know what happened, leading up to the stabbing."

"I understand," I said. "But I was in the car."

Simeon sat up almost at attention. "In the *car*," he said. "Not at the door with Sergeant Morgan."

"That's right."

164

"So you didn't hear what was said — or *not* said," he said, raising one eyebrow high enough that it might almost pass for a tiny toupee on that shiny bald head.

"That's right."

Cappuccio leaned in and said. "But you said in your statement that Sergeant Morgan showed her badge."

"Yes," I said. "I saw her."

"And he was sitting in the car, HOW far away?" Simeon said. "Do you know what I could do with that in court?"

Matthews cleared his throat. "Let's not, um — court is not, uh, we don't have to assume this will end in court," he said.

"I was a lot closer when he tried to stab me," I said, hoping to be a little helpful.

But Simeon waved that off. "Self-defense," he said. "If she failed to properly identify herself as an officer of the law, he had every right to defend himself!"

"She showed her badge, I'm sure of it," I said.

"You CAN'T be sure — not from fifty feet away!" Simeon said.

"I saw it," I said, and I hoped I didn't sound petulant. "Besides, Deborah would never forget that — she's known the correct procedure since she could walk."

Simeon waved a very large index finger at

me. "And that's another thing I really don't like here — exactly *what* is your relationship to Sergeant Morgan?"

"She's my sister," I said.

"Your *sister,*" he said, making it sound somehow like he was saying, "Your evil henchman." He shook his head theatrically and looked around the room. He definitely had everyone's attention, and he was clearly enjoying it. "This just gets better and better," he said, with a much nicer smile than Cappuccio's.

Salguero spoke up for the first time. "Deborah Morgan has a clean record. She comes from a police family, and she is clean in every way, and always has been."

"A police family does not mean clean," Simeon said. "What it means is the Blue Wall, and you know it. This is a clear case of self-defense, abuse of authority, and cover-up." He threw his hands up and went on. "Obviously, we are never going to find out what really happened, not with all these byzantine family and police-department connections. I think we will just have to let the courts figure this out."

Ed Beasley spoke up for the first time, in a gruff and non-hysterical way that made me want to give him a hearty handshake. "We have an officer in intensive care," he said. "Because your client stuck a knife in her. And we don't need a court to figure that out, Kwami."

Simeon turned a row of bright teeth on Beasley. "Maybe not, Ed," he said. "But until you guys succeed in throwing out the Bill of Rights, my client has that option."

He stood up. "In any case," he said, "I think I have enough to get my client out on bail." He nodded at Cappuccio and left the room.

There was a moment of silence, and then Matthews cleared his throat. "Does he have enough, Irene?"

Cappuccio snapped the pencil she was holding. "With the right judge? Yeah," she said. "Probably."

"The political climate is not good right now," Beasley said. "Simeon can stir things up and make this stink. And we can't afford another stink right now."

"All right then, people," Matthews said. "Let's batten down the hatches for the coming shit-storm. Lieutenant Stein, you've got your work cut out for you. Get something on my desk for the press ASAP — before noon."

Stein nodded. "Right," he said.

Israel Salguero stood up and said, "I have my work, too, Captain. Internal Affairs will have to start a review of Sergeant Morgan's behavior right away."

"All right, good," Matthews said, and then he looked at me. "Morgan," he said, shaking his head, "I wish you could have been a little more helpful."

FOURTEEN

So Alex Doncevic was out on the street long before Deborah was even awake. In fact, Doncevic was out of the detention center at 5:17 that afternoon, which was only an hour and twenty-four minutes after Deborah opened her eyes for the first time.

I knew about Deborah because Chutsky called me right away, as excited as if she had just swum the English Channel towing a piano. "She's gonna be okay, Dex," he said. "She opened her eyes and looked right at me."

"Did she say anything?" I asked.

"No," he said. "But she squeezed my hand. She's gonna make it."

I was still not convinced that a wink and a squeeze were accurate signs that a complete recovery was at hand, but it was nice to know that she had made some progress. Especially since she would need to be fully conscious to face Israel Salguero and Internal Affairs.

And I knew when Doncevic was released from the detention center because in the time between the meeting in the conference room and Chutsky's call, I had made a decision.

Dexter is not delusional; he knows better than most that life is not fair. Humans invented the idea of fairness to try to level the playing field and make things a little more challenging for the predators. And that's fine. Personally, I welcome the challenge.

But although Life is not fair, Law and Order was supposed to be. And the idea that Doncevic might go free while Deborah wasted away in a hospital with so many tubes going in and out of her just seemed so very, kind of . . . All right, I will say it: it wasn't fair. I mean, I am sure there are other available words here, but Dexter will not dodge merely because this truth, like most others, is a relatively ugly one. I felt a sharp sense of not-fairness to the whole thing, and it made me ponder what I might do to set things back in their proper order.

I pondered through several hours of routine paperwork and three cups of somewhat horrible coffee. And I pondered through a below-average lunch at a small place claiming to be Mediterranean, which was only true if we accept that stale bread, clotted mayonnaise, and greasy cold cuts are Mediterranean. And then I pondered through another few minutes of pushing things around on the desk in my little cubby.

And finally, somewhere in the distant fog of Dexter's diminished brainscape, a small and faint gong sounded a tiny tinny note. *Bong,* it said softly, and murky light slowly flooded into Dexter's Dim Noggin.

I had been scolded for being not very helpful, and I believe that I had been feeling the truth of that accusation. Dexter had not, in fact, been helpful; he had been sulking in the car when Debs was hurt, and he had failed to protect her once again from the attack of the shiny-headed lawyer.

But there was a way I could be very very helpful, and it was something that I was particularly good at. I could make a whole handful of problems go away: Deborah's, the department's, and my own very special ones, all at the same time, with one smooth stroke — or several choppy ones, if I was feeling particularly playful. All I had to do was relax and be wonderful special Me, while helping poor deserving Doncevic to see the error of his ways.

I knew Doncevic was guilty — I had seen

him stab Deborah with my own eyes. And there was a very good chance he had killed and arranged the bodies that were causing such an uproar and harming our vital tourist economy. Disposing of Doncevic was practically my civic duty. Since he was out on bail, if he turned up missing, everyone would assume he had run. The bounty hunters would make a stab at finding him, but no one would care when they failed.

I felt a very strong satisfaction with this solution: it's nice when things can work out so nicely, and the neatness of it appealed to my inner monster, the tidy one that likes to see problems properly bagged up and thrown away. Besides, it was only fair.

Wonderful: I would spend some quality time with Alex Doncevic.

I began by checking online to see his status, and rechecking every fifteen minutes when it became clear that he was about to be released. At 4:32 his paperwork was in its final stages, and I moseyed down to the parking lot and drove over to the front door of the detention center.

I got there just in time, and there were plenty of people there ahead of me. Simeon really knew how to throw a party, especially if the press were involved, and they were all there waiting in a huge, unruly mob, the vans and satellite dishes and beautiful haircuts all competing for space. When Doncevic came out on Simeon's arm, there was a clatter of cameras and the multiple thud of many elbows trying to clear a way, and the crowd surged forward like a pack of dogs pouncing on raw meat.

I watched from my car as Simeon made a long and heart-warming statement, answered a few questions, and then pushed through the crowd, towing Doncevic with him. They got into a black Lexus SUV and drove away, and after a moment, I followed.

Following another car is relatively simple, particularly in Miami, where there is always traffic, and it always acts irrationally. Since it was rush hour, all these things were even more so. I just had to stay back a bit, leaving a couple of cars between me and the Lexus. Simeon did nothing to show that he thought he was being followed. Of course, even if he spotted me he would assume I was a reporter hoping for a candid shot of Doncevic weeping with gratitude, and Simeon would do nothing more than make sure his good side was to the camera.

I followed them across town to North Miami Avenue, and dropped back a little as they turned onto Northeast Fortieth Street. I was fairly confident I knew where they were going now, and sure enough, Simeon pulled over in front of the building where Deborah had first met my new friend Doncevic. I drove past, circled the block once, and came back in time to see Doncevic get out of the Lexus and head into the building.

Happily for me, there was a parking spot where I could see the door. I pulled into it, turned off the engine, and waited for darkness, which would come as it always did, to find Dexter ready for it. And tonight, at last, after such a long and dreary stay in the daytime world, ready to join with it, revel in its sweet and savage music, and play a few chords of Dexter's own minuet. I found myself impatient with the ponderous, slowly sinking sun, and eager for the night. I could feel it stretching out for me, leaning in to spread through me, flexing its wings, easing the knots out of the too-long-unused muscles and preparing to spring —

My phone rang.

"It's me," said Rita.

"I'm sure it is," I said.

"I think I have a really good — what did you say?"

"Nothing," I said. "What's your really good?"

"What?" she said. "Oh — I've been thinking about what we said. About Cody?"

I pulled my mind back from the pulsing darkness I had been feeding and tried to remember what we had said about Cody. It had been something about helping him come out of his shell, but I did not remember that we had actually decided anything beyond a few vague platitudes designed to make Rita feel better while I carefully placed Cody's feet on the Harry Path. So I just said, "Oh, right. Yes?" in the hope of drawing her out just a bit.

"I was talking to Susan? You know, over on One hundred thirty-seventh? With the big dog," she said.

"Yes," I said. "I remember the dog." As indeed I did — it hated me, like all domestic animals do. They all recognize me for what I am, even if their masters do not.

"And her son, Albert? He's been having a really positive experience with the Cub Scouts. And I thought, that might be just right for Cody."

At first the idea didn't make any sense at all. Cody? A Cub Scout? It seemed like serving cucumber sandwiches and tea to Godzilla. But as I stammered for a reply, trying to think of something that was neither outraged denial nor hysterical laughter, I actually caught myself realizing that it was not a bad idea. It was, in fact, a very good idea that would mesh perfectly with the plan to make Cody fit in with human children. And so, caught halfway between irritated denial and enthusiastic acceptance, I quite distinctly said, "Hi didda yuh-kay."

"Dexter, are you all right?" Rita said.

"I, uh, you caught me by surprise," I said. "I'm in the middle of something. But I think it's a great idea."

"Really? You really do?" she said.

"Absolutely," I said. "It's the perfect thing for him."

"I was hoping you'd say so," she said. "But then I thought, I don't know. What if — I mean, you really do think so?"

I really did, and eventually I made her believe me. But it took several minutes, since Rita is able to speak without breathing and, quite often, without finishing a sentence, so that she got out fifteen or twenty disconnected words for every one of mine.

By the time I finally persuaded her and hung up, it was slightly darker outside, but unfortunately much lighter inside me. The opening notes of Dexter's Dance Suite were muted now, some of the rising urgency blurred by the sound track of Rita's call. Still, it would come back, I was quite sure.

In the meantime, just to look busy, I called Chutsky.

"Hey, buddy," he said. "She opened her eyes again a few minutes ago. The doctors think she's starting to come around a little bit."

"That's wonderful," I said. "I'm coming by a little later. I just have some loose ends to take care of."

"Some of your people have been coming by to say hi," he said. "Do you know a guy named Israel Salguero?"

A bicycle went by me in the street. The rider thumped my side mirror and went on past. "I know him," I said. "Was he there?"

"Yeah," said Chutsky. "He was here." Chutsky was silent, as if waiting for me to say something. I couldn't think of much, so finally he said, "Something about the guy."

"He knew our father," I said.

"Uh-huh," he said. "Something else."

"Um," I said. "He's from Internal Affairs. He's investigating Deborah's behavior in this whole thing."

Chutsky was very silent for a moment. "HER behavior," he said at last.

"Yes," I said.

"She got *stabbed.*"

"The lawyer said it was self-defense," I said.

"Son of a bitch," he said.

"I'm sure there's nothing to worry about," I said. "It's just regulations, he has to investigate."

"Son of a goddamn bitch," Chutsky said. "And he comes around here? With her in a fucking coma?"

"He's known Deborah a long time," I said. "He probably just wanted to see if she was okay."

There was a very long pause, and then Chutsky said, "Okay, buddy. If you say so. But I don't think I'm going to let him in here next time."

I was not really sure how well Chutsky's hook would match up with Salguero's smooth and total confidence, but I had a feeling it would be an interesting contest. Chutsky, for all his bluff and phony cheerfulness, was a cold killer. But Salguero had been in Internal Affairs for years, which made him practically bulletproof. If it came to a fight, I thought it might do quite well on pay-per-view. I also thought I should probably keep that idea to myself, so I just said, "All right. I'll see you later," and hung up.

And so, with all the petty human details taken care of, I went back to waiting. Cars went by. People walked past on the sidewalk.

I got thirsty, and found half a bottle of water on the floor in the backseat. And finally, it got completely dark.

I waited a little longer to let the darkness settle over the city, and over me. It felt very good to shrug into the cold and comfy night jacket, and the anticipation grew strong inside with whispered encouragement from the Dark Passenger, urging me to step aside and give it the wheel.

And finally, I did.

I put the careful noose of nylon fishing leader and a roll of duct tape in my pocket, the only tools I had in my car at the moment, and got out.

And hesitated: too long since the last time, far too long since Dexter had done the deed. I had not done my research and that was not good. I had no plan and that was worse. I did not really know what was behind that door or what I would do when I got inside. I was uncertain for a moment and I stood beside the car and wondered if I could improvise my way through the dance. The uncertainty ate away my armor and left me standing on one foot in the dangerous dark without a way to move forward in the first knowing step.

But this was silly, weak, and wrong — and very much Not Dexter. The Real Dexter lived in the Dark, came alive in the sharp night, took joy in slashing out from the shadows. Who was this, standing here hesitating? Dexter does not dither.

I looked up into the night sky and breathed it in. Better: there was only a chunk of rotten yellow moon, but I opened up to it and it howled at me, and the night pounded through my veins and throbbed into my fingertips and sang across the skin stretched tight on my neck and I felt it all change, all grow back into what We must be to do what We would do, and then We were ready to do it.

This was now, this was the night, this was Dark Dexter's Dance, and the steps would come, flowing from our feet as they had always known they must.

And the black wings reached out from deep inside and spread across the night sky and carried us forward.

We slid through the night and around the block, checking the entire area carefully. Down at the far end of the street there was an alley and we went down it into deeper darkness, cutting back toward the rear of Doncevic's building. There was a battered van parked at a covered and well-masked loading dock at the back of it — a quick and dry whisper from the Passenger saying,

Look: this is how he moved the bodies out and took them to their display points. And soon he would leave the same way.

We circled back around and found nothing alarming in the area. An Ethiopian restaurant around the corner. Loud music three doors down. And then we were back at the front door and we rang the bell. He opened the door and had one small moment of surprise before we were on him, putting him quickly facedown on the floor with the noose on his neck as we taped his mouth, hands, and feet. When he was secure and quiet, we moved quickly through the rest of the place and found no one. We did find some few items of interest; some very nice tools in the bathroom, right next to a large bathtub. Saws and snips and all, lovely Dexter Playtime Toys, and it was quite clearly the white porcelain background from the home movie we had seen at the Tourist Board and it was proof, all the proof we needed now, in this night of need. Doncevic was guilty. He had stood here on the tile by the tub holding these tools and done unthinkable things — exactly the unthinkable acts that we were thinking and would now do to him.

We dragged him into the bathroom and put him in the tub and then we stopped again, just for a moment. A very small and insistent whisper was hinting that all was not right, and it went up our spine and into our teeth. We rolled Doncevic into the tub, facedown, and went quickly through the place again. There was nothing and no one, and all was well, and the very loud voice of the Dark Driver was drowning out the feeble whisper and once again demanding that we steer back to the Dance with Doncevic.

So we went back to the tub and went to work. And we hurried a little because we were in a strange place without any real planning, and also because Doncevic said one strange thing before we took the gift of speech away from him forever. "Smile," he said, and that made us angry and he was quickly unable to say anything very definite again. But we were thorough, oh yes, and when we were done, we were quite pleased with a job well done. Everything had gone very well indeed, and we had taken a very large step toward getting things back to the way things must be.

And they were that way until it ended, with nothing left but a few bags of garbage and one small drop of Doncevic's blood on a glass slide for my rosewood box.

And as always, I felt a whole lot better afterward.

FIFTEEN

It was the next morning that things began to unravel. I went into work tired but content from my happy chores and the late night they had put me through. I had just settled down with a cup of coffee to attack a heap of paperwork when Vince Masuoka poked his head in the door. "Dexter," he said.

"The one and only," I said with proper modesty.

"Did you hear?" he said with an irritating bet-you-didn't-hear smirk.

"I hear so many things, Vince," I said. "Which one do you mean?"

"The autopsy report," he said. And because it was apparently important to him to stay as annoying as possible, he said nothing else, just looked at me expectantly.

"All right, Vince," I said at last. "Which autopsy report did I not hear about that will change the way I think about every-thing?"

He frowned. "What?" he said.

"I said, no, I didn't hear. Please tell me."

He shook his head. "I don't think that's what you said," he said. "But anyway, you know those wacky designer bodies, with all the fruit and stuff in them?"

"At South Beach, and Fairchild Gardens?" I said.

"Right," he said. "So they get them to the morgue for the autopsy, and the M.E. is like, whoa, great, they're back."

I don't know if you have noticed this, but it is quite possible for two human beings to have a conversation in which one or both parties involved have absolutely no idea what they're talking about. I seemed to be in one of those brain-puzzling chats right now, since so far the only thing I'd gotten from talking to Vince was a profound sense of irritation.

"Vince," I said. "Please use small and simple words and tell me what you're trying to say before you force me to break a chair over your head."

"I'm just saying," he said, which at least was true and easy to understand, as far as it went, "the M.E. gets those four bodies and says, these were stolen from here. And now

185

they're back."

The world seemed to tilt to one side ever so slightly, and a heavy gray fog settled over everything and made it hard to breathe. "The bodies were *stolen* from the morgue?" I said.

"Yeah."

"Meaning, they were already dead, and somebody took them away and then did all the weird stuff to them?"

He nodded. "It's just like the craziest thing I ever heard," he said. "I mean, you steal dead bodies from the morgue? And you play with 'em like that?"

"But whoever did it didn't actually kill them," I said.

"No, they were all accidental death, just lying there on their slabs."

Accidental is such a terrible word. It stands for all the things I have fought against my whole life: it is random, messy, unplanned, and therefore dangerous. It is the word that will get me caught someday, because in spite of all the care in the world, something accidental can still happen and, in this world of ragged chaotic chance, it always does.

And it just had. I had just last night filled a half-dozen garbage bags with someone who was more or less accidentally innocent.

"So it isn't murder after all," I said.

He shrugged. "It's still a felony," he said. "Stealing a corpse, desecrating the dead, something like that. Endangering public health? I mean, it's gotta be illegal."

"So is jaywalking," I said.

"Not in New York. They do it all the time."

Learning more about the jaywalking statutes in New York did nothing at all to fill me with good cheer. The more I thought about it, the more I would have to say that I was skating perilously close to having real human emotions about this, and as the day went on I thought about it more and more. I felt a strange kind of choking sensation just below my throat, and a vague and aimless anxiety that I could not shake, and I had to wonder: Is this what guilt feels like? I mean, supposing I had a conscience, would mine be troubled now? It was very unsettling, and I didn't like it at all.

And it was all so pointless — Doncevic had, after all, stuck a knife in Deborah, and if she wasn't dead, it was not from lack of trying on his part. He was guilty of *something* rather naughty, even if it was not the more final version of the deed.

So why should I "feel" anything? It is all very well for a human being to say, "I did something that made me feel bad." But how could cold and empty Dexter possibly say anything of the sort? Even if I *did* feel something, the odds are very good that it would be something that most of us would agree is, after all, kind of bad. This society does not look with approval on emotions like "Need to Kill," or "Enjoying Cutting," and realistically those would be the most likely things to pop up in my case.

No, there was nothing to regret here — it was one small accidental and impulsive tiny little dismemberment. Applying the smooth and icy logic of Dexter's great intellect resulted in the same bottom line no matter how many times I ran through it: Doncevic was no great loss to anybody, and he had at least tried to kill Deborah. Did I have to hope she would die, simply so I could feel good about myself?

But it was bothering me, and it continued to rankle throughout the morning and on into the afternoon when I stopped at the hospital on my lunch break.

"Hey, buddy," Chutsky said wearily as I came into the room. "Not much change. She's opened her eyes a couple of times. I think she's getting a little stronger."

I sat in the chair on the opposite side of the bed from Chutsky. Deborah didn't look stronger. She looked about the same — pale, barely breathing, closer to death than life. I had seen this expression before, many times, but it did not belong on Deborah. It belonged on people I had carefully fitted out to wear that look as I pushed them down the dark slope and away into emptiness as the reward for the wicked things they had done.

I had seen it just last night on Doncevic — and even though I had not carefully chosen him, I realized the look truly belonged there, on him. He had put this same look on my sister, and that was enough. There was nothing here to stir unease in Dexter's nonexistent soul. I had done my job, taken a bad person out of the crawling frenzy of life, and hurried him into a cluster of garbage bags, where he belonged. If it was untidy and unplanned, it was still righteous, as my law enforcement associates would say. Associates like Israel Salguero, who would now have no need to harass Deborah and damage her career just because the man with the shiny head was making noise in the press.

When I ended Doncevic, I had ended that mess, too. A small weight lifted. I had done what Dexter does, and done it well, and my little corner of the world was just a tiny bit better. I sat in the chair and chewed on a really terrible sandwich, chatting with

Chutsky and actually getting to see Deborah open her eyes one time, for a full three seconds. I could not say for sure that she knew I was there, but the sight of her eyeballs was very encouraging and I began to understand Chutsky's wild optimism a little more.

I went back to work feeling a great deal better about myself and things in general. It was a lovely and gratifying way to roll in from lunch, and the feeling lasted all the way into the building and up to my cubicle, where I found Detective Coulter waiting for me.

"Morgan," he said. "Siddown."

I thought it was very nice of him to invite me to sit in my own chair, so I sat down. He looked at me for a long moment, chewing on a toothpick that stuck out of one corner of his mouth. He was a pear-shaped guy, never terribly attractive, and at the moment even less so. He had crammed his sizable buttocks into the extra chair by my desk and, aside from the toothpick, he was working on a giant bottle of Mountain Dew, some of which had already stained his dingy white shirt. His appearance, together with the way he stared silently at me as if hoping I would burst into tears and confess to something, was extremely annoying, to say the least. So fighting off the temptation to collapse into a weeping heap, I picked up a lab report from my in-basket and began to read.

After a moment Coulter cleared his throat. "All right," he said, and I looked up and raised a polite eyebrow at him. "We gotta talk about your statement."

"Which one?" I said.

"When your sister got stabbed," he said. "Couple of things don't add up."

"All right," I said.

Coulter cleared his throat again. "So, uh — Tell me again what you saw."

"I was sitting in the car," I said.

"How far away?"

"Oh, maybe fifty feet," I said.

"Uh-huh. How come you didn't go with her?"

"Well," I said, thinking it was really none of his business, "I really didn't see the point."

He stared some more and then shook his head. "You coulda helped her," he said. "Maybe stopped the guy from stabbing her."

"Maybe," I said.

"You coulda acted like a partner," he said. It was clear that the sacred bond of partnership was still pulling strongly at Coulter, so I bit back my impulse to say something, and after a moment he nodded and went on.

"So the door opens and boom, he sticks a knife in?"

"The door opens and Deborah showed her badge," I said.

"You sure about that?"

"Yes."

"But you're fifty feet away?"

"I have really good eyesight," I said, wondering if everyone who came in to see me today was going to be profoundly annoying.

"Okay," he said. "And then what?"

"Then," I said, reliving that moment with terrible slow-motion clarity, "Deborah fell over. She tried to get up and couldn't and I ran to help her."

"And this guy Dankawitz, whatever, he was there the whole time?"

"No," I said. "He was gone, and then he came back out as I got close to Deborah."

"Uh-huh," Coulter said. "How long was he gone?"

"Maybe ten seconds tops," I said. "Why does that matter?"

Coulter took the toothpick out of his mouth and stared at it. Apparently it even looked awful to him, because after a moment of thinking about it, he threw it at my wastebasket. He missed, of course. "Here's the problem," he said. "The fingerprints on the knife aren't his."

About a year ago I'd had an impacted tooth removed, and the dentist had given me nitrous oxide. For just a moment I felt the same sense of dizzy silliness whipping through me. "The — urm — fingerprints . . . ?" I finally managed to stutter.

"Yeah," he said, swigging briefly from the huge soda bottle. "We took his prints when we booked him. Naturally." He wiped the corner of his mouth with his wrist. "And we compared them to the ones on the handle of that knife? And hey. They don't match. So I'm thinking, what the fuck, right?"

"Naturally," I said.

"So I thought, what if there was *two* of 'em, 'cuz what else could it be, right?" He shrugged and, sadly for all of us, fumbled another toothpick out of his shirt pocket and began to munch on it. "Which is why I had to ask you again what you think you saw."

He looked at me with an expression of totally focused stupidity and I had to close my eyes to think at all. I replayed the scene in my memory one more time: Deborah waiting by the door, the door opening. Deborah showing her badge and then suddenly falling — but all I could see in my memory was the man's profile with no details. The door opens, Deborah shows the badge, the profile . . . No, that was it. There was no more detail. Dark hair and a light shirt, but that was true of half the world, including the Doncevic I had kicked in the head a moment later.

I opened my eyes. "I think it was the same guy," I said, and although for some reason I was reluctant to give him any more, I did. He was, after all, the representative of Truth, Justice, and the American Way, no matter how unattractive. "But to be honest, I can't really be sure. It was too quick."

Coulter bit down on the toothpick. I watched it bobble around in the corner of his mouth for a moment while he tried to remember how to speak. "So it coulda been two of 'em," he said at last.

"I suppose so," I said.

"One of 'em stabs her, runs inside like, shit, what'd I do," he said. "And the other one goes, shit, and runs out to look, and you pop him one."

"It's possible," I said.

"Two of 'em," he repeated.

I did not see the point of answering the same question twice, so I just sat and watched the toothpick wiggle. If I had thought I was filled with unpleasant rumblings before, it was nothing to the whirlpool of unease that was forming in me now. If Doncevic's fingerprints were not on the knife, he had not stabbed Deborah; that was elementary, Dear Dexter. And if he had not stabbed Deborah, he was innocent and I had made a very large mistake.

This really should not have bothered me. Dexter does what he must and the only reason he does it to the well deserving is because of Harry's training. For all the Dark Passenger cares, it could just as easily be random. The relief would be just as sweet for us. The way I choose is merely the Harry-imposed icy logic of the knife.

But it was possible that Harry's voice was in me deeper than I had ever thought, because the idea that Doncevic might be innocent was sending me into a tailspin. And even before I could get a grip on this nasty uncomfortable sensation, I realized Coulter was staring at me.

"Yes," I said, not at all sure what that meant.

Coulter once again threw a mangled toothpick at the trash can. He missed again. "So where's the other guy?" he said.

"I don't know," I told him. And I didn't.

But I really wanted to find out.

SIXTEEN

I have heard coworkers speak of having "the Blahs," and always thought myself blessed that I lacked the ability to provide a host for anything with such an unattractive name. But the last few hours of my workday could be described in no other way. Dexter of the Bright Knife, Dexter the Duke of Darkness, Dexter the Hard and Sharp and Totally Empty, had the Blahs. It was uncomfortable, of course, but due to the very nature of the thing, I did not have the energy to do anything about it. I sat at my desk and pushed paper clips around, wishing I could just as easily push the pictures out of my head: Deborah falling, my foot connecting to Doncevic's head, the knife going up, the saw coming down . . .

Blah. It was as stupid as it was embarrassing and enervating. Okay, technically speaking, Doncevic had been sort of innocent. I had made one lousy little mistake. Big deal.

Nobody's perfect. Why should I even pretend to be? Was I really going to imagine that I felt bad about ending an innocent life? Preposterous. And anyway, what is innocent, after all? Doncevic had been playing around with dead bodies, and he had caused millions of dollars in damage to the city budget and the tourist industry. There were plenty of people in Miami who would gladly have killed him just to stop the bleeding.

The only problem was that one of those people was not me.

I was not much, I knew that. I never pretended to have any real humanity, and I certainly didn't tell myself that what I did was all right just because my playmates were cut from the same cloth. In fact, I was fairly certain that the world would be a much better place without me. Mind you, I have never been in a very big hurry to make the world a better place in that regard, either. I wanted to stick around as long as possible, because when you die either everything stops forever, or else Dexter was in for a very warm surprise. Neither option seemed like much of a choice.

So I had no illusions about my worth to the rest of the world. I did what I did and didn't ask for any thanks. But always before, every time since the very first, I had done it by the rules laid down by Saint Harry, my near-perfect adoptive father. This time I had broken the rules, and for reasons that were not clear to me, that made me feel like I deserved to be caught and punished. And I could not convince myself that this was a healthy feeling.

So I battled the Blahs until quitting time and then, without any real increase in energy, I drove over to the hospital again. The rush-hour traffic did nothing to cheer me up. Everybody seemed to be just going through the motions without any real, genuine homicidal rage. A woman cut me off and threw half an orange at my windshield, and a man in a van tried to run me off the road, but to me they seemed to be doing it mechanically, not really putting their hearts into it.

When I got to Deborah's room, Chutsky was asleep in his chair, snoring loud enough to rattle the windows. So I sat for a little while, watching Deborah's eyelids quiver. I thought that was probably a good thing, indicating she was getting her REM sleep and therefore getting better. I wondered what she would think of my little mistake when she woke up. Considering what her attitude had been just before she got stabbed, it didn't seem likely that she would be terribly understanding about even such a minor slipup. After all, she was as much in the grip of Harry's Shadow as I was, and if she could barely tolerate what I did when it was Harry Approved, she would never go along with something outside his careful limits.

Debs could never know what I had done. Not a big deal, considering I had always hidden everything from her until recently. But it didn't make me feel any better this time, for some reason. After all, I had done this one for *her,* as much as anything else — the first time I had ever acted out of noble impulses, and it had turned out very badly. My sister made a really poor Dark Passenger.

Debs moved her hand, just a twitch, and her eyes blinked open. Her lips parted slightly and I was certain she actually focused on me for a moment. I leaned toward her and she watched me, and then her eyelids drifted closed again.

She was slowly getting better, and she was going to make it, I was sure. It might be weeks rather than days, but sooner or later she was going to get up out of that awful steel bed and get to work at being her old self again. And when she did . . .

. . . what would she do about me?

I didn't know. But I had a very bad feeling that it wouldn't be much fun for either of us; because as I had realized, we were both still living in Harry's shadow, and I was pretty sure I knew what Harry would say.

Harry would say it was wrong, because this was not the way he had designed Dexter's life, as I remembered oh so well.

Harry usually looked very happy when he came in the front door from work. I don't think he ever was truly happy, of course, but he always *looked* like it, and this was one of my first very important lessons from him: *make your face fit the occasion.* It may seem like a small and obvious point, but to a fledgling monster still figuring out that he was very different, it was a vital lesson.

I remember sitting in the great banyan tree in our front yard one afternoon because, frankly, that is what the other kids in the neighborhood did, even long after what one what might call optimum tree-climbing age. Those trees were a great place to sit, with their wide horizontal branches, and they served as a clubhouse for everyone under the age of eighteen.

So I sat in mine that afternoon, hoping

the rest of the neighborhood would mistake me for normal. I was at an age when everything was starting to change, and I had begun to notice that I was changing in a very different way. For one thing, unlike the other boys, I was not totally consumed with trying to see under Bobbie Gelber's skirt when she climbed up into the tree. And for another . . .

When the Dark Passenger started whispering wicked thoughts, I realized that it was a Presence that had always been there; it just had not spoken until now. But now, when my contemporaries were starting to pass around copies of *Hustler,* it was sending me dreams of a different kind of illustration, perhaps from *Vivisection Monthly.* And although the images that came to me were disturbing at first, they started to seem more and more natural, inevitable, desirable, and finally, necessary. But another voice, equally strong, told me this was wrong, crazy, very dangerous. And for the most part the two voices fought to a tie and I did nothing but dream, just like all the human boys my age.

But one wonderful night the two whispering armies came together when I realized that the Gelbers' dog, Buddy, was keeping Mom awake with its nonstop barking. And this was not a good thing. Mom was dying of some untreatable mysterious thing called a lymphoma, and she needed her sleep. And it occurred to me that if I could help Mom sleep, this would be a very good thing, and both voices agreed that this was so — one somewhat reluctantly, of course, but the other, Darker one, with an eagerness that made me dizzy.

And so it was that Buddy, the loud-mouthed little dog, launched Dexter on his way. It was clumsy of course, and much messier than I had planned on, but it was also oh so good and right and necessary . . .

In the following months there were a few more minor experiments; carefully spaced, playmates more carefully chosen, since even in my hot-blooded phase of self-discovery, I understood that if all the pets in the neighborhood disappeared, someone was bound to ask questions. But there was a stray, and a bicycle trip to a different area, and somehow young Luke Darkwalker got by, slowly learning to be happily me. And because I felt so *attached* to my small experiments, I buried them close at hand, behind a row of bushes in our backyard.

I certainly know better than that now. But at the time, everything seemed so innocent and wonderful, and I wanted to look out at the bushes and bask in the warm glow of the memories from time to time, and I had made my first mistake.

And so that lazy afternoon I sat in my banyan tree and watched as Harry parked the car, got out, and paused. He had on his work face, the one that said, I have seen it all and don't like most of it. And he stood beside the car for a long moment with his eyes closed, doing nothing more complicated than breathing.

When he opened his eyes again he had an expression on his face that said, I am home and feel very good about that. He took a step toward the front door and I jumped down out of the tree and went to him.

"Dexter," he said. "How was your day at school?"

In truth it had been just about like all the others, but even then I knew that wasn't the appropriate response. "Good," I said. "We're studying communism."

Harry nodded. "That's important to know about," he said. "What's the capital of Russia?"

"Moscow," I said. "It used to be St. Petersburg."

"Really," said Harry. "Why did they change it?"

I shrugged. "They're atheists now," I said. "They can't have a Saint anything, because they don't believe in them."

He put a hand on my shoulder and we started walking to the house. "That can't be much fun," he said.

"Didn't you, um, *fight* communists?" I asked him, wanting to say *kill* but not quite daring. "In the Marines?"

Harry nodded. "That's right," he said. "Communism threatens our way of life. So it's important to fight it."

We were at the front door, and he gently pushed me in ahead of him, into the smell of the fresh coffee that Doris, my adoptive mom, always had ready for Harry when he came home from work. She was not yet too sick to move, and she was waiting for him in the kitchen.

They went through their ritual of drinking coffee and talking quietly, as they did every day, and it was such a perfect Norman Rockwell picture that I would certainly have forgotten it almost instantly if not for what happened later that evening.

Doris was already in bed. She had taken to going to sleep earlier and earlier as her cancer got worse and she needed more pain medicine. Harry, Deborah, and I had gathered in front of the TV set as we usually did. We were watching a sitcom, I don't remember which. There were so many of them at the time that they all could have been lumped together under the title of *Funny Minority and the White Guy.* The whole purpose of all these shows seemed to be letting us all know that in spite of our small differences we were really all the same. I kept waiting for some clue that this might include me, but neither Freddie Prinze nor Redd Foxx ever chopped up a neighbor. Still, everyone else seemed to enjoy the show. Deborah laughed out loud now and then, and Harry kept a contented smile on his face, and I did my best just to keep a low profile and fit in amid the hilarity.

But in the middle of the climactic scene, right when we were about to learn that we are all the same and then hug, the doorbell rang. Harry frowned a little bit, but he got up and went to the door with one eye still on the TV. Since I had already guessed how the show would end and I was not particularly moved by artificial hugs of compassion, I watched Harry. He turned on the outside light, peeked through the eyehole, and then unlocked and opened the door.

"Gus," he said, with surprise. "Come on in."

Gus Rigby was Harry's oldest friend on the force. They had been best man at each other's wedding, and Harry was godfather to Gus's daughter, Betsy. Since his divorce, Gus was always at our house for holidays and special occasions, although not as often now that Doris was sick, and he always brought a key lime pie.

But he didn't look terribly social now, and he was not carrying a pie. He looked angry and frazzled, and he said, "We gotta talk," and pushed past Harry into the house.

"About what?" Harry said, still holding the door open.

Gus turned and snarled at him, "Otto Valdez is out on the street."

Harry stared at him. "How did he get out?"

"That lawyer he's got," Gus said. "He said it was excessive force."

Harry nodded. "You were rough on him, Gus."

"He's a baby-raper," Gus said. "You want me to kiss him?"

"All right," Harry said. He closed and locked the door. "What is there to talk about?" he said.

"He's after me now," Gus said. "The phone rings and nobody's there, just breathing. But I know it's him. And I got a note under my front door. At my *home,* Harry."

"What did the lieutenant say?"

Gus shook his head. "I want to do this

206

myself," he said. "On the side. And I want your help."

With the wonderful timing that happens only in real life, the TV show came to an end and the laugh track blasted out right on the toes of Gus's words. Deborah laughed, too, and finally looked up. "Hi, Uncle Gus," she said.

"Hello, Debbie," Gus said. "You're more beautiful every day."

Debs scowled. Even then she was embarrassed by her good looks, and she didn't like being reminded of it. "Thank you," she said grumpily.

"Come on into the kitchen," Harry said, taking Gus by the elbow and leading him away.

I knew perfectly well that Harry was taking Gus into the kitchen to keep me and Deborah from hearing what would be said, and naturally enough that made me want to hear it all the more. And since Harry had not specifically said, "Stay here and do not listen . . . ," why, it would hardly be eavesdropping at all!

So I got up from in front of the TV set very casually and went down the hall toward the bathroom. I paused in the hallway and looked back: Deborah was already engrossed in the next program, and so I slid into a small patch of shadow and listened.

". . . courts will handle it," Harry was saying.

"Like they handled it so far?" Gus said, sounding angrier than I had ever heard him. "Come on, Harry, you know better than that."

"We're not vigilantes, Gus."

"Well maybe we should be, goddamn it."

There was a pause. I heard the refrigerator door open and then the sound of a beer can opening. A moment went by and nothing was said.

"Listen, Harry," Gus said at last. "We've been cops for a long time now."

"Coming up on twenty years," Harry said.

"And from the first day on the job, didn't it hit you that the system just doesn't work? That the biggest assholes always find a way to fall out of jail and back onto the streets? Huh?"

"That doesn't mean we have the right to —"

"Then who does have the right, Harry? If not us, who does?"

There was another longish pause. Finally, Harry spoke, very softly, and I had to strain to make out the words.

"You weren't in Vietnam," Harry said. Gus didn't respond. "Something I learned there is that some people can kill in cold blood, and others can't. And most of us can't," Harry said. "It does bad things to you."

"So what are you saying, you agree with me, but you can't do it? If ever anybody deserved it, Harry, Otto Valdez . . ."

"What are you doing?" came Deborah's voice, approximately eight inches from my ear. I jumped so hard I bumped my head on the wall.

"Nothing," I said.

"Funny place to do it," she said, and since she showed no inclination to move on, I decided I was done listening and I went back to zombie land in front of the TV. I had certainly heard enough to understand what was going on, and I was fascinated. Dear sweet kindly Uncle Gus wanted to kill somebody, and wanted Harry to help him. My brain whirled with the excitement of it, frantically searching for a way to persuade them to let me help — or at least watch. Where was the harm in that? It was almost a civic duty!

But Harry refused to help Gus, and a little while later Gus left the house looking like someone had let all the air out of him. Harry came back to the TV with me and Debs, and spent the next half hour trying to get his happy face back on.

Two days later they found Uncle Gus's body. It had been mutilated and beheaded and apparently tortured first.

And three days after that, unknown to me, Harry found my little pet memorial under the bushes in the backyard. Over the next week or two I caught him staring at me more than once with his work face on. I did not know why at the time, and it was somewhat intimidating, but I was far too much of the young gawp to be able to phrase a statement like, Dad, why are you staring at me with that particular expression?

And in any case, the Why of it very soon became apparent. Three weeks after Uncle Gus met his untimely end, Harry and I went on a camping trip to Elliott Key, and with a few simple sentences — starting with, "You're different, son" — Harry changed everything forever.

His plan. His design for Dexter. His perfectly crafted, sane, and sensible road map for me to be eternally and wonderfully me.

And now I had stepped off the Path, taken a small and dangerous back-road detour. I could almost see him shake his head and turn those ice-cold blue eyes on me.

"We've got to get you squared away," Harry would have said.

SEVENTEEN

A particularly loud snore from Chutsky brought me back to the present. It was loud enough that one of the nurses stuck her head in the door, and then checked all the dials and gauges and whirling machinery before going away again, with a suspicious backward glance at the two of us, as if we had deliberately made terrible noises in order to upset her machines.

Deborah moved one leg slightly, just enough to prove she was still alive, and I pulled myself all the way back from meandering down memory lane. Somewhere, there was somebody who actually was guilty of putting the knife into my sister. That was all that mattered. Someone had actually done this thing. It was a large and untidy loose end wandering around and I needed to grab hold and snip it back into neatness. Because the thought of such a large piece of unfinished and unpunished business gave me the urge to clean the kitchen and make the bed. It was messy, plain and simple, and Dexter doesn't like disorder.

Another thought poked its nose into the room. I tried to shoo it away, but it kept coming back, wagging its tail and demanding that I pet it. And when I did, it seemed to me to be a good thought. I closed my eyes and tried to picture the scene one more time. The door swings open — and it stays open as Deborah shows her badge and then falls. And it is still open when I get to her side . . .

. . . which means that someone else could very well have been inside and looking out. And that meant that somewhere, there just might be somebody who knew what I looked like. A second person, just like Detective Coulter had suggested. It was a little insulting to admit that a drooling dolt like Coulter might be right about something, but after all, Isaac Newton didn't reject gravity just because the apple had a low IQ.

And happily for my self-esteem, I was one step ahead of Coulter, because I might know this hypothetical second person's name. We had been going to ask someone named Brandon Weiss about his threats to the Tourist Board, and somehow ended up with Doncevic instead. So there might well have been two of them, living together —

Another small train chugged into the station: Arabelle, the cleaning woman at Joe's, had seen two gay tourists, with cameras. And I had seen two men who fit that description at Fairchild Gardens, also with cameras, filming the crowd. A film of the crime scene arriving at the Tourist Board had started all this. It was not conclusive, but it was certainly a nice start, and I was pleased, since it proved that a certain amount of mental function might well be returning to Cyber-Dex.

And as if to prove it, I had one more thought. Taking it a step further, if this hypothetical Weiss had followed the story in the media, which seemed very likely, he would know who I was, and quite possibly consider me a person worth talking to, in the strictly Dexter-ian sense of the word. Dexter-ose? Probably not — this was not a sweet thought, and it did not fill me with sociable good cheer. It meant that either I would have to defend myself successfully when he came, or let him do unto me. Either way there would be a mess, and a body, and a great deal of publicity, and all of them attached to my secret identity, Daytime Dexter, which was something I would very much like to avoid if possible.

All that meant one simple thing: I had to find him first.

This was not a daunting task. I have spent my adult life getting very good at finding things, and people, on the computer. In fact, it was this particular talent that had gotten Debs and me into our current mess, so there was a certain symmetry to the idea that this same skill would get me out of it now.

All right then: to work. Time to heed the clarion call and strap myself into my trusty computer.

And as always seems to happen when I have reached the point where I am ready to take decisive action, everything began to happen at once.

As I took a breath in preparation for standing up, Chutsky suddenly opened his eyes and said, "Oh, hey, buddy, the doctor said —" and was interrupted by the sound of my cell phone ringing, and as I reached to answer it, a doctor stepped into the room and said, "All right," to two interns following close behind him.

And then in rapid-fire confusion I heard, from the doctor, the phone, and Chutsky, "Hey, buddy, it's the doc — Cub Scouts, and Astor's friend has the mumps — the higher nerve center seems to be responding to . . ."

Once again I was very pleased to be abnormal, because a normal human being would certainly have flung his chair at the doctor and run screaming from the room. Instead, I waved at Chutsky, turned away from the doctors, and concentrated on the phone.

"I'm sorry, I couldn't hear you," I said. "Can you say it again?"

"I said, it would be a big help if you could come home," Rita said. "If you're not too busy? Because Cody has his first Cub Scout meeting tonight, and Astor's friend Lucy has the mumps? Which means she can't go over there, so one of us should stay with her at home? And I thought, you know. Unless you're stuck at work again?"

"I'm at the hospital," I said.

"Oh," Rita said. "Well then, that's — Is she any better?"

I looked over at the small clot of doctors. They were examining a small heap of documents apparently relating to Deborah. "I think we're about to find out," I said. "The doctors are here now."

"Well, if it's — I guess I could just — I mean, Astor could go along to Cub Scouts if —"

"I'll take Cody to Scouts," I said. "Let me just talk to the doctor first."

"If you're sure," she said. "Because if it's, you know . . ."

"I know," I said, although I actually didn't. "I'll be right home."

"All right," she said. "Love you."

I hung up and turned back to the doctors. One of the interns had peeled back one of Deborah's eyelids and was glaring at her eyeball with the aid of a small flashlight. The real doctor was watching him, holding the clipboard.

"Excuse me," I said, and he glanced up at me.

"Yes," he said, with what I recognized as a fake smile. It was not nearly as good as mine.

"She's my sister," I said.

The doctor nodded. "Next of kin, all right," he said.

"Is there any sign of improvement?"

"Well," he said. "The higher nerve functions seem to be coming back online, and the autonomic responses are good. And there's no fever or infection, so the prognosis seems favorable for a slight upgrade in condition within the next twenty-four hours."

"That's good," I said hopefully.

"However, I do have to warn you," he said, with an equally phony frown of importance and seriousness. "She lost an awful lot of blood, which can sometimes lead to permanent impairment of brain functions."

"But it's too soon to tell?" I said.

"Yes," he said, nodding vigorously. "Exactly."

"Thank you, Doctor," I said, and I stepped around him, to where Chutsky was now standing, wedged into a corner, so the doctors could have full access to Debs.

"She'll be fine," he told me. "Don't let these guys scare you, she's gonna be absolutely fine. Remember, I had Doc Teidel here." He lowered his voice to just above a whisper. "No offense to these guys, but Teidel's a hell of a lot better. He put me back together, and I was a whole lot worse than this," he said, nodding at Deborah. "And I didn't have any brain damage, either."

Considering the Pollyanna optimism he was showing, I wasn't sure about that, but it didn't seem worth arguing about. "All right," I said. "Then I'll check back with you later. I have a crisis at home."

"Oh," he said, with a frown. "Everybody okay?"

"All fine," I said. "It's the Cub Scouts I'm

worried about."

And although I meant that as a light-hearted exit line, isn't it funny how often these little jokes come true?

EIGHTEEN

The Cub Scout den that Rita had found for Cody met at Golden Lakes Elementary School, a few miles from our house. We got there a little early and sat in the car for a minute, and Cody watched without expression as a handful of boys his approximate age ran into the school wearing their blue uniforms. I let him sit and watch, thinking that a little preparation time might do us both some good.

A few cars pulled up. More boys in blue uniforms ran into the building, apparently eager to get inside. Anyone equipped with a heart would certainly have found it warming at the sight — one parent was so enamored of the scene that he stood beside his van and videotaped the stream of boys running past and inside. But Cody and I simply sat and watched.

"They're all the same," Cody said softly.

"Just on the outside," I said. "It's something you can learn to do."

He looked at me blankly.

"It's just like putting on one of those uniforms," I said. "When you *look* the same, people think you *are.* You can do this."

"Why," he said.

"Cody," I said, "we have talked about how important it is to look normal." He nodded. "This will help you figure out how to act like other kids. It's part of your training."

"Other part?" he said, with the first eagerness he had shown, and I knew he was longing for the simple clarity of the knife.

"If you do this part well, we will do the other part," I said.

"An animal?"

I looked at him, saw the cold gleam in his small blue eyes, and knew there was no going back from he where he already was; the only thing I could hope for was the long and difficult shaping that had been done to me. "All right," I said at last. "Maybe we can do an animal."

He watched me for another long moment, and then he nodded back, and we climbed out of the car and followed the pack into the cafeteria.

Inside, the other boys — and one girl — ran around making lots of loud noise for the first few minutes. Cody and I sat quietly in our tiny, molded plastic chairs, at a table just barely tall enough to smack you in the kneecaps if you tried to walk around it. He watched the others at their noisy play without expression and without any attempt to join in, and that was a starting point, something I could do with him. He was far too young to be known as a brooding loner — we needed to get his disguise in gear.

"Cody," I said, and he looked at me with the same lack of expression. "Look at the other kids."

He blinked, and then swiveled his head to take in the rest of the room. He watched without comment for a minute, and then turned back to me. "Okay," he said softly.

"It's just that they're all running around and having fun, and you're not," I said.

"No," he said.

"So you will stand out," I said. "You have to pretend you're having fun here."

"I don't know how," he said, a major speech for him.

"But you have to learn," I said. "You have to look like all the others, or . . ."

"Well, well, what's wrong with you, little guy?" a voice boomed out. A large and offensively cheerful man came over and put his hands on his bare knees so he could shove his face closer to Cody's. He was bursting out of a Cub Scout leader's uniform, and the sight of his hairy legs and large belly seemed very wrong. "You're not feeling shy, are you?" he said with a huge and terrible grin.

Cody stared back at him without blinking for a long moment, and the man's grin began to fade a little. "No," Cody said at last.

"Well, good," the man said, straightening up and moving back a step.

"He's not really shy," I said. "He's just a little tired today."

The man turned his grin on me, looked me over for a moment, then stuck out his hand. "Roger Deutsch," he said, holding out his hand. "I'm the den master. I just like to get to know everybody a little before we start."

"Dexter Morgan," I said, shaking his hand. "This is Cody."

Deutsch held his hand out to Cody. "Hi, Cody, glad to meet you." Cody looked at the hand, then at me; I nodded at him, and he put his small hand into the meaty paw held out in front of him. "Hi," he said.

"So," Deutsch said relentlessly, "what brings you to Scouting, Cody?"

Cody glanced at me. I smiled, and he turned back to Deutsch. "Have fun," he said, his small, deadpan face looking like he was at a funeral.

"Great," said Deutsch. "Scouting should be fun. But there's a serious part, too. You can learn about all kinds of cool things. Is there anything special you really want to learn about, Cody?"

"Animal carving," Cody said, and I had to fight not to fall out of my tiny chair.

"Cody," I said.

"No, that's okay, Mr. Morgan," Deutsch said. "We do lots of crafts. We can start with soap carving and move on to wood." He winked at Cody. "If you're worried about him working with knives, we won't let him hurt himself."

It didn't seem politic to say that I wasn't worried about Cody hurting *himself* with a blade in his hand. He already knew very well which end to hold, and he had shown a precocious talent for finding the right way to put in the point. But I was fairly certain Cody could not learn the kind of animal carving he wanted in Scouting — at least not until the Eagle Scout level. So I simply said, "We'll talk it over with Mom, and see what she says," and Deutsch nodded his head.

"Great," he said. "In the meantime, don't

be shy. You just jump in here with both feet, buddy."

Cody looked at me, and then nodded at Deutsch.

"All right," Deutsch said, finally straightening up. "Well, let's get this thing started, then." He nodded at me and turned back to begin rallying the troops.

Cody shook his head and whispered something. I leaned a little closer to him. "What?" I said.

"Both feet," he said.

"It's just an expression," I told him.

He looked at me. "Stupid expression," he said.

Deutsch had moved across the room, calling for quiet, getting all the kids together, and they were now assembling in the front of the room. It was time for Cody to jump in, even if it was only with one foot at first. So I stood up and held out a hand to him. "Come on," I said. "This will work out fine."

Cody didn't look convinced, but he stood up and looked at the group of normal boys converging on Deutsch. He pulled himself as straight and tall as possible, took a deep breath, and said, "Okay," and marched over to join the group.

I watched him push carefully through the crowd to find his spot and then stand there, all alone and being as brave as he could be. This was not going to be easy — not for him, and not for me. There would be a very natural awkwardness for him as he tried to fit into a group that he had nothing in common with. He was a tiny wolf trying to grow lamb's wool and learn to say *baaa!* And if he howled at the moon even once, the game was over.

And for me? I could only watch, and possibly give him a few pointers in between rounds. I had gone through a similar phase myself, and I still remembered the terrible pain of it: realizing that this was all and forever something for the others and never for me — that laughter, friendship, the sense of belonging, were things I would never really feel. And even worse, once I realized that I was outside all of it, I had to pretend to feel it, learn to show the mask of happiness in order to hide the deadly emptiness inside.

And I remembered the dreadful clumsiness of those first years of trying; the first horrible attempts at laughter, always at the wrong time and always sounding so very inhuman. Even speaking to the others naturally, easily, about the right things and with the right manufactured feelings. Slowly, painfully, awkwardly learning, watching how the others did these things so effortlessly and feeling the added pain of being outside that graceful easiness of expression. A small thing, knowing how to laugh. So very inconsequential, unless you don't know how and have to learn it from watching others, as I did.

As Cody would have to do now. He would have to go through the whole vile process of understanding that he was different and always would be, and then learning to pretend he was not. And that was just the starting point, the first easy leg of the Harry Path. After that, things got even more complicated, more difficult and painful, until an entire artificial life was built and hammered into place. All fake, all the time, with only the short and far-too-rare intervals of razor-edged reality to look forward to — and I was passing all this on to Cody, that small and damaged creature who stood up there now so stiffly, watching with such intense focus for a hint of belonging that would never come.

Did I really have the right to force him into this agonizing mold? Merely because I had gone through this, did that truly mean HE had to? Because if I was honest with myself, it had not been working terribly well for me lately. The Harry Path, a thing that had seemed so clear, clean, and clever, had taken a turn into the underbrush. Deborah, the one person in the world who should understand, doubted that it was right, that it was even real, and now she lay in the ICU while I floundered around the city slaughtering the innocent.

Was this really what I wanted for Cody?

I watched him follow along through the Pledge of Allegiance, and found no answers there.

And so it was a very thoughtful Dexter who eventually tottered home after the meeting, with a wounded and uncertain Cody in tow.

Rita met us at the door, a look of worry on her face. "How did it go?" she asked Cody.

"Okay," he said, with a look on his face that said it was not okay.

"It was fine," I said, sounding a little more convincing. "And it will get much better."

"Has to," Cody said softly.

Rita looked from Cody to me and then back again. "I don't — I mean, did you, did you . . . Cody. Are you going to keep going?"

Cody looked at me and I could almost see a small and sharp blade flashing in his eyes. "I'll go," he said to his mother.

Rita looked relieved. "That's wonderful," she said. "Because it really is — I know that you'll, you know."

"I'm sure he will," I said.

My cell phone began to chirp and I answered it. "Yes," I said.

"She woke up," Chutsky said. "And she spoke."

"I'll be right there," I said.

NINETEEN

I don't really know what I was expecting when I got to the hospital, but I didn't get it. Nothing seemed to have changed. Deborah was not sitting up in bed and doing the crossword puzzle while listening to her iPod. She still lay motionless, surrounded by the clutter of machinery and Chutsky. And he sat in the same position of supplication in the same chair, although he had managed to shave and change his shirt somewhere along the way.

"Hey, man!" he called out cheerfully as I pushed in to Deborah's bedside. "We're on the mend," he said. "She looked right at me, and she said my name. She's gonna be totally fine."

"Great," I said, although it didn't seem clear to me that saying a one-syllable name meant that my sister was rocketing back to full, unimpaired normality. "What did the doctors say?"

Chutsky shrugged. "Same old shit. Not to get my hopes up too high, too soon to be sure, autonomic nervous blah blah blah." He held up his hand in a what-the-hell gesture. "But they didn't see it when she woke up and I did. She looked into my eyes, and I could tell. She's still in there, buddy. She's gonna be fine."

There seemed to be very little to say to that, so I muttered a few well-meaning and empty syllables and sat down. And although I waited very patiently for two and a half hours, Debs did not leap out of bed and begin to do calisthenics; she did not even repeat her parlor trick of opening her eyes and saying Chutsky's name, and so I finally tottered home to bed without feeling any of Chutsky's magical certainty.

The next morning when I arrived at my job, I was determined to get to work right away and find out all I could about Doncevic and his mysterious associate. But I barely had time to put my coffee cup down on my desk when I received a visitation from the Ghost of Christmas Gone Terribly Wrong, in the person of Israel Salguero, from Internal Affairs. He came wafting silently in and sat in the folding chair across from me without a sound. There was a sense of velvet menace to his movement that I

231

would have admired, if it had not been aimed at me. I watched him, and he watched me for a moment, before he finally nodded and said, "I knew your father."

I nodded and took the very great risk of sipping my coffee — but without taking my eyes off Salguero.

"He was a good cop, and a good man," Salguero said. He spoke softly, fitting his way of moving so silently, and he had the slight trace of an accent that many Cuban Americans of his generation had. He had, in fact, known Harry very well, and Harry had thought highly of him. But that was in the past, and Salguero was now a very respected and very feared IA lieutenant, and no good could come of having him investigating either me or Deborah.

And so, thinking that it was probably best just to wait him out and let him get to the point, if there was one, I took another sip of my coffee. It did not taste nearly as good as it had before Salguero's arrival.

"I would like to be able to get this thing cleared up as quickly as possible," he said. "I'm sure that neither you or your sister have anything to worry about."

"No, of course not," I said, wondering why I didn't feel reassured — unless of course it was because my entire life was built around the idea of escaping notice, and having a trained investigator peering in under the edges was not terribly comforting.

"If there is anything you care to tell me at any time," he said, "my office door is always open to you."

"Thank you very much," I said, and since there didn't seem to be anything else to say, I didn't say it. Salguero watched me for a moment, then nodded and slid up from his chair and out the door, leaving me wondering just how much trouble the Morgans were in. It took me several minutes and a full cup of coffee to clear his visit from my head and concentrate on the computer.

And when I did, what a wonderful surprise I got.

Just as a matter of reflex, I glanced at my e-mail in-box as I went to work. There were two departmental memos that demanded my immediate inattention, an ad promising me several inches of unspecified additional length, and a note with no title that I almost deleted, until I saw who it was from: bweiss@aol.com.

It really shouldn't have, but it took a moment for the name to register, and my finger was literally poised on the mouse to delete the message when something clicked in my head and I paused.

Bweiss. The name seemed familiar some-how. Perhaps it was "Weiss, first initial *B*," like most e-mail addresses. That would make sense. And if the *B* stood for Brandon, that would make even more sense. Because it was the name of the person I had just sat down to investigate.

How thoughtful of him to get in touch.

I opened Weiss's e-mail with more than usual interest, very eager to find out what he might have to say to me. But to my great disappointment, he apparently had nothing at all to say. There was merely an Internet link, underlined and in blue letters, stuck in the middle of the page with no comment at all.

http://www.youtube.com/watch?v=99lrj?42r

How very interesting. Brandon wanted to share his videos with me. But what kind of video could it possibly be? Perhaps his favorite rock band? Or an edited montage of clips from his favorite TV show? Or even more of the kind of footage he had sent to the Tourist Board? That would be very thoughtful.

And so with a warm and fuzzy glow grow-ing in the spot where my heart should have been, I clicked on the link and waited impatiently for the screen to open. Finally, the small box showed up and I clicked on the play button.

For a moment there was just darkness. Then once again a grainy picture blossomed and I was looking down at white porcelain from a fixed camera perched somewhere near the ceiling — the same shot featured in the video sent to the Tourist Board. I felt mildly disappointed — he had just sent me a link to a copy of something I had already seen. But then there was a sound of soft slithering, and movement started in the corner of the screen. A dark figure lurched into the frame and dumped something onto the white porcelain.

Doncevic.

And the dark figure? Dashing Dimpled Dexter, of course.

My face was not visible, but there was no doubt. That was Dexter's back, his seventeen-dollar haircut, the collar of Dexter's lovely dark shirt curled around Dexter's wonderful precious neck —

My sense of disappointment was completely gone. This was a brand-new video after all, something I had never seen, and I was immediately very anxious to see it for the first time.

I watched as Dexter Past straightened up, looked around — still, happily, without showing his face to the camera. Clever boy. Dexter walked out of the frame and was gone. The lump in the tub moved slightly, and then Dexter came back and picked up the saw. The blade whirred, the arm went up —

And darkness. End of video.

I sat in a quiet and stunned stupor for several minutes. There was a clatter of some kind in the hall. Someone came into the lab and opened a drawer, closed it again, and left. The phone rang; I didn't answer it.

That was me. Right there on YouTube. In full glorious living and slightly grainy color. Dexter of the Deadly Dimples, now starring in a minor motion-picture classic. Smile at the camera, Dexter. Wave to the nice audience. I had never been very fond of home movies, and this one left me even colder than ever. But there I was — not merely captured on film but posted on YouTube for all the world to see and admire. It was more than I could wrap my mind around; my thoughts just moved in a circle, like a film clip in a loop. That was me; it couldn't be me but it was; I had to do something, but what could I do? Don't know, but something — because that was me . . .

Things were certainly getting interesting, weren't they?

All right; that was me. Obviously, there was a camera hidden somewhere above the tub. Weiss and Doncevic had used it for their decorative projects, and it was still there when I showed up. Which meant that Weiss was still somewhere in the area —

But no, it didn't mean that at all. It was ridiculously easy to connect a camera to the Internet and monitor from a computer. Weiss could be anywhere, collecting the video and sending it on to me —

To me, precious anonymous me, Dexter the mostly modest, who toiled in the shadows and never ever looked for publicity of any kind for his good works. But of course, in the hideous clamor of media attention that had surrounded this whole thing, including the attack on Deborah, my name had almost certainly been mentioned somewhere. Dexter Morgan, unassuming forensic whiz, brother of the nearly-slain. One picture, one frame of evening news footage, and he would have me.

A cold and awful lump began to grow in my stomach. It was just that easy. So simple a deranged decorator could figure out who and what I was. I had been too clever for too long and grown accustomed to being the only tiger in the forest. And I had forgotten that when there is only one tiger, it's awfully easy for the hunter to follow the tracks.

And he had. He had followed me to my den and taken pictures of Dexter at play, and there it was.

My finger twitched almost unwillingly on the mouse and I watched the video again.

It was still me. Right there on the video. It was me.

I took a deep breath and let the oxygen work its magic on my thought process, or what was left of it. This was a problem, to be sure, but it had a solution like every other problem. Time to apply logic, turn the full power of Dexter's icy biocomputer on the problem. First: What did this guy want? Why had he done this? Obviously, he wanted some reaction from me — but which one? The most obvious would be that he was looking for revenge. I had killed his friend — partner? Lover? It didn't matter. He wanted me to know that he knew what I had done, and, and . . .

And he had sent the clip to me, not to someone who would presumably do something about it, like Detective Coulter. Which meant that this was a personal challenge, something that he was not going to make public, at least not yet.

Except that it *was* public — it was on YouTube, and it was only a matter of time before someone else stumbled onto it and saw the clip. And that meant that there was a time element. So what was he saying? Find me before *they* find *you?*

Okay so far. But then what? An Old West showdown — power saws at ten paces? Or was the idea just to torture me, keep me chasing until I made a mistake, or until he grew bored and sent the whole thing on to the evening news?

It was enough to create at least the idea of panic in a lesser being. But Dexter is made of far sterner stuff. He wanted me to try to find him — but he could not know that I had my varsity letter in finding. If I was even half as good as modesty let me admit I was, I would find him a great deal quicker than he thought I could. Fine: if Weiss wanted to play, I would play.

But we were going to play by Dexter's rules, not his.

TWENTY

First things first has always been my motto, mostly because it makes absolutely no sense — after all, if first things were second or third, they wouldn't be first things, would they? Still, clichés exist to comfort the feeble-minded, not to provide any actual meaning. Since I was feeling somewhat weak between the ears at the moment, I took a little bit of consolation from the thought as I pulled up the police records on Brandon Weiss.

It wasn't much; there was a parking ticket that he had paid, and the complaint filed against him by the Tourist Board. He had no outstanding warrants, no special permits beyond a driver's license, no permit to carry a concealed firearm — or a concealed power saw, for that matter. His address was the one I knew, where Deborah had been stabbed. With a little digging, I found one previous address, in Syracuse, New York.

Before that he had lived in Montreal, Canada. A quick check showed that he was still a Canadian citizen.

No real leads there; nothing that qualified as a clue of any kind. I hadn't really expected anything, but my job and my adoptive father had taught me well that due diligence paid off from time to time. This was just the beginning.

The next step, Weiss's e-mail address, was a little harder. With a certain amount of slightly illegal maneuvering, I got into AOL's subscriber list and found out just a little more. The same address in the Design District was still given as his home address, but there was also a cell-phone number. I wrote it down in case I needed it later. Other than that, there was nothing helpful here, either — surprising, really, that an organization like AOL fails to ask simple and vital questions, like, "Where would you hide if Dexter was after you?"

Still, nothing worth doing is ever easy — another fascinatingly stupid cliché. After all, breathing is fairly easy, for the most part, and I think many scholars would agree it pays handsome dividends. In any case, I got no real information from the AOL file, except the phone number, which I set aside to use as a last resort. The telephone company's records would tell me much the same thing as AOL's, but there was a chance I could track down the location of the cell phone itself, a trick I had done once before when I very nearly saved Sergeant Doakes from being surgically modified.

For no particular reason I went back to YouTube. Perhaps I just wanted to see me one more time, relaxing and being myself. It was, after all, something I had never seen before, and never expected to see. Dexter in action, as only he can do it. I watched the video one more time, marveling at how graceful and natural I looked. What a wonderful sense of style I showed as I swung the saw up toward the camera. Beautiful. A true artist. I should do more film work.

And with that, another thought popped into my slowly awakening brain. Beside the screen, the e-mail address was highlighted. I really didn't know much about YouTube, but I knew that if an e-mail address was highlighted, it led somewhere. So I clicked on it and almost immediately an orange background came up on-screen and I was on a YouTube personal page. And in large fiery letters across the top of the page, it said THE NEW MIAMI. I scrolled partway down to a box that said VIDEOS (5), with a row of thumbnail shots of each video. The one showing my back was number four.

In an effort to be methodical and not simply watch my riveting performance again, I clicked on the first one, which showed a man's face twisted into a grimace of disgust. The video began, and again the title appeared on the screen in fiery letters: THE NEW MIAMI, #1.

Then there was a very nice sunset shot of lush tropical vegetation — a row of lovely orchids, a line of birds landing on a small lake — and then the camera pulled back to show the body we had found at Fairchild Gardens. There was a terrible groan off-camera and a somewhat strangled voice said, "Oh, Jesus," and then the camera followed his back as a piercing scream ripped out of the speaker. It sounded strangely familiar, and for a moment that puzzled me, and I paused the video, rewound, and played the scream again. Then I had it; it was the same scream that had been on the first video, the one we had seen at the Tourist Board. For whatever strange reasons, Weiss had used the same scream here. Possibly it was just brand continuity, like McDonald's using the same clown.

I started up the video again; the camera was moving through the crowd in the Fairchild Gardens parking lot, picking out faces that looked shocked, disgusted, or merely curious. And again the screen whirled and lined up the expressive faces in a row of boxes against a background of the opening sunset shot of the vegetation, and the letters supered in on top:

THE NEW MIAMI: PERFECTLY NATURAL

If nothing else, it removed any lingering doubt I might have had about Weiss's guilt. I was quite sure the other videos would show the other victims, complete with re-action shots of the crowd. But just to be thorough, I decided to watch them all in order, all five of them —

But wait a second: there should only be *three* spots, one for each of the sites we had found. One more for Dexter's great perfor-mance and that would be four — what was the other one? Was it possible that Weiss had included something else, something more personal that might give some clue to where I could find him?

There was a loud clatter in the lab, and Vince Masuoka called out, "Yo, Dexter!" and I quickly clicked off the browser. It wasn't just false modesty that made me reluctant to share my wonderful acting work with Vince. Explaining the performance would be far too difficult. And just as my monitor went blank, Vince pushed in to my little cubby, carrying his forensic kit.

"You don't answer your phone anymore?" he said.

"I must have been in the restroom," I said.

"No rest for the wicked," he said. "Come on, we gotta go to work."

"Oh," I said. "What's up?"

"I don't know, but it's got the uniforms on-site almost hysterical," Vince said. "Something down in Kendall."

Of course awful things happen in Kendall all the time, but very few of them require my professional attention. In retrospect, I suppose I should have been more curious, but I was still distracted by the discovery of my unwilling stardom on YouTube, and I really wanted to see the other videos. So I rode along with Vince exchanging half-conscious pleasantries and wondering what Weiss might have revealed in that last, unseen video. And therefore it was with a very real sense of shock that I recognized our destination when Vince pulled into the parking lot, turned off the engine, and said, "Let's go."

We were parked at a large public building I had seen before. In fact, I had seen it only a day ago, when I had taken Cody to his Cub Scout meeting.

We had just parked at Golden Lakes Elementary School.

Of course, it had to be mere happenstance. People get killed all the time, even at elementary schools, and to assume this was any more than one of those funny co-incidences that make life so interesting was to believe that the entire world revolved around Dexter — which was true in a rather limited way, of course, but I was not deranged enough to believe in it in a literal way.

So a bemused and slightly unsettled Dexter trudged after Vince, under the yellow crime-scene tape, and over to the side door of the building, where the body had been discovered. And as I approached the carefully guarded spot where it lay in all its glory, I heard a strange and near-idiot whistling sound, and realized it was me. Because in spite of the see-through plastic mask glued to the face, in spite of the yawning body cavity which was filled with what appeared to be Cub Scout uniform items and paraphernalia, and in spite of the fact that it was completely impossible that I was right, I recognized the body from ten feet away.

It was Roger Deutsch, Cody's scoutmaster.

TWENTY-ONE

The body had been propped in the recess around the side door of the building, the door that served as an emergency exit for the combination cafeteria and auditorium of the school. One of the servers had stepped outside for a smoke and seen it, and had to be sedated, which was easy for me to understand after I took a quick look. And after a second, more careful examination, I very nearly needed a sedative myself.

Roger Deutsch had a lanyard around his neck with a whistle hanging from it. And as before, the body cavity had been scooped out and then filled with interesting things — in this case, a Cub Scout uniform, a colorful book that said *BIG BEAR Cub Scout Handbook* on the cover, and some other gear. I could see the handle of a hand ax sticking up, and a pocketknife with the Cub Scout logo on it. And as I bent closer to look, I also saw a grainy picture, printed on regular white paper, with BE PREPARED printed on it in large black letters. The picture showed a blurry shot, taken from some distance away, of several boys and one adult going into this same building. And although it was impossible to prove, I knew quite well who the adult and one of the children were.

Me and Cody.

There was no mistaking the familiar curve of Cody's back. And there was no mistaking the message, either.

It was a very odd moment, kneeling there on the pavement and looking at a blurry, indistinct picture of myself and Cody, and wondering if anybody would see me if I took it. I had never tampered with evidence before, but then again, I had never been part of it, either. And it was quite clear that this was meant for me. BE PREPARED, and the photo. It was a warning, a challenge. I know who you are, and I know how to hurt you. And here I come.

BE PREPARED.

And I was not prepared. I did not yet know where Weiss might be, and I did not know what or when his next move would be, but I did know that he had moved everything several notches ahead of me, and he had raised the stakes considerably at the same time. This was not a stolen dead body, and it was not anonymous. Weiss had killed Roger Deutsch, not just modified his body. And he had chosen this victim carefully, deliberately, in order to get at me.

It was a complex threat, too. Because the picture added another dimension — it said that I may get you, and I may get Cody, or I may simply expose you for what we both know you are. And on top of that was the sure knowledge that if I was exposed and slapped in jail, Cody would have no protection at all against whatever Weiss might do.

I looked hard at the picture, trying to decide if anyone else could tell it was me, and whether taking it was worth the risk. But before I could make any decision, the feather stroke of an invisible black wing brushed across my face and raised the hair along my neck.

The Dark Passenger had been very quiet through this whole thing so far, contenting himself with a disinterested smirk from time to time and offering no really cogent observations. But now the message was clear, and it echoed the one on the photograph: *Be prepared. You are not alone.* And I knew just as certainly as I possibly could that somewhere nearby something was looking at me and harboring wicked thoughts, watching me as the tiger watches its prey.

Slowly, carefully, as if I had simply forgotten something in the car, I stood up and walked back toward where we had parked. As I walked I casually scanned the parking area; not looking for anything in particular, just Dopey Dexter ambling along in a perfectly normal way, and under the nonchalant and distracted smile, the black smoke boiled and I looked for something that I knew was looking at me.

And found it.

Over there, in the nearest row of the parking lot, maybe a hundred feet away, right where it would provide the best view, a small bronze-colored sedan was parked. And through the windshield, something winked at me; sunlight off the lens of a camera.

Still so very careful-casual, even though the darkness was roaring through me with a knife edge blossoming, I took a step toward the car. Across the distance I saw the bright flash of the camera coming down, and the small pale face of a man, and the black wings rattled and crashed between us for one very long second —

— and then the car started up, backed out of the parking spot with a small squeal of rubber, and disappeared out of the lot and away into traffic. And although I sprinted forward, the most I could see of the license plate was the first half: OGA and three numbers that might have been anything, although I thought the middle one was either a three or an eight.

But with the description of the car, it was enough. I would at least find the registry of the car. It would not be registered to Weiss, couldn't be. Nobody is that stupid, not in this day of nonstop police drama in all the media. But a small hope flickered. He had left quickly, not wanting me to see him or his car, and just this once I might have some small bit of luck.

I stood there for nearly a minute, letting the wild wind inside me settle back down into a neatly coiled and steadily purring thing. My heart was pumping as it seldom did in the light of day, and I realized that it was a very good thing that Weiss had been just a little bit shy and had taken off so readily. After all, what would I have done otherwise? Pulled him out of the car and cut him into a dozen neat pieces? Or had him arrested and flung into a squad car so he could begin to tell everyone who would listen all about Dexter?

No, it was just as well that he had escaped. I would find him, and we would meet on my terms, in the suitable dark of a night that could not come soon enough for me.

I took a deep breath, plastered my best phony working smile back onto my face, and walked back to the pile of decorative meat that had been Cody's scoutmaster.

Vince Masuoka was squatting by the body when I got there, but instead of doing something useful, he was simply staring at the stuff shoved into the cavity and frowning. He looked up as I approached and said, "What do you think it means?"

"I'm sure I have no idea," I said. "I just do blood spatter. They pay detectives to figure out what it means."

Vince cocked his head and looked at me as if I had told him we were supposed to eat the body. "Did you know that Detective Coulter is in charge of the investigation?" he said.

"Maybe they pay him for something else," I said, and I felt a small surge of hope. I had forgotten this detail, but it was worth remembering. With Coulter in charge, I could confess to the murder, hand him videos of me performing it, and he would still find a way not to prove it.

So it was with something approaching good cheer that I went back to work — tempered with very real impatience to get it finished and get back to my computer to track down Weiss. Happily, there was very little blood spatter on-site —Weiss appeared to be the kind of neatnik I admired — and therefore there was almost nothing for me to do. I finished up shortly and begged a ride back to headquarters with one of the squad cars. The driver, a large white-haired guy named Stewart, talked about the Dolphins the whole way, apparently not really caring if I responded.

But by the time we got back to headquarters, I had learned some wonderful things about the approaching football season and what we should have done during the off-season but had somehow, inexplicably, managed to bungle once again, which would certainly lead to another season of ineptitude and shameful losses. I thanked Stewart for the ride and the vital information and fled for my computer.

The database for automobile registration is one of the most basic tools of police work, both in reality and in fiction, and it was with a slight sense of shame that I went to it now. It really seemed just too easy, straight out of a rather simpleminded television drama. Of course, if it led to finding Weiss, I would somehow overcome the feeling that this was almost like cheating, but for the time being

I really kind of wished for a clue that would call for something a little more clever. Still, we work with the tools we are given, and hope that someone asks us later for constructive criticism.

After only fifteen minutes I had combed the entire Florida state database, and found three small bronze-colored vehicles with the letters OGA on their license tag. One of them was registered in Kissimmee, which seemed like a bit of a commute. Another was a 1963 Rambler, and I was reasonably sure that I would have noticed something that distinctive.

That left number three, a 1995 Honda, registered to a Kenneth A. Wimble on Northwest Ninety-eighth Street in Miami Shores. The address was in an area of modest homes, and it was relatively close to the place in the Design District where Deborah had been stabbed. It really wouldn't even be a terribly long walk — so that, for example, if the police came to your little nest on Northeast Fortieth, you could easily hop out the back door and amble a few blocks over until you found an unattended car.

But then what? If you are Weiss, where do you take this car? It seemed to me that you would take it far away from wherever you stole it. So probably the very last place on earth that he would be was the house on Northwest Ninety-eighth Street.

Unless there was some connection between Weiss and Wimble. It would be perfectly natural to borrow a friend's car; just some casual butchery, buddy — back in a couple of hours.

Of course, for some bizarre reason, we don't have a National Registry of Who Your Friends Are. One would have thought that they would have made that a vital part of the Patriot Act, and rammed it through Congress. It would certainly make my work easier now. But no such luck; if Weiss and Wimble were indeed chums, I would have to find out the hard way, by a personal visit. It was merely due diligence in any case. But first I would see if I could uncover anything at all about Kenneth A. Wimble.

A quick check of the database showed that he had no criminal record, at least not under that name. His utilities were paid, although payment on his propane bill had been late several times. Digging a little deeper, going into the tax records, I discovered that Wimble was self-employed, and his occupation was listed as video editor.

Coincidence is always possible. Strange and improbable things happen every day, and we accept them and simply scratch our heads like rubes in the big city, and say, "Gollee, ain't that somethin'." But this seemed to be stretching coincidence past the breaking point. I had been following a writer who had left a video trail, and now the trail had led me to a video professional. And since there comes a time and place when the seasoned investigator must accept the fact that he has stumbled on something that is probably NOT coincidence, I murmured, "Aha," very quietly to myself. I thought I sounded quite professional saying it, too.

Wimble was in on this in some way, tied up with Weiss in making and sending the videos and, therefore, presumably in arranging the bodies and finally in killing Roger Deutsch. So when Deborah came knocking at the door, Weiss fled to his other partner, Wimble. A place to hide, a small bronze-colored car to borrow, and on with the show.

All right then, Dexter. Mount up and move out. We know where he is, and now is the time to go get him — before he decides to put my name and picture on the front page of the *Miami Herald*. Up and away. Let's go.

Dexter? Are you there, buddy?

I was there. But I suddenly found, oddly

enough, that I really missed Deborah. This was exactly the kind of thing I should be doing with her — after all, it was bright daylight out there, and that was not truly Dexter's Dominion. Dexter needs darkness to blossom into the real life-of-the-party that he is deep inside. Sunlight and hunting did not mix. With Deborah's badge I could have stayed hidden in plain sight, but without it . . . I was not actually nervous, of course, but I was a little bit uneasy.

But there was no choice at all. Deborah was lying in a hospital bed, Weiss and his dear friend Wimble were giggling at me in a house on Ninety-eighth Street, and Dexter was dithering about daylight. And that would not do, not at all.

So stand, breathe, stretch. Once more into the breach, dear Dexter. Get up and be gone. And I did, and I headed out the door to my car, but I could not shake the strange feeling of unease.

The feeling lasted all the way over to Northeast Ninety-eighth Street, even through the soothing homicidal rhythm of the traffic. Something was wrong somewhere and Dexter was headed into it somehow. But since there was nothing more definite than that, I kept going, and wondering what was really chewing at the bottom corner of my brain. Was it really just fear of daylight? Or was my subconscious telling me that I had missed something important, something that was getting ready to rear up and bite me? I went over it all in my head, again and again, and it all added up the same way, and the only thing that really stuck out was the thought that it was all very simple, perfectly connected, coherent and logical and right, and I had no choice but to act as quickly as I could, and why should that be bothersome? When did Dexter ever have any choice anyway? When does anyone really have a choice of any kind, beyond occasionally being able to say — on those very few good days we get — I choose ice cream instead of pie?

But I still felt invisible fingers tickling at my neck when I parked the car, across the street and halfway down the block from Wimble's house. And so for several long minutes I did nothing more than sit in the car and look up the street at the house.

The bronze-colored car was parked in the street right in front of the house. There was no sign of life, and no large heap of body parts dragged to the curb to wait for pickup. Nothing at all but a quiet house in an ordinary Miami neighborhood, baking in the midday sun.

And the longer I sat there in the car with the motor off, the more I realized that I was baking, too, and if I stayed in the car a few more minutes, I would be watching a crisp dark crust form on my skin. Whatever faint tremors of doubt I felt, I had to do something while there was still breathable air in the car.

I got out and stood blinking in the heat and light for several seconds, and then moved off down the street, away from Wimble's house. Moving slowly and casually, I walked around the block one time, looking at the house from the rear. There was not much to see; a row of hedges growing up through a chain-link fence blocked any view of the house from the next block over. I continued around the block, crossed the street, and walked on back to my car.

And stood there again, blinking in the brightness, feeling the sweat roll down my spine, across my forehead, into my eyes. I knew that I could not stand there a great deal longer without drawing attention. I had to do something — either approach the house, or get back into my car, drive home, and wait to see myself on the evening news. But with that nasty, annoying little voice still squeaking in my brain that something was just not right, I stood there a little longer, until some small and brittle thing inside snapped, and I finally said, Fine. Let it come, whatever it might be. Anything is better than standing here counting the droplets of sweat as they fall.

I remembered something helpful for a change, and opened the trunk of my car. I had thrown a clipboard in there; it had been very useful for several past investigations into the lifestyles of the wicked and infamous, and there was a clip-on tie as well. It has been my experience that you can go anywhere, day or night, and no one will question you if you wear a clip-on tie and carry a clipboard. Luckily today I was wearing a shirt that actually buttoned at the neck, and I hung the tie on my collar, picked up the clipboard and a ballpoint pen, and walked up the street to Wimble's house. Just another semi-important official somebody or other, here to check on something.

I glanced up the street; it was lined with trees, and several of the houses had visible fruit trees in their yard. Fine: today I was Inspector Dexter, from the State Board of Tree Inspection. This would allow me to move close to the house with a semilogical activity to cloak me.

And then what? Could I really get inside and take Weiss by surprise, in broad daylight? The hot glare of the sun made it seem vastly unlikely somehow. There was no comforting darkness, no shadows to hold me and hide my approach. I was as completely visible and obvious as could be, and if Weiss glanced out the window and recognized me, the game was up before it properly began.

But what choice did I have? It was him or me, and if I did nothing at all, he would most likely do a great deal of something, starting with exposing me and moving down the list to hurting Cody or Astor, or who knows what. I had to head him off and stop him, now.

And as I straightened up to do so, a most unwelcome thought shoved its way in: Was this the way Deborah thought of me? Did she see me as a sort of wild obscenity, slashing its way across the landscape with random ferocity? Was that why she had been so unhappy with me? Because she had formed an image of me as a ravening monster? It was such a painful notion that for a moment I could do nothing but blink away the drops of sweat rolling down my forehead. It was unfair, totally unjustified; of course I was a monster — but not that kind. I was neat, focused, polite, and very careful not to cause the tourists any inconvenience with random body parts scattered about. How could she fail to see that? How could I make her see the well-ordered beauty of the way Harry had set me up?

And the first answer was, I could not — not if Weiss stayed alive and at liberty. Because once my face was on the news, my life was over and Deborah would have no more choice than I would; no more choice than I had right now. Sunlight or not, I had to do this, and I had to do it quickly and well.

I took a deep breath and moved up the street to the house next to Wimble's, looking intently at the trees along the drive and scribbling on the clipboard. I moved slowly up the driveway. No one leaped out at me with a machete in their teeth, so I walked back down the driveway, paused in front of the house, and then went on to Wimble's.

There were suspicious trees to examine there, too, and I looked up at them, made notes, and moved a bit farther up the driveway. There was no sight nor sound of life from the house. Even though I did not know what I hoped to see, I moved closer, looking for it, and not just in the trees. I looked carefully at the house, noting that all the windows seemed to have shades drawn down. Nothing could see in or out. I got far enough up the driveway to notice that there was a back door, located at the top of two concrete steps. I moved toward it very casually, listening for any small rustling or whispering or shouts of "Look out! He's here!" Still nothing; I pretended to notice a tree in the backyard, close to a propane tank and only about twenty feet from the door, and I went over to it.

Still nothing. I scribbled. There was a window in the top half of the door, with no shade pulled down. I walked over to it, mounted the two steps, and peeked inside. I was looking into a darkened hallway, lined with a washing machine and dryer, and a few brooms and mops held in clamps on the wall. I put a hand on the doorknob and turned very slowly and quietly. It was unlocked. I took a deep breath —

— and very nearly fell out of my skin as a horrible, shattering scream came from inside. It was the sound of anguish and horror and such a clear call for help that even Disinterested Dexter moved reflexively forward, and I had one foot actually inside the house when a tiny little question mark scuttled across the floor of my brain and I thought, *I've heard that scream before.* And as my second foot moved forward, farther into the house, I thought, *Really? Where?*

The answer came quite quickly, which was comforting: it was the same scream that was on the "New Miami" videos that Weiss had made.

— which meant that it was a recorded scream.

— which meant it was intended to lure me inside.

— which meant that Weiss was ready and waiting for me.

It is not terribly flattering to my own special self, but the truth is that I actually paused for a split second to admire the speed and clarity of my mental process. And then, happily for me, I obeyed the shrill interior voice that was screaming *Run, Dexter, Run!* and bolted out of the house and down the driveway, just in time to see the bronze-colored car screech away down the street.

And then a huge hand rose up behind me and slammed me to the ground, a hot wind blew past, and Wimble's house was gone in a cloud of flame and showering rubble.

Twenty-Two

"It was the propane," Detective Coulter told me. I leaned against the side of the EMS truck holding an ice pack to my head. My wounds were very minor, considering, but because they were on me they seemed more important, and I was not enjoying them, nor the attention I was getting. Across the street the rubble of Wimble's house smoldered and the firefighters still poked and squirted at steaming piles of junk. The house was not totally destroyed, but a large chunk of the middle of it from roof to foundation was gone and it had certainly lost a great deal of market value, dropping instantly into the category of Very Airy Fixer-Upper.

"So," Coulter said. "He lets the gas out from the wall heater in that soundproof room, tosses in something to set it off, we don't know what yet, and he's out the door and away before it all goes *boom.*" Coulter paused and took a long swig from the large plastic bottle of Mountain Dew he carried. I watched his Adam's apple bob under two thick rolls of grimy flab. He finished drinking, poked his index finger into the mouth of the bottle, and wiped his mouth on his forearm, staring at me as if I was keeping him from using a napkin.

"Why would he have a soundproof room, you think?" he said.

I shook my head very briefly and stopped because it hurt. "He was a video editor," I said. "He probably needed it for recording."

"Recording," said Coulter. "Not chopping people up."

"That's right," I said.

Coulter shook his head. Apparently it didn't hurt him at all, because he did it for several seconds, looking over at the smoking house. "So, and you were here, because why?" he said. "I'm not real clear on that part, Dex."

Of course he was not real clear on that part. I had done everything I could to avoid answering any questions about that part, clutching my head and blinking and gasping as if in terrible pain every time someone approached the subject. Of course I knew that sooner or later I would have to provide a satisfactory answer, and the sticky part was that "satisfactory" thing. Certainly I could claim I'd been visiting my ailing granny, but the problem with giving such answers to cops is that they tend to check them, and alas, Dexter had no ailing granny, nor any other plausible reason to be here when the house exploded, and I had a very strong feeling that claiming coincidence would not really get me terribly far, either.

And in all the time since I had picked myself up off the pavement and staggered over to lean on a tree and admire the way I could still move all my body parts — the whole time I was getting patched up and then waiting for Coulter to arrive — all these long minutes-into-hours, I had not managed to come up with anything that sounded even faintly believable. And with Coulter now turning to stare at me very hard indeed, I realized my time was up.

"So, what then?" he said. "You were here because why? Picking up your laundry? Part-time job delivering pizza? What?"

It was one of the biggest shocks of a very unsettling day to hear Coulter revealing a faint patina of wit. I had thought of him as an exceedingly dull and dim lump of dough, incapable of anything beyond filling out an accident report, and yet here he was making amusing remarks with a very professional deadpan delivery, and if he could do that, I had to assume he might have an outside chance of putting two and two together and coming up with me. I was truly on the spot. And so, throwing my cunning into high gear, I decided to go with the time-honored tactic of telling a big lie wrapped in a small truth.

"Look, Detective," I said, with a painful and somewhat hesitant delivery that I was quite proud of. Then I closed my eyes and took a deep breath — all real Academy Award stuff, if you asked me. "I'm sorry, I'm still a little fuzzy. They say I sustained a minor concussion."

"Was that before you got here, Dex?" Coulter said. "Or can you remember that far back, about why you were here?"

"I can remember," I said reluctantly. "I just . . ."

"You don't feel so good," he said.

"Yeah, that's right."

"I can understand that," he said, and for one wild, irrational moment I thought he might let me go. But no: "What I can't understand," he went on relentlessly, "is what the fuck you were doing here when the fucking house blew the fuck up."

"It's not easy to say," I said.

"I guess not," said Coulter. " 'Cause you

haven't said it yet. You gonna tell me, Dex?" He popped his finger out of the bottle, took a sip, pushed the finger back in again. The bottle was more than half empty now, and it hung there like some kind of strange and embarrassing biological appendage. Coulter wiped his mouth again. "See, I kind of need to know this," he said. " 'Cuz they tell me there's a body in there."

A minor seismic event worked its way down my spine, from the top of my skull all the way down to my heels. "Body?" I said with my usual incisive wit.

"Yeah," he said. "A body."

"That's, you mean — dead?"

Coulter nodded, watching me with distant amusement, and I realized with a terrible shock that we had switched roles, and now I was the stupid one. "Yeah, that's right," he said. " 'Cuz it was inside the house when it went *ka-boom,* so you would have to figure it would be dead. Also," he said, "it couldn't run away, being tied up like that. Who would tie a guy up when the house was gonna blow like that, do you figure?"

"It, uh . . . must have been the killer," I stammered.

"Uh-huh," said Coulter. "So you figure the killer killed him, that it?"

"Uh, yes," I said, and even through the

growing pounding in my head, I could tell how stupid and unconvincing that sounded.

"Uh-huh. But not you, right? I mean, you didn't tie the guy up and toss in a Cohiba or something, right?"

"Look, I saw the guy drive away as the house went up," I said.

"And who was that guy, Dex? I mean, you got a name or anything? 'Cuz that would really help a lot here."

It might have been that the concussion was spreading, but a terrible numbness seemed to be taking me over. Coulter suspected something, and even though I was relatively innocent in this case, any kind of investigation was bound to have uncomfortable results for Dexter. Coulter's eyes had not left my face, and he had not blinked, and I had to tell him something, but even with a minor concussion I knew that I could not give him Weiss's name. "I, it — the car was registered to Kenneth Wimble," I said tentatively.

Coulter nodded. "Same guy owns the house," he said.

"Yes, that's right."

He kept nodding mechanically as if that made sense and said, "Sure. So you figure Wimble ties up this guy — in his own house — and then blows up his own house and drives away in his car, like to the summer place in North Carolina, maybe?"

Again it came across to me that there was more to this man than I had thought there was, and it was not a pleasant realization. I thought I was dealing with SpongeBob, and he had turned out to be Colombo instead, hiding a much sharper mind than the shabby appearance seemed to allow for. I, who'd worn a disguise my entire life, had been fooled by a better costume, and looking at the gleam of previously hidden intelligence in Coulter's eyes, I realized that Dexter was in danger. This was going to call for a great deal of skill and cleverness, and even then I was no longer sure it would be enough.

"I don't know where he went," I said, which was not a great start, but it was all I could come up with.

" 'Course not. And you don't know who he is, either, right? 'Cuz you'd tell me if you did."

"Yes, I would."

"But you don't have any idea."

"No."

"So great, then why'n't you tell me what you were doing here instead?" he said.

And there it was, full circle, back to the real question — and if I answered it right, all was forgiven, and if I did not respond in a way that would make my suddenly smart friend happy, there was a very real possibility that he would follow through and derail the Dexter Express. I was waist-deep in the outhouse without a rope, and my brain was throbbing, trying to push through the fog to top form, and failing.

"It's . . . it's . . ." I looked down and then far away to my left, searching for the right words for a terrible and embarrassing admission. "She's my sister," I said at last.

"Who is?" said Coulter.

"Deborah," I said. "Your partner. Deborah Morgan. She's in the ICU because of this guy, and I . . ." I trailed off very convincingly and waited to see if he could fill in the blanks, or if the cute remarks had been a coincidence.

"I knew that," he admitted. He took another sip of soda and then jammed his fingertip back into the mouth of the bottle and let it dangle again. "So you find this guy how?"

"At the elementary school this morning," I said. "He was shooting video from his car, and I got the tag. I traced it to here."

Coulter nodded. "Uh-huh," he said. "And instead of telling me, or the lieutenant, or even a school crossing guard, you figure to take him on by yourself."

"Yes," I said.

"Because she's your sister."

"I wanted to, you know," I said.

"Kill him?" he said, and the words hit me with an icy shock.

"No," I said. "Just, just —"

"Read him his rights?" said Coulter. "Handcuff him? Ask him some tough questions? Blow up his house?"

"I guess, um," I said, as if reluctantly letting out ugly truth. "I wanted to, you know. Rough him up a little."

"Uh-huh," said Coulter. "And then what?"

I shrugged, feeling somewhat like a teenage boy caught with a condom. "Then bring him in," I said.

"Not kill him?" Coulter said, raising one badly trimmed eyebrow.

"No," I said. "How could I, um . . . ?"

"Not stick a knife in him and say, This is for what you did to my sister?"

"Come on, Detective. Me?" And I didn't quite bat my eyes at him, but I did my best to look like the charter member of the Geek Patrol that I was in my secret identity.

And Coulter simply stared at me for a long and very uncomfortable minute. Then he shook his head again. "I dunno, Dex," he said. "Doesn't really add up."

I gave him a look of pained confusion, which wasn't entirely acting. "What do you mean?"

He took another swig of soda. "You always play by the rules," he said. "Your sister's a cop. Your dad was a cop. You never get in any kind of trouble, ever. Mr. Boy Scout. And now you decide you're Rambo?" He made a face as if somebody had put garlic in his Mountain Dew. "Am I missing something? You know, something that makes sense?"

"She's my sister," I said, and it sounded incredibly feeble, even to me.

"Yeah, I got that already," he said. "You got nothing else?"

I felt trapped in slow motion while large and ponderous things whizzed past me. My head throbbed and my tongue was too thick, and all my legendary cleverness had deserted me. Coulter watched me as I numbly and painfully shook my head, and I thought, *This is a very dangerous man.* But out loud, all I could manage was, "I'm sorry."

He looked at me for just a moment longer, then turned away. "I think maybe Doakes was right about you," he said, and then he walked across the street to talk to the firefighters.

Well. The mention of Doakes was the perfect end to an absolutely enchanting conversation. I just barely stopped myself from shaking my head again, but the temptation was strong, because it seemed to me that what had been a sane and well-ordered universe just a few days ago was suddenly beginning to spin wildly out of control. First I walked into a trap and nearly turned into the Inhuman Torch, and then a man I had regarded as a foot soldier in the war against intelligence turned out to be a covert general — and to top it off, he was apparently in league with the last few living pieces of my nemesis, Sergeant Doakes, and he seemed very likely to take up where Doakes had left off, in the pursuit of poor persecuted Dexter. Where would this end?

And if this was not bad enough — which, frankly, I thought it was — I was still in terrible danger from Weiss and whatever his plan of attack might be.

All in all, it occurred to me that this would be a very good time to be somebody else. Unfortunately, that was a trick I had so far failed to master. With nothing else to do except ponder the almost certain doom headed toward me at such terrible speed from so many different directions, I walked down the block to my car. And of course, because apparently I had not suffered nearly enough, a slim and ghostly figure came off the curb and glided into step beside me.

"You were here when this happened," said Israel Salguero.

"Yes," I said, wondering if next a satellite would fall from orbit and onto my head.

He was silent for a moment and then he stopped walking, and I turned to face him. "You know I am not investigating you," he said.

I thought that was very nice to hear, but considering how things had gone the last few hours, I thought it would be best just to nod, so I did.

"But apparently what happened here is connected to the incident involving your sister, and that I *am* investigating," he said, and I was glad I hadn't said anything. So glad, in fact, that I decided that silence would be a good policy to continue.

"You know that one of the most important things I am charged to uncover is any kind of vigilante activity on the part of any of our officers," he said.

"Yes," I said. After all, only one word.

He nodded. He still had not taken his eyes off my face.

"Your sister has a very promising career ahead of her," he said. "It would be a very great shame if something like this hurt her."

"She's still unconscious," I said. "She hasn't done anything."

"No, she hasn't done anything," he said. "What about you?"

"I just tried to find the guy who stabbed her," I said. "I didn't do anything wrong."

"Of course," he said. He waited for me to say something else, but I didn't, and so after what seemed like several weeks, he smiled and patted my arm and walked away across the street to where Coulter was standing and swigging from his Mountain Dew bottle. I watched as the two of them spoke, turned to face me, and then turned away again to look at the smoldering house. And thinking that this afternoon couldn't possibly get any better, I turned and trudged to my car.

The windshield was cracked from a flying piece of house.

I managed not to burst into tears. I got in and drove home, peering through the cracked glass and listening to my head throb.

Twenty-Three

Rita was not home yet when I arrived, since I'd gotten there a bit early as a result of my explosive misfortune. The house seemed very empty, and I stood inside the front door for a minute just listening to the unnatural silence. A pipe ticked in the back of the house, and then the air conditioner came on, but these were not living sounds and I still felt as if I had stumbled into a movie where everyone else had been whisked away in a spaceship. The lump on my head was still throbbing, and I was very tired and very alone. I went to the couch and fell onto it as if I suddenly had no bones left to hold me up.

I lay there for some time in a kind of strange interval in the urgency. I knew I still had to explode into action, track down Weiss, head him off at the pass, and beard him in his den, but for some reason I was completely unable to move, and the mean e voice that had been urging me on did ..ot sound terribly convincing at the moment, as if it, too, needed a coffee break. So I just lay there, facedown, trying to feel the sense of emergency that had deserted me, and failing to feel anything except, as mentioned, fatigue and pain. And if somebody had shouted at me, "Look out behind you! He's got a gun!" I would have replied with no more than a weary mumble, "Tell him to take a number and wait."

I woke up, I don't know how much later, to an overwhelming sense of blue, which made no sense at all until I was able to focus my eyes. And there stood Cody, no more than six inches away from my head, in his apparently brand-new Cub Scout uniform. I sat up, which caused my head to clang like a gong, and looked at him.

"Well," I said. "You certainly look official."

"Look stupid," he said. "Shorts."

I looked at him in his dark blue shirt and shorts, the little hat perched on top of his head and the neckerchief in its slide around his neck, and it didn't seem fair to pick on the shorts. "What's wrong with shorts?" I said. "You wear shorts all the time."

"*Uniform* shorts," he said, as if it was some kind of impossible assault on the last frontier of human dignity.

"Lots of people wear uniform shorts," I said, desperately flinging my battered brain through its paces in search of an example.

Cody looked very doubtful. "Who?" he said.

"Well, ah, the mailman wears shorts —" I broke off quickly; the look he was giving me was louder and more pointed than anything he could have said. "And, um, the British soldiers wore shorts in India," I said, with incredibly feeble hope.

He stared at me for a moment longer without saying anything, as if I had let him down badly when all the chips were on the table. And before I could think of another brilliant example, Rita came charging into the room.

"Oh, Cody, you didn't wake him up, did you? Hello, Dexter, we've been shopping, we got ALL the things Cody needs for the Cub Scouts, he doesn't like the shorts, I think because Astor said something, my God, what happened to your head?" she said, running through two octaves and eight emotions without breathing.

"It's nothing," I said, "just a flesh wound," which was something I'd always wanted to say, even though I didn't really know what that meant. Weren't ALL wounds flesh wounds, unless they bypassed the flesh somehow and went right to the bone?

Nevertheless, Rita responded with a gratifying circus of concern, shooing away Cody and Astor and getting me an ice pack, a comforter, and a cup of tea before flinging herself down beside me on the couch and demanding to know what had happened to my poor dear head. I filled her in on all the dreadful details — leaving out one or two things with no real relevance, like what I had been doing at a house that blew up in an attempt to kill me — and as I spoke, I watched with dismay as her eyes got big and moist, until they began to overflow and tears ran down her cheeks and across her face. It was really quite flattering to think that minor damage to my skull could cause such a display of hydrotechnics, but at the same time it left me slightly uneasy about what my response ought to be.

Luckily for my reputation as a Method actor, Rita left me in no doubt at all about how I should behave. "You stay right here and rest," she said. "Quiet and rest when you get a bump on the head like that. I'm going to make you some soup."

I had not known that soup was good for concussions, but Rita seemed very sure about it, and with a few gentle strokes on my face and a light kiss near the bump, she was off the couch and into the kitchen, where she immediately began a muted clatter that very soon smelled like garlic, onion, and then chicken, and I drifted into a state of half sleep where even the faint throbbing of my head seemed distant, cozy, and almost pleasant. I wondered if Rita would bring me soup if I was arrested. I wondered if Weiss had anyone to bring him soup. I hoped not — I was starting to dislike him, and he certainly didn't deserve soup.

Astor suddenly appeared beside the couch, interrupting my reverie. "Mom says you got hit on the head," she said.

"Yes, that's right," I said.

"Can I see it?" she asked, and I was so deeply touched by her concern that I bowed my head to reveal the lump and the matted hair around it where it had bled. "It doesn't look so bad," she said, sounding a little disappointed.

"It isn't," I told her.

"So you're not going to die, are you?" she asked politely.

"Not yet," I said. "Not until after you do your homework."

She nodded, glanced toward the kitchen, and said, "I hate math." Then she wandered away down the hall, presumably to hate her math at closer range.

drifted awhile longer. The soup finally came, and while I would not absolutely insist that it was good for my head injury, it certainly did me no harm. As I may have mentioned before, Rita in the kitchen can do things that are far beyond mortal ken, and after a big portion of her chicken soup I began to think that the world at large might deserve one last chance. She fussed over me the whole time, which was not really my favorite thing, but at the moment it seemed kind of soothing and I let her fluff the pillows, mop my brow with a cool cloth, and rub my neck when the soup was all gone.

Before too long, the entire evening had passed, and Cody and Astor came in to say muted good nights. Rita herded them away to bed and tucked them in, and I staggered down the hall to the bathroom to brush my teeth. Just as I got the toothbrush going in a really good rhythm, I caught sight of myself in the mirror over the sink. My hair stuck up in all directions, there was a bruise on one cheek, and the normal sprightly emptiness of my eyes seemed hollow. I looked like a very unflattering mug shot, the kind where the recently arrested is still sobering up and trying to figure out what he did and how he got caught. I hoped it was not an omen of what was to come.

In spite of an evening of nothing more strenuous than lounging on the couch and dozing, I was nearly overwhelmed with sleepiness, and the toothbrushing had taken the last of my energy. Still, I made it all the way to the bed under my own power, and I flopped down onto the pillows thinking that I would just drift off into slumberland and worry about everything else in the morning. But alas, Rita had other plans.

After the hushed murmur of bedtime prayers had died away down the hall in the children's room, I heard her come into the bathroom and run water for a while, and I had almost fallen asleep when the sheets rustled and something that smelled like very aggressive orchids slid into bed beside me.

"How do you feel?" Rita said.

"Much better," I said, and giving credit where it was due, I added, "The soup seemed to help."

"Good," she whispered, and she put her head down on my chest. For a while she just lay there, and I could feel her breath blowing across my chest and I wondered if I could really get to sleep with the weight of her head pressed onto my ribs like that. But then the pattern of her breathing changed, got slightly percussive, and I realized she was crying.

There are few things in the world that make me feel more clueless than a woman's tears. I know that I am supposed to do something comforting and then go slay whatever dragon caused the crying fit, but it has been my experience, in my limited dealings with women, that the tears never come when they should, and they are never about what you might think, and consequently you are reduced to truly stupid options like patting her head and saying, "There there," in the hopes that at some point she will let you in on what the display is actually about.

But Dexter is nothing if not a team player, and so I slid my arm up across her back, put the palm of my hand on her head, and patted. "It's okay," I said, and no matter how stupid that sounded, I thought it was a tremendous improvement over "there there."

And true to form, Rita's reply came out of absolutely nowhere that I could hope to predict. "I can't lose you," she said.

I certainly had no plans to be lost, and I would gladly have told her so, but she was just hitting her stride now, and the silent sobs were jerking her body and sending a small rivulet of salt water rolling down my chest. "Oh, Dexter," she sobbed, "what would I do if I lost you, too?"

And now, with that word *too,* I had some-how joined a completely unexpected and unknown company, presumably of people Rita had carelessly left lying around where they had been easily lost, and she had given me no clue how I had managed to get a seat with that group, or even who they were. Did she mean her first husband, the addict who had beaten and tormented her, Cody, and Astor, until they were traumatized into becoming my ideal family? He was in prison now, and I certainly agreed that being lost that way was a bad idea. Or was there some other string of misplaced persons who had slipped through the cracks of Rita's life and been washed away by the rains of mis-chance?

And then, as if I needed further proof that her thoughts were being beamed to her from a mother ship in orbit beyond Pluto, Rita began to slide her face down my chest, across my stomach — still sobbing, you understand, and leaving a trail of tears that quickly turned cool.

"Just lie still," she sniffled. "You shouldn't exert yourself with a concussion."

As I said, you never really know what the program is going to be when a woman switches on the tears.

Twenty-Four

In the middle of the night I woke up and thought, *But what does he want?* I don't know why I hadn't asked that question before, and I don't know why it came to me now, lying in my comfy bed next to a gently snoring Rita. But there it was — it was bobbling around on the surface of Lake Dexter now, and I had to do something with it. The inside of my head still felt stiff, as if it was packed with wet sand, and for several minutes I lay there unable to do anything with my thought except to repeat it: *What does he want?*

What did Weiss want? He was not simply feeding a Passenger of his own, I was reasonably sure of that. I had felt no sympathy twinges from my own anywhere near either Weiss or his handiwork, which ordinarily I would, in the presence of another Presence.

And the way he went about it, starting

with already-dead bodies instead of creating his own — until he had killed Deutsch — argued that he was after something altogether different.

But what? He made videos of the bodies. He made videos of people looking at the bodies. And he had made a video of me at play — unique footage, yes, but it all added up to nothing that made any sense to me. Where was the fun in all that? I saw none — and that made it impossible for me to get inside Weiss's head and figure him out. With normal, well-adjusted psychopaths who killed because they must and took a simple, honest pleasure from their work, I never had that problem. I understood them all too well, since I was one. But with Weiss, there was no point of contact, no place to feel empathy, and because of that I had no idea of where he would go or what he would do next. I had a very bad feeling that whatever it was, I would not like it — but I had no feeling at all of what it would be, and I didn't like that at all.

I lay there in bed for a while thinking about it — or trying to think about it, since the good ship Dexter was clearly not yet ready to raise full steam. Nothing came to me. I didn't know what he wanted. I didn't know what he would do next. Coulter was out to get me. So was Salguero, and of course, Doakes had never given up. Debs was still in a coma.

On the plus side, Rita had made me some very good soup. She was really very good to me — she deserved better, even though she clearly didn't know that. She thought she had everything, apparently, between me, the children, and our recent trip to Paris. And although she did, in fact, have these things, none of them remotely resembled what she thought they were. She was like a mother lamb in a wolf pack, and she only saw white fluffy wool all around her when in fact the pack was licking its lips and waiting for her to turn her back. Dexter, Cody, and Astor were monsters. And Paris — well, they did actually speak French there, just as she had hoped. But Paris had proved to have its own unique kind of monster, too, as our wonderful interval at the art gallery had shown. What was it called? *Jennifer's Leg.* Very interesting; after all my years of toiling in the fields it was still possible for me to see something that surprised me, and for that reason I felt a certain warmth for Paris nowadays.

Between Jennifer and her leg, and Rita's eccentric performance, and whatever it was that Weiss was doing, life was just full of surprises lately, and they all boiled down to one thing: People really deserve whatever happens to them, don't they?

It may not do me very much credit, but I found this thought very comforting, and I drifted back to sleep soon after.

The next morning my head had cleared a great deal; whether it was from Rita's attentions or just my naturally chipper metabolism, I couldn't say. In any case, I jumped out of bed with a fully functioning and powerfully effective brain at my service once again, which was all to the good.

The downside to that, however, was that any effective brain, realizing it was in the situation in which I found myself, would also find itself fighting down a very strong urge to panic, pack a bag, and run for the border. But even with my mental powers in high gear, I could not think of a border that would protect me from the mess I was in.

Still, life gives us very few real choices, and most of them are awful, so I headed for work, determined to track down Weiss and not to rest until I had him. I still did not understand him, or what he was doing, but that did not mean I couldn't find him. No, indeed; Dexter was part bloodhound and part bulldog, and when he is on your trail, you might as well give up and save yourself the needless bother. I wondered if there was a way to get that message to Weiss.

I got to work a little bit early and so managed to grab a cup of coffee that almost tasted like coffee. I took it to my desk, sat at the computer, and got down to work. Or to be perfectly accurate, I got down to staring at my computer screen and trying to think of the right way to go to work. I had used up most of my clues already and felt like I was at something of a dead end. Weiss had stayed one step ahead of me, and I had to admit that he could be anywhere now; holed up somewhere nearby or even back in Canada, there was no way to know. And although I had thought my brain was fully functional once again, it was offering me no way to find out.

And then, far away, on top of an ice-covered peak in the distant skyline of Dexter's mind, a signal flag rose up the pole and fluttered in the wind. I stared across the distance, trying to read the signal, and finally I got it: *Five!* it said. I blinked against the glare and read it again. *Five.*

A lovely number, five. I tried to remember if it was a prime number, and discovered I could not recall what that meant. But it was a very welcome number right now, because I had remembered why it was important, prime or not.

There were five videos on Weiss's YouTube page. One each for the sites where Weiss had left his modified bodies, one of Dexter at play . . . and one more that I had not seen yet when Vince clattered in and called me away to work. It could not be another "New Miami" commercial featuring Deutsch's body, because Weiss had still been filming that when I arrived at the crime scene. So it showed something else. And although I did not really expect it to tell me how to get to Weiss, it would almost certainly tell me something I did not know.

I grabbed my mouse and eagerly drove to YouTube, undeterred by the fact that I had watched myself on YouTube more often than modesty would really permit. I clicked through to the "New Miami" page. It was unchanged, the orange background still lighting up the screen behind the blazing letters. And on the right side were the five videos, neatly lined up in a thumbnail gallery, just as I remembered them.

Number five, the last one down, showed no picture in its box, just an area of blurry darkness. I moved the cursor over it and clicked. For a moment nothing happened; then a thick white line pulsed across the screen from left to right, and there was a blare of trumpets that was oddly familiar. And then a face appeared on the screen — Doncevic, smiling, his hair puffed out — and a voice began to sing, "Here's the story —" and I realized why it had sounded familiar.

It was the opening to *The Brady Bunch.*

The horribly cheerful music bumped out at me and I watched as the voice warbled, "Here's the story, of a guy named Alex, who was lonely, bored, and looking — for a change." Then the first three arranged corpses appeared to the left of Doncevic's happy face. He looked up at them and smiled as the song went on. They even smiled back, thanks to the plastic masks glued onto their faces.

The white line slid across the screen again, and the voice went on. "It's the story, of a guy named Brandon, who had time of his own on his hands." A picture of a man's face appeared in the middle — Weiss? He was thirty or so, about the same age as Doncevic, but he was not smiling as the song continued. "They were two guys — living all together, until suddenly Brandon was alone." Three boxes appeared on the right side of the screen, and in each one a dark and blurry frame appeared that was just as familiar as the song, but in a very slightly different way: these were three action shots lifted from the video of Dexter at play.

The first showed Doncevic's body dumped in the tub. The second showed Dexter's arm raising the saw, and the third was the saw slashing down on Doncevic. All three were short, two-second loops that repeated, over and over, as the song lurched on.

From the middle box Weiss looked on as the voice sang, "Until one day Brandon Weiss will get this fellow, and I promise he will not be saved by luck. There is nothing you can do to escape me. Because you have made me a crazy fuck."

The cheerful tune crashed on as Weiss sang, "A crazy fuck. A crazy fuck. When you killed Alex — I became — a crazy fuck."

But then, instead of a happy smile and dissolve to the first commercial, Weiss's face swelled up to fill the whole screen and he said, "I loved Alex, and you took him away from me, just when we were getting started. In a way it's very funny, because he was the one who said we shouldn't kill anybody. I thought it would have been . . . truer . . ." He made a face and said, "Is that a word?" He gave a short and bitter laugh and went on. "Alex came up with the idea of taking bodies from the morgue so we didn't have to kill anybody. And when you took him, you took away the only thing that stopped me from killing."

For a moment he just stared at the camera. Then, very softly, he said, "Thank you. You're right. It's fun. I'm going to do it some more." He gave a kind of twisted smile, as if he found something funny but didn't feel like laughing. "You know, I kind of admire you."

Then the screen went black.

When I was much younger, I used to feel cheated by my lack of human feelings. I could see the huge barrier between me and humanity, a wall built of feelings I would never feel, and I resented it very much. But one of those feelings was guilt — one of the most common and powerful, in fact — and as I realized that Weiss was telling me I had turned him loose as a killer, I also realized that I really ought to feel a little guilt, and I was very grateful that I did not.

Instead of guilt, what I felt was relief. Chilled waves of it, pulsing through me and snapping the tension that had been winding itself tighter and tighter inside me. I was well and truly relieved — because now I knew what he wanted. He wanted me. It had not been said out loud, but it was there: *the next time it will be you and yours.* And

296

following the relief came a sense of cold urgency, a slow spreading and flexing of dark interior talons as the Dark Passenger caught the challenge in Weiss's voice and responded in kind.

This was a great relief, too. Up until now the Passenger had been silent, having nothing at all to say about borrowed bodies, even when they were converted into patio furniture or gift baskets. But now there was menace, another predator sniffing down our back trail and threatening a territory we had already marked. And this was a challenge we could not allow, not for a moment. Weiss had served notice that he was coming — and finally, at last, the Passenger was rising from its nap and polishing its teeth. We would be ready.

But ready for what? I did not believe for a moment that Weiss would run away; that was not even a question. So what would he do?

The Passenger hissed an answer, an obvious one, but I felt its rightness because it was what *we* would have done. And Weiss had as much as told me himself: "I loved Alex and you took him away . . ." So he would go after someone close to me. And by leaving the photo on Deutsch's body, he had even told me who. It would be Cody and Astor, because that would hit me the same way I had hit him — and it would also bring me to him, and on his terms.

But how would he do it? That was the big question — and it seemed to me that the answer was fairly obvious. So far Weiss had been very straightforward — there is nothing terribly subtle about blowing up a house. I had to believe that he would move quickly, when he felt the odds favored him most. And since I knew he had been watching me, I had to assume he knew my daily routine — and the routine the children followed. They would be most vulnerable when Rita picked them up from school, coming out of a secure environment and into anything-goes Miami: I would be far away at work, and he could certainly overcome one relatively frail and unsuspecting woman to grab at least one of the kids.

So what I had to do was get into position first, before Weiss, and watch for him to arrive. It was a simple plan, and not without risk — I might well be wrong. But the Passenger was hissing agreement, and it is rarely wrong, so I resolved to leave work early, right after lunch, and get into position at the elementary school to intercept Weiss.

And once again, as I gathered myself for a great leap at the jugular vein of the impending foe — my telephone rang.

"Hey, buddy," Kyle Chutsky said. "She's awake, and she's asking for you."

TWENTY-FIVE

They had moved Deborah out of the intensive care unit. I had one moment of disjointed confusion when I stared into the empty ICU. I had seen this in a half-dozen movies, where the hero looks at the empty hospital bed and knows that it means whoever had been there is now dead, but I was quite sure Chutsky would have mentioned it if Debs had died, so I just went back down the hall to the reception area.

The woman at the desk made me wait while she did mysterious and very slow things with a computer, answered the phone, and talked with two of the nurses who were leaning nearby. The air of barely controlled panic that everyone had shown in the ICU was completely gone now, replaced by an apparently obsessive interest in phone calls and fingernails. But finally the woman admitted that there was a slim possibility of finding Deborah in room 235, which was on the second floor. That made so much sense I actually thanked her, and trudged off to find the room.

It was indeed on the second floor, and right next to room 233, so with a feeling that all was right with the world, I stepped in to see Deborah propped up in bed, with Chutsky on the far side of the bed in virtually the same position he had held in the ICU. There was still an impressive array of machinery surrounding Deborah, and the tubes still went in and out, but as I entered the room she opened one eye and looked at me, managing a modest half smile for my benefit.

"Alive, alive, oh," I said, thinking that quaint good cheer was called for. I pulled a chair up beside the bed and sat.

"Dex," she said in a soft and hoarse voice. She tried to smile again, but it was even worse than the first attempt, and she gave up and closed her eyes, seeming somehow to be receding into the snowy distance of the pillows.

"She's not too strong here yet," Chutsky said.

"I guessed that," I said.

"So, uh, don't get her tired, or anything. The doctor said."

I don't know if Chutsky thought I was going to suggest a game of volleyball, but I nodded and just patted Deborah's hand. "It's nice to have you back, sis," I said. "You had us worried."

"I feel," she said in a feeble husky voice. But she did not tell us what she felt; instead, she closed her eyes again and parted her lips for a ragged breath, and Chutsky leaned forward and put a small chip of ice between her lips.

"Here," he said. "Don't try to talk yet."

Debs swallowed the ice, but frowned at Chutsky anyway. "I'm okay," she said, which was certainly a bit of an exaggeration. The ice seemed to help a little, and when she spoke again, her voice did not sound quite so much like a rat-tail file on an old door-knob. "Dexter," she said, and the sound of it was unnaturally loud, as if she was shout-ing in church. She shook her head slightly and, to my great amazement, I saw a tear roll out of the corner of her eye — some-thing I had not seen from her since she was twelve. It slid across her cheek and down onto the pillow, where it disappeared.

"Shit," she said. "I feel so totally . . ." Her hand fluttered feebly, the one that Chutsky was not holding.

"You should," I said. "You were practi-cally dead."

She lay there for a long moment, unspeaking, eyes closed, and then finally said, very softly, "I don't want to do this anymore."

I looked at Chutsky across Deborah; he shrugged. "Do what, Debs?" I said.

"Cops," she said, and when I finally understood what she was saying, that she didn't want to be a cop anymore, I was as shocked as if the moon had tried to resign.

"Deborah," I said.

"Doesn't make sense," she said. "End up here . . . For what?" She opened her eyes and looked at me, and shook her head very slightly. "For what?" she said.

"It's your job," I said, and I admit it wasn't terribly moving, but it was all I could think of under the circumstances, and I didn't really think she wanted to hear about Truth, Justice, and the American Way.

She apparently didn't want to hear that it was her job, either, because she just looked at me and then turned her head and closed her eyes again. "Shit," she said.

"All right now," said a loud and cheerful voice from the door, in a thick Bahamian accent. "Gentlemen must go." I looked; a large and very happy nurse had come into the room and was advancing on us rapidly. "The lady must rest, which she cannot do when you are bothering her," the nurse said.

She said "boddering," and for a second I found it so charming that I did not realize she was shooing me out.

"I just got here," I said.

She planted herself right in front of me and crossed her arms. "Then you will save big money on parking, because you got to go now," she said. "Come on, gentlemen," she said, turning to face Chutsky. "Boat of you."

"Me?" he said with a look of great surprise.

"You," she said, leveling a massive finger at him. "You been here too long already."

"But I have to stay here," he said.

"No, you have to go," the nurse said. "Doctor wants her to rest awhile. Alone."

"Go ahead," Debs said softly, and Chutsky looked at her with an expression of hurt. "I'll be fine," she said. "Go on."

Chutsky looked from her to the nurse, and then back at Deborah again. "All right," he said at last. He leaned forward and kissed her cheek, and she did not object. He stood up and raised an eyebrow at me. "Okay, buddy," he said. "Guess we're evicted."

As we left, the nurse was battering at the pillows as if they had misbehaved.

Chutsky led me down the hall to the elevator, and as we waited for it he said,

"I'm a little bit worried." He frowned and poked at the down button several more times.

"What," I said. "You mean about, um, brain damage?" Deborah's statement that she wanted to quit was still ringing in my ears, and it was so completely unlike her that I was a little worried, too. The image of vegetable Debbie drooling in a chair while Dexter spoon-fed her oatmeal still seemed hauntingly awful to me.

Chutsky shook his head. "Not exactly," he said. "More like psychological damage."

"How do you mean?"

He made a face. "I dunno," he said. "Maybe it's just the trauma. But she seems . . . very weepy. Anxious. Not like, you know. Herself."

I have never been stabbed and then lost most of my blood, and in any case I could not remember reading anything that explained how you are supposed to feel under the circumstances. But it seemed to me that being weepy and anxious when these things happened to you was a relatively reasonable reaction. And before I could think of a tactful way to say so, the elevator doors slid open and Chutsky charged in. I followed.

As the doors slid shut, he went on. "She didn't really know me at first," he said.

"Right when she opened her eyes."

"I'm sure that's normal," I said, although I was not really sure at all. "I mean, she's been in a coma."

"She looked right at me," he said, as if I hadn't spoken at all, "and she was like, I dunno. Scared of me. Like, who am I and what am I doing there."

To be perfectly honest, I had wondered the same thing over the last year or so, but it hardly seemed proper to say so. Instead, I just said, "I'm sure it takes time to —"

"Who am I," he said, again apparently without noticing that I had spoken. "I sat there the whole time, never left her side longer than five minutes at a time." He stared at the elevator's control panel as it chimed to let us know we had arrived. "And she doesn't know who I am."

The doors slid open, but Chutsky did not notice at first.

"Well," I said, hoping to break him out of his freeze.

He looked up at me. "Let's get a cup of coffee," he said, and headed out the elevator door, pushing past three people in light green scrubs, and I trudged along behind.

Chutsky led me out the door and over to the small restaurant on the ground floor of the parking garage, where somehow he managed to get two cups of coffee rather quickly, without anyone shoving in front of him or elbowing him in the ribs. It made me feel slightly superior: obviously, he was not a Miami native. Still, there was something to be said for results, and I took the coffee and sat at a small table wedged into the corner.

Chutsky didn't look at me, or anything else for that matter. He didn't blink, and the expression on his face didn't change. I couldn't think of anything to say that was worth the air it would take, so we sat in chummy awkwardness for several minutes, until he finally blurted out, "What if she doesn't love me anymore?"

I have always tried to maintain a modest outlook, particularly when it comes to my own talents, and I know very well that I am really only good at one or two things, and advice to the lovelorn was very definitely not one of them. And since I do not actually understand love, it seemed a little unfair to expect me to comment on its possible loss.

Still, it was quite clear that some kind of comment was called for, and so, dropping the temptation to say, "I don't really know why she loved you in the first place," I fumbled in my bag of clichés and came up with, "Of course she does. She's just had a terrible strain — it takes time to recover."

Chutsky watched me for a few seconds to see if there was any more, but there wasn't. He turned away and sipped at his coffee. "Maybe you're right," he said.

"Of course I am," I said. "Give her time to get well. Everything will be fine." No lightning struck me when I said it, so I suppose it was possible that I was right.

We finished our coffee in relative silence, Chutsky brooding on the possibility that he was no longer beloved, and Dexter anxiously gazing at the clock as it approached noon, the time for me to leave and get in place to ambush Weiss, and so it was something less than chummy when I finally drained my cup and stood up to go. "I'll come back later," I said, but Chutsky just nodded and took another forlorn sip of his coffee.

"Okay, buddy," he said. "See you."

Twenty-Six

The Golden Lakes area went boldly against the canon law of Miami real estate; in spite of the fact that the word *lakes* was in its name, there were actually several lakes in the area, and one of them butted up against the far side of the school's playground. In truth, it did not look terribly golden to me, more of a milky green, but there was no denying that it was actually a lake, or at least a large pond. Still, I could appreciate the difficulty of trying to sell an area called "Milky Green Pond," so perhaps the developers had known what they were doing after all, which would be yet another violation of custom.

I got to Golden Lakes well before school was over for the day, and I drove around the perimeter a couple of times, looking for a likely place for Weiss. There was none. The road on the east side ended where the lake came up almost to one side of the fence.

And the fence was the tall chain-link variety and it went all around the school without a break, even on the lakeside — just in case a hostile frog tried to get on the grounds, I'm sure. Almost to the spot where the side road ended at the lake, there was a gate in the fence at the far side of the playfield, but it was securely closed with a chain and a large padlock.

Other than that, the only way through the fence was in front of the school, and it was blocked by a guard booth, with a police car parked beside it. Try to get through during school hours and the guard or the cop would stop you. Try to get through during drop-off or pickup and hundreds of teachers, moms, and crossing guards would stop you, or at least make things too difficult and chancy for comfort.

So the obvious answer for Weiss was to get in position early. And I had to figure out where. I put my Dark Thoughts Thinking Cap on and went slowly around the perimeter one more time. If I wanted to grab somebody from the school, how would I do it? First, it would have to be going in or coming out, since it would be too hard to breach school security in the middle of class. And that meant at the front gate — which is, naturally enough, why all the security was there, everything from the cop on duty to the very mean shop teacher.

Of course, if you could somehow get inside the fence first, and strike while all the security was focused at the front gate, that would make things much easier. But to do that, you would have to come through the fence, or over it, at a spot where you were not likely to be noticed — or at a spot where you could be inside the school quickly enough that it wouldn't matter if you were seen.

But as far as I could tell, there was no such spot. I drove around the perimeter one more time; nothing. The fence was set well back from the buildings on all sides except the front. The one apparent weak spot was at the pond. There was a clump of pine trees and scrub brush between the pond and the fence, but the whole thing was too far from the school's buildings. You could never get over the fence and across the field without being extremely visible.

And I could not drive around again without raising suspicion. I nosed the car onto a street off to the south side of the school, parked, and thought about it. All my keen reasoning led me to believe that Weiss would try to get the kids here, this afternoon, and this icy impeccable logic was seconded by a hot and inarguable blast of certainty from the Passenger. But how? From where I sat, I looked out at the school, and I had a very strong sense that somewhere nearby Weiss was doing the same thing. But he would not simply bust through the fence and hope he got lucky. He had been watching, making note of the details, and he would have a plan. And I had about half an hour now to figure out what that plan was and come up with a way to stop it.

I looked diagonally at the clump of trees by the lake. It was the only place where there was any kind of cover. But so what, if that cover vanished at the fence? Then something caught my eye just to the left, and I turned to look.

A white van pulled up and parked by the padlocked gate and a figure got out, wearing a lime-green shirt with matching cap and carrying a toolbox, very visible even from far away. The figure walked to the gate, set down the toolbox, and knelt down at the chain.

Of course. The best way to be invisible is to be completely, obviously visible. I am scenery; I belong here. I am just here to fix the fence, and there is no need to look at me at all, ha ha.

I started the car. Moving slowly back

around the perimeter, keeping my eye on that bright green blob, I felt the cold wings unfold in me. I had him — right where he was supposed to be. But of course, I couldn't just park and jump out; I would have to approach cautiously, assuming he knew what my car looked like, taking for granted that he would have both eyes wide open and watching for the possibility of Dexter.

So slow down, think this through; don't simply count on the dark wings to carry you over all obstacles. Look carefully, and notice things: like, Weiss had his back to the van — and the van was parked sideways, nose in to the fence, blocking off the view of the pond. Because obviously nothing could come at him from that side.

Which naturally meant that Dexter would.

Driving slowly and taking great care not to attract any attention, I turned the car around and headed back to the south side of the school grounds. I followed the fence to the end, where the road ended and the pond began. I parked at the very end of the road in front of the metal barricade, invisible to Weiss at the padlocked gate, and got out. I moved quickly to the narrow path between the lake and the fence and hurried forward.

From the distant school building the bell rang. School was over for the day and Weiss would have to make his move now. I could see him, still kneeling at the padlock. I didn't see the large handles of a bolt cutter sticking up, and it would take him a few minutes either to pick the lock or cut it. But once inside he could simply move along the fence leisurely, pretending to inspect the chain link. I reached the edge of the clump of trees and hurried through. I stepped carefully over small heaps of garbage — beer cans, plastic soda bottles, chicken bones, and other, less pleasant objects — and came to the far end, pausing only for a moment at the last tree to make sure that Weiss was still there, fiddling with the lock. The van was in the way and I could not see him, but as far as I could tell the gate was still closed. I took a deep breath, drawing in the darkness and letting it flow through me, and then I stepped out into the bright sun.

I moved to the right, almost at a run, to come at him from the rear, around the back end of the van. Silently, carefully, feeling the stretch of dark wings all around me, I crossed the space to the van, came around the back end, and paused as I saw the figure kneeling by the gate.

He looked back over his shoulder and saw

me. "Whus hapnin'," the man said. He was about fifty, black, and very definitely not Weiss.

"Oh," I said, with my usual wit. "Hello."

"Damn kids put Super Glue in the lock," he said, turning back around to face the lock.

"What were they thinking?" I said politely. But I never got to find out what they were thinking, because far away across the field, in the street in front of the main gate, I heard the sound of car horns, followed by the crunch of metal. And much closer at hand, actually inside my head, in fact, I heard a voice hissing, *Stupid!* And without pausing to wonder how I knew that the accident had been Weiss ramming Rita, I jumped up onto the fence, hooked myself over to the other side, and took off at a run across the playing field.

"Hey!" the man at the lock called, but for once I did not mind my manners and wait to hear what he had to say.

Of course Weiss would not cut the lock — he didn't need to. Of course he didn't have to get into the school and try to outwit or overcome hundreds of wary teachers and savage children. All he had to do was wait outside in the traffic, like a shark swimming the edge of the reef and waiting for Nemo to swim out. Of course.

I ran hard. The field seemed a little un-even, but it was all short and well-kept grass and I was able to hit a very good pace. I was just congratulating myself on being in good enough shape to stay at top speed when I raised my eyes for a moment to see what was going on. It was not a good idea; my foot caught on something almost in-stantly and I pitched face forward at a really wonderful velocity. I tucked into a ball and rolled through a somersault and a half before I flopped out flat on my back on top of something lumpy. I jumped up and took off running again, with a slight limp from a twisted ankle, and a vague picture of a fire-ant mound, now flattened by my human cannonball act.

Closer now; voices raised in alarm and panic from the street — and then a scream of pain. I could see nothing but a jumble of cars and a clot of people straining forward to look at something in the middle of the road. I went through the small gate in the fence, onto the sidewalk, and around to the front of the school. I had to slow down to work my way through the crowd of kids, teachers, and parents, clustered at the pickup spot at the front door, but I pushed through as quickly as I could and on out into the street. I moved back up to a run to cover the last hundred and fifty feet or so, to where traffic had stopped and coalesced around two cars that had come together in an untidy clump. One of them was Weiss's bronze-colored Honda. The other car was Rita's.

There was no sign of Weiss. But Rita herself leaned against the front bumper of her car with a look of numb shock on her face, holding Cody by one hand and Astor by the other. Seeing them all together, safe and sound, I slowed to a walk for the last few paces. She looked at me with no change in expression. "Dexter," she said. "What are you doing here?"

"I was just in the neighborhood," I said. "Ouch." And the *ouch* was not mere random cleverness: all across my back, dozens of fire ants I had apparently picked up when I fell bit me at the same time as if by some telepathic signal. "Is everyone all right?" I said, pulling frantically to get my shirt off.

I pulled the shirt over my head to see the three of them staring at me with a look of mildly annoyed concern. "Are *you* okay?" Astor said. "Because you just took your shirt off in the middle of the street."

"Fire ants," I said. "All over my back." I slapped at my back with the shirt, which

317

did no good at all.

"A man rammed us with his car," Rita said. "And he tried to grab the children."

"Yes, I know," I said, twisting myself into shapes a pretzel would envy as I tried to get at the fire ants.

"What do you mean, you know?" Rita said.

"He got away," a voice said behind us. "Moved pretty fast, considering." I turned in mid–ant slap to see a uniformed cop, panting from his apparent chase of Weiss. He was a youngish guy, rather fit-looking, and his name tag said LEAR. He had stopped and was staring at me. "This isn't clothing optional here, pal," he said.

"Fire ants," I said. "Rita, could you give me a hand, please?"

"You know this guy?" the cop asked Rita.

"My husband," she said, and she let go of the children's hands, somewhat reluctantly, and began to slap at my back.

"Well," Lear said, "anyway, the guy got away. He ran clear over to U.S. 1 and headed for the strip malls. I called it in, they'll do a BOLO, but . . ." He shrugged. "Gotta say he ran pretty good for having a pencil stuck in his leg."

"My pencil," Cody said with his strange and very rare smile.

"AND I punched him really hard in the crotch," Astor said.

I looked down at the two of them through my red cloud of ant-bite pain. They looked so smug and pleased with themselves; and to be honest, I was very pleased with them, too. Weiss had done his worst — and theirs was just a bit worse. My little predators. It was almost enough to stop the ant bites from hurting. But only almost — especially since Rita was smacking the bites as well as the ants, causing added pain.

"Got yourself a couple of real scouts here," Officer Lear said, looking at Cody and Astor with an expression of slightly worried approval.

"Just Cody," Astor said. "And he's only been to one meeting."

Officer Lear opened his mouth, realized he had nothing to say, and closed it again. He turned to me instead and said, "The tow truck will be here in a couple of minutes. And EMS will want to take a look, just to make sure everybody's okay."

"We're *okay*," said Astor.

"So," Lear went on, "if you wanna stay with your family, I can maybe get this traffic going?"

"I think that will be all right," I said. Lear looked at Rita and raised an eyebrow, and she nodded.

"Yes," she said. "Of course."

"All right," he said. "The feds will probably want to talk to you. I mean, about the attempted kidnapping."

"Oh my God," Rita said, as if hearing that word made it all real.

"I think the guy was just a random crazy," I said hopefully. After all, I already had enough trouble without the FBI looking into my family life.

Lear was not impressed. He looked at me very sternly. "It's KIDnapping," he said. "With your *kids.*" He stared at me for a moment to make sure I knew that word, then turned and waggled his finger at Rita. "Make sure you all see the EMS people." He looked back at me with no expression. "And maybe you better get dressed, all right?" And then he turned and stepped out into the street and began to wave at the cars in an attempt to get traffic moving again.

"I think I got them all," Rita said with a last slap at my back. "Give me your shirt." She took it, shook it out vigorously, and handed it back to me. "Here, you better put this back on," she said, and although I could not imagine why all of Miami was suddenly so obsessed with fighting partial nudity, I put the shirt back on, after looking suspiciously inside for any lingering fire ants.

When I poked my head out of the shirt and into the daylight again, Rita had already grabbed Cody and Astor by the hand again. "Dexter," she said. "You said — how could you, I mean . . . Why are you here?"

I was not sure how little I could tell her and still answer satisfactorily, and unfortunately, I didn't think I could just clutch at my head and moan again — I was pretty sure I'd worn that out yesterday. And to say that the Passenger and I had agreed that Weiss would come here and take the children because that's what we would have done in his place probably would not go down well, either. So I decided to try a rather diluted version of the truth. "It, ah — it's this guy who blew up the house yesterday," I said. "I just had a hunch that he might try again." Rita just looked at me. "I mean, to grab the kids as a way to get at me."

"But you're not even a real policeman," Rita said with a certain amount of outrage in her voice, as if somebody had broken a basic rule. "Why would he try to get at you?"

It was a good point, particularly since in her world — and generally speaking, in my world, too — blood spatter experts don't end up in blood feuds. "I think it's about Deborah," I said. After all, she *was* a real policeman, and she wasn't here to contradict me. "It's somebody she was after when she got stabbed and I was there."

"And so now he tries to hurt my children?" she said. "Because Deborah tried to arrest him?"

"That's the criminal mind," I said. "It doesn't work like yours." Of course, it actually *did* work like mine, and right now the criminal mind was working on a thought about what Weiss might have left behind in his car. He had not expected to flee on foot — it was quite possible that there was some kind of hint in the car about where he would go and what his next move would be. And more — there might be some kind of horrible clue that pointed a blood-soaked finger in my direction. With that thought, I realized I needed to go through his car now, while Lear was busy and before any other cops arrived on the scene.

And seeing that Rita was still looking at me expectantly, I said, "He's crazy. We may never really understand what he's thinking." She looked nearly convinced, so in the belief that a quick exit was often the most persuasive argument, I nodded at Weiss's car. "I should probably see if he left anything important. Before the tow truck gets here." And I stepped around the hood of Rita's car and up to the front door of Weiss's, which was hanging open.

The front seat held the usual assortment of car garbage. Gum wrappers littered the floor, a water bottle lay on the seat, an ashtray held a handful of quarters for tolls. No butcher knives, bone saws, or bombs; nothing interesting at all. I was just about to slide into the car and open the glove compartment when I noticed a large notebook on the backseat. It was an artist's sketchbook, with the edges of several loose pages sticking out, all held together with a large rubber band, and as I saw it the voice in the back of Dexter's Dark Room called out, *Bingo!*

I stepped out of the car and tried to open the back door. It was jammed shut, dented in from impact with Rita's car. So I knelt on the front seat and leaned over, grabbing the notebook and pulling it out. A siren wailed nearby, and I stepped away from Weiss's car and moved over next to Rita, clutching the book to my chest.

"What is it?" she said.

"I don't know," I said. "Let's have a look."

And thinking only innocent thoughts, I removed the rubber band. A loose page fluttered to the ground and Astor pounced on it. "Dexter," she said. "This looks just like you."

"That's not possible," I said, taking the page from her hand.

But it was possible. It was a nice drawing, very well done, showing a man from the waist up, in a kind of mock-heroic Rambo-esque pose, holding a large knife that dripped blood, and there was no doubt about it.

It was me.

Twenty-Seven

I only had a few seconds to admire the splendid likeness of myself. And then, in rapid succession, Cody said, "Cool," Rita said, "Let me see," and — happiest of all — the ambulance arrived. In the confusion that followed I managed to slip the portrait back into the notebook and usher my little family over to talk to the medical techs for a brief but thorough examination. And although they were reluctant to admit it, they could find no severed limbs, missing skulls, or mangled internal organs at all and so, eventually, they were forced to allow Rita and the kids to go, with dire warnings about what to watch out for just in case.

The damage to Rita's car was mostly cosmetic — one headlight was broken and the fender was pushed in — so I bundled the three of them into the car. Normally, Rita would drop them at an after-school program and go back to work, but there is an unwritten law granting you the rest of the day off when you and your children are attacked by a maniac, so she decided to take them all home to recover from the trauma. And since Weiss was still out there somewhere, we decided that I had better do the same, and come home to protect them. So I waved them away into traffic and started the long and weary walk back to where I had parked my car.

My ankle was throbbing and the sweat that ran down my back irritated the ant bites, so in order to take my mind off the pain I flipped open Weiss's notebook and paged through it as I walked. The shock of that picture of me was past, and I needed to find out what it meant — and where it might be leading Weiss. I was reasonably sure it was not a mere doodle, something he had absentmindedly scratched out while talking on the telephone. After all, who did he have left to talk to? His lover Doncevic was dead, and he had killed his dear pal Wimble himself. Besides, everything he had done so far had been pointed at a very specific purpose, and without exception it had been a purpose that I could do without quite happily.

So I studied the drawing of me again. It was idealized, I suppose — I could not remember noticing that I had such clearly defined washboard abs when last I looked. And the overall impression of a vast and happy menace was, while perhaps accurate, something I tried very hard not to show. But I had to admit he had captured something here, possibly even suitable for framing.

I went through the other pages. It was quite interesting stuff, and the drawings were good, especially the ones that featured me. I was sure I didn't look that noble, happy, and savage, but perhaps that was what artistic license is all about. And as I looked at the other drawings and began to get an idea of what it was all leading up to, I was also quite sure that I didn't like it, no matter how flattering. Not at all.

Many of the drawings showed ideas for ways to decorate anonymous bodies in the spirit of what Weiss had already done. There was one that featured a woman with six breasts; where the extras would come from was not mentioned. She was wearing a flamboyant feathered hat and a thong, the kind of costume we had seen at the Moulin Rouge in Paris. It hid almost nothing, but made everything seem so glamorous, and the effect of the sequined bras that barely covered all six breasts was absolutely riveting.

The next page had a letter-size piece of paper wedged into the binding. I took it out and unfolded it. It was an airline schedule from Cubana de Aviación, printed from a computer and listing its flights from Havana to Mexico. It was tucked in with a drawing that depicted a man wearing a straw hat and holding an oar. A line had been drawn through it and next to it in bold and neat block letters was written REFUGEE! I shoved the Aviación printout back in and flipped the page. The next page showed a man with an opened body cavity stuffed with what appeared to be cigars and rum bottles. He was propped up in a vintage convertible car with the top down.

But by far the more interesting drawings — at least to me — were the series featuring one strong central image of Dauntless Dimpled Dexter. It may not say a great deal about me that I found these pictures of myself so much more compelling than the ones that featured butchered strangers, but there is something endlessly fascinating about looking at drawings of yourself you've discovered in a homicidal psychopath's notebook. In any case, it was this final series that took my breath away. And if Weiss actually created this, it would take my breath away literally and forever.

Because these, done in much more detail, were taken from the film loop that showed me working on Doncevic. They were accurately copied, showing almost exactly what I remembered from seeing that video so many times; almost. In several of the frames, Weiss had sketched in a slight change of angle so that the face showed.

My face.

Attached to the body doing all the chopping.

And just to underscore the threat, Weiss had written in PHOTOSHOP underneath these pictures, underlining it. I am not really current on video technology, but I can put two and two together as well as anyone else. Photoshop is a program for manipulating film images, and you could use it to alter the images, put in things that didn't belong. I had to assume it could be done just as easily with video. And I knew Weiss had enough video to last for several wicked lifetimes — video of me, and Cody, and gawkers at crime scenes, and Dark Passenger knows what else.

So he was clearly going to modify the clip of me working on Doncevic so that my face showed. As well as I was coming to know

Weiss, or at least his handiwork, I knew this would not be a make-work project. He was going to use this to make some lovely piece of decoration that would destroy me. And all because of an hour's frolic with his sweetheart, Doncevic.

I had done it, of course, and rather enjoyed it, too. But this seemed like cheating — it was unfair to put my face in after the fact, wasn't it? Especially since, added afterward or not, it would be more than enough to start a series of very awkward questions coming my way.

The final drawing was the most terrifying of all. It showed a giant and wickedly smiling Dexter from the film loop raising up the power saw, projected onto the facade of a large building, while below him on the ground crouched what appeared to be a half-dozen or so ornamental corpses, all adorned with the sort of accessories that Weiss had used on his other bodies so far. The whole thing was framed by a double row of royal-palm trees, and it was such a beautiful picture of tropical and artistic splendor that it might have brought a tear to my eye if modesty hadn't interfered.

It all made perfect sense in a Weiss-y sort of way. Use the film he already had, subtly changed to feature *moi* in a starring role, and project it onto a very public building so there could be no doubt at all that we were seeing Decapitating Dexter at work. Throw me to the sharks *and* at the same time create a large communal artwork for all to admire. A perfect solution.

I arrived at my car and sat in the driver's seat, looking through the notebook one more time. Of course it was possible that these were just sketches, a paper-and-pencil fantasy that would never see the light of day. But this had all started with Weiss and Doncevic making public displays out of bodies, and the only difference here was one of scale — that and the fact that at some point in the last few days Dexter had become Weiss's art-fair project. The *Mona Dexter.*

And now Weiss planned to make me a great public-works project, too. Dexter the Magnificent, who doth bestride the world like a Colossus, many lovely corpses at his feet, brought to you in living color just in time for the evening news. Oh, Mama, who is that large and handsome man with the bloody saw? Why, that's Dexter Morgan, dear, the horrible man they arrested a little while ago. But Mama, why is he smiling? He likes his work, dear. Let that be a lesson to you — always find a worthy job that keeps you happy.

I had learned enough in college to appreciate the fact that a civilization is judged by its art. It was humbling to think that, if Weiss is successful, future generations would look back on the twenty-first century and weigh its accomplishments with my image. This kind of immortality was a very tempting idea — but there were a few drawbacks to this particular invitation to eternal fame. First of all, I am far too modest, and second — well, there was the whole thing about people discovering what I really am. People like Coulter and Salguero, for example. Which they certainly would, if this video of my image was projected onto a large public building with a pile of corpses at its feet. Really a lovely thought, but unfortunately it would lead these people to ask certain questions, make a few connections, and before long the meal of the day would be Cream of Dexter Soup, lovingly cooked on Old Sparky and served up to you on the front page of the *Herald.*

No, this was very flattering, but I was not really prepared to become a living icon of twenty-first-century art. With all possible reluctance, I would have to extend my regrets and decline the honor.

And how?

It was a fair question, after all. The pic-

tures told me what Weiss wanted to do —
but they told me nothing about how far
along his plans were, or when he wanted to
do it, or even where —

But wait a minute: they did tell me where.
I turned to the last picture again, the one
that showed the whole lunatic project in
brightly colored detail. The drawing of the
building that served as a projection screen
was very specific and looked familiar — and
the two rows of royal palms I had seen
somewhere before, I was quite sure. Someplace I had actually been, too; but where
and when? I stared at the picture and let
my giant brain whirl. I had been there in
the not-too-distant past. Perhaps only a year
or so before I got married?

And with that one word, *married*, I remembered. It had been just about a year and a
half ago. Rita's friend from work, Anna, had
gotten married. It had been a lavish and
remarkably expensive wedding, owing to the
bride's family's wealth, and Rita and I had
attended the reception at a ridiculously posh
old hotel called The Breakers in Palm
Beach. The building pictured here was
unmistakably the front of The Breakers.

Wonderful; now I knew exactly where
Weiss planned to set up this noble Dexterama. So what did I do with that knowledge?

I couldn't very well stake out the hotel night and day for the next three months and wait for Weiss to show up with the first load of bodies. But I also couldn't afford to do nothing. Sooner or later he would either set it up or — or was it possible that this was another trap of some kind, intended only to draw me away to Palm Beach while Weiss did something else down here in Dade County?

But that was silly; he hadn't planned to limp away over the horizon with a pencil in his leg and the imprint of a small fist in his crotch, leaving his drawings behind. This was his plan, for better or worse — and I had to believe it was for worse, at least as far as my reputation was concerned. So the only remaining question was: When did he plan to do it? The only answer I could come up with was "soon," and that really didn't seem specific enough.

There was really no other way — I would have to take some time off from work and wait at the hotel. That meant leaving Rita and the kids alone and I didn't like that, but I could not see anything else to do. Weiss had been moving very fast, from one idea to the next, and I thought he would most likely concentrate on this one project and act quickly. It was a huge gamble, but it was certainly worth it if I could stop him from projecting a giant image of me onto the front of The Breakers.

All right; I would do it. When Weiss began in Palm Beach, I would be there waiting for him. And with that settled, I flipped open the notebook for one last look at handsome Comic-Book Dexter. But before I could really sink into a self-admiring trance, a car pulled up next to mine and a man get out.

It was Coulter.

TWENTY-EIGHT

Detective Coulter came around the rear end of his car and paused, looked at me, and then went back to the driver's side of his car and disappeared for a moment. I used the time to slip the notebook under my seat, and Coulter popped right back up and again came around the tail end of the car, this time with his two-liter bottle of Mountain Dew dangling from the end of his index finger. He leaned his backside against his car, looked at me, and took a large sip of soda. Then he wiped his mouth on the back of his arm.

"You weren't in your office," he said.

"No, I wasn't," I said. After all, here I was.

"So when the call comes on the radio, it's your wife, I look in to tell you," he said, and he shrugged. "You're not there. You're here already, right?" He didn't wait for an answer, which was just as well, since I didn't have one. Instead, he took another swig from his soda bottle, wiped his mouth again, and said, "Same school where we got that Scout leader guy, too, huh?"

"That's right."

"But you were already here when it happened?" he said, trying to look innocently surprised. "How'd that happen, anyway?"

I was very sure that telling Coulter I'd had a hunch would not make him want to shake my hand and congratulate me. So launching myself off my legendary wit once again, I heard myself saying, "I thought I'd come down and surprise Rita and the kids."

Coulter nodded as if he found that very believable. "Surprise 'em," he said. "Guess somebody else beat you to it."

"Yes," I said carefully. "It certainly looks like it."

He took another long pull on the soda bottle, but this time he didn't wipe his mouth; he just turned and stared back at the main road where the tow truck was now hauling away Weiss's car. "You got any idea who that might have been that did this to your wife and kids?" he said without looking back at me.

"No," I said. "I guess I just assumed it was, you know. An accident?"

"Huh," he said, and now he was staring at me. "An accident. Jeez, I hadn't even thought of that one. 'Cause, you know. It's the same school where that Cub Scout guy was killed. And also it's you here again. So, hey. An accident. Really? You think?"

"I . . . I just — why wouldn't it be?" I have practiced a lifetime, and my expression of surprise was certainly a very good one, but Coulter didn't look terribly convinced.

"This guy Donkeywit," he said.

"Doncevic," I said.

"Whatever." He shrugged. "Looks like he's disappeared. You know anything about that?"

"Why would I know about that?" I said, putting as much astonishment on my face as I could.

"Just skipped bail, run away from his boyfriend, and disappeared," he said. "Why would he do that?"

"I really don't know," I said.

"You ever read, Dexter?" he said, and the way he used my first name worried me — it sounded like he was talking to a suspect. And of course he was, but I was still hoping he wouldn't think of me that way.

"Read?" I said. "Um, not a whole lot, no. Why?"

"I like to read," he said. And then, apparently shifting gears, he went on, "Once is happenstance, twice is coincidence, three

338

times is enemy action."

"Excuse me?" I said. He had lost me somewhere around "I like to read."

"It's from *Goldfinger*," he said. "Where he's telling James Bond, I come across you three times where you don't belong, it ain't a coincidence." He sipped, wiped his mouth, and watched me sweat. "Love that book. Must of read it like three, four times," he said.

"I haven't read it," I said politely.

"So we got you here," he went on. "And we got you at the house that blows up. And that's two times we shouldn't have you anywhere around. Am I s'posed to think that's coincidence?"

"What else would it be?" I said.

He just looked without blinking. Then he took another sip of his Mountain Dew. "I don't know," he said at last. "But I know what Goldfinger would say it is if there's a third time."

"Well, let's hope there isn't," I said, and I truly meant it this time.

"Yeah," he said. He nodded, stuck his index finger back into the mouth of the soda bottle, and stood up. "Let's just hope the shit out of that," he said. He turned away, walked back around his car, got in, and drove away.

If I had been a little bit more of a fond observer of human foible I'm sure I would have taken great joy in discovering new depths in Detective Coulter. How wonderful to find that he was a devotee of the literary arts! But the joy of this discovery was diminished by the fact that I really had no interest in what Coulter did with his time, provided he did it away from me. I had barely gotten Sergeant Doakes off perpetual Dexter watch, and now here came Coulter to take his place. It was like I was the victim of some strange and sinister Dexter-persecuting Tibetan sect — whenever the old Dexter-hating Lama died, a new one was born to take his place.

But there was very little I could do about that right now. I was about to become a major work of art, and at the moment that was a far more pressing problem. I got into my car, started the engine, and drove home.

When I got to the house, I had to stand outside and knock for several minutes, since Rita had decided to fasten the security chain on the inside of the door. I suppose I was lucky that she had not piled the couch and the refrigerator in front of the door as well. Possibly that was only because she needed to use the couch; she had huddled on it with the two children clutched tightly to her, one

on each side, and after letting me in —
somewhat reluctantly — she resumed her
position, throwing a protective arm around
each child. Cody and Astor had almost
identical looks of annoyed boredom on their
faces. Apparently, cringing in terror in the
living room was not the sort of quality
bonding time they truly appreciated.

"You took so long," Rita said as she slid
the chain back on the door.

"I had to talk to a detective," I said.

"Well, but," she said, sliding back onto
the couch between the children. "I mean,
we were worried."

"WE weren't worried," Astor said, rolling
her eyes at her mother.

"Because I mean, that man could be
anywhere right now," Rita said. "He could
be right outside, right now." And even
though none of us really believed that —
not even Rita — all four of us swiveled our
heads to the door for a look. Happily for us,
he wasn't there, at least not as far as we
could tell by trying to look through a closed
and locked door.

"Please, Dexter," Rita said, and the edge
of fear was so sharp in her voice I could
smell it. "Please, this is — what is . . . why
is this happening? I can't —" She made
several large but incomplete motions with

her hands and then dropped them into her lap. "This has to stop," she said. "Make it stop."

In all honesty, I could only think of a few things I would rather do than make it stop — and several of those things could easily be part of making it stop, just as soon as I caught Weiss. But before I could really concentrate on making happy plans, the doorbell rang.

Rita responded by lurching up into the air and then settling back down again with one child pulled in tight on each side of her. "Oh God," she said. "Who could that be?"

I was pretty sure it was not a Mormon Youth Ministry, but I just said, "I'll get it," and went to the door. Just to be safe, I peeked through the little spy hole — Mormons can be so persistent — and what I saw was even scarier.

Sergeant Doakes stood on my doorstep.

He was clutching the little silver computer that now spoke for him, and at his elbow was a clean-cut middle-aged woman in a gray suit, and even though she was not wearing a fedora, I was reasonably sure she was the fed I had been threatened with, to investigate the attempted kidnapping.

Looking at the two of them and thinking of all the trouble they might represent, I actually considered leaving the door bolted and pretending we weren't home. But it was an idle thought; I have found that the faster you run from trouble, the quicker it catches you, and I was quite sure that if I did not let in Doakes and his new friend, they would be right back with a warrant, and probably Coulter and Salguero as well. So thinking unhappy thoughts and trying to settle my face into the right mixture of surprise and weary shock, I opened the door.

"Move. It. Motherfucker!" Doakes's cheerful artificial baritone voice called out as he stabbed his claw three times at the keyboard of his little silver box.

The fed put a restraining hand on him, and then glanced back at me. "Mr. Morgan?" she said. "Can we come in?" She held up her credentials patiently while I looked at them; apparently she was Special Agent Brenda Recht of the FBI. "Sergeant Doakes offered to bring me down here to talk to you," she said, and I thought about what a nice thing that was for Doakes to do.

"Of course you can come in," I said, and then I had one of those happy inspirations that sometimes come at just the right time and I added, "But the children have had such a shock — and Sergeant Doakes kind of scares them. Can he wait out here?"

"Motherfucker!" Doakes said, sounding like he was happily calling out, Howdy, neighbor!

"Also, his language is a bit rough for the kids," I added.

Special Agent Recht glanced at Doakes. As an FBI agent, she could not admit that anything scared her, even Doakes the cyborg, but she looked like she thought that was a very good idea. "Sure," she said. "Why don't you wait out here, Sergeant?"

Doakes glared at me for a very long moment, and in the dark distance I could almost hear the angry scream of his Passenger. But all he did was raise one silver claw, glance at his keyboard, and punch one of his prerecorded sentences. "I am still watching you, motherfucker," the cheerful voice assured me.

"That's fine," I said. "But watch me through the door, all right?" I motioned Recht inside, and as she brushed past Doakes and came in, I closed the door behind her, leaving an unblinking Doakes to glare at the outside of the door.

"He doesn't seem to like you," Special Agent Recht observed, and I was impressed with her keen eye for detail.

"No," I said. "I think he blames me for

what happened to him," which was at least partly true, even though he had disliked me well before he lost his hands, feet, and tongue.

"Uh-huh," she said, and although I could see she was thinking about that, she didn't say anything more on the subject. Instead, she moved on over to the couch, where Rita still sat clutching Cody and Astor. "Mrs. Morgan?" she said, holding up her credentials again. "Special Agent Recht, FBI. Can I ask you a few questions about what happened this afternoon?"

"FBI?" Rita said, as guiltily as if she was sitting on stolen bearer bonds. "But that's — why would — yes, of course."

"Do you have a gun?" Astor said.

Recht looked at her with a sort of wary fondness. "Yes, I do," she said.

"Do you get to shoot people with it?"

"Only if I have to," Recht said. She glanced around and found the nearby easy chair. "Can I sit down and ask you a few questions?"

"Oh," Rita said. "I'm so sorry. I was only — yes, please sit down."

Recht settled herself onto the edge of the chair and looked at me before addressing Rita. "Tell me what happened," she said, and when Rita hesitated, she went on, "You had the kids in the car, you pulled out onto U.S. 1 . . ."

"He just, he came out of nowhere," Rita said.

"Boom," Cody added softly, and I looked at him with surprise. He was smiling just a little, which was equally alarming. Rita looked at him with dismay, and then went on.

"He hit us," she said. "And while I was still — before I could — he just, he was there at the door, grabbing at the children."

"I punched him in the crotch," Astor said. "And Cody stabbed him with a pencil."

Cody frowned at her. "I stabbed *first,*" he said.

"Whatever," Astor said.

Recht looked at the two of them with mild astonishment. "Good for you both," she said.

"And then the policeman came over and he ran away," Astor said, and Rita nodded.

"And how did you come to be there, Mr. Morgan?" she said, swinging her head toward me with no warning.

I had known that she would ask this, of course, but I had still not come up with any really socko answer. My claim to Coulter that I had wanted to surprise Rita had fallen very, very flat, and Special Agent Recht seemed to be considerably sharper — and she was looking at me expectantly as the seconds ticked by, waiting for a sane and logical reply that I did not have. I had to say something, and soon; but what?

"Um," I mumbled, "I don't know if you heard I had a concussion . . . ?"

The interview with Special Agent Brenda Recht of the FBI will never appear on any highlight reel that wants my endorsement. She did not seem to believe that I had gone home early because I felt bad, stopping at the school because it was that time of day — and I can't really say I blamed her. It sounded remarkably feeble, but since it was all I could come up with, I had to stick with it.

She also seemed to have trouble accepting my statement that whoever had attacked Rita and the children was a random maniac, the product of road rage, Miami traffic, and too much Cuban coffee. She did, however, finally accept that she was not going to get any other answer. She stood up at last, looking at me with an expression that might best be called thoughtful. "All right, Mr. Morgan," she said. "Something doesn't quite add up here, but I guess you're not going to tell me what it is."

"There's really nothing to tell," I said, perhaps too modestly. "These things happen all the time in Miami."

"Uh-huh," she said. "The problem is, they seem to be happening around you an awful lot."

Somehow, I stopped myself from saying, "If you only knew . . ." and I ushered her to the front door.

"We'll keep a cop posted here for a couple of days, for safety's sake," she said, which was not really welcome news, and with unfortunate timing, as she said it I swung open the door to reveal Sergeant Doakes in almost the exact position we had left him, staring malevolently at the door. I said my fond good-byes to them both, and as I closed the door the last thing I saw was Doakes's unblinking glare, for all the world like the Cheshire cat's evil twin.

The FBI's interest had done very little to make Rita feel better, however. She still clutched at the children and spoke in jangled half sentences. So I reassured her the best I could, and for a while we all sat there together on the couch, until finally the squirming of Cody and Astor made it too difficult to sit all together like that. Rita gave up and put on a DVD for them to watch and went into the kitchen, where she began her alternative comfort therapy by rattling pots and pans, and I went down the hall to the small extra room she called "Dexter's Office" to look at Weiss's sketchbook again and think dark thoughts.

The list of people who could not be considered friendly was certainly growing: Doakes, Coulter, Salguero, and now the FBI.

And of course, Weiss himself. He was still out there, and he still wanted to get at me to get his revenge. Would he come after the children again, limping out of the shadows to grab them, perhaps wearing Kevlar pants and a groin protector this time? If so, I would have to stay with the kids until it was over, which was not the best way to catch him — especially not if he tried something different. And if he wanted to kill me, staying with Cody and Astor endangered them; judging by his exploding-house trick, he clearly didn't worry about collateral damage.

But I did — I had to. I was worried about the children, and protecting them was a top priority. It was a very strange epiphany, to realize that I was concerned with their safety as much as with protecting my secret identity. It did not fit with how I thought of myself, how I had built up my careful self-image. Of course I had always taken special delight in tracking down predators who preyed on children, but I had never really thought about why that was. And certainly I planned to do my duty to Cody and Astor, both as their stepfather and, far more importantly, as their guide onto the Harry Path. But to see myself spinning in mother-hen circles at the thought of someone trying to hurt them was new and somewhat unsettling.

So stopping Weiss was important in a brand-new way. I was Daddy Dexter now, and I had to do it for the children, as well as for myself, and I was experiencing a surge of something dangerously close to emotion at the thought of any attempt to harm them.

All right then, I clearly had to figure out Weiss's next move and try to stop him before he could pull it off. I picked up his notebook and flipped through the drawings one more time, perhaps unconsciously hoping I had missed something before — an address where I could find Weiss, perhaps, or even a suicide note. But the pages were still the same, and truthfully the novelty had worn off and I took no real joy in looking at the pictures of me. I have never been all that interested in looking at me, and looking at me in a series of pictures intended to depict me-as-I-really-am to the world at large took any possible vestigial joy out of it.

And what was the point of all this? To expose me? To create a great work of art? I paused and studied several of the detailed drawings, the ones depicting the other elements of the display. It may sound self-centered for me to say so since, after all, they were competing for space with the pictures of me, but they were really not very interesting. You could probably call them clever, but no more. They lacked any real originality and seemed rather lifeless — even for dead bodies.

And to be brutally honest, even the pictures of me were something any talented high school kid might have done. They might be projected in huge scale on the front of The Breakers Hotel, but they were not in the same class as anything I had seen so recently in Paris — not even the stuff in the small galleries. Of course, there was that last piece, *Jennifer's Leg*. It had used amateurish videos, too — but there the whole point had been the audience's reaction and not the . . .

For a moment there was absolute silence in Dexter's brain, a silence so thick it obscured everything else. And then it rolled away to reveal a jabbering little monkey of a thought.

Audience reaction.

If you were interested in the reaction, then the quality of the work is not so important, as long as it provokes shock. And you would arrange to capture that reaction — for example, on videotape. And perhaps you would have the services of a video professional — someone like, just for example, Kenneth Wimble, whose house Weiss had blown up. It made much more sense to think of Wimble as one of them, rather than a random victim.

And when Weiss had made the jump to full-scale murder, instead of stealing bodies to play with, Wimble had probably gotten squeamish, and Weiss had blown him up in his own house at the same time that he tried to take out irreplaceable me.

But Weiss was still video-ing, even without his expert. Because that was what this was about for him. He wanted pictures of people seeing what he had done. More and more he wanted to do it, too — with the Scout leader and with Wimble and the attempt on me. But the video, that was what mattered. And he would happily kill to get it.

No wonder the Dark Passenger had been bemused. Ours was very much a hands-on kind of art, and the results were extremely private. Weiss was different. He might want his revenge on me, but he would happily take it indirectly, something the Passenger and I would never consider. To Weiss, the art still mattered. He needed his pictures.

I looked at the last large, full-color rendering of ME projected onto The Breakers Hotel. The picture was clearly drawn and you could easily see the basic architecture of the place. The front was U-shaped, with the front door in the center and a wing sticking forward on each side. There was a long mall leading up to the front door, with its rows of royal-palm trees, a perfect place for a crowd to gather and gape in horror. Weiss would be there somewhere in the crowd with his camera, getting pictures of the faces. But as I looked at the picture I realized that even before that, he would want to get a room in one of the wings overlooking the front, where the projection was displayed, and he would set up a camera there, something like one of the remote cameras he had used already but this time with a really good lens, to capture the faces of the people seeing it.

The whole trick would be to stop him before he set things up — stop him when he arrived at the hotel. And to do that, all I had to do was find out when he checked in. That would be very simple if only I had access to the hotel's records — which I didn't — or knew a way to force my way into them — which I didn't. But as I thought about it, I realized something.

I knew somebody who did.

TWENTY-NINE

Kyle Chutsky sat across from me at the same small corner table in the snack bar located on the ground floor of the coffee shop at the hospital. In spite of the fact that I didn't think he'd left the grounds in several days, he was clean-shaven and wore what seemed to be a clean shirt, and he looked across the table at me with a look of amusement that moved the corners of his mouth up and crinkled the skin around his eyes but did not touch the eyes themselves, which stayed cold and watchful.

"That's funny," he said. "You want me to help you hack into registration at this hotel, The Breakers? Ha." He gave a short laugh that was not very convincing. "Why do you think I can help you do that?"

Unfortunately, it was a fair question. I did not, in fact, *know* that he could help me, not based on anything he had said or done. But the little I did know about Chutsky indicated that he was a member in good standing of the shadow government, the deliberately nonmonitored and unconnected clan of people who worked for various alphabet agencies that were more or less affiliated with the federal government, and sometimes even with one another. And as such, I was quite confident that he would know any number of ways to find out when Weiss registered at the hotel.

But there was the small problem of protocol, that I was not supposed to know and he was not supposed to admit it. And to get past that I had to impress him with something that was urgent enough to overcome his instinctive reluctance. I can think of almost nothing more important than the pending demise of Dashing Dexter, but somehow I did not think that Chutsky would share my high self-evaluation. He would probably put higher ratings on foolish trifles like national security, world peace, and his own relatively worthless life and limb.

But it occurred to me that he also put a very high rating on my sister, and this provided at least a potential opening. So with my best artificial manly directness I said, "Kyle — this is the guy that stabbed Deborah."

And in any scene of any macho TV show I had ever seen, that would have been more than enough; but apparently Chutsky did not watch a great deal of TV. He just raised one eyebrow and said, "So?"

"So," I said, somewhat taken aback, and trying to remember a few more specifics from those scenes on TV, "he's out there, and, um, getting away with it. Uh — and he might do it again."

This time he raised both eyebrows. "You think he might stab Deborah again?" he said.

This was really not going well, not at all the way I'd thought it would. I had assumed that there was some kind of Man-of-Action Code in place, and all I had to do was bring up the subject of direct action and express my eagerness to be up and at 'em, and Chutsky would leap to his feet equally eager and we would charge up Pork Chop Hill together. But instead, Chutsky was looking at me as if I had suggested an enema.

"How can you not want to catch this guy?" I said, and I made a little bit of awkward desperation slide into my voice.

"It's not my job," he said. "And it's not your job, either, Dexter. If you think this guy is going to check into this hotel, tell the cops. They got plenty of guys they can use to stake it out and grab him. You just got you, buddy — and don't take this wrong, but this could be a little rougher than you are used to."

"The cops will want to know how I know," I said, and I regretted it instantly.

And Chutsky picked it up just as quickly. "Okay. So how DO you know?" he said.

There comes a time when even Disingenuous Dexter has to place at least one or two cards faceup on the table, and clearly it had arrived. And so throwing my inborn inhibitions out the window, I said, "He's stalking me."

Chutsky blinked. "What does that mean?" he said.

"It means he wants me dead," I said. "He's made two tries already."

"And you think he's about to try again? At this hotel, The Breakers?"

"Yes."

"So why don't you just stay home?" he said.

I am not really being conceited when I say that I am not used to having all the cleverness on the other side of a conversation. But Chutsky was clearly leading in this dance, and Dexter was several steps behind, limping along on two left feet with blisters blossoming on heel and toe. I had walked into this with a very clear picture of Chutsky as a real two-fisted man, even though one of the fists was now a steel hook — but nevertheless the kind of gung-ho, over-the-top, damn-the-torpedoes guy who would leap into battle at the merest suggestion, especially when it concerned getting his hook on the man who had stabbed his true love, my sister Deborah. Clearly, I had miscalculated.

But this left a very large question mark: Who was Chutsky, in fact, and how did I get his help? Did I need some cunning stratagem to bend him to my will, or would I have to resort to some form of the unprecedented uncomfortable unspeakable truth? The very thought of committing honesty made me tremble in every leaf and branch — it went against everything I had ever stood for. But there seemed no way out; I would have to be at least marginally truthful.

"If I stay home," I said, "he is going to do something terrible. To me, and maybe the kids."

Chutsky stared at me, then shook his head. "You were making more sense when I thought you wanted revenge," he said. "How can he do anything to you if you're at home and he's in the hotel?"

At a certain point you really have to accept the fact that there are days when you have not brought your A game, and this was one of them. I told myself that I was most likely still suffering from my concussion, but my self answered back that this was a pitiful and now overused excuse at best, and with much more self-annoyance than I could remember experiencing for quite some time, I pulled out the notebook I had taken from Weiss's car and flipped it open to the full-color drawing of Dexter the Dominator on the front of The Breakers Hotel.

"Like this," I said. "If he can't kill me, he'll get me arrested for murder."

Chutsky studied the picture for a long moment, and then whistled quietly. "Boy howdy," he said. "And these things down here around the bottom . . . ?"

"Dead bodies," I said. "Fixed up like the ones that Deborah was investigating when this man stabbed her."

"Why would he do this?" he said.

"It's a kind of art," I said. "I mean, he thinks it is."

"Yeah, but why would he do this to YOU, buddy?"

"The guy that was arrested when Deborah was stabbed," I said. "I kicked him hard, right in the head. That was his boy-friend."

"Was?" said Chutsky. "Where is he now?"

I have never really seen the point in self-mutilation — after all, life itself is on the job and doing really well at it. But if I could have taken back that word *was* by biting down hard on my own tongue, I would cheerfully have done so. However, it had been said and I was stuck with it, and so, floundering about for a small chunk of my formerly sharp wit, I found a little piece of it and came out with, "He skipped bail and disappeared," I said.

"And this guy blames you because his boyfriend took off?"

"I guess so," I said.

Chutsky looked at me and then looked down at the drawing again. "Listen, buddy," he said. "You know this guy, and I know you gotta go with your gut feeling. It's always worked for me, nine times out of ten. But this is, I don't know." He shrugged. "Kind of, really thin, don't you think?" He flipped a finger at the picture. "But anyway, you were right about one thing. If he's going to do this, you do need my help. A lot more than you thought."

"What do you mean?" I asked politely.

Chutsky smacked the drawing with the

back of his hand. "This hotel," he said. "It isn't The Breakers. It's the Hotel Nacional. In Havana." And seeing that Dexter's mouth was hanging open in a most unbecoming way, he added, "You know, Havana. The one in Cuba."

"But that's not possible," I said. "I mean, I've been there. That's The Breakers."

He smiled at me, the irritating, superior kind of smile that I would love to try sometime when I wasn't in disguise. "You didn't read your history, did you?" he said.

"I don't think this chapter was assigned. What are you talking about?"

"Hotel Nacional and The Breakers were built from the same blueprint, to save money," he said. "They're virtually identical."

"Then why are you so sure this isn't The Breakers?"

"Lookit," Chutsky said. "Look at the old cars. Pure Cuba. And see the little golf-cart thing, with the bubble top? That's a Coco Loco, and you only find 'em there, not Palm Beach. And the vegetation. That stuff on the left? You don't see that at The Breakers. Definitely only in Havana." He dropped the notebook and leaned back. "So actually, I'd say problem solved, buddy."

"Why would you say that?" I said, irritated

both at his attitude and at the lack of any sense in what he said.

Chutsky smiled. "It's just too hard for an American to get over there," he said. "I don't think he could pull it off."

A small nickel dropped through the slot and a light went on in Dexter's brain. "He's Canadian," I said.

"All right," he said stubbornly. "So he *could* go down there." He shrugged. "But hey — you maybe don't remember that things are sort of tight down there? I mean — there's no way he gets away with anything like this —" He smacked the notebook with the back of his hand. "Not in Cuba. The cops would be all over him like . . ." Chutsky frowned and thoughtfully raised his bright silver hook toward his face. He caught himself just before he put the hook into his eye. "Unless . . ." he said.

"What?" I said.

He shook his head slightly. "This guy's pretty smart, right?"

"Well," I said grudgingly, "I know HE thinks so."

"So he's gotta know. Which maybe means . . ." Chutsky said, politely refusing to finish a sentence with anything resembling a noun. He fumbled out his phone, one of those larger ones with the bigger screen. Holding it in place on the table with his hook, he began to poke rapidly at the keyboard with a finger, muttering, "Damn . . . okay . . . Uh-huh," and other bright observations under his breath. I could see that he had Google on the screen, but nothing else was legible from across the table. "Bingo," he said at last.

"What?"

He smiled, clearly pleased with how smart he was. "They do all these festivals down there," he said. "To prove how sophisticated and free they are." He pushed the phone across the table at me. "Like this one," he said.

I pulled the phone to me and read the screen. "Festival Internacional de Artes Multimedia," I said, scrolling down.

"It starts in three days," Chutsky said. "And whatever this guy does — projectors or film clips or whatever — the cops will have orders to back off and let him do his thing. For the festival."

"And the press will be there," I said. "From all over the world."

Chutsky made a gesture with his hook that would have been putting a hand palm up, if only it was a hand. Of course, hooks don't have palms, but the meaning was still clear. "Things being what they are," he said, "it gets coverage in Miami just like it was *in* Miami."

And it was true. Miami got official and unofficial coverage of everything that happened in Havana — with more detail than we got about the happenings in Fort Lauderdale, which was right next door. So if I was implicated in Havana, I would be convicted in Miami, with the added bonus that I could do nothing about it. "Perfect," I said. And it was — Weiss had a free pass to set up his awful project, and then collect all the attention he so desperately craved, all in one gift-wrapped holiday package. Which did not seem like it could possibly be a good thing for me. Especially since he knew that I could not get to Cuba to stop him.

"All right," Chutsky said. "It might make sense. But why are you so sure he *will* go there?"

It was, unfortunately, a fair question. I thought about it. First of all, was I really sure? Casually, not wanting to startle Chutsky in any way, I sent a careful, silent question mark to the Dark Passenger. *Are we sure about this?* I asked.

Oh, yes, it said with a sharp-toothed smirk. *Quite sure.*

All right then. That was settled. Weiss

would go to Cuba to expose Dexter. But I needed something a little more convincing than silent certainty; what proof did I really have, aside from the drawings, which were probably not admissible in a court of law? It was true that some of them were very interesting — the image of the woman with the six breasts, for example, was the kind of thing that really stuck in your head.

I remembered that drawing, and this time there was a nearly audible *clang* as a very, very big nickel dropped.

There had been a piece of paper wedged into the binding at the page in question.

It had listed airline flights from Havana to Mexico.

Just exactly the kind of thing you might like to know about if, for example, you thought you would need to leave Havana in a hurry. If, just hypothetically, you had just scattered some unusual dead bodies around in front of the city's flagship five-star hotel.

I reached for the notebook, fished out the flight schedule, and flipped the paper onto the table. "He'll be there," I said.

Chutsky picked up the paper and unfolded it. "Cubana de Aviación," he read.

"From Havana to Mexico," I said. "So he can do it and then get out in a hurry."

"Maybe," he said. "Uh-huh, could be."

He looked up at me and cocked his head to one side. "What's your gut telling you?"

Truthfully, the only thing my gut ever told me was that it was dinnertime. But it was obviously very important to Chutsky, and if I stretched the definition of *gut* to include the Passenger, my gut was telling me that there was absolutely no doubt about it. "He'll be there," I said again.

Chutsky frowned and looked down at the drawing again. Then he started nodding his head, slowly at first and then with increasing energy. "Uh-huh," he said, and then he looked up, flipped the flight schedule to me, and stood up. "Let's go talk to Deborah," he said.

Deborah was lying in her bed, which should not really have been a surprise. She was staring at the window, even though she couldn't see out from her bed, and in spite of the fact that the television was on and broadcasting scenes of unearthly merriment and happiness. Debs didn't seem interested in the cheerful music and cries of bliss coming from the speaker, however. In fact, if you were to judge strictly from the look on her face, you would have to say she had never felt happiness in her life, and never intended to if she could help it. She glanced at us without interest as we came in, just long enough to identify us, and then looked back in the direction of the window.

"She's feeling kind of low," Chutsky muttered to me. "Happens sometimes after you get chopped up." From the number of scars all over Chutsky's face and body, I had to assume he knew what he was talking about, so I just nodded and approached Deborah.

"Hey, sis," I said, in the kind of artificially cheerful voice I had always understood you were supposed to use at an invalid's bedside.

She turned to look at me, and in the deadness of her face and the deep blue emptiness of her eyes, I saw an echo of her father, Harry; I had seen that look before, in Harry's eyes, and out of those blue depths a memory came out and wrapped itself all around me.

Harry lay dying. It was an awkward thing for all of us, like watching Superman in the throes of Kryptonite. He was supposed to be above that kind of common weakness. But for the last year and a half he had been dying, slowly, in fits and starts, and now he was very close to the finish line. And as he lay there in his hospice bed, his nurse had decided to help. She had been deliberately and lethally increasing the dose of his pain medicine and feeding on Harry's death, savoring his shrinking away, and he had known it and told me. And oh the joy and bliss, Harry had given me permission to make this nurse my very first real live human playmate, the first ever I had taken away with me to the Dark Playground.

And I had done so. First Nurse became the very first small drop of blood on the original glass slide in my brand-new collection. It had been several hours of wonder, exploration, and ecstasy, before First Nurse went the way of all flesh, and the next morning when I went to the hospice to report to Harry, the experience still filled me with brilliant darkness.

I came into Harry's room on feet that barely touched the ground, and as Harry opened his eyes and looked into mine he saw this, saw that I had changed and become the thing that he had made me, and as he watched me the deadness came into his eyes.

I sat anxiously beside him, thinking he might be at some new crisis. "Are you okay?" I said. "Should I call the doctor?"

He closed his eyes and slowly, fragilely, shook his head.

"What's wrong?" I insisted, thinking that since I felt better than I ever had before, everyone else really ought to cheer up a little, too.

"Nothing wrong," he said, in his soft, careful, dying voice. And he opened his eyes again and looked at me with that same glazed look of blue-eyed emptiness. "So you did it?"

I nodded, almost blushing, feeling that talking about it was somehow embarrassing.

"And after?" he said.

"All cleaned up," I said. "I was really careful."

"No problems?" he said.

"No," I told him, and blurted out, "It was wonderful." And seeing the pain on his face and thinking I could help, I added, "Thank you, Dad."

Harry closed his eyes again and turned his head away. For six or seven breaths, he stayed like that, and then, so softly I almost couldn't hear him, he said, "What have I done . . . Oh, Jesus, what have I done . . ."

"Dad . . . ?" I said. I could not remember that he had ever spoken like this, saying bad words and sounding so very anguished and uncertain, and it was very unsettling and absolutely took the edge off my euphoria. And he just shook his head, eyes closed, and would say nothing more.

"Dad . . . ?" I said again.

But he said nothing, just shook his head a few more painful times and then lay there quietly, for what seemed to me like a very long time, until at last he opened his eyes and looked at me, and there it was, that dead-eyed blue gaze that had moved beyond all hope and light and into the darkest place there is. "You are," he said, "what I have made you."

"Yes," I said, and I would have thanked him again, but he spoke.

"It's not your fault," he said, "it's mine," and I did not know then what he meant by that, although these many years later I think I have begun to understand. And I still wish I could have done or said something then, some small thing that would have made it easier for Harry to slide happily into the final dark; some carefully crafted sentence that made the self-doubt go away and let the sunlight back into those empty blue eyes.

But I also know, these many years later, that there is no such sentence, not in any language I know. Dexter is what Dexter must be, always and evermore, world without end, and if Harry saw that at the end and felt a final surge of horror and guilt — well, I really am sorry, but what else is there? Dying makes everyone weaker, subject to painful insight, and not always insight into any kind of special truth — it's just the approaching end that makes people want to believe they are seeing something in the line of a great revelation. Believe me, I am very much an expert in what dying people do. If I were to catalog all the strange things that my Special Friends have said to me as I helped them over the edge, it would make a very interesting book.

So I felt bad about Harry. But as a young and awkward geek of a monster, there was very little I could have said to make it easier on him.

And all these years later, seeing the same look in Deborah's eyes, I felt the same unhappy sense of helplessness wash over me. I could only gawk at her as she turned away and looked at the window once more.

"For Christ's sake," she said, without looking away from the window, "quit staring at me."

Chutsky slid into a chair on the opposite side. "She is a little cranky lately," he said.

"Fuck you," she said without any real emphasis, tilting her head to look around Chutsky and keep her focus on the window.

"Listen, Deborah," he said. "Dexter knows where this guy is that hurt you." She still didn't look, just blinked her eyes, twice.

"Uh, and he was thinking that him and me might go get him actually. And we wanted to talk to you about it," Chutsky said. "See how you feel about it."

"How I feel," she said with a flat and bitter voice, and then she turned to face us with a pain in her eyes that was so terrible even I could feel it. "Do you want to know what I really feel?" she said.

"Hey, it's okay," said Chutsky.

"They told me I was dead on the table," she said. "I feel like I'm still dead. I feel like I don't know who I am or why or anything and I just . . ." A tear rolled down her cheek and, again, it was very unsettling. "I feel like he cut out all of me that matters," she said, "and I don't know if I will ever get it back." She looked back at the window again. "I feel like crying all the time, and that's not me. I don't cry, you know that, Dex. I don't cry," she repeated softly as another tear rolled down the track made by the first one.

"It's okay," Chutsky said again, even though it clearly wasn't.

"I feel like everything I always thought is wrong now," she went on. "And I don't know if I can go back to being a cop if I feel like this."

"You're gonna feel better," Chustky said.

"It just takes time."

"Go get him," she said, and she looked at me with a little trace of her good old anger showing now. "Get him, Dexter," she said. "And do what you have to do." She held my gaze for a moment, then turned back to the window.

"Dad was right," she said.

THIRTY

And that is how early next morning I found myself standing at a small building on the outer edge of the runway at Miami International, clutching a passport in the name of David Marcey, and wearing what can only be called a leisure suit, green, with bright yellow matching belt and shoes. And next to me stood my associate director at Baptist Brethren International Ministries, the Reverend Campbell Freeney, in an equally hideous outfit and a big smile that changed the shape of his face and even seemed to hide some of the scars.

I am not truly a clothing-oriented person, but I do have some basic standards of sartorial decency, and the outfits we were wearing crushed them utterly and spat them into the dust. I had protested, of course, but Reverend Kyle had told me there was no choice. "Gotta look the part, buddy," he said, and he brushed a hand against his red sport coat. "This is Baptist missionary clothing."

"Couldn't we be Presbyterians?" I asked hopefully, but he shook his head.

"This is the pipeline I got," he said, "and this is how we gotta do it. Unless you speak Hungarian?"

"Eva Gabor?" I said, but he shook his head.

"And don't try to talk about Jesus all the time, they don't do that," he said. "Just smile a lot and be kind to everybody, and you'll be fine." He handed me another piece of paper, and said. "Here. This is your letter from Treasury to allow you to travel to Cuba for missionary work. Don't lose it."

He had been a fountain of a great deal more information in the few short hours between deciding he would take me to Havana and our dawn arrival at the airport, even remembering to tell me not to drink the water, which I thought was close to quaint.

I'd barely had time to tell Rita something almost plausible — that I had an emergency to take care of and not to worry, the uniformed cop would stay at her front door until I got back. And although she was quite smart enough to be puzzled by the idea of emergency forensics, she went along with it, reassured by the sight of the police cruiser parked in front of the house. Chutsky, too, had done his part, patting Rita on the shoulder and saying, "Don't worry, we'll take care of this for you." Of course this confused her even more, since she had not requested any blood spatter work, and if she had, Chutsky would not have been involved. But overall, it seemed to give her the impression that somehow vital things were being done to make her safe and everything would soon be all right, so she gave me a hug with minimal tears, and Chutsky led me away to the car.

And so we stood there together in the small building at the airport waiting for the flight to Havana, and after a short spell we were out the door and onto the runway, clutching our phony papers and our real tickets and taking our fair share of elbows from the rest of the passengers as we all scuttled onto the plane.

The airplane was an old passenger jet. The seats were worn and not quite as clean as they could have been. Chutsky — I mean Reverend Freeney — took the aisle seat, but he was big enough that he still crowded me over against the window. It would be a tight fit all the way to Havana, tight enough that I would have to wait for him to go to the restroom before I could inhale. Still, it seemed a small price to pay for bringing the Word of the Lord to the godless communists. And after only a few minutes of holding my breath, the plane rattled and bumped down the runway and into the air, and we were on our way.

The flight was not long enough for me to suffer too much from oxygen deprivation, especially since Chutsky spent much of the time leaning into the aisle and talking to the flight attendant; in only about half an hour we were banking in over the green countryside of Cuba and thumping onto a runway that apparently used the same paving contractor as Miami International. Still, as far as I could tell, the wheels did not actually fall off, and we rolled along up to a beautiful modern airport terminal — and rolled right past it until we finally came to a halt next to a grim old structure that looked like the bus station for a prison camp.

We trooped down off the plane on a rolling stairway, and crossed the tarmac into the squat gray building, and the inside was not a great deal more welcoming. Some very serious-looking uniformed men with mustaches stood around inside clutching automatic weapons and glaring at everyone. As a bizarre contrast, several television sets hung down from the ceiling, all playing what seemed to be a Cuban sitcom, complete with a hysterical laugh track that made its U.S. counterpart sound bored. Every few minutes one of the actors would shout something I couldn't decipher, and a blast of music would rise up over the laughter.

We stood in a line that moved slowly toward a booth. I could see nothing at all on the far side of the booth and for all I knew they could be sorting us into cattle cars to take us away to a gulag, but Chutsky didn't seem terribly worried, so it would have been poor sportsmanship for me to complain.

The line inched ahead and soon, without saying a word to me, Chutsky stepped up to the window and shoved his passport in through a hole at the bottom. I could not see or hear what was said, but there were no wild shouts and no gunfire and after a moment he collected his papers and vanished on the far side of the booth and it was my turn.

Behind the thick glass sat a man who could have been the twin of the nearest gun-toting soldier. He took my passport without comment and opened it, looked inside, looked up at me, and then pushed it back to me without a word. I had expected some kind of interrogation — I suppose I'd thought he might rise up and smite me for being either a capitalist running dog, or possibly a paper tiger — and I was so startled at his complete lack of response that I stood there for a moment before the man behind the glass jerked his head at me to go, and I did, heading around a corner the way Chutsky had gone and into the baggage-claim area.

"Hey, buddy," Chutsky said as I approached the spot he had staked out by the unmoving belt that would soon, I hoped, bring our bags out. "You weren't scared, were you?"

"I guess I thought it would be a little more difficult than that," I said. "I mean, aren't they kind of mad at us or something?"

Chutsky laughed. "I think you're gonna find out that they *like* you," he said. "It's just your government they can't stand."

I shook my head. "Can they really separate them like that?"

"Sure," he said. "It's simple Cuban Logic."

And as nonsensical as that seemed, I had grown up in Miami and knew perfectly well what that was; Cuban Logic was a running joke in the Cuban community, placed right before being *Cubanaso* in the emotional spectrum. The best explanation I'd ever had was from a professor in college. I'd taken a poetry course in the vain hope of learning to see into the human soul, since I don't have one. And the professor had been reading aloud from Walt Whitman — I still remembered the line, since it is so utterly human. "Do I contradict myself? Well then, I contradict myself. I am large. I contain multitudes." And the professor had looked up from the book and said, "Perfect Cuban Logic," waited for the laugh to die down, and then gone back to reading the poem.

So if the Cuban people disliked America and liked Americans, it involved no more mental gymnastics than I had seen and heard nearly every day of my life. In any case, there was a clatter, a buzzer blasted a loud note, and our baggage began to come out on the belt. We didn't have a lot, just one small bag each — just a change of socks and a dozen Bibles — and we wrestled the bags out past a female customs agent who seemed more interested in talking to the guard beside her than in catching us smuggling in weapons or stock portfolios. She merely glanced at the bags and waved us through, without losing a syllable of her rapid-fire monologue. And then we were free, walking improbably out the door and into the sunshine outside. Chutsky whistled up a taxi, a gray Mercedes, and a man stepped out in gray livery and matching cap and grabbed our bags. Chutsky said, "Hotel Nacional" to the driver, who threw our bags in the trunk, and we all climbed in.

The highway into Havana was badly pockmarked, but it was very close to deserted. We saw only a few other cabs, a couple of motorcycles, and some army trucks moving slowly along, and that was it — all the way in to the city. Then the streets suddenly exploded into life, with ancient cars, bicycles, crowds of people flowing over the sidewalks, and some very strange-looking buses that were pulled by diesel trucks. They were twice as long as an American bus, and shaped something like the letter *M* with the two ends going up like wings and then sloping down to a flat-roofed low spot in the middle. They were all packed so full of people that it seemed impossible for anyone else to get on, but as I watched one of them stopped, and sure enough, another clump of people crowded in.

"Camels," Chutsky said, and I stared at him curiously.

"Excuse me?" I said.

He jerked his head at one of the strange

buses. "They're called camels," he said. "They'll tell you it's because of the shape, but my guess is it has to do with the smell inside at rush hour." He shook his head. "You get four hundred people inside there, coming home from work, no air-conditioning and the windows don't open. Unbelievable."

It was a fascinating tidbit of information, or at least Chutsky apparently thought so, because he had nothing more profound to offer, even though we were moving through a city I had never seen before. But his impulse to be a tour guide was apparently dead, and we slid through traffic and onto a wide boulevard that ran along the water. High up on a cliff on the other side of the harbor I could see an old lighthouse and some battlements, and beyond that a black smudge of smoke climbing into the sky. Between us and the water there was a broad sidewalk and a seawall. Waves broke on the wall, sending spray up into the air, but nobody seemed to mind getting a little wet. There were throngs of people of all ages sitting, standing, walking, fishing, lying, and kissing on the seawall. We passed some strange contorted sculpture, thumped over a rough patch of pavement, and turned left up a short hill. And then there it was, the

Hotel Nacional, complete with its facade that would soon feature the smirking face of Dexter, unless we could find Weiss first.

The driver stopped his car in front of a grand marble staircase, a doorman dressed like an Italian admiral stepped up and clapped his hands, and a uniformed bellboy came running out to grab our bags.

"Here we are," said Chutsky, somewhat unnecessarily. The admiral opened the door and Chutsky climbed out. I was allowed to open my own door, since I was on the side away from the marble stairs. I did so, and climbed out into a forest of helpful smiles. Chutsky paid the driver, and we followed the bellboy up the stairs and into the hotel.

The lobby looked like it had been carved out of the same block of marble as the stairs. It was somewhat narrow, but it stretched away past the front desk and vanished in the misty distance. The bellboy led us right up to the desk, past a cluster of plush chairs and a velvet rope, and the clerk at the desk seemed very glad to see us.

"Señor Freeney," he said, bowing his head happily. "So very good to see you again." He raised an eyebrow. "Surely, you are not here for the Art Festival?" His accent was less than many I had heard in Miami, and

Chutsky seemed very pleased to see him, too.

Chutsky reached across the counter and shook his hand. "How are you, Rogelio?" he said. "Nice to see you, too. I'm here to break in a new guy." He put his hand on my shoulder and nudged me forward, as if I was a sullen boy being forced to kiss Granny on the cheek. "This is David Marcey, one of our rising stars," he said. "Does a hell of a sermon."

Rogelio shook my hand. "I am very pleased to meet you, Señor Marcey."

"Thank you," I said. "You have a very nice place here."

He gave a half bow again and began to tap on a computer keyboard. "I hope you will enjoy your stay," he said. "If Señor Freeney does not object, I will put you on the executive floor? That way you are closer to the breakfast."

"That sounds very nice," I said.

"One room or two?" he said.

"I think just one this time, Rogelio," Chutsky said. "Gotta watch the old expense account this trip."

"Of course," Rogelio said. He tapped out a few more quick keystrokes and then, with a grand flourish, slid two keys across the desk. "Here you go," he said.

Chutsky put his hand on the keys and leaned in a little closer. "One more thing, Rogelio," he said, lowering his voice. "We have a friend coming in from Canada," he said. "Name of Brandon Weiss." He pulled the keys toward himself over the counter, and a twenty-dollar bill lay on the counter where they had been. "We'd like to surprise him," he said. "It's his birthday."

Rogelio flicked out a hand and the twenty-dollar bill disappeared like a fly grabbed by a lizard. "Of course," he said. "I will let you know immediately."

"Thanks, Rogelio," Chutsky said, and he turned away, motioning me to follow. I trailed along behind him and the bellboy with our bags, to the far end of the lobby, where a bank of elevators stood ready to whisk us up to the executive floor. A crowd of people dressed in very nice resort wear stood waiting, and it may have been only my feverish imagination, but I thought they glared in horror at our missionary clothing. Still, there was nothing for it but to follow the script, and I smiled at them and managed to avoid blurting out something religious, possibly from Revelation.

The door slid open and the crowd surged into the elevator. The bellboy smiled and said, "Go ahead, sir, I follow in two minute," and the Right Reverend Freeney and I climbed in.

The doors closed. I caught a few more anxious glances at my shoes, but no one had anything to say, and neither did I. But I did wonder why we had to share a room. I hadn't had a roommate since college, and that hadn't really worked out very well. And I knew full well that Chutsky snored.

The doors slid open and we stepped out. I followed Chutsky to the left, to another reception area, where a waiter stood beside a glass cart. He bowed and handed us each a tall glass.

"What's this?" I asked.

"Cuban Gatorade," Chutsky said. "Cheers." He drained his glass and put the empty down on the cart, so I allowed myself to be shamed into doing the same. The drink tasted mild, sweet, slightly minty, and I found that it did, indeed, seem to be kind of refreshing in the way that Gatorade is on a hot day. I put the empty down next to Chutsky's. He picked up another one, so I did, too. *"Salud,"* he said. We clinked glasses and I drank. It really did taste good, and since I'd had almost nothing to eat or drink in the scramble of getting to the airport, I let myself enjoy it.

Behind us, the elevator door slid open and

our bellboy dashed out clutching our bags. "Hey, there you are," Chutsky said. "Let's see the room." He drained his glass, and I did, too, and we followed the bellboy down the hall.

About halfway down the hall I began to feel a little bit odd, as if my legs had suddenly been turned into balsawood. "What was in that Gatorade?" I asked Chutsky.

"Mostly rum," he said. "What, you never had a mojito before?"

"I don't think so," I said.

He gave a short grunt that might have been intended as a laugh. "Get used to it," he said. "You're in Havana now."

I followed him down the hall, which had suddenly grown longer and a little brighter. I was feeling very refreshed now. But somehow I made it all the way to the room and through the door. The bellboy heaved our suitcases up onto a stand and flung open the curtains to reveal a very nice room, tastefully furnished in the classical style. There were two beds, separated by a nightstand, and a bathroom to the left of the room's door.

"Very nice," said Chutsky, and the bellboy smiled and gave him a half bow. "Thanks," Chutsky said, and held out his hand with a ten-dollar bill in it. "Thanks very much."

The bellboy took the money with a smile and a nod and promised that we only had to call and he would move heaven and earth to help fulfill our slightest whim, and then he disappeared out the door as I flopped facedown onto the bed nearest the window. I chose that bed because it was closest, but it was also much too bright with the sun rocketing in through the window so aggressively, and I closed my eyes. The room did not spin, and I did not suddenly slip into unconsciousness, but it seemed like a very good idea to lie there for a while with my eyes closed.

"Ten bucks," Chutsky said. "That's what most of the people here make in a month. And *boom-bah* — he gets it for five minutes' work. He's probably got a PhD in astrophysics." There was a short and welcome pause, and then Chutsky said, in a voice that seemed much farther away, "Hey, you all right, buddy?"

"Never better," I said, and my voice was kind of far away, too. "But I think I'll just take a nap for a minute."

Thirty-One

When I woke up the room was quiet and dark and my mouth was very dry. I fumbled around on the nightstand for a moment until I found a lamp, and I switched it on. In its light I saw that Chutsky had closed the curtains and then gone out somewhere. I also saw a bottle of drinking water beside the lamp, and I grabbed it and ripped the top off, gratefully sucking down about half the bottle in one fell swoop.

I stood up. I was a little bit stiff from sleeping on my face, but other than that I felt surprisingly good, as well as hungry, which was not surprising. I went to the window and opened the curtains. It was still bright daylight, but the sun had moved off to one side and calmed down a little, and I stood looking out at the harbor and the seawall and the large sidewalk that ran along beside it filled with people. None of them seemed in any hurry; they were strolling rather than going anywhere, and groups of them collected here and there for talking, singing, and, from what I could gather from some of the visible activity, advice to the lovelorn.

Farther out in the harbor a large inner tube bobbed in the swell, a man dangling through its center and holding what looked to be a Cuban yo-yo, which is a spool of fishing line with no reel or pole. And farther still, just on the inside of the horizon, three large ships were steaming past, whether freighters or passenger liners I couldn't tell. The birds wheeled above the waves, the sun sparkled off the water; all in all it was a beautiful sight, and it made me realize that there was absolutely nothing to eat at the window, so I found my room key on the bedside table and headed down to the lobby.

I found a very large and formal dining room on the far side of the elevators from the front desk, and tucked into a corner beside it was a dark wood-paneled bar. They were both very nice, but not really what I was looking for. The bartender told me, in perfect English, that there was a snack bar in the basement, down the stairs at the far side of the lobby, and I thanked him, also in perfect English, and headed for the stairs.

The snack bar was decorated in tribute to

the movies, and I had a bad moment until I saw the menu and realized they served more than popcorn. I ordered a Cuban sandwich, naturally, and an Iron Beer, and sat at a table contemplating lights, camera, and action with just a trace of bitterness. Weiss was somewhere nearby, or about to be, and he had promised to make Dexter a big star. I did not want to be a star. I much preferred toiling in shadowy obscurity, quietly compiling a record of flawless excellence in my chosen field. This would soon be utterly impossible unless I managed to stop Weiss, and since I was not really sure how I planned to do that, it was a very distressing prospect. Still, the sandwich was good.

When I had finished eating, I went back up the stairs and, on a whim, down the grand marble staircase and outside to the front of the hotel, where a line of taxis stood guard. I walked aimlessly by them and up the long sidewalk, past a row of ancient Chevys and Buicks, and even a Hudson — I had to read the name off the front end. Several very happy-looking people leaned against the cars, and all of them were eager to take me for a ride, but I smiled my way past them and headed for the distant front gate. Beyond these was an untidy heap of what seemed to be golf carts with brightly colored plastic shells attached to them. Their drivers were younger and not quite so high end as those attending the Hudson, but they were equally eager to prevent me from having to use my legs. Nevertheless, I managed to get through them as well.

At the gate I paused and looked around. Ahead of me was a crooked street that led past a bar or nightclub. To my right a road led downhill to the boulevard that ran along the seawall, and to my left, also down a hill, I could see what looked like a movie theater on the corner and a row of shops. And as I was contemplating all this and trying to decide which way to go, a taxi stopped beside me, the window rolled down, and Chutsky called to me urgently from inside. "Get in," he said. "Come on, buddy. In the cab. Hurry up." I had no idea why it was so important, but I climbed in and the cab took us on up to the hotel, turning right before the front door and pulling into a parking lot that butted up against one wing of the building.

"You can't be wandering around out front," Chutsky said. "If this guy sees you, the game's over."

"Oh," I said, feeling slightly stupid. He was right, of course; but Dexter was so unused to daytime stalking that it had not occurred to me.

"Come on," he said, and he climbed out of the cab, holding a new leather briefcase. He paid the driver and I followed him through a side door that led past a few shops and right to the elevators. We went straight up to our room with nothing else to say, until we got inside. Chutsky threw the briefcase on the bed, flung himself into a chair, and said, "Okay, we got some time to kill, and it's best to do it right here in the room." He gave me a look that one might give to a very slow child and added, "So this guy doesn't know we're here." He looked at me for a moment to see if I understood him and then, apparently figuring out that I did, he pulled out a battered little booklet and a pencil, opened the book, and began to do Sudoku.

"What's in your briefcase?" I said, mostly because I was a little irritated.

Chutsky smiled, pulled the case toward him with his steel hook, and flipped it open. It was full of cheap souvenir percussion instruments, most of them stamped CUBA.

"Why?" I asked him.

He just kept smiling. "You never know what might turn up," he said, and turned back to his no-doubt-fascinating Sudoku puzzle. Left to my own devices, I pulled the other chair in front of the television, switched it on, and watched Cuban sitcoms.

We sat there peacefully enough until very close to dusk. Then Chutsky glanced at the clock and said, "Okay, buddy, let's get going."

"Going where?" I said.

He winked at me. "Meet a friend," he said, and he would say no more. He picked up his new briefcase and headed out the door. So even though it was a little bit disturbing to be winked at, I had no real choice, and I followed meekly along out of the room, out the hotel's side door again, and into a waiting taxi.

The streets of Havana were even busier in the fading light. I rolled down my window to see, hear, and smell the city, and was rewarded by an ever-changing but never-stopping surge of music, seemingly coming from every door and window we passed, as well as from the many groups of musicians clustered on the street. Their song rose and fell and mutated as we drove through the city, but somehow it always seemed to come back to the chorus of "Guantanamera."

The cab followed a tortured path over rough cobbled streets, always through crowds of people singing, selling things, and, strangely, playing baseball. I lost all sense of direction very quickly, and by the time the cab stopped at a barrier of large iron globes in the middle of the road, I had no idea what direction we had come from. So I followed Chutsky up a side street, through a plaza, and into an intersection in front of what seemed to be a hotel. It was bright orange pink in the light of the setting sun, and Chutsky led me in, past a piano bar and a number of tables spread with pictures of Ernest Hemingway that looked like they'd been painted by elementary school children.

Beyond these was an old-fashioned elevator cage at the far end of the lobby, and we went over to it and Chutsky rang the bell. As we waited I looked around me. Off to one side was a row of shelves containing merchandise of some kind and I wandered over for a look. There were ashtrays, mugs, and other items, all containing a likeness of Ernest Hemingway, in this case done by someone a bit more skillful than the grade school artists.

The elevator arrived and I walked back to get in. A massive gray iron gate slid open to reveal the inside, complete with a grim old man operating the controls. Chutsky and I got in. A few more people crowded in with us before the operator slid the iron gate shut and cranked the handle into the up position. The cage lurched and we began to move slowly upward, until we reached the fifth floor. Then the elevator operator yanked the handle and we thumped to a stop. "The room of Hemingway," he said. He pulled the gate open and the rest of the people on board skittered out. I glanced at Chutsky, but he shook his head and pointed up, so I stood and waited until the gate slid shut again and we jerked our way up two more flights before staggering to a halt. The man slid the gate open and we stepped gratefully out into a small room, really no more than a roof over the elevator and the top of a flight of stairs. I could hear music playing nearby, and Chutsky, with a wave of his hand, led me out onto the roof and toward the music.

A trio was playing a song about *ojos verdes* as we walked around a trellis to where the musicians were set up, three men in white pants and guayaberas. A bar was against the wall beyond them, and on the other two sides there was just the city of Havana spread out below us in the orange light of the setting sun.

Chutsky led the way to a low table with a cluster of easy chairs around it and he nudged his briefcase under the table as we sat down. "Pretty nice view, huh?" he said.

"Very pretty," I said. "Is that why we came here?"

"No, I told you," he said. "We're gonna meet a friend."

And whether he was kidding me or not, that was apparently all he was going to say on the subject. In any case, the waiter appeared at our table at that point. "Two mojitos," Chutsky said.

"Actually, I think I'll stick to beer," I said, remembering my mojito-induced nap a little earlier.

Chutsky shrugged. "Suit yourself," he said. "Try a Crystal, it's pretty good."

I nodded at the waiter; if I could trust Chutsky for anything at all, I was pretty sure it would be beer selection. The waiter nodded back and went to the bar to get our drinks and the trio launched into "Guantanamera."

We'd had no more than one sip of our drinks when I saw a man approaching our table. He was very short and dressed in brown slacks and a lime-green guayabera, and he carried a briefcase that looked very much like Chutsky's.

Chutsky jumped up and held out his hand. "Ee-bangh!" he yelled, and it took me a moment to realize that Chutsky was not experiencing a sudden attack of Tourette's syndrome, but only the Cuban pronunciation of the newcomer's name, Iván. Eebangh held out his hand, too, and embraced Chutsky as they shook hands.

"Cahm-BEYL!" Ee-bangh said, and again it took a moment — this time because I hadn't really remembered that Chutsky was Reverend Campbell Freeney. By the time all the gears had meshed, Ivan had turned to look at me with one raised eyebrow. "Oh, hey," Chutsky said, "this is David Marcey. David, Iván Echeverría."

"Mucho gusto," Iván said, shaking my hand.

"Nice to meet you," I told him in English, since I was not sure whether "David" spoke any Spanish at all.

"Well, sit down," Chutsky said, and he waved at the waiter as Iván sat. The waiter hurtled over to our table and took Iván's order for a mojito, and when it arrived, Chutsky and Iván sipped and talked cheerfully in very rapid Cuban Spanish. I could probably have followed along if I had really worked at it, but it seemed like an awful lot of hard labor for what seemed to be a private conversation made up mostly of fond memories — and in truth, even if they had been discussing something far more interesting than What Happened That Time,

I would have tuned it out; because it was full night now, and coming up over the rim of the roof was a huge, reddish-yellow moon, a bloated, simpering, bloodthirsty moon, and the first sight of it turned every inch of my skin into a chilled carpet of goose bumps, all the hairs on my back and arms stood up and howled, and running through every corridor of Castle Dexter was a small and dark footman carrying orders to every Knight of the Night to Go Now and Do It.

But of course it was not to be. This was not a Night of Letting Go; it was very unfortunately a Night of Clamping Down. It was a night to sip rapidly warming beer, pretend I could hear and enjoy the trio; a night to smile politely at Ee-bahng and wish it was all over and I could get back to being happy homicidal me in peace and tranquillity. It was a night to endure, and hope that someday soon would find me with a knife in one hand and Weiss in the other.

Until then, I could only take a deep breath, a sip of beer, and pretend to enjoy the lovely view and the wonderful music. Practice that winning smile, Dexter. How many teeth can we show? Very good; now without teeth, just the lips. How far up can you make the corners of your mouth go before it looks like you are in very great internal pain?

"Hey, you all right, buddy?" Chutsky called some twenty minutes later. Apparently I had let my face stretch past Happy Smile and into Rictus.

"I'm fine," I told him. "Just, ah — fine, really."

"Uh-huh," he said, though he didn't look convinced. "Well, maybe we better get you back to the hotel." He drained his glass and stood up, and so did Iván. They shook hands, and then Iván sat back down and Chutsky grabbed his briefcase and we headed for the elevator. I looked back to see Iván ordering another drink, and I raised an eyebrow at Chutsky.

"Oh," he said. "We don't want to leave together. You know, at the same time."

Well, I suppose that made as much sense as anything else, since we were now apparently living in a spy movie, so I watched everyone else carefully, all the way down in the elevator, to make sure they weren't agents of some evil cartel. Apparently they weren't, since we made it safely all the way down and into the street. But as we crossed the street to find a taxi, we passed a horse and buggy waiting there, something I really should have noticed and avoided, because animals don't like me, and this horse reared up — even though he was old and tired and had been placidly chewing something in a nose bag. It was not a very impressive maneuver, hardly a John Wayne moment, but he did get both front feet off the ground and make a noise of extreme displeasure at me, which startled his driver nearly as much as it did me. But I hurried on by and we managed to get into a taxi without any clouds of bats swarming out to attack me.

We rode back to the hotel in silence. Chutsky sat with his briefcase on his lap and looked out the window, and I tried not to listen to that fat overwhelming moon. But that didn't work very well; it was there in every postcard view of Havana we drove through, always bright and leering and calling out wonderful ideas, and why couldn't I come out to play? But I could not. I could only smile back and say, Soon. It will be soon.

Just as soon as I could find Weiss.

Thirty-Two

We got back to our room without incident and with no more than a dozen words between the two of us. Chutsky's lack of wordiness was proving to be a really charming personality trait, since the less he talked, the less I had to pretend I was interested, and it saved wear on my facial muscles. And in fact, the few words he did say were so pleasant and winning that I was almost ready to like him. "Lemme put this in the room," he said, holding up the briefcase. "Then we'll think about dinner." Wise and welcome words; since I would not be out in the wonderful dark light of the moon tonight, dinner would be a very acceptable substitute.

We took the elevator up and strolled down the hall to the room, and when we got inside, Chutsky put the briefcase carefully on the bed and sat beside it, and it occurred to me that he had brought it with us to the rooftop bar for no reason I could see, and was now being rather careful of it. Since curiosity is one of my few flaws, I decided to indulge it and find out why.

"What's so important about the maracas?" I asked him.

He smiled. "Nothing," he said. "Not a single damn thing."

"Then why are you carrying them all over Havana?"

He held the briefcase down with his hook and opened it with his hand. "Because," he said, "they're not maracas anymore." And sliding his hand into the briefcase, he pulled out a very serious-looking automatic pistol. "Hey, presto," he said.

I thought of Chutsky lugging the briefcase all over town to meet Ee-bangh, who then came in with an identical briefcase — both of which were shoved under the table while we all sat and listened to "Guantanamera."

"You arranged to switch briefcases with your friend," I said.

"Bingo."

It does not rank among the smartest things I ever said, but I was surprised, and what came out of my mouth was "But what's it for?"

Chutsky gave me such a warm, tolerant, patronizing smile that I would gladly have turned the pistol on him and pulled the trigger. "It's a pistol, buddy," he said. "What do you think it's for?"

"Um, self-defense?" I said.

"You do remember why we came here, right?" he said.

"To find Brandon Weiss," I said.

"FIND him?" Chutsky demanded. "Is that what you're telling yourself? We're going to FIND him?" He shook his head. "We're here to kill him, buddy. You need to get that straight in your head. We can't just find him, we have to put him down. We've got to kill him. What'd you think we were going to do? Bring him home with us and give him to the zoo?"

"I guess I thought that sort of thing was frowned on here," I said. "I mean, this isn't Miami, you know."

"It isn't Disneyland, either," he said, unnecessarily, I thought. "This isn't a picnic, buddy. We're here to kill this guy, and the sooner you get used to that idea the better."

"Yes, I know, but —"

"There ain't no *but,*" he said. "We're gonna kill him. I can see you have a problem with that."

"Not at all," I said.

He apparently didn't hear me — either that or he was already launched into a preexisting lecture and couldn't stop himself. "You can't be squeamish about a little blood," he went on. "It's perfectly natural. We all grow up hearing that killing is wrong."

It kind of depends on who, I thought, but did not say.

"But the rules are made by people who couldn't win without 'em. And anyway, killing isn't *always* wrong, buddy," he said, and oddly enough he winked. "Sometimes it's something you have to do. And sometimes, it's somebody who deserves it. Because either a whole lot of other people will die if you don't do it, or maybe it's, get him before he gets you. And in this case — it's both, right?"

And although it was very odd to hear this rough version of my lifelong creed from my sister's boyfriend, sitting on the bed in a hotel room in Havana, it once again made me appreciate Harry, both for being ahead of his time and also for being able to say all this in a way that didn't make me feel like I was cheating at Solitaire. But I still couldn't warm to the idea of using a gun. It just seemed wrong, like washing your socks in the baptismal font at church.

But Chutsky was apparently very pleased with himself. "Walther, nine-millimeter.

Very nice weapons." He nodded and reached into the briefcase again and pulled out a second pistol. "One for each of us," he said. He flipped one of the guns to me and I caught it reflexively. "Think you can pull the trigger?"

I do know which end of a pistol to hold on to, whatever Chutsky might think. After all, I grew up in a cop's house, and I worked with cops every day. I just didn't like the things — they are so impersonal, and they lack real elegance. But he had thrown it at me as something of a challenge, and on top of everything else that had happened, I was not about to ignore it. So I ejected the clip, worked the action one time, and held it out in the firing position, just like Harry had taught me. "Very nice," I said. "Would you like me to shoot the television?"

"Save it for the bad guy," Chutsky said. "If you think you can do it."

I tossed the gun on the bed beside him. "Is that really your plan?" I asked him. "We wait for Weiss to check in to the hotel and then play O.K. Corral with him? In the lobby, or at breakfast?"

Chutsky shook his head sadly, as if he had tried and failed to teach me how to tie my shoes. "Buddy, we don't know when this guy is going to turn up, and we don't know what he's going to do. He may even spot us first." He raised both eyebrows at me, as if to say, *Ha* — didn't *think of that, did you?*

"So we shoot him wherever we find him?"

"The thing is, to just be ready, whatever happens," he said. "Ideally, we get him off someplace quiet and do it. But at least we're ready." He patted the briefcase with his hook. "Iván brought us a couple of other things, just in case, too."

"Like land mines?" I said. "Maybe a flame thrower?"

"Some electronic stuff," he said. "State-of-the-art stuff. For surveillance. We can track him, find him, listen in on him — with this stuff we can hear him fart from a mile away."

I really did want to get into the spirit of things here, but it was very hard to show any interest in Weiss's digestive process, and I hoped it wasn't absolutely essential for Chutsky's plan. In any case, his entire James Bond approach was making me uncomfortable. It may be very wrong of me, but I began to appreciate just how lucky I had been so far in life. I had managed very well with only a few shiny blades and a hunger — nothing state-of-the-art, no vague plots, no huddling in foreign hotel rooms awash with uncertainty and firepower. Just happy, carefree, relaxing carnage. Certainly it seemed primitive and even slapdash in the face of all this high-tech steel-nerved preparation, but it was at least honest and wholesome labor. None of this waiting around spitting testosterone and polishing bullets. Chutsky was taking all the fun out of my life's work.

Still, I had asked for his help, and now I was stuck with it. So there was really nothing to do but put the best possible face on things and get on with it. "It's all very nice," I said, with an encouraging smile that did not even fool me. "When do we start?"

Chutsky snorted and put the guns back in the briefcase. He held it up to me, dangling it from his hook. "When he gets here," he said. "Put this in the closet for now."

I took the briefcase from him and carried it to the closet. But as I reached to open the door I heard a faint rustling of wings somewhere in the distance and I froze. *What is it?* I asked silently. There was a slight inaudible twitch, a raising of awareness, but no more.

So I reached into the briefcase and got my ridiculous gun, holding it at the ready as I reached for the closet's doorknob. I opened the door — and for a moment I could do nothing but stare into the unlit space and wait for an answering darkness to spread protective wings over me. It was an impossible, surreal, dream-time image — but after staring at it for what seemed like an awfully long time, I had to believe it was true.

It was Rogelio, Chutsky's friend from the front desk, who was going to tell us when Weiss checked in. But it certainly didn't look like he was going to tell us much of anything, unless we listened to him with a Ouija board. Because if appearances were any guide at all, judging by the belt so tightly wrapped around his neck and the way his tongue and eyes bulged out, Rogelio was extremely dead.

"What is it, buddy?" Chutsky said.

"I think Weiss has already checked in," I said.

Chutsky lumbered up from the bed and over to the closet. He stared for a moment and then said, "Shit." He reached his hand in and felt for a pulse — rather unnecessary, I thought, but I suppose there's a protocol for these things. He felt no pulse, of course, and mumbled, "Fucking *shit*." I didn't see how repetition would help, but of course he was the expert, so I just watched as he slid a hand into each of Rogelio's pockets in turn. "His passkey," he said. He put that into his pocket. He turned out the usual junk — keys, a handkerchief, a comb, some money. He looked carefully at the cash for a moment. "Canadian twenty here," he said. "Like somebody tipped him for something, huh?"

"You mean Weiss?" I said.

He shrugged. "How many homicidal Canadians you know?"

It was a fair question. Since the NHL season had ended a few months ago, I could only think of one — Weiss.

Chutsky pulled an envelope out of Rogelio's jacket pocket. "Bingo," he said. "Mr. B. Weiss, room 865." He handed the envelope to me. "I'm guessing it's complimentary drink tickets. Open it up."

I peeled back the flap and pulled out two oblongs of cardboard. Sure enough: two complimentary drinks at the Cabaret Parisien, the hotel's famous cabaret. "How did you guess?" I said.

Chutsky straightened up from his ghoulish search. "I fucked up," he said. "When I told Rogelio it was Weiss's birthday, all he could think was to make the hotel look good, and maybe pick up a tip." He held up the Canadian twenty-dollar bill. "This is a month's pay," he said. "You can't blame him." He shrugged. "So I fucked up, and he's dead. And our ass is deep in the shit."

Even though he had clearly not thought through that image, I got his point. Weiss knew we were here, we had no idea where he was or what he was up to, and we had a very embarrassing corpse in the closet.

"All right," I said, and for once I was glad to have his experience to lean on — which was assuming, of course, that he had experience at fucking up and finding strangled bodies in his closet, but he was certainly more knowledgeable about it than I was. "So what do we do?"

Chutsky frowned. "First, we have to check his room. He's probably run for it, but we'd look really stupid if we didn't check." He nodded at the envelope in my hand. "We know his room number, and he doesn't necessarily *know* that we know. And if he *is* there — then we have to, what'd you call it, play O.K. Corral on his ass."

"And if he's not there?" I said, because I, too, had the feeling that Rogelio was a farewell gift and Weiss was already sprinting for the horizon.

"If he's not in his room," Chutsky said, "and even if he IS in his room and we take him out — either way, I'm sorry to say it, buddy, but our vacation is over." He nodded at Rogelio. "Sooner or later they find this, and then it's big trouble. We gotta get the hell out of Dodge."

"But what about Weiss?" I said. "What if he's already gone?"

Chutsky shook his head. "He's got to run for his life, too," he said. "He knows we're after him, and when they find Rogelio's body, somebody will remember them together — I think he's already gone, heading for the hills. But just in case, we gotta check his room. And then beat feet out of Cuba, *muy rápido.*"

I had been terribly afraid he would have some high-tech plan for getting rid of Rogelio's body, like dipping it in laser solution in the bathtub, so I was very relieved to hear that for once he was speaking sound common sense. I had seen almost nothing of Havana except the inside of a hotel room and the bottom of a mojito glass, but it was clearly time to head for home and work on Plan B. "All right," I said. "Let's go."

Chutsky nodded. "Good man," he said. "Grab your pistol."

I took the cold and clunky thing and shoved it into the waistband of my pants, pulling the awful green jacket over it, and as Chutsky closed the closet door I headed for the hallway.

"Put the 'Do Not Disturb' sign on the

door," he said. An excellent idea, proving that I was right about his experience. At this point it would be very awkward to have a maid come in to wash the coat hangers. I hung the sign on the doorknob and Chutsky followed me out of the room and down the hallway to the stairs.

It was very, very strange to feel myself stalking something in the brightly lit hall, no moon churning through the sky over my shoulder, no bright blade gleaming with anticipation, and no happy hiss from the dark backseat as the Passenger prepared to take the wheel; nothing at all except the *lump-thump* of Chutsky's feet, the real one and the metal one alternating, and the sound of our breathing as we found the fire door and climbed up the stairs to the eighth floor. Room 865, just as I had guessed, overlooked the front of the hotel, a perfect spot for Weiss to place his camera. We stood outside the door quietly while Chutsky held his pistol with his hook and fumbled out Rogelio's passkey. He handed it to me, nodded at the door, and whispered, "One. Two — three." I shoved the key in, turned the doorknob, and stepped back as Chutsky rushed into the room with his gun held high, and I followed along behind, self-consciously holding my pistol at the ready, too.

I covered Chutsky as he kicked open the bathroom door, then the closet, and then relaxed, tucking the pistol back into his pants. "And there it is," he said, looking at the table by the window. A large fruit basket sat there, which I thought was a little ironic, considering what Weiss was known to do with them. I went over and looked; happily, there were no entrails or fingers inside. Just some mangoes, papayas, and so on, and a card that said, *Feliz Navidad. Hotel Nacional.* A somewhat standard message; nothing at all out of the ordinary. Just enough to get Rogelio killed.

We looked through the drawers and under the bed, but there was nothing at all there. Aside from the fruit basket, the room was as empty as the inside of Dexter on the shelf marked SOUL.

Weiss was gone.

THIRTY-THREE

As far as I know, I have never sauntered. To be completely honest, I doubt very much that I have even strolled, but sauntering is far beyond me. When I go somewhere, it is with a clear purpose in mind, and although I hesitate to sound boastful, more often than not I tend to stride.

But after leaving Weiss's empty hotel room and stepping into the elevator, Chutsky spoke as he stuffed the guns back into the briefcase and impressed upon me the importance of looking casual, unhurried, and unworried, to such an extent that as we stepped into the lobby of the Hotel Nacional, I believe I actually did, in fact, saunter. I am quite sure that's what Chutsky was doing, and I hoped I looked more natural at it than he did — of course, he had one artificial foot to deal with, so perhaps I really did look better.

In any case, we sauntered through the

lobby, smiling at anyone who bothered to glance at us. We sauntered out the door, down the front steps, and over to the man in the admiral's uniform, and then sauntered behind him to the curb as he called up the first taxi in the row of waiting cars. And our slow and happy meanderings continued inside the cab, because Chutsky told the driver to take us to El Morro Castle. I raised an eyebrow at him, but he just shook his head and I was left to puzzle it out for myself. As far as I knew, there was no secret tunnel out of Cuba from El Morro. It was one of the most crowded tourist destinations in Havana, absolutely overrun with cameras and the scent of sunscreen. But I tried to think like Chutsky for a moment — which is to say, I pretended to be a conspiracy buff — and after only a moment of reflection, I got it.

It was precisely the fact that it was a popular tourist spot that led Chutsky to tell the driver to take us there. If the worst happened, and I had to admit that's the way things were going right now, then our trail would end there, in a crowd, and tracking us down would be just a little bit harder.

So I sat back and enjoyed the ride and the splendid moonlit view and the idea that I had absolutely no idea where Weiss would go now and what he would do next. I found some comfort in thinking that he probably didn't know, either, but not enough to make me really happy.

Somewhere this same soothing glow of happy laughing light from a pale moon was shining on Weiss. And perhaps it whispered the same terrible, wonderful things into his inner ear — the sly and smiling ideas for things to do tonight, now, very soon — I had never felt such a strong pull on the tidal pool of Dexter Beach from such a paltry moon. But there it was, its soft chortles and chuckles filling me with such a static charge that I felt like I had to burst into the darkness and slash the first warm-blooded biped I could find. It was probably just the frustration of missing Weiss again, but it was very strong, and I chewed my lip all the way up the road to El Morro.

The driver let us out by the entrance to the fortress, where a great crowd swirled about waiting for the evening show, and a number of vendors had set up their carts. An elderly couple in shorts and Hawaiian shirts climbed into the cab as we got out and Chutsky stepped over to one of the vendors and bought two cold green cans of beer. "Here you go, buddy," he said, handing me one can. "Let's just stroll down this way."

First sauntering and now strolling — all in one day. It was enough to make my head spin. But I strolled, I sipped my beer, and I followed Chutsky about a hundred yards to the far end of the crowd. We stopped once at a souvenir cart and Chutsky bought a couple of T-shirts with a picture of the lighthouse on the front, and two caps that said CUBA on the front. Then we strolled on to the end of the pavement. When we got there, he took a casual look around, threw his beer can into a trash barrel, and said, "All right. Looks good. Over here." He moved casually toward an alley between two of the old fort buildings and I followed.

"Okay," I said. "Now what?"

He shrugged. "Change," he said. "Then we go to the airport, get the first flight out, no matter where it's going, and head for home. Oh — here," he said. He reached inside the briefcase and pulled out two passports. He flipped them open and handed me one, saying, "Derek Miller. Okay?"

"Sure, why not. It's a beautiful name."

"Yeah, it is," he said. "Better than Dexter."

"Or Kyle," I said.

"Kyle who?" He held up his new passport. "It's Calvin," he said. "Calvin Brinker. But you can call me Cal." He started taking things out of his jacket pockets and transferring them to his pants. "We need to lose the jackets now, too. And I wish we had time for a whole new outfit. But this will change our profile a little. Put this on," he said, handing me one of the T-shirts and a cap. I slipped out of my awful green jacket, quite gratefully, really, and the shirt I had on as well, quickly pulling on my brand-new wardrobe. Chutsky did the same, and we stepped out of the alley and stuffed the Baptist missionary outfits into the trash.

"Okay," he said, and we headed back to the far end, where a couple of taxis were waiting. We hopped into the first one, Chutsky told the driver "Aeropuerto José Martí," and we were off.

The ride back to the airport was pretty much the same as the ride in. There were very few cars, except for taxis and a couple of military vehicles, and the driver treated it like an obstacle course between potholes. It was a little tricky at night, since the road was not lighted, and he didn't always make it, and several times we were bounced severely, but we got to the airport eventually without any life-threatening injuries.

This time the cab dropped us at the beautiful new terminal, instead of the gulag building where we had come in. Chutsky went straight to the screen showing departures.

"Cancún, leaving in thirty-five minutes," he said. "Perfect."

"And what about your James Bond briefcase?" I asked, thinking it might be a slight inconvenience at security, since it was loaded with guns and grenade launchers and who knew what.

"Not to worry," he said. "Over here." He led the way to a bank of lockers, shoved in a few coins, and stuffed the briefcase inside. "All right," he said. He slammed the locker shut, took the key, and led the way to the AeroMéxico ticket counter, pausing on the way to drop the locker's key into a trash bin.

There was a very short line, and in no time at all we were buying two tickets to Cancún. Sadly, there were no vacancies outside of first class, but since we were fleeing from the repression of a communist state, I thought the extra expense was justified, even poetically fitting. The nice young woman told us they were boarding now and we must hurry, and we did, pausing only to show our passports and pay an exit tax, which was not as bad as it sounds, since I had expected a little more difficulty with the passports, frankly, and when there was none, I didn't mind paying the tax, no matter how ridiculous the idea seemed.

We were the last passengers to board, and I am sure the flight attendant would not have smiled so pleasantly if we were flying coach. We even got a glass of champagne to thank us for being wonderful enough to arrive late in first class, and as they closed and locked the cabin door and I began to think we might really get away, I found that I actually enjoyed the champagne, even on an empty stomach.

I enjoyed it even more when we were finally up in the air, wheels up, and headed for Mexico, and I probably would have had more when we landed in Cancún after our short flight, but the flight attendant didn't offer me any. I suppose my first class status had worn off somewhere along the line, leaving just enough to earn me a polite smile as we left the plane.

Inside the terminal, Chutsky went to arrange the rest of our trip home, and I sat in a shiny restaurant and ate enchiladas. They tasted like airport food everywhere else I had ever had them — a bland and strange approximation of what they were supposed to taste like, and bad, but not so clinically vile that you could demand your money back. It was hard work, but I had finished them by the time Chutsky got back with our tickets.

"Cancún to Houston, Houston to Miami," he said, handing me a ticket. "We'll get in around seven A.M."

After spending most of the night in molded plastic chairs, I can't remember a time when my hometown looked quite so welcoming, as when the rising sun lit up the runway and the plane finally landed and rolled up to the Miami International terminal. I was warmed by that special feeling of homecoming as we fought our way through the hysterical and often violent crowd and out to get a shuttle to long-term parking.

I dropped Chutsky at the hospital to reunite with Deborah, at his request. He climbed out of the car, hesitated, and then stuck his head back in the door. "I'm sorry it didn't work out, buddy," he said.

"Yes," I said. "So am I."

"You let me know if I can help out in any way to finish this thing," he said. "You know — if you find the guy and you're feeling squeamish, I can help."

Of course that was the one thing I was certainly not feeling squeamish about, but it was such a thoughtful gesture on his part to offer to pull the trigger for me, I just thanked him. He nodded, said, "I mean it," and then closed the car door and limped on into the hospital.

And I headed home against the rush-hour traffic, making fairly good time, but still arriving too late to see Rita and the kids. So I consoled myself with a shower, a change of clothes, and then a cup of coffee and some toast before heading back across town to work.

It was no longer full rush hour, but as always there was still plenty of traffic, and in the stop-and-go on the turnpike I had time to think, and I didn't like what I came up with. Weiss was still at large, and for all intents and purposes he was now impossible to find. I was reasonably sure that nothing had happened to make him change his mind about me and move on to somebody else. He would find another way, soon, either to kill me or make me wish he had. And as far as I could tell, there was nothing I could do about it except wait — either for him to do something, or for some wonderful idea to fall out of the sky and hit me on the head.

Traffic wound to a stop. I waited. A car roared past on the shoulder of the road, blasting its horn, and several other cars blasted back, but no ideas fell on me. I was just stuck in traffic, trying to get to work, and waiting for something awful to happen. I suppose that is a terrific description of the human condition, but I had always thought I was immune.

Traffic lurched forward. I crawled slowly past a flatbed truck that was pulled off onto the grass beside the road. The hood of the truck was up. Seven or eight men in dingy clothes sat on the bed of the truck. They were waiting, too, but they seemed a little happier about it than I was. Maybe they weren't being pursued by an insane homicidal artist.

Eventually I made it in to work, and if I had been hoping for a warm welcome and a cheery hello from my coworkers, I would have been bitterly disappointed. Vince Masuoka was in the lab and glanced up at me as I came in. "Where have you been?" he said, in a tone of voice that sounded like he was accusing me of something terrible.

"Fine, thanks," I said. "Very glad to see you, too."

"It's been crazy around here," Vince said, apparently without hearing me at all. "The migrant-worker thing, and on top of that, yesterday some douche bag killed his wife and her boyfriend."

"I'm sorry to hear it," I said.

"He used a hammer, and if you think that was fun . . ." he said.

"Doesn't sound like it," I said, mentally adding, *except for him.*

"Could have used your help," he said.

"It's nice to be wanted," I said, and he looked at me with disgust for a moment before turning away.

The day didn't get much better. I ended up at the site where the man with the hammer had given his little party. Vince was right — it was an awful mess, with the now-dried blood spattered across two and a half walls, a couch, and a large section of formerly beige carpet. I heard from one of the cops on the door that the man was in custody; he'd confessed and said he didn't know what came over him. It didn't make me feel any better, but it's nice to see justice done once in a while, and the work took my mind off Weiss for a while. It's always good to stay busy.

But it didn't drive away the bad feeling that Weiss would probably think so, too.

THIRTY-FOUR

I did stay busy, and Weiss did, too. With Chutsky's help, I learned that he had taken a flight to Toronto that left Havana just about the time we arrived at the Havana airport. But what he did after that no amount of computer snooping could uncover. A small voice inside me was stuttering hopefully that maybe he would give up and stay home, but this little voice was answered by a large and very loud bray of laughter from most of the other voices inside me.

I did the very few small things I could think of; I ran some Internet searches that technically I should not have been able to do, and I managed to find a little bit of credit-card activity, but all of it in Toronto. This led me to Weiss's bank, which was easy enough to make me a little bit indignant: Shouldn't people guarding our sacred money be a little bit more careful about it?

Weiss had made a cash withdrawal of a few thousand dollars, and then that was it. No activity at all for the next few days.

I knew that the cash withdrawal would somehow turn into bad news for me, but beyond that I could think of no way to turn that certainty into any kind of specific threat. In desperation, I went back to Weiss's YouTube page. Shockingly, the whole "New Miami" motif was completely gone, as were all the little thumbnail film boxes. Instead, the background was a dull gray and there was a rather horrible picture, a nasty-looking nude male body, with the privates partially hacked off. Underneath it was written, *Schwarzkogler was just the beginning. The next step is on the way.*

Any conversation that starts with *Schwarzkogler was just the beginning* is not going anywhere that a rational being could possibly want to go. But the name sounded vaguely familiar to me and, of course, I could not possibly leave a potential clue unexamined, and so I did my due diligence and ran a Google check.

The Schwarzkogler in question turned out to be Rudolf, an Austrian who considered himself an artist, and in order to prove it he reportedly sliced his penis off a little bit at a time and took photographs of the process.

This was such an artistic triumph that he continued his career, until his masterpiece finally killed him. And I remembered as I read it that he had been an icon of the group in Paris who had so brilliantly given us *Jennifer's Leg.*

I don't know much about art, but I like hanging on to my body parts. So far even Weiss had proven to be stingy with his limbs, in spite of my best effort. But I could see that this whole artistic movement would have a very definite aesthetic appeal to him, particularly if he took it one step further, as he said he was doing. It made sense; why create art with your own body when you can do the same thing with someone else's and it won't hurt? And your career would last a lot longer, too. I applauded Weiss's great common sense, and I had a very deep feeling that I was going to see the next step in his artistic career sometime soon, and someplace far too close to Dexter the Philistine.

I checked the YouTube page several more times over the next week, but there was no change, and the rhythm of a very busy week at work began to make it all seem like an unpleasant memory.

Things at home were no easier; a cop was still waiting at our door when the kids came home, and although most of them were very nice, their presence added to the strain. Rita got a little bit distant and distracted, as though she was perpetually waiting for an important long-distance telephone call, and this caused her usually excellent cooking to suffer. We had leftovers twice in one week — previously unheard of in our little house. And Astor seemed to pick up on the weirdness and, for the only time since I had known her, she got relatively silent, sitting in front of the TV with Cody and watching all her favorite DVDs over and over, with no more than two or three words at a time for the rest of us.

Cody, oddly enough, was the only one showing any kind of animation. He was very eagerly looking forward to his next Cub Scout meeting, even though it meant wearing his dreaded uniform shorts. But when I asked him why he'd had a change of heart, he admitted it was only because he was hoping the new den leader might turn up dead, too, and this time he might see something.

So the week dragged on, the weekend was no relief, and Monday morning came around again as it almost always seems to do. And even though I brought a large box of doughnuts in to work, Monday had nothing much to offer me in return, either, except more work. A drive-by shooting in Liberty City took me out onto the hot streets for several unnecessary hours. A sixteen-year-old boy was dead, and it was obvious from one quick look at the blood pattern that he had been shot from a moving vehicle. But "obvious" is never enough for a police investigation, so there I was sweating under the hot sun and doing things that came perilously close to physical labor, just so I could fill out the correct forms.

By the time I got back to my little cubby at headquarters, I had sweated away most of my artificial human covering and I wanted nothing more out of life than to take a shower, put on some dry clothes, and then possibly slice up somebody who thoroughly deserved it. And of course that led my slowly chugging train of thought straight down the track to Weiss, and with nothing else to do except admire the feel and the smell of my own sweat, I checked his YouTube page one more time.

And this time there was a brand-new thumbnail waiting for me at the bottom of the page.

It was labeled DEXTERAMA!

There wasn't any realistic choice in the matter. I clicked on the box.

There was an unfocused blur, and then

the sound of an orchestra that led into noble-sounding music that reminded me of high school graduation. And then a series of pictures; the "New Miami" bodies, intercut with reaction shots from people seeing them, as Weiss's voice came in, sounding like a wicked version of a newsreel announcer.

"For thousands of years," he intoned, "terrible things have happened to us —" and there were some close-up shots of the bodies and their plastic-masked faces. "And man has asked the same question: Why am I here? And for all that time, the answer has been the same . . ." A close-up of a face from the crowd at Fairchild Gardens, looking puzzled, confused, uncertain, and Weiss's voice coming over it in dopey tones. "I dunno . . ."

The film technique was very clumsy, nothing at all like the earlier stuff, and I tried not to be too critical — after all, Weiss's talents were in another area, and he had lost his first partner, and killed his second, who had been good at editing.

"So man has turned to art," Weiss said with artificially solemn breathlessness, and there was a picture of a statue with no arms and legs. "And art has given us a much better answer . . ." Close-up of the jogger finding the body on South Beach, followed by Weiss's famous scream.

"But conventional art can only take us so far," he said. "Because using traditional methods like paint and stone create a barrier between the artistic event and the *experience* of art. And as artists, we have to be all about breaking down barriers . . ." Picture of the Berlin Wall falling as a crowd cheered.

"So guys like Chris Burden and David Nebreda began to experiment and make *themselves* the art — one barrier down! But it's not enough, because to the average audience member" — another dopey face from the crowd — "there's no difference between a lump of clay and some crazy artist; the barrier is still there! Bummer!"

Then Weiss's face came on-screen; the camera jiggled a little, as if he was positioning the camera as he talked. "We need to get more immediate. We need to make the audience *part* of the event, so the barrier disappears. And we need better answers . . . to the bigger questions. Questions like, 'What is truth? What is the threshold of human agony?' And most important" — and here the screen showed that awful loop of Dexter Dumping Doncevic into the white porcelain tub — " 'What would Dexter do

— if he became part of the art, instead of being the artist?' "

And here there was a new scream — it was muffled, but it sounded tantalizingly familiar; not Weiss's, but something I had heard before, although I couldn't place it, and Weiss was back on-screen, smiling slightly and glancing over his shoulder. "At least we can answer that last one, can't we?" he said. And he picked up the camera and twirled it around off his face and onto a twitching heap in the background. The heap swam into focus and I realized why the scream had sounded familiar.

It was Rita.

She lay on her side with her hands tied behind her and her feet bound at the ankles. She squirmed furiously and made another loud and muffled sound, this time one of outrage.

Weiss laughed. "The audience is the art," he said. "And you're going to be my master-piece, Dexter." He smiled, and even though it was not an artificial smile, it was not particularly pretty, either. "It's going to be an absolute . . . Art-stravaganza," he said. And then the screen went dark.

He had Rita — and I know very well that I should have leaped up, grabbed my squirrel gun, and charged into the tall pine screaming a war cry — but I felt a curious calmness spread over me, and I simply sat there for a long moment, wondering what he would do to her, before I finally realized that, one way or another, I really did have to do something. And so I started to take a large breath to get me out of the chair and through the door.

But I had time for only one small breath, not even enough to get one foot on the floor, when a voice came from close behind me.

"That's your wife, right?" said Detective Coulter.

After I peeled myself from the ceiling I turned and faced him. He stood just inside the door, several feet away, but close enough that he must have seen and heard everything. There was no way to dodge his question.

"Yes," I said. "That's Rita."

He nodded. "That looked like you, with the guy in the bathtub."

"That . . . I," I stammered. "I don't think so."

Coulter nodded again. "That was you," he said. And since I had nothing to say and didn't want to hear myself stammer again, I just shook my head.

"You going to just sit there, guy got your

wife?" he said.

"I was just about to get up," I said.

Coulter cocked his head to one side. "You get the feeling this guy doesn't like you or something?" he said.

"It's starting to look like that," I admitted.

"Why do you think that is?" he said.

"I told you. I hurt his boyfriend," I said, which sounded very weak, even to me.

"Yeah, that's right," Coulter said. "The guy that disappeared. You still don't know where he went, do you?"

"No, I don't," I said.

"You don't," he said, cocking his head. "Because that wasn't him in the bathtub. And it wasn't you standing over him with a saw."

"No, of course not."

"But this guy maybe thinks it was, 'cuz it looks like you," he said, "so he took your wife. Kind of a trade thing, right?"

"Detective, I don't know where the boyfriend is, really," I said. And it was true, considering tide, current, and the habits of marine scavengers.

"Huh," he said, and he put an expression on his face that I assumed was meant to look thoughtful. "So he just decides to, what . . . ? Make your wife into some kind of art, right? Because . . . ?"

"Because he's crazy?" I said hopefully. And that was true, too, but that didn't mean that Coulter would be impressed.

Apparently he wasn't. "Uh-huh," he said, looking a little dubious. "He's crazy. That would make sense, right." He nodded, like he was trying to convince himself. "Okay, so we got a crazy guy, and he's got your wife. And so what now?" He raised his eyebrows at me with a look that said he hoped I might come up with something really helpful.

"I don't know," I said. "I guess I should report this."

"Report it," he said, nodding his head. "Like to the police. Because last time when you didn't do that, I spoke harshly to you on the subject."

Intelligence is generally praised as a good thing, but I really have to admit that I had liked Coulter a lot more when I thought he was a harmless idiot. Now that I knew he was not, I was caught between the urge to be very careful what I said to him and an equally powerful desire to break my chair over his head. But good chairs are expensive; caution won.

"Detective," I said. "This guy has my wife. Maybe you've never been married —"

"Twice," he said. "It didn't work."

"Well, it works for me," I said. "I'd like to get her back in one piece."

He stared at me for a very long moment before he finally said, "Who is this guy? I mean, you know."

"Brandon Weiss," I said, not sure where this was going.

"That's just his name," he said. "Who the fuck IS he?"

I shook my head, not truly sure what he meant, and even less sure that I wanted to tell him.

"But this is the guy that, you know. Did all those fancy dead-body displays that the governor was pissed off about?"

"I'm pretty sure he did," I said.

He nodded and looked at his hand, and it occurred to me that there was no Mountain Dew bottle hanging from it. The poor man must have run out.

"Be a good thing to nail this guy," he said.

"Yes, it would," I said.

"Make all kinds of people happy," he said. "Good for the career."

"I suppose so," I said, wondering if perhaps I should have hit him with the chair, after all.

Coulter clapped his hands. "All right," he said. "Let's go get him."

It was a wonderful idea, very decisively

delivered, but I saw one small problem with it. "Go where?" I said. "Where has he taken Rita?"

He blinked at me. "What. He told you," he said.

"I don't think so," I said.

"Come on, you don't watch public television?" he said, sounding like I had committed some kind of crime with small animals.

"Not very much," I admitted. "The kids have outgrown *Barney.*"

"They been running promos for it for three weeks," he said. "The Art-stravaganza."

"The what?"

"The Art-stravaganza, at the Convention Center," he said, starting to sound like the promo. "Over two hundred cutting-edge artists from across North America and the Caribbean, all under one roof."

I could feel my mouth moving in a game attempt to make words, but nothing came out. I blinked and tried again, but before I could make any sound at all, Coulter jerked his head at the door and said, "Come on. Let's go get 'em." He took one step backward. "Afterward we can talk about why that looks like you with the guy in the tub."

This time I actually got both of my feet

on the floor, together, ready to propel me up and out — but before I could take it any further my cell phone rang. Out of habit more than anything else, I answered it. "Hello," I said.

"Mr. Morgan?" a tired young female voice asked.

"Yes," I said.

"This is Megan? At the after-school program? That, you know, um, with Cody? And Astor?"

"Oh, yes," I said, and a new alarm began to clatter on the main floor of my brain.

"It's like five after six?" Megan said. "And I gotta go home now? 'Cause I have my accounting class tonight? Like, at seven?"

"Yes, Megan," I said, "how can I help you?"

"Like I said? I need to go home?" she said.

"All right," I said, wishing I could reach through the telephone and fling her away to her house.

"But your kids?" she said. "I mean, your wife never came for them? So they're here? And I'm not supposed to go if there are kids here?"

It seemed like a very good rule — especially since it meant that Cody and Astor were both all right, and not in Weiss's clutches. "I'll come get them," I said. "I'll be there in twenty minutes."

I snapped the telephone shut and saw Coulter looking at me expectantly. "My kids," I said. "Their mother never picked them up, and now I have to."

"Right now," he said.

"Yes."

"So you're gonna go get them?"

"That's right."

"Uh-huh," he said. "You still want to save your wife?"

"I think that would be best," I said.

"So you'll get the kids and come for your wife," he said. "And not, like, try to leave the country or anything."

"Detective," I said, "I want to get my wife back."

Coulter looked at me for a long moment. Then he nodded. "I'll be at the Convention Center," he said, and turned around and walked out the door.

THIRTY-FIVE

The park where Cody and Astor went after school each day was only a few minutes from our house, but it was the far side of town from my office, and so it was a bit more than twenty minutes before I finally got there. Since it was rush-hour traffic, I suppose you could say it was lucky that I got there at all. But I had plenty of time to reflect on what might be happening to Rita, and I found to my surprise that I actually hoped she was all right. I was just starting to get used to her. I liked having her cooking every night, and certainly I could not manage both kids on a full-time basis and still have the freedom to blossom in my chosen career — not yet, not for a few more years, when they had both been trained.

So I hoped that Coulter had taken reliable backup, and that they would have Weiss tucked away and Rita secured, perhaps sipping coffee and wrapped in a blanket, like on television.

But that brought up an interesting point, one that filled the rest of my otherwise pleasant drive through the homicidal homeward-bound crowd with genuine worry. Suppose they *did* have Weiss all safely cuffed and Mirandized? What would happen when they started to ask him questions? Things like, why did you do it? And more importantly, why did you do it to Dexter? What if he had the very poor taste to answer them truthfully? So far he had showed an appalling willingness to tell everyone all about me, and although I am not particularly shy, I would rather keep my real accomplishments hidden from the public eye.

And if Coulter added the things Weiss might blather to what he already suspected from seeing the video, things might get very unhappy in Dexterville.

It would have been a much better thing if I had been able to confront Weiss by myself — settle things amicably, mano a mano — or possibly *cuchilla a cuchilla* — and solve the problem of Weiss's urge to communicate by feeding my Passenger. But I'd had no real choice in the matter — Coulter had been there and heard it, and I'd had to go along. After all, I was a law-abiding citizen — I really was, technically speaking; I mean,

443

innocent until proven guilty in a court of law, right?

And it was looking more and more like it would come down to a court of law, starring Dexter in an orange jumpsuit and leg irons, which I could not look forward to at all — orange is a very bad color for me. And of course being accused of murder would really be a major roadblock to my true happiness. I don't have any illusions about our legal system; I see it on the job every day, and I am quite sure that I could beat it, unless they actually catch me in the act, on film, in front of a bus filled with U.S. senators and nuns. But even an open accusation would put me under the kind of scrutiny that would spell an end to my playtime activities, even if I was found to be completely innocent. Just look at poor O.J.; in his last years of freedom he couldn't even play golf anymore without someone accusing him of something.

But what could I do about it? My options were very limited. I could either let Weiss talk, in which case I was in trouble, or stop him from talking — in which case, exact same result. There was no way around it. Dexter was in deep, and the tide was rising.

It was therefore a very thoughtful Dexter who finally pulled up at the community hall at the park. Good Old Megan was still there, holding Cody and Astor by the hand, and hopping from one foot to the other in her anxiety to be rid of them and off into the exciting world of accounting class. They all seemed happy to see me, in their own individual ways, which was so gratifying that I forgot all about Weiss for three or four full seconds.

"Mr. Morgan?" Megan said. "I really gotta go." And I was so stunned to hear her complete a sentence that was not a question, I merely nodded and pried Cody and Astor's hands from hers. She skittered away to a small beat-up Chevy and raced off into the evening traffic.

"Where's Mom?" Astor demanded.

I am sure there is a caring and sensitive and very human way to tell children that their mother is in the clutches of a homicidal monster, but I did not know what it was, so I said, "That bad guy has her. The one that crashed into your car."

"The one I got with a pencil?" Cody asked me.

"That's right," I said.

"I hit him in the crotch," Astor said.

"You should have hit him harder," I said. "He's got your mom."

She made a face at me that showed she

was deeply disappointed in my dorkiness. "Are we going to go get her?"

"We're going to help," I said. "The police are there now."

They both looked at me like I was crazy. "The *police?!*" Astor said. "You sent the *police?!*"

"I had to come get you two," I said, surprised to find myself on the defensive all of a sudden.

"So you're going to let this guy GO, and he'll just go to JAIL?" she demanded.

"I had to," I said, and suddenly I felt like I really was in court and I had already lost. "One of the cops found out, and I had to come get you."

They exchanged one of their silent but very meaningful looks, and then Cody looked away. "Are you taking us with you now?" Astor asked.

"Uh," I said, and it really didn't seem fair to have first Coulter and now Astor reduce honey-tongued Dashing Dexter to monosyllabic idiocy in the same day, but there it was. Things being what they were — exceedingly unpleasant and uncertain — I had not really thought this through. But of course I could not take them with me to corner Weiss. I knew that his whole performance was aimed at me, and it would not really start until I got there, if he could help it; I could not be certain that Coulter had him cornered, and it would be far too dangerous.

And as if she heard me thinking it, Astor said, "We already beat him once."

"He wasn't expecting anything from you then," I said. "This time he will be."

"This time we'll have more than a pencil," Astor said, and the cool ferocity she said it with absolutely warmed my heart — but it was still out of the question.

"No," I said. "It's too dangerous."

Cody muttered, "Promise," and Astor rolled her eyes in an epic fashion and blew out a matching breath. "You keep saying we can't do *anything,*" she said. "Not until you teach us. And we say go ahead and teach us, and we don't do anything. And now when we have a chance to really learn something real, you say it's too dangerous."

"It IS too dangerous," I said.

"Then what are we supposed to do while you go doing something dangerous?" she demanded. "And what if you don't save Mom and you both never come back?"

I looked at her, and then at Cody. She was glaring at me with her lower lip quivering, while he settled for a stony-faced expression of contempt, and once again the best I could manage was to open my mouth soundlessly a few times.

And that is how I ended up driving to the Convention Center, going slightly faster than the speed limit, with two very excited children in the backseat. We got off I-95 at Eighth Street and headed over to the Convention Center on Brickell. There was a lot of traffic and no place to park — apparently a lot of other people had been watching public television and were aware of the Artstravaganza. Under the circumstances, it seemed a little silly to waste time looking for a parking spot, and just as I decided to park on the sidewalk police-style, I saw what had to be Coulter's motor-pool car, and I pulled up onto the walk beside it and slapped my department placard on the dashboard and turned to face Cody and Astor.

"Stay with me," I said, "and don't do anything without asking me first."

"Unless it's an emergency," Astor said.

I thought about how they'd done so far in emergencies; pretty good, in fact. Besides, it was almost certainly all over by now. "All right," I said. "If it's an emergency." I opened the car door. "Come on," I said.

They didn't budge. "What?" I said.

"Knife," Cody said softly.

"He wants a knife," Astor said.

"I'm not giving you a knife," I said.

"But what if there IS an emergency?" Astor demanded. "You said we could do something if there's an emergency, but then you won't let us have anything to DO it with!"

"You can't wander around in public holding a knife," I said.

"We can't go totally defenseless," Astor insisted.

I blew out a long breath. I was reasonably sure that Rita would be safe until I got there, but at this rate, Weiss would die of old age before I found him. So I opened the glove compartment and took out a Phillips-head screwdriver and handed it to Cody. After all, life is all about compromise. "Here," I said. "That's the best I can do."

Cody looked at the screwdriver and then looked at me.

"It's better than a pencil," I said. He looked at his sister, and then he nodded. "Good," I said, reaching once again to open the door. "Let's go."

This time they followed me, up across the sidewalk and to the main entrance of the big hall. But before we got there, Astor stopped dead.

"What is it?" I asked her.

"I have to pee," she said.

"Astor," I said. "We have to get moving here."

"I have to pee really bad," she said.

"Can't it wait five minutes?"

"No," she said, shaking her head vigorously. "I gotta go *now.*"

I took a very deep breath and wondered if Batman ever had this problem with Robin. "All right," I said. "Hurry."

We found the restroom over to one side of the lobby and Astor hurried in. Cody and I just stood and waited. He changed his grip on the screwdriver a few times, and finally settled for the more natural blade-forward position. He looked at me for approval, and I nodded, just as Astor came out again.

"Come on," she said. "Let's go." She breezed past us toward the door to the main hall and we followed. A doughy man with large glasses wanted to collect fifteen dollars from each of us to let us enter, but I showed him my police credentials. "What about the kids?" he demanded.

Cody started to raise his screwdriver, but I motioned him back. "They're witnesses," I said.

The man looked like he wanted to argue, but when he saw the way Cody was holding the screwdriver, he just shook his head. "All

450

right," he said with a very large sigh.

"Do you know where the other officers went?" I asked him.

He just kept shaking his head. "There's only one officer that I know of," he said, "and I am QUITE sure I would know if there were more, since they all think they can just parade past me without paying." He smiled to show that he really did mean it as an insult, and beckoned us forward into the hall. "Enjoy the show."

We went into the hall. There were actually several booths showing things that were recognizable as art — sculpture, paintings, and so on. But there were many more that really seemed to be working a little too hard at stretching the boundaries of the human experience into new frontiers of perception. One of the very first we saw was nothing more than a pile of leaves and twigs with a faded beer can lying beside it. Two more featured multiple TV monitors; one showed a fat man sitting on a toilet, the other an airplane flying into a building. But there was no sign of Weiss, Rita, or Coulter.

We walked down to the far end of the hall and turned, glancing up each aisle as we passed. There were many more interesting and horizon-expanding displays, but none of them involved Rita. I began to wonder if

I had been wrong to think Coulter was secretly smart. I had blindly accepted his statement that Weiss would be here — but what if he was wrong? What if Weiss was somewhere else, happily carving up Rita, while I looked at art that merely added depth and understanding to a soul that I really didn't have?

And then Cody stopped in his tracks and slowly came up on point. I turned to see what he was looking at, and I came to a point, too.

"Mom," he said.

And it was.

THIRTY-SIX

A crowd of about a dozen people had gathered in the far corner of the room, beneath a flat-screen TV monitor that had been mounted to the wall. And on the monitor was a close-up of Rita's face. She had a gag pulled between her teeth, but her eyes were as wide open as they could possibly be and she was tossing her head from side to side in terror. And before I could do anything but lift a foot, Cody and Astor were already plunging ahead to save their mother.

"Wait!" I called to them, but they did not, so I hurried after them, scanning frantically for Weiss. The Dark Passenger was completely quiet, silenced by my near-panicked concern for Cody and Astor, and in my rapidly skittering imagination Weiss was waiting to jump out at them from behind every easel, ready to lurch out from under every table, and I did not like rushing to meet him blind and sweating, but the children running to Rita left me no choice at all. I went faster, but they were already pushing through the small crowd to their mother's side.

Rita was bound as well as gagged and strapped down to a table saw. The blade was whirling between her ankles, and the implication was clear that some very bad person was ready and willing to push her forward toward the shiny teeth of the saw. A sign taped to the front side of the table said WHO CAN SAVE OUR NELL? and below that, in block letters, PLEASE DO NOT DISTURB THE PERFORMERS. Around the edge of the space ran a model train, towing a series of flatcars with a sign propped up on them that said THE FUTURE OF MELODRAMA.

And finally I saw Coulter — but it was not a happy and reassuring sighting. He was propped up in a corner, head lolling to one side. Weiss had put an old-fashioned conductor's hat on his head, and a heavy electric cable was attached to his arms by large jumper-cable clips. A sign was propped in his lap: SEMI-CONDUCTOR. He was not moving, but I could not tell if he was dead or merely unconscious, and considering the circumstances, finding out was not high on my list.

I pushed into the crowd, and as the model train went by again I heard Weiss's patented prerecorded scream played in a taped loop that repeated every few seconds.

And I still did not see Weiss — but as I reached the crowd the image on the TV monitor changed — to my face. I spun frantically, searching for the camera, and found it, mounted on a pole on the far side of the exhibit's space. And before I could spin back around again, I heard a whistling sound and a loop of very heavy fishing line whipped tight around my neck. As things started to go dark and whirly I had only a moment to appreciate the bitter irony that Weiss was using a fishing-line noose, one of my own techniques; the phrase *my own petard* trundled through my brain, and then I was on my knees and stumbling dreadfully forward in the direction of Weiss's exhibit.

With a noose that tight around your neck, it's really quite remarkable how quickly you lose interest in everything and slide into a dim region of distant sounds and dark lights. And even though I felt the pressure slacken slightly, I couldn't raise enough interest to use the looseness to get free. I slumped on the floor, trying to remember how to breathe, and from far away I heard a woman's voice saying, "That isn't right —

stop them!" And I was mildly grateful that someone was going to stop them until the voice went on, "Hey, you kids! It's an art exhibit! Get away from there!" And it filtered through to me that somebody wanted to stop Cody and Astor from ruining the piece by saving their mother.

Air came in through my throat, which suddenly felt sore and much too big; Weiss had let go of the noose and picked up his camera. I took a ragged breath and managed to focus one eye on his back as he began to pan across the crowd. I took another breath; pain raced through my throat, but it felt pretty good, and enough light and thought came back with the breath that I managed to get up on one knee and look around.

Weiss was pointing the camera at a woman on the edge of the crowd — the woman who had scolded Cody and Astor for interfering. She was fiftyish, dressed very stylishly, and she was still yelling at them to back away, leave it alone, somebody call security, and happily for us all, the kids were not listening. They had freed Rita from the table, although her hands and feet were still bound, and the gag was still wedged into her mouth. I stood up — but before I could take more than a half step toward them,

Weiss grabbed my leash again and pulled tight, and I went back into the midnight sun.

Dimly, from very far away, I heard scuffling, and the line around my throat went slack again as Weiss said, "Not this time, you little shit!" There was a smacking sound and a small thump, and as a little light came back into my world, I saw Astor lying on the floor and Weiss struggling to take the screwdriver away from Cody. I raised a hand to my neck and scrabbled feebly at the line, and got it loose enough to take a huge breath, which was probably the right thing to do, but nonetheless caused a fit of the most painful coughing I have ever experienced, so very choked and dry that the lights went out once more.

When I could breathe again, I opened my eyes to see that Cody was on the floor next to Astor, on the far side of the exhibit space beyond the table saw, and Weiss stood over them with the screwdriver in one hand and his video camera in the other. Astor's leg twitched, but other than that they did not move. Weiss stepped toward them and raised the screwdriver, and I lurched drunkenly up to my feet to stop him, knowing I could never get there in time and feeling all the darkness drain out of me and puddle around my shoes at the thought of my helplessness.

And at the last possible second, as Weiss stood gloating over the small still bodies of the children and Dexter leaned forward with horrible slowness, Rita stumbled forward into the picture — hands still tied, mouth still gagged, but feet fast enough to bring her charging into Weiss, slamming him with a deadly hip that sent him twirling sideways, away from the children, and straight at the table saw. And as he staggered upright she bumped him again, and this time his feet tangled together and he fell, the arm holding his camera flailing out protectively to keep him from falling onto the spinning saw blade. And he almost succeeded — almost.

Weiss's hand slapped the table on the far side of the blade, but the force of his fall brought all his weight down, and with a grinding whine an explosive red mist shot into the air as Weiss's forearm, hand still clutching the camera, came off altogether and thumped onto the model-train track at the edge of the crowd. The spectators gasped and Weiss stood slowly upright, staring at the stump of his arm as the blood pumped out. He looked at me and tried to say something, shook his head and stepped toward me, and looked at his rapidly squirting stump again, and then came another step toward me. And then, almost like he was walking down a flight of invisible stairs, he walked slowly down onto his knees and knelt there, swaying, only a few feet away from me.

And I, paralyzed by my fight with the noose and my fear for the children and above all the sight of that awful wet nasty viscous horrible blood pouring out and onto the floor — I simply stood there as Weiss looked up at me one last time. His lips moved again, but nothing came out and he shook his head slowly, carefully, as if he was afraid that it, too, might fall off and onto the floor. With exaggerated care he locked his eyes onto mine and very carefully, very distinctly, he said, "Take lots of pictures." And he smiled a faint and very pale smile and pitched face forward into his own blood.

I took a step back as he fell and looked up; on the TV screen the model train chugged forward and slammed into the camera still clutched in the hand at the end of Weiss's severed arm. The wheels churned for a moment, and then the train fell over.

"Brilliant," said the stylish older lady in the front of the crowd. "Absolutely brilliant."

EPILOGUE

The emergency medics in Miami are very good, partly because they get so much practice. But alas, they did not manage to save Weiss. He had very nearly bled out by the time they got to his side, and at the urging of a frantic Rita, the meds spent a crucial two more minutes looking at Cody and Astor as Weiss slipped away down the long dark slope into the pages of art history.

Rita hovered anxiously while the EMS guys got Cody and Astor to sit up and look around. Cody blinked and tried to reach for his screwdriver, and Astor immediately started to complain about how rotten the smelling salts smelled, so I was reasonably sure they were going to be all right. Still, they almost certainly had minor concussions, which gave me a warm feeling of family togetherness; so young, and already following in my footsteps. And so the two of them were sent off to the hospital for twenty-four hours of observation, "just to be safe." Rita went along, of course, to protect them from the doctors.

When they were gone, I stood and watched the two EMS techs who knelt beside Coulter. They had brought the defribillator paddles out, but after a few moments of poking at the body, they shook their heads, stood up, and walked away. I thought they looked a little disappointed that they hadn't had a chance to yell "Clear!" and release the charge, but maybe I was reading into it. I was still feeling a little woozy from my time in Weiss's noose, and a little strange at the way things had wobbled away from me so quickly. Normally, I am Dexter on the Spot, at the center of all important action, and to have so much death and destruction all around me and not be a crucial part of it didn't seem right. Two whole bodies, and me no more than an observer with the vapors, fainting on the outskirts of the drama like a Victorian maiden.

And Weiss: he actually looked peaceful and content. Extremely pale and dead, too, of course, but still — what could he be thinking? I had never seen such an expression on the face of the dear departed, and it was a bit unsettling. What did he have to feel happy about? He was absolutely, certifiably dead, and that did not seem to me like anything that should inspire good cheer. Maybe it was just a trick of the facial muscles settling into death. Whatever it was, my pondering was interrupted by a hurried scuffle behind me and I turned around.

Special Agent Recht came to a halt a few feet away and stood looking at the carnage with a face locked rigidly into a professional mask, even though it did not hide the shock, or the fact that she was rather pale. Still, she didn't faint or throw up, so I thought she was well ahead of the game.

"Is that him?" she said in a voice as tightly locked as her face. She cleared her throat before I could answer and added, "Is that the man who attempted to kidnap your children?"

"Yes," I said, and then, showing that my giant brain was at last swimming back to the controls, I anticipated the awkward question and said, "My wife was sure that's him, and so were the kids."

Recht nodded, apparently unable to take her eyes off Weiss. "All right," she said. I couldn't tell what that meant, but it seemed like an encouraging sign. I hoped it meant that the FBI would lose interest in me now. "What about him?" Recht said, nodding toward the back of the exhibit where the EMS guys were finishing their examination of Coulter.

"Detective Coulter got here before me," I said.

Recht nodded. "That's what the guy on the door says," she said, and the fact that she had asked about that was not terribly comforting, so I decided that a few careful dance steps might be called for.

"Detective Coulter," I said carefully, as if fighting for control — and I have to admit that the rasp remaining in my voice from the noose was very effective — "He got here first. Before I could . . . I think he — He gave his life to save Rita."

I thought that sniffling might be overkill, so I held back, but even I was impressed with the sound of the manly emotion in my voice. Alas, Special Agent Recht was not. She looked at Coulter's body again, and at Weiss's, and then at me. "Mr. Morgan," she said, and there was official doubt in her voice. For a moment I thought she was going to arrest me anyway, and possibly she thought so, too. But then she just shook her head and turned away.

And in a sane and well-ordered universe, any ruling deity would have said that was enough for one day. But things being what they are, it was not. Because I turned around to leave and bumped directly into Israel Salguero.

"Detective Coulter is dead?" he said, sliding a step back without blinking.

"Yes," I said. "Um, before I got here."

Salguero nodded. "Yes," he said. "That's what the witnesses said."

On the one hand, it was very good news that the witnesses said that, but on the other, it was very bad that he had already asked them, since it meant his first concern was, *Where was Dexter when the bodies began to fall?* And so, thinking that some grand, emotional flummery might save the day, I looked away and said, "I should have been here."

There was such a long silence from Salguero that I finally had to turn back and look at him, if only to make sure he had not drawn his weapon and pointed it at my head. Happily for Dexter's Dome, he had not. Instead, he was just looking at me with his completely detached and emotionless gaze. "I think it is probably a very good thing that you were not here," he said at last. "Good for you, and your sister, and the memory of your father."

"Um . . . ?" I said, and it is a testament to Salguero's savvy that he knew exactly what

I meant.

"There are now no witnesses . . ." He paused and gave me a look very much like what you might see if cobras ever learn to smile. "No *surviving* witnesses," he said, "to anything that happened, in any of these . . . circumstances." He made a slight movement of his shoulders that was probably a shrug. "And so . . ." He did not finish the sentence, letting it dangle so it might mean, "and so that's the end of it," or "and so I will simply arrest you," or even, "and so I will kill you myself." He watched me for a moment and then repeated, "And so," this time so that it sounded like a question. Then he nodded and walked away, leaving me with the image of his bright and lidless gaze burned into my retinas.

And so.

That was, happily, just about the last of it. There was a minor bit of excitement provided by the stylish lady from the front of the crowd, who turned out to be Dr. Elaine Donazetti, a very important figure in the world of contemporary art. She pushed her way through the perimeter and began taking Polaroids, and had to be restrained and led away from bodies. But she used the pictures and some of the videotape Weiss had made and published a series of illustrated articles that made Weiss semifamous with the people who like that sort of thing. So at least he got his last request for pictures. It's nice when things work out, isn't it?

Detective Coulter was just as lucky. Department gossip told me that he had been passed over for promotion, twice, and I suppose he thought he could jump-start his career by making a dramatic arrest single-handedly. And it worked! The department decided it needed some good publicity out of this whole dreadful mess, and Coulter was all they had to work with. So he was promoted posthumously for his heroism in single-handedly almost saving Rita.

Of course I went to Coulter's funeral. I love the ceremony, the ritual, the outpouring of all that rigid emotion, and it gave me a chance to practice some of my favorite facial expressions — solemnity, noble grief, and compassion, all rarely used and in need of a workout.

The whole department was there, in uniform, even Deborah. She looked very pale in her blue uniform, but after all, Coulter had been her partner, at least on paper, and honor demanded that she attend. The hospital fussed, but she was close enough to being released anyway that they didn't stop her. She did not cry, of course — she had never been nearly as good at hypocrisy as I was. But she looked properly solemn when they lowered the coffin into the ground, and I did my best to make the same kind of face.

I thought I did it rather well, too — but Sergeant Doakes did not agree. I saw him glaring at me from the ranks, as if he thought I had personally strangled Coulter, which was absurd; I had never strangled anyone. I mean, a little noose play now and then, but all in good fun — I don't like that kind of personal contact, and a knife is so much cleaner. Of course I had been very pleased to see Coulter pronounced dead and Dexter therefore off the hook, but I'd had nothing at all to do with it. As I said, it's just nice when things work out, isn't it?

And life staggered back onto its feet and lurched into its old routines once again. I went to work, Cody and Astor went to school, and two days after Coulter's funeral Rita went to a doctor's appointment. That night after she tucked the children in, she settled down beside me on the couch, put her head on my shoulder, and pried the remote control out of my hands. She turned off the TV and sighed a few times, and finally, when I was mystified beyond endurance, I said, "Is something wrong?"

"No," she said. "Not wrong at all. I mean, I don't think so. If you don't, um, think so."

"Why would I think so?" I said.

"I don't know," she said, and she sighed again. "It's just, you know, we never talked about it, and now . . ."

"Now *what?*" I said. It was really too much; after all I had gone through, to have to endure this kind of circular nonconversation, and I could feel my irritation level rising rapidly.

"Now, just," she said. "The doctor says I'm all right."

"Oh," I said. "That's good."

She shook her head. "In *spite* of," she said. "You know."

I didn't know, and it didn't seem fair that she expected me to know, and I said so. And after a great deal of throat clearing and stammering, when she finally told me, I found that I lost the power of speech just as she had, and the only thing I could manage to say was the punch line of a very old joke that I knew was not the right thing to say, but I could not stop it and it came out anyway, and as if from a great distance, I heard Dexter's voice calling out:

You're going to have a WHAT?!

We hope you have enjoyed this Large Print book. Other Thorndike, Wheeler, Kennebec, and Chivers Press Large Print books are available at your library or directly from the publishers.

For information about current and upcoming titles, please call or write, without obligation, to:

Publisher
Thorndike Press
295 Kennedy Memorial Drive
Waterville, ME 04901
Tel. (800) 223-1244

or visit our Web site at:

http://gale.cengage.com/thorndike

OR

Chivers Large Print
published by BBC Audiobooks Ltd
St James House, The Square
Lower Bristol Road
Bath BA2 3SB
England
Tel. +44(0) 800 136919
email: bbcaudiobooks@bbc.co.uk
www.bbcaudiobooks.co.uk

All our Large Print titles are designed for easy reading, and all our books are made to last.